LOVE'S NOT OVER 'TIL IT'S OVER

A NOVEL

Dear Julie

I hope you enjoy this

"back in the day" story

All the best,

Ed B

LOVE'S NOT OVER 'TIL IT'S OVER

A NOVEL

Edward T. Byrne

SIXBY LITERARY COMPANY, LLC

This book is dedicated to Donald T. Byrne, Matthew E. Byrne, and all fathers and sons who have ever loved each other.

Prologue
October 1981

H E WANTED TO TAKE THE SUBWAY, even with its graffiti and variety of shady characters, Number 7 train to the end of the line. Then the bus. The Q-12. Just like the old days.

James Devlin stood on the platform at the lowest level of Grand Central Station. There was a loud magnetic click, announcing that his wait was almost over. The whisper from the dark tunnel escalated to a roar as the defaced train entered the station, trailing the procession of litter it blew down the tracks.

He left his seat as the train pulled out of Vernon Jackson station. Back to the other passengers, he pressed his shoulder against the door as the train left the tunnel, then snaked on the elevated track over Queensboro Plaza and the dreary railroad yards, up Queens Boulevard, then down Roosevelt Avenue.

Even from high above, he could identify the old neighborhoods of Queens. Sunnyside. Woodside. Jackson Heights. Corona. It looked as though the neighborhoods had not changed, but how could that be? People move on. Loved ones die. Families dissolve. Newcomers replace them, again huddling around the el, as if trying to draw power from the subway's third rail.

The doors opened at Main Street in Flushing, and he waded into the crowd of passengers waiting to get on board and go in the opposite direction.

Once on the street, he traced his old path to the Q-12. Nothing looked the same, but at least the bus stop hadn't moved. When the bus's brakes alerted him to its arrival, the doors swooshed open and he rooted through his change to pay the full, astronomical fare, not the nickel he once paid as a student with a pass.

He gazed out the window, except for a few glances past the other scattered passengers, never at them. While the bus lurched out of Flushing, bits and pieces of James's past confronted him. Nothing important, silly things. The time he fell asleep and almost missed his stop. Another time when he tried to study for a Latin quiz, attempting to keep the book balanced on his knees while the bus jerked to a halt every few blocks. His mind kept filling with thoughts, mundane ones appearing while more consequential memories stayed hidden. Maybe that was why he felt so overgrown, so swollen as he kept shifting in the seat that had once fit well.

He purposely let the bus pass Douglaston Parkway without ringing the bell. It then rocked past St. Aidan's Church and School. *You'll like St. Aidan's just fine. I'll bet they've got a lot of great kids there, just like you.* He pushed this memory away as the bus gathered speed heading into Little Neck. When he snapped the string for the warning bell, the driver pulled over at Marathon Parkway. James staggered into the stairwell, pushed open the door and went out onto the curb. The bus continued on its journey while James stood there noticing the fast food restaurants now dotting Northern Boulevard. But some of the old haunts across the Boulevard were still there. Mary's Delicatessen. The auto body shop. He turned and headed back toward 248th Street, making a left toward the playground.

He tugged at his tie, feeling odd walking this route in a business suit instead of blue jeans and sneakers. So much had changed, in the neighborhood, in his life. The aroma of autumn, from dead flowers and decaying leaves, wafted around him. Breathing in, he recalled the season vividly. How he'd refused to bounce the basketball home until the last ray of daylight deserted him. Those familiar odors convinced him the important things would be as he remembered, but once he reached the entrance of the park he realized he'd been mistaken. Deceived.

He stopped. The once imposing wrought iron gate lay on the ground, ripped off its hinges. Not because it had ever succeeded in keeping anyone out. Something told him to turn around, but instead he stepped over the gate, walking past peeling chain link fences, going further into a place he remembered more clearly than anywhere he'd ever lived.

Time for you skins to take the suckers' walk. Other echoes of the past bombarded him. "The Eve of Destruction" blasting from scratchy portable radios sitting on giant stone checkerboard tables that were now smashed to pieces. He couldn't help but shake his head that the song's prophecy had been fulfilled.

Hey, guys, this is Jimmy Devlin, the Gonzaga Flash. Maddest dog in this park and the brightest son of a bitch you'll ever meet.

The park benches where girls sat on their infrequent visits had also been destroyed. All the slats were gone, along with the heavy, scoop-shaped concrete supports. Weeds that had managed to break through the blacktop brushed at the cuffs of his pants as he headed toward the park house. His mouth was dry, but when he reached the brick fountain, he saw that the spigot had been knocked out. That's when he noticed the entire park house was charred. Who knew how to set a brick building on fire? Sheet-metal windows stared back at him. He forced himself to keep going.

He trudged up the ramp, avoiding the edge where a railing had once been, keeping his gaze downward. This was supposed to be the past, but he couldn't recognize it at all. Once he reached the top, he looked up to see what was left of the place where he once felt most at home.

All the other guys are going out for the team. I played a couple of times down the schoolyard with the big kids and...I, well, I like it.

The basketball court was covered with shattered glass from broken beer bottles. The basket on one side was gone. The rim on the other was bent downward. LIFE SUCKS was spray painted across the perforated backboard. James closed his eyes tightly, maybe for a minute.

He had never come back to the park since that March night when he had also been alone. He should not have returned today. Some things are better left alone. His memories had been vandalized too. He could no longer deny it. Everything he remembered had been torn apart.

He turned, heading back to Northern Boulevard, wishing he could leave his regrets behind as well. The detour had been a disaster. Hopefully things would go better when he reached his real destination.

PART ONE

I
January 1955

JAMES THOMAS DEVLIN, JUST THREE YEARS OLD, squinted from the glare of the sun bouncing off the deep piles of snow. He wanted to reach out of his stroller, being pushed by his mother, and touch the white cold fluff, but he was pinned by bags of groceries on each side.

His mother struggled to get the stroller through the narrow path, finally reaching the corner of 37th Avenue and 104th Street.

"Well, aren't you ambitious, Peg!"

James looked up to see a strapping woman in a cloth coat and kerchief wrapped tight to her head. When he didn't recognize her, he fixed his gaze on what appeared to be man's galoshes on her feet. She bent over and mechanically patted him on the head.

"Marketing all done 'fore the rest of the world has a chance to clear its walks," the woman wheezed.

"I've got a husband and two children who eat, Mrs. Shea," his mother replied. "Snow or no snow. And with my sick mother to shop for, too, I've got no time to be wasting."

While Mrs. Shea and his mother discussed the unexpected storm that had passed through the night before, James fidgeted in his stroller. He managed to twist himself so that he could see the candy store across the avenue. He watched two elderly men, each with a newspaper tucked under his arm, walk out of the store, onto the sidewalk, and then next door into Gavitt's Tavern.

The conversation between his mother and Mrs. Shea seemed to shift in tone with Mrs. Shea saying, "I for one like to keep on top of things. Here's a for instance." Although her voice lowered, her unfamiliar words sounded even clearer to the boy. "I'll bet you didn't know that two of those black bastards up the Boulevard froze to death last night."

"That's dreadful," James's mother said, reaching down and wrapping the scarf around her son's neck. Although talking to the woman, his mother looked at him.

13

"Was an older brother and sister," Mrs. Shea continued. "Hadn't paid the rent and the super turned off the heat. Then the Edison turned off the juice yesterday, so their space heater did them no good."

James's mother grasped the stroller's handlebars and began to push, but Mrs. Shea didn't stop talking.

"Cops found them huddled together this morning, dead as doornails. I say their type hasn't sense to come in from the rain...or go back south to see their relatives in winter."

"Our landlords are the Pritchards," his mother said. "They're colored and as nice as anyone in the neighborhood."

"I know the jigs who own that building you live in—and so does the rest of Corona," Mrs. Shea sneered, her mouth curling up in a smug smile.

Using her foot to give the wheel a push, James's mother leaned into the handles, coaxing the stroller out of the snow and murmured, "I better be going. We've got to stop at the church and get Jimmy back for his lunch and nap. Good day, Mrs. Shea."

"Goodbye, dearie," Mrs. Shea said. She attempted to give James another pat on the head, but his mother managed to give the stroller a strong push, leaving Mrs. Shea standing there with her hand out.

Moments later, they were at the bottom of the stone steps leading up to Our Lady of the Crucifixion. "We'll make this a short visit," his mother said, swinging the stroller around and straining as she pulled it backwards up the steep stairs, causing James to bounce with each step. He was familiar with the routine, but it seemed more difficult this time due to the snow.

When they reached the top, his mother jerked open the heavy wooden door, holding it open with her foot so that she could pull the stroller up the last half-step into the foyer. They entered the dark, high-ceiling building, causing James to focus in the dim lighting. Eventually, he was able to make out the backs of people standing solemnly before those pictures along the church's wall. His mother wheeled him down an aisle, lifted him by the snowsuit from the stroller, and deposited him in a pew. Everything was hushed. She slid alongside him and unfastened his chin strap to remove his hat. A swipe of her fingers pushed the hair off his forehead before she unbuttoned her frayed tweed coat but left her own felt hat devoutly in place. She then took her rosaries and prayer book from her purse and looked down.

James began his repertoire of silent distractions. He leaned over, playing with the clasp. His mother had once told him it was to hold men's hats. Again and again, he let it pinch his chubby fingers, always making sure it didn't snap against the pew and give him away. When that bored him, he stood on the kneeler, rocking back and forth, then crouched straddling it, lifting it up and down without being noticed by his mother who was whispering and fingering her beads.

He then looked for that contorted figure of Jesus mounted on a large cross. What was he doing there? He looked back at his mother who was flipping the pages to her prayer book. He looked over to see holy pictures tucked in as reminders of dead relatives and neighbors. She'd told James that they were keepsakes from wakes she'd attended. He wasn't quite sure what any of that meant, but was more interested in playing on the kneeler until he slipped and flopped back on the pew.

His mother yanked him toward her, lifting him toward the stroller, and dropping him back down in between the two bags of groceries. She grabbed her things and pushed the stroller to the side altar at the front of the church where they stopped. James tried to get a closer look at the figures partially hidden behind racks of unlit votive candles, at the mournful face of the woman and unclad body of the man draped across her, the blood trickling from his open palms.

"All right, James," his mother said. "Do you think I should let you put the money in the box even though you weren't a very good boy this time?"

James looked up at his mother to see she held a coin in her hand. He waited in anticipation, his expression brightening as she handed him the quarter. Immediately, he knew what to do and leaned over the stroller's side and pushed the coin into the box hanging below the candle rack. He smiled to hear it clatter. He then watched his mother take a needly stick, touch it to the flame of one and light another candle. She then bowed her head and closed her eyes for a moment, before exhaling and gripping the stroller's handlebar, wheeling James toward the exit. She bent down to put his hat back on and make sure he was bundled.

James kicked his legs excitedly, happy to be leaving such a gloomy place. His mother gazed at him. "James," she said, "this is God's house. He's happy when we come visit Him."

James stretched his neck and looked back. God's house was like none other he'd seen.

"God is the Father of all of us and we're here on earth to do His will." She slipped her glove on her hand. "You see, God's will is different for each of us. We have to listen to Him very closely to find out what He wants us to do." She leaned in closer to James's face. "And pray hard for His help in discovering the purpose He has for each of our lives."

James just kept fidgeting, wanting to get to his own house that had toys and a television. His mother stopped talking, stood and leaned into the door to hold it open while she pushed the stroller out. The sun was hidden behind a stray cloud and the wind felt more piercing. His entire body bounced as his mother guided the stroller down the steps. Once they reached the bottom, she said. "You like coming to church, Jimmy, right?"

The young boy knew how he was expected to respond and nodded in the affirmative. He understood his mother, but had no idea what this God wanted. He slid the counting beads on the stroller bar back and forth, hoping the questions would stop.

His mother sighed and pushed him and the groceries through the snow to the Devlins' apartment. Before they arrived, James forgot all about the unseen man God his mother seemed to know.

II
October 1957

LIKE MANY OTHERS IN NEW YORK CITY, Corona, Queens was a neighborhood in transition. Before World War II, Corona had been inhabited
almost entirely by immigrants from Europe and their native-born descen-
dants. In apartments over the stores fronting Northern Boulevard a few black
families lived, headed by maintenance men and domestics who worked in the
community. This small "colored" population was not deemed significant by the
majority of Corona residents; it was condescendingly treated by the whites as an
aberration.

V-J Day in 1945 had signaled the start of a great upheaval in the neighborhood. The unfolding suburbs of Long Island began enticing lifelong residents and
returning veterans alike away from their small houses in Corona, which were attached or stood within feet of each other. The departing occupants were rapidly
replaced by middle-class black families. To these former renters from Manhattan
and Brooklyn, the cramped quarters they could purchase in Corona seemed el-
egant.

The original narrow strip of black families lining Northern Boulevard, one of
two major thoroughfares, first bulged in a northward direction. It soon encom-
passed the entire portion of the town above Northern Boulevard, and crossed into
East Elmhurst. Then, the turnover of homes took a new direction: south, toward
Roosevelt Avenue, the other main drag. Within a year or two, a near-complete ex-
odus of the old residents would occur. In the meantime, the process spread to the
two adjacent blocks, and began working across the avenue that connected them.

Dave Devlin had married Peg Connolly shortly after his return from the War.
Within a year, their daughter, Nora, was born. Housing had been tight, so Dave
insisted they return to his old neighborhood where they managed to snap up a
one-bedroom walkup on 107th Street, close to where he'd grown up, on a block
that had long since "tipped". The Devlins considered the owners of the building, Mr. and Mrs. Samuel G. Pritchard, Jr., the finest sort of colored people. They

lived on the first floor and kept all four of the rental units as well-maintained as their own apartment. The Pritchards had only one greater virtue in Dave Devlin's mind: they were probably the only landlords in town charging a rent that his meager salary could cover.

Dave had rejected the Navy's advice to use his corpsman's training to pursue a career in medicine, and he wasn't interested in preparing for the civil service test that so many of his friends took. Instead, convincing Peg to bet on their future, he chose to start off in a large advertising agency's mailroom where many of the top executives reportedly launched their careers. His bet was already looking good. After a year in the mailroom, he moved up to a traffic spot, then soon after, became junior man on an account team.

Peg went along with Dave's decisions on pretty much about everything, but she did not share her husband's dreamy colorblind notions. Intellectually, spiritually, she knew he was right, but realistically, she could not shake her upbringing in Woodside, an Irish enclave, by a stevedore father who proudly called a spade a spade. For her, the situation on the block had become a crisis. Her reaction was to draw the family circle closer until she could convince Dave to move. Meanwhile, life went on and they had a son, James.

Peg was determined to keep her children safe. She and James would escort Nora to her third grade class at Our Lady of the Crucifixion every morning before she would do the family's shopping or go help her own mother with her chores. At quarter to three on the dot, however, Peg and James would be waiting for Nora outside of her school, no matter the weather.

For playtime outside of the apartment, Peg would take her children to the local playground. Peg didn't mind when it was deserted, since she was better able to keep an eye on the children. Nora, who was eight years old, had little interest in playing with her five year old brother, but the children managed to keep themselves entertained until it was time for Peg to bring them home to prepare the evening meal. With the exception of summertime, when the buses of Catholic Day Camp picked up the children at the doorstep in early morning and dropped them off in late afternoon, Peg knew where Nora and James were at all times.

It was late October when Peg approached Dave, who was standing at the full-length mirror fastened to the bedroom door straightening his tie.

"You have that new campaign today?" Peg asked.

He nodded. "Got to look sharp for it," he said.

"Don't worry. You do." She smiled, hesitated, then added, "I wonder if you mind if I attend a one-day retreat that Our Lady of the Crucifixion is sponsoring. It's on Tuesday."

"I don't know how you could pray more that day than any other." He glanced over to see her hurt expression. "What about the kids?"

"Well, I could drop Nora off at school as usual," she said. "You would just have to bring James to kindergarten on your way to work."

"Kindergarten?" Dave raised an eyebrow.

"The sisters agreed to watch the preschool children, for those taking part in the retreat."

The idea of his son mixing with some children his own age was appealing to Dave. Peg had held back their son after he'd had one of his periodic bouts with bronchitis that late summer. Dave had acquiesced in her decision reluctantly, suspecting that Peg was looking for an excuse to postpone her baby's departure from her side.

He said, "It'll be good for him to get in there with other kids."

"So, you'll do it?" Peg asked.

Dave slipped on his suit jacket, gave Peg a kiss on the cheek and said, "I'll do it."

The day of the retreat, Peg and Nora were up and dressed early. Dave, on the other hand, dragged himself into the bathroom with his son following. Dave glanced down to see James wearing his old canvas combat leggings pulled awkwardly over his pajamas and slippers, and towing a toy tommy gun behind him.

Dave, clad in lightweight pajama bottoms, lathered shaving cream on his face while smoke from his cigarette curled up around him from the ashtray resting on the sink.

"Pow! Pow!" James shouted, pointing the gun at no one in particular, as far as Dave could tell. "I got another one!"

He gazed down at his young boy, images flashing in his mind. He said, "It's easy to pretend, son, but you have to remember that war isn't a game. You can't make any mistakes once it really counts. You have to be brave all the time. No matter what."

James stared at his father, hearing but not understanding the urgency in his voice.

"Otherwise, you'll never be a man." He looked back in the mirror at his half-shaven face as the smoke rising from the ashtray curled downward toward his son's nostrils. There was that same haunted look in his eyes. It'd been thirteen years, and it was still there. Once again, he was taken back to 1942, when it had all started.

*

The national war mobilization was shifting into full gear. As the youths of Corona reached the minimum age to serve, they hurriedly enlisted in their favorite branch of the armed forces. It seemed as though every house had at least one son in service, and David Thomas Devlin at sixteen ached for adventure while enduring endless school days. When his last class let out each afternoon, he'd rush to Hoffman's, the candy store, have a quick smoke with the boys, then head into

Manhattan for his porter job at the Horn & Hardart Automat. It was no different this particular day.

"Well, at long-awaited last!" Sonny announced. "Don't tell us you sat through that French class again, Darin' Dave."

Dave approached the group of young men milling around a beat-up Coca-Cola cooler on the sidewalk in front of the store. No doubt they were debating the merits of the Army, Navy and Marines. Dragging on their cigarettes, it was always the same: each boasting how the tide of battle would shift once he got into the action.

Dave shot back, "You're so goddamn stupid, Sonny. You'll be the first one shipped to France and you won't be able to ask where the bathroom is."

"Very funny, Darin', but you're wasting time if you think you're going to *parlez vous* with all those French whores."

Dave laughed along with the others, in spite of himself.

"Really, Darin'," Sonny said, waving his cigarette, "what's your plans? You gonna enlist?"

Dave pulled one last time on his cigarette before flicking it to the ground and exhaling through his nostrils. "March 15, I'm gone." He met Sonny's eyes.

Sonny raised his eyebrows while the others watched. "Right in the middle of the semester?" Sonny pressed. "Your folks don't mind?"

"Pop's going to sign me into the Marines on my birthday."

Sonny whistled, shaking his head. "Well, I've got my old man convinced to sign me up for the Army. I wanna join the Air Corps. Flying airplanes seems way better than slogging around the Pacific, but my mother's giving him a hard time."

Dave nodded, but thought, *talk's cheap.* He doubted many of his friends would follow through and actually leave school to enlist. But that wouldn't stop him. Being accepted by these guys once seemed so important to him, and after slamming wise-mouth Sonny's head into the locker in response to one too many insults, Sonny and the rest respected Dave. But playing high school big shot had become yesterday's news. It was time to move on to something different, something that mattered and would give him a chance to prove himself.

"Well," Dave said, "I got to get to work. See you later."

*

Not only was the idea of joining the Marines enticing to Dave, but so was getting out of a house with five sisters and his mother Beatrice ruling the cramped roost. He was choking on femininity. Christ, he couldn't even take a shower without moving half a dozen pieces of ladies' undergarments—at the risk of severe scolding if he got any of them wet again.

He considered his father, Thomas James Devlin, to be some sort of saint because he never complained. He was hard-pressed to recall if his father ever raised his voice. He would just keep smiling no matter what Beatrice said to him.

And she said plenty.

Family members loved to tell Dave and his sisters how Beatrice had been the belle of Corona. "She could have had her pick of suitors," one aunt told him, "but she chose your father. Ah, he was handsome, but that didn't mean her family approved."

In their eyes, Tom's intelligence, manners and accounting training hadn't offset the disfigurement that would catch people off guard: a claw-like right hand consisting of just a thumb, forefinger, and pulpy knob of bone and flesh, the result of a childhood accident on the old trolley tracks.

Beatrice's father called him "the cripple" and felt Tom was too content to accept his physical disqualification and stay home with the women instead of joining the Expeditionary Force during World War I. As he bounced from job to job during the Depression, he became the disappointment that Beatrice's father had predicted. In turn, even though Dave could not recall his mother ever spelling it out, one condescending remark or another conveyed her growing disdain for his father. She could not let it go when telling Dave he needed to find an afterschool job to help out financially without adding "because your father can't feed his family."

Dave was often drilled by Beatrice on how to get ahead, about how to be more aggressive than the other fellow. "You must *will* yourself to come out on top," she stressed.

Dave's younger sisters would often watch him receive his lecture while their father just stood on the side, smiling, then kissing each pajama-clad daughter goodnight while his wife continued instructing their son.

All Dave knew was that he had to leave. Yes, he loved his country and felt the call to do his part, but he felt the need to get away just as strongly. He would rather face the entire Japanese Army than spend another night witnessing the subtle abuse of his father, who refused to say a word in his own defense.

But the problem was: how was he going to get his parents' permission? He was sure his father knew very little about war, especially since he never addressed the topic with his son. Just before Christmas, Dave decided to risk tipping his hand. He took a Monday night off from work. While Beatrice put the wet dishes in the rack and his father dried them, Dave, standing in the kitchen doorway, cleared his throat and asked, "Dad, can I go with you to devotions and Benediction tonight?"

His father gave him a curious look. His sisters shared their father's religious fervor, but Dave never had. He felt as little interest in religion as in school, maybe less since being one of the few males in a church full of women made him uncomfortable, but going with his father that evening would mean he'd get him alone.

"Sure," his father said, seemingly pleased.

Not much later they walked toward Our Lady of the Crucifixion without speaking. Somewhere along the line, silence had begun dominating the little time they spent together. Dave wasn't sure whether to pop his question before or after church, but he had to somehow get a conversation going. He decided to pick a topic that still seemed to put them on common ground.

"Those Giants must be really desperate to get back on top and beat the Yanks," he said. After waiting a beat or two and not getting a reply, he continued. "Did you read how they traded three players to the Cardinals for Johnny Mize and paid $50,000 to boot?"

His father glanced in his direction. "That's insanity."

"I don't know," Dave said, keeping in stride with his father. "Big Cat had an off year, but he's always been an All Star. I bet the Cards gave up on him too soon."

"No one man is worth three others," Tom said. "Never mind the money."

Dave wasn't in agreement with his father, who didn't seem to know what it took to win. Instead he just nodded. The church was just up ahead so he would have to broach the topic on his mind on the walk back home.

Soon, sitting in the pew next to his father while the congregation was chanting, he ignored the smell of incense from the swinging, clicking thurible and began mentally rehearsing what he would say on their way back home. He was relieved when the last hymn concluded and the priests and attendants marched to the rear of the church. His father made the sign of the cross, fastened his coat and shuffled out from the pew with Dave following behind.

Once again, they walked in silence side by side. Dave noticed his father's mood seemed serene and he didn't want to ruin it. However, as they almost reached the stoop to the Devlin house, he blurted, "Pop, I want to enlist. In the Marines."

His father stopped, his gaze on the ground.

"Will you sign the consent when I turn seventeen?"

"I...I guess I knew this was coming," his father stammered. "All...all right."

Dave waited for more, but there wasn't. He whispered, "Thanks," then followed his father up the stoop and into the house.

*

Dave didn't need any help waking up the morning of his seventeenth birthday. Instead of waiting for his father to nudge him awake, he jumped up, folded the daybed and rolled it into the corner of the porch that doubled as his bedroom. Wearing only boxer shorts, he walked into the living room tight with furniture his mother had acquired over the years. His father was at his desk, tucked in the corner under the staircase, his head bent over the Bible he read every morning.

Tom flicked off the small brass desk lamp and said, as if to himself, "John, fifteenth chapter, verse thirteen." He then looked over at Dave. "I made you oatmeal."

"Thanks," Dave said. "Let me get dressed first. Don't want to be late."

Tom arched an eyebrow behind his wire-rimmed glasses. "Sure," he said, his tone sounding resigned.

After breakfast, they left the house before any of the women stirred. Dave's pace was slightly ahead of his father's so he slowed himself down. He broke the silence by asking, "You think the Yanks can do it again this year?" Sports. They could still talk about sports.

"I do." Tom grinned. "DiMaggio's got them back on the right track." He stopped short on the sidewalk and tried to imitate the slugger's right-handed stance.

Dave thought, *If Joe D. looked like that at the plate, the Yanks would be in big trouble.*

"But they'll never have another Gehrig," Tom said as he resumed walking.

Dave smiled with the memory of a summer Sunday when he'd sat next to his father in the upper deck of Yankee Stadium as Gehrig came to bat. The crowd had just finished moaning as Ruth uncoiled from one of his ever more frequent strikeouts. He grinned, recalling anticipating how Lou, his favorite Yankee, was about to crush one.

"Here," his father interrupted his thoughts as they reached the staircase to the el.

Dave looked down to see Tom holding out a nickel for him. "That's okay, Pop" he said. "I've got it." He pulled a nickel from his pocket and climbed the steps, his father behind him. They stood together shivering on the windswept platform, until the train pulled into the station. They boarded an empty car and took a seat on a wicker-covered side bench. Two stops later, father and son squeezed through the throng of Manhattan-bound riders anxiously scrambling past them for seats.

The joint Navy/Marine recruiting booth was located on a traffic island in the middle of Northern Boulevard, a few blocks north of the station. "Here we are," Dave said, peering through the steamed-up windows.

Inside, a small space heater glowed brightly in the corner. Dave approached the middle-aged man wearing multiple campaign bars on his uniform shirt pocket. He said, "Sergeant Donovan, this is my father, Thomas Devlin."

The sergeant stood and extended his hand. "Glad to meet you, sir. You should be proud of the very patriotic thing you're doing."

Tom stared blankly at the sergeant. "What do I have to sign?"

The man reached down toward his desk. "Just these three consent forms." He pushed the papers across the desk toward Tom. "You're doing the right thing, sir."

Tom looked at the forms without reading them. "I'll only sign him into the Navy." He turned toward Dave, his face reddening. "I'm sorry, but that's as far as I'll go. I'm not willing to say it's okay for you to invade some island, trying to take another man's life while he tries to take yours. If you want to join the Navy, I won't stop you, even though I should. At least there's less chance of my only son getting killed."

It was the most Dave had heard his father say on the subject. He exchanged glances with the sergeant. The sergeant spoke. "That's fine, Mr. Devlin. No problem, right, Dave?"

Tom looked at his son, hesitating again before closing his eyes for a moment.

"You'll just have to sign these forms instead, Mr. Devlin," the sergeant said.

Tom opened his eyes and immediately scratched his name across each of the forms. He then headed directly to the door.

"I'll be here at one o'clock on Sunday, Sergeant," Dave said. He stood straight, giving the marine a crisp salute before turning and following his father outside. They stood waiting for the light to change. "Thanks again, Pop," he said. "I told you it wouldn't take long."

"You were right," Tom said, his tone sounding distant. This time the silence felt even more awkward.

"Well, I guess I may as well head up to school and clean out my locker," Dave said, hitching his shoulders up.

"Yes, you do that," Tom said. "I'll take the subway back to Manhattan and see if I can get to work on time."

"How's this job?"

"Not half bad, but it's only temporary. Probably be let go when tax season is over."

Dave noticed tears streaming down his father's face and his stomach clenched. But it was done, decided. What else was there to say? Nothing, except to remember that, although it would not make a difference, his old man had surprised him. He had cared enough about him to take a stand.

"See you later," Dave said in a whisper. Then he crossed over to the far side of Northern Boulevard and started trotting toward Flushing High with a lump in his throat.

*

Like all his other rides on landing craft, this one struck Dave as strangely peaceful. Huddled down among heavily armed men of his unit, the young corpsman felt oddly detached. Perhaps it was his different assignment; he wasn't supposed to hurt anyone. His job was to keep the ones who got hurt alive. Whatever the reason, he felt no real involvement in the impending killing and confusion. He shrugged off his comrades' unspoken fear that their high-walled vehicle would be blown out of the water before it reached the shore. That had not happened on any prior invasion. It surely would not happen today. They would hear the scraping of sand under the craft and its gate would plunge inevitably into the shallow surf. Word had even filtered down from command that the invasion of this funny-sounding island, Peleliu, would be a piece of cake—a quick mop-up action.

Dave had followed a back-door route to the service branch of his choice. As a Navy corpsman, he'd requested an assignment to a Marine unit. He hadn't been disappointed by the Corps. They were indeed the elite group he had sought. The plan was always right. You did not have to understand it, only execute it, letting the reflexes embedded in you by training take over.

This mechanical approach to life and death had worked well for Dave during his prior landings. As the First Marine Division advanced island by island, the combat had been gory. The corpsman's job was especially grim: "collecting" the initial casualties on the beach before setting up an aid station. Yet, Dave had been trained not to react, to expect the carnage, to welcome the opportunity to use his skills. The drilling had made the task manageable. He found he could efficiently tend the wounded and retrieve the dead while maintaining a calm exterior.

As the landing craft continued to lurch toward Peleliu, Dave felt for his pack of cigarettes. Next to him, Johnny D'Amato was pulling the straps of his haversack repeatedly, trying to make them tighter than they would go. As Dave watched his friend fidgeting, he realized that the trenching tools and provisions stuffed in their packs and extra canteens hanging from their web belts would be a blessing if they made it onto the coral island, but a huge problem if they were dropped in deep water.

Ever since his mother had insisted he work after high school, instead of going out for track, he'd longed to be a part of something. Now he looked at the young men around him while waves splashed over the side of the craft, and thought, *I'm certainly part of a team now. Dear God, I really must be crazy. I honestly enjoy this.*

The background thunder of the artillery from the Navy ships faded as the first wave of LVTs approached shore. Whenever he headed into combat, Dave's senses seemed particularly sharp. He could just make out intermittent bursts of machine gun fire whenever his landing craft glided on a breaker. The acrid, smoky sky above the landing boat's sides perfectly matched its steely color. He turned to Johnny. "Race ya to the bathhouse, D. Loser buys the pizza back home."

"Not that slop from Leo's in Corona, Davey," D'Amato replied.

One of the new guys asked, "Pizza? What's that?"

A sergeant growled, "Don't know, but I'm gonna find out, if we get home alive."

Johnny and Dave had been together since basic training. Cut from the same cloth, Johnny came from nearby Astoria. The pair turned all the drudgery of life in the Corps into a game, to be overcome as quickly and easily as possible. Their lives became a continuous contest between the fair and skinny Irish kid from Corona and his dark complexioned and chunky Italian counterpart from Astoria, except for battalion baseball games. Then Johnny demanded to be captain and would argue, bargain, and threaten until he had rigged the sides so he teamed up with his friend as a keystone combination, Dave at shortstop and Johnny at second base.

Dave looked Johnny straight in the eyes as they hunched below the starboard wall of the LVT. "Good luck, buddy," he whispered so the others wouldn't hear.

The LVT ground into the coral. Johnny nodded, kissed the Miraculous Medal around his neck, then made a speedy Sign of the Cross. "Mother Cabrini, pray for us," he said in a low voice.

There was a surge of men going down the rear ramp. Dave and D'Amato sunk into knee-deep surf, then turned toward the beach. As soon as Dave had stepped off the ramp, still hugging the side of the landing craft as he headed for shore, he realized the intensity of enemy fire was unlike anything he'd previously experienced. What they were encountering could only be described as devastating.

He and Johnny struggled out of the water already crowded with bobbing bodies, the blueish-green hue turning to a ghastly violet from the blood. When the pair dove face first among Marines felled at the high-tide mark, Dave began shaking. An odor of fresh death filled his nostrils and lungs. He gagged, panicked to think that if he swallowed enough, it would surely prove fatal.

As rounds zinged over them and mortar shells exploded around them, Dave lay paralyzed in the sand next to D'Amato. His heart pumped audibly, making his blood ebb and flow in exaggerated fashion, his breath coming only in forced, wheezed gasps. In earlier landings, he'd acknowledged his own death was possible, but he'd been able to brush the thought aside without real impact on his conduct. This time, as he lay shivering on the steamy beach, his death became not only likely, but an imminent occurrence. He and his buddies were about to be dismembered on this coral island. The idea that he couldn't correctly spell or pronounce the name of the place where they would die disturbed him unduly.

There were moans and pitiful cries for a corpsman all around him. He heaved himself to his side, snorting each breath. "D," he grunted, "got to..."

D'Amato, half buried in the sand, rolled his head toward his friend. The glistening eyes of the men met for a moment, sharing an expectation bordering on certainty that this would be their last morning together. In unison, they rose to their knees, then dashed to the right toward the nearest cries for help.

They worked feverishly through midday, like two misplaced sandpipers running parallel courses on the beach, unconcerned for their own safety. It seemed as though each man they reached was in worse shape than the last, yet more expectant of the miracle they could not possibly perform. Marines with their guts and innards bubbling out clutched onto them, their expressions fearful and wide, trying to mouth their final words. Others dropped by head wounds lay still, their eyes alone briefly searching for an explanation.

Dave and Johnny became little more than witnesses to death. By late afternoon, the overwhelming number of casualties stripped Dave of all detachment. He fell to the sand, cradling the bare head of a fading young Marine on his blood-soaked sleeve.

"Not so bad, am I, Doc?" the young man pleaded.

Dave looked at the boy's shredded trousers, emptied from the crotch down by the mortar, revealing scant remnants. Choking on his words, Dave sputtered, "Naw, pal. You're not too bad." He hoped the boy didn't see the tears in his eyes. "I've seen a lot worse here today."

The boy smiled weakly, then convulsed in his grip.

Dave sat straight up, blinded by tears. "D!" he screamed. "I can't take any more of this. Oh, God," he begged, "let it be my turn and get it over with."

Johnny headed toward his buddy, hunched over. There was a whir, followed by a thud of a shell landing in the sand between them. The impact of the mortar flattened both of them, but Dave managed to scramble to his feet and rush to D'Amato. Johnny was stretched on his back, an ugly wedge of shrapnel protruding from his neck.

"No!" Dave roared, as he absorbed the sight. "D, I'm sorry. No!" he bellowed, before the contents of his stomach rushed up to the back of his mouth.

"Gung...gung," Johnny rasped.

"Don't you leave me here, D!" Dave howled, ripping the cover from a bandage he'd pulled from his haversack. He pressed it down on the gurgling wound.

Johnny grabbed Dave's hand with surprising strength and pulled it away, down to his chest. He held it there, staring plaintively at his friend.

"Our Father," Dave wept, "who art in heaven..."

Johnny's eyes turned placid, scanning the sky.

"Forgive us our trespasses, as we forgive those who trespass against us..."

Johnny clamped down on Dave's hand, his olive skin blanching through his heavy, sand-covered beard as he bled out from his neck and unseen wounds to his back.

Dave grabbed him by the collar, shaking him. "D, don't leave me..."

Johnny's gaze clouded. He shuddered and grew limp. Dave hugged him close to his chest, then pushed him to the sand, prying Johnny's clenched jaws apart, giving him mouth-to-mouth. As his lips touched those of his friend, he felt a terrible chill, but forced himself to exhale steadily into D'Amato's open mouth, pausing as he should, waiting for a response. His answer was an ungodly whistle as the air he breathed in escaped out the edges of the oozing shrapnel wound in Johnny's throat.

Dave could never remember how long he worked on Johnny that day. He came to believe that he had exhaled his own soul in trying to revive his dead pal. At dusk, two Marines pulled him off the already brittle D'Amato without a struggle, and led him to a foxhole scratched painfully into the coral surface. The battle had subsided for the moment but, within hours, the Japanese had regrouped and commenced a nighttime lunge at the shore position. Flares lit up the sky. The enemy's mortars and larger guns randomly pounded the Marines' makeshift entrenchment.

Dave awoke from a sleep that bordered unconsciousness. He felt surprisingly refreshed by his brief rest; his composure had been restored. If anything, he was further removed from his comrades than ever before. He had been cut completely adrift from the others by Johnny's death, and was unable to look at them, unable to speak to them. Isolated, half of a dismembered pair, he awaited the onslaught without a trace of emotion. Once again, the Japanese shells and bullets began to find their targets and the shrill cries for a corpsman rose again.

Dave moved into action, slowly at first, but then he gathered momentum, rushing from casualty to casualty. He soon abandoned all caution, sprinting straight into the fire to reach any fallen Marine, living or dead. As he dragged another lifeless body back toward their lines, he heard the same eerie descending whistle as before. *A little short*, he thought, as the dark world around him flashed red, and the idea was wrenched from his mind.

Like a boxer after a slip to the canvas, Dave bounced to his feet, his ears ringing from the shell's explosion.

"Come on, you mothers, try me again. You had your chance earlier but you blew it. Damn you all to hell!" He stood erect but shaking, his helmet knocked yards away, his face pockmarked by tiny bits of shrapnel. A steady flow of blood ran from his skull down the back of his neck and into his shirt.

Dave blinked hard, then stiffly dropped to a crouch. He dragged the corpse back to the line, completing his delivery. A fellow corpsman led Dave away, submissive and unaware of the chaos around him.

*

Dave flinched at the sound of Peg's voice.

"Hurry out of there, you two, or you'll surely be late!" his wife yelled.

Dave tried to shake the memory. He stood in front of the bathroom mirror, the razor in his hand. His eyes were wet again. He glanced down to see Jimmy looking at him. Quickly, he collected himself.

"Your mom's right," Dave said. He wiped the excess lather from his shaving mug, rinsed the soft bristles of the brush, and placed them back in the medicine cabinet. "Time to get a move on. Get dressed. I'll time you."

James raced out of the bathroom without saying a word. Dave watched his son nearly trip as he tried to run in the oversized leggings. *He's as stumpy as D'Amato.*

He chuckled softly and headed to his bedroom. James's clothes had been neatly spread on Dave and Peg's double bed, which occupied the center of the small room. Dave began putting on his own clothes while supervising his son's frantic efforts to dress himself.

Peg and Nora came into the bedroom. Peg said, "Goodbye and good luck." Dave bent down to receive a kiss first from his daughter, who then dashed out of the bedroom, and then his wife.

"Peg," Dave whispered, "I'll be late tonight. I better get over to the hospital again."

Peg's hazel eyes softened. "How is he?"

Dave's expression was somber. "Not good."

Peg mouthed, "I'm sorry," and squeezed his hand before turning to leave.

"Ready, Daddy!" Jimmy shouted, just as the apartment door banged shut behind Peg and Nora. "Stop the clock."

Dave turned to look at his son. "Pretty good, Jim," he said. "Why, yes, I do believe you've just broken the Corona and northern Queens' records for your age group. Next time you'll have to shoot for the county mark. Wait a second, though." Dave glanced at his watch, shaking his head. "What about the shoes?"

"Oh, Daddy," James said. "I need help to tie them."

Dave smiled. "I know, I know, but you keep working on that, too." He bent down in front of his small boy to tie his shoes. Without warning, James threw his arms around Dave's neck and leapt at him, almost knocking him to the floor.

"Love you!" James said, looking his father in the eyes and planting a sloppy kiss on his lips.

For an instant, Dave closed his eyes and let himself feel the child's warmth. He squeezed his son tightly and said, "I love you, too." The boy's arms circled his head. "Come on, we'd better hurry."

In minutes they were clattering down the single flight of stairs to the street. James fought to keep up as they headed down the block. He took at least two quick steps for every one of his father's as they turned the corner and headed toward Our Lady of the Crucifixion. The morning sun projected their outlandishly thin shadows before them on the avenue while the chill penetrating their light jackets promised to give way to a warm midday.

Dave noticed James's tiny hand holding his side rib. "You okay down there, buddy?"

James took a deep breath, nodded and picked up his pace to prove as much. He then said, "Nora and I are almost ready for the test. We been practicing that song a lot."

At Dave's insistence, the children had already mastered the Marine Corps Hymn. This time he promised them a lunchbox and schoolbag, respectively, if they learned "God Bless America" by heart.

James began belting the song out as they continued walking. "...Stand beside her, and guide her, through the night with the kite up above–"

"Though the night with a light from above," Dave corrected. "I think you ought to keep practicing." Dave gently patted his son on the head. "But you'll be ready real soon." They neared the school and Dave looked down at his son with a twinkle in his eye. "Now listen, Jimmy. This is an important day for you. You're probably not going to know any of the other kids, but I've got a solution for that." He straightened his tie and crouched down to be face to face with his son.

James paid close attention.

"When you go into the classroom, go up to each kid and say, "Hi, my name's James Devlin. What's yours?"

"Can I shake their hand, like you do?"

Dave suppressed a grin, thinking, *this is bound to be interesting*. He said, "Sure. That would be real nice." He stood up and they entered the school, proceeding to the kindergarten room.

They walked into the classroom. James halted, dazzled by the brightly colored playhouse to his left. A smiling, young-looking nun approached them.

"My name's James Devlin," James said, thrusting out his hand. "What's yours?"

After a moment's hesitation, the nun said, "Why...why I'm Sister Maureen." She took James's outstretched hand and shook it. "Why don't you join the other children?"

"Okay," James replied, walking over to a group of children seated at a table. One by one, he told them his name, asked them theirs, and stuck out his hand. They regarded him cautiously.

"Is he considering a career in politics?" Sister Maureen said, her tone wry.

Dave grinned, obviously proud of his son. "I wouldn't be surprised, Sister." *Whatever he wants. Anything at all. He's going to be the one*. He called over to James, telling him goodbye, but then noticed a black child sitting alone at a table under the window. He motioned for his son to come over to him.

"What, Dad?" James said, running up to his father.

"You see the colored boy at that table?"

James turned and looked. "I told him my name, but he didn't tell me his."

"That's Lance Pritchard. His grandma and grandpa are our landlords. Why don't you sit with him?"

James shrugged, as if that would be just fine with him. Dave leaned over and kissed him. "See you later tonight," he said.

James nodded and immediately headed over to Lance's table.

"Have fun," Dave said, walking out of the room. As he headed toward the el, he was glowing. There was no denying that he was fully taken with the boy. James's innocence was total, his trust complete. Dave had never known anyone like that, child or otherwise, untouched by shame or embarrassment. He certainly did not remember being like that when he was a kid, even when he was James's age. Dave wondered if it could possibly last.

*

Lance rose as James approached him. James noticed he had dark, warm eyes and skin so smooth it seemed liquid. James said, "Hi again."

Lance looked James over and asked, "How old are you?"

"Five," James said.

"I'm six," Lance said. He stood with his legs spread apart. "I'll be seven years old in December, though."

James nodded. "Your grandma and grandpa own my building."

Lance scowled. "I'm living with my grandma and grandpa."

"Why?" James asked. He noticed that Lance kept rubbing his wrist.

Lance shrugged. "My mom and dad had to go away."

James's eyes widened. "For how long?"

Another shrug. "Grandma says just for a while."

It occurred to James that Lance must be living in the same building as he did. He smiled at his new friend, pulled out a chair and sat down. Lance followed suit. As he lowered his gaze from across the table, James noticed that Lance's thumb looked as white as his own. He pointed to it and asked, "What happened to your thumb?"

Lance hesitated before replying. "I got burned when it went into some really hot water."

"Does it hurt?"

Lance shook his head. "Not anymore."

James sucked up some air. "My grandpa hurt his hand, too." He looked directly at Lance. "Can I touch it?"

Lance shrugged. "Sure."

James reached out and gently touched Lance's thumb and, for some reason, laughed nervously.

"We call it a zebra stripe."

James laughed again.

Lance pulled his hand away, reached into his pocket and pulled out two miniature plastic soldiers. "Want to play?"

James examined the green figurines. They had their own base, which let them stand upright when placed on the table. He looked back at Lance and said, "We could play war instead." He motioned to the playhouse. "We could play over there."

"Okay!" Lance exclaimed, giggling. His dancing eyes transformed his face into that of a mischievous dark elf. He stuck the toy soldiers back into his pocket and took James's extended hand and walked toward the playhouse crowded with kindergarten veterans.

"I'll be the Marine and you be the Jap. I'll give you a head start. I'm counting to ten, but when I catch you, I get to kill you."

"Sounds like fun." Lance said, running behind the playhouse in search of a place to hide.

III
October 1957

D AVE KEPT HIS CHAIR PRESSED into the corner across from the turquoise curtain separating his father's half of the room from the other patient's. There was only one other chair, and his mother occupied it, right at the head of the bed, which had been cranked up as high as it went so that Tom could almost sit up straight. Between Dave and Beatrice, four of his five sisters fluttered in tight formation, taking turns chatting with their father and each other. It was an old habit of Dave's to keep distance from his sisters, even though he had to admit they'd grown up nicely.

While he was gone to war for more than three years, he'd missed the part where they had changed from girls to women. There was no mistaking their kinship; not just the cookie-cutter Irish faces, but their clothes, which mimicked his mother's attire: belted, buttoned-up dresses with demure hemlines down to their shins. In a word, they were proper, but they were no prissy slackers.

Like him, one had joined the Navy as a WAVE, another became a nurse, and two others USO volunteers. Each had done her part for the war effort in his absence, even the sister in the convent who prayed for all of them and victory. Strange as it was, each sister reminded him of his father. It struck him as odd that Tom's influence had taken root so naturally with his daughters, while his only son always tried to fight it off.

Constance, Dave's oldest sister, said, "You look terribly tired, Mother. Let's take you home now."

The others nodded in agreement across the cramped hospital room.

"That's a good idea, Beatrice," a gaunt Thomas Devlin chimed in. "One of us has to keep up strength. Besides, David here can keep me company 'til curfew."

"Yes, my dear," Beatrice replied limply, displaying her fatigue. In a bustle of activity, her daughters helped her with her coat and hat. She then gave her husband a hug and kiss, followed by perfunctory pecks from Dave's sisters before the entourage shuffled out of the room.

As soon as their steps began to fade down the hallway, Tom said, "Did you know that your mother was the only woman I ever wanted?" He looked over at his son. "I never looked at anyone else. I thought I had no chance, with this ugly hand of mine, but I wound up with her after all. How many people can say that they got the one thing they wanted most in life?" He smiled weakly. "Now, it didn't turn out like I hoped. Couldn't make her happy. Guess I had to be punished for that." He shrugged. "I accepted it. I always felt sorry for people who spend their lives wondering how things would've been if they'd gotten what they wanted. I was never tortured by what ifs. I knew how it felt to get exactly what you asked for."

Dave didn't know how to respond, embarrassed by the mention of his parents' relationship. Tom grew quiet as well, and the silence began snowballing in Dave's mind. Rather than being just the absence of sound, the quiet took on an oppressive quality. If he did not break the silence, he'd forfeit his power ever to do so again. He noticed his father's face was so thin, Dave could see his cheekbones in relief. He cleared his throat.

"Have they let you follow the Series? Burdette's been killing the Yanks. I hear he'll pitch again, if there's game seven. Let me get you a television in here for the last games."

Tom raised an eyebrow. "David, I'm finished. Do you understand? I'm through. Nobody gets over with what's wrong with me. It'll be a miracle if you see me tomorrow." Tom started hacking, a painful cough that thumped him back against the pillows.

The force in his father's voice stunned Dave. He stood with tears running down his face.

Once Tom's spell passed, he said, "Take it easy now, David. I'm not trying to upset you."

Dave was surprised by his father's peaceful expression. He was also more alert than he had been in days.

"Let's lay it on the line, not just pass the time." His blue eyes searched for his son's assent.

Dave nodded and sat back down.

"Good," Tom said. "Now, how about getting my pipe and tobacco?" He motioned toward the nightstand.

Dave got back up and did as his father requested. He remembered fetching the tobacco for him from the wooden humidor when he was a little boy. It was one of their private rituals. He wondered whether the tobacco would still be Prince Albert. It was. He handed everything to his father, including a book of matches.

"Pull up your chair," Tom said, as he began packing the bowl with tobacco and then lit it with his good left hand. Once Dave was settled again, sitting up alongside the bed, Tom continued. "There's no need for a lot of gloom." He took a puff.

"This tumor is squeezing me from the inside out. I've come to realize I am nobody today, and tomorrow I'm going to be nothing at all. Insignificance incarnate. All our lives we struggle against and deny that fact. Every blessed thing we do cries out, 'Look at me. I'm somebody. I'm important.' But in the final analysis, all any of us can ever be is nobody going on nothing."

David looked down. "You know," he said, "I saw a lot of guys die overseas. Not one of them knew their number was up until it happened to them." He paused and looked up at his father. "Are you afraid?"

Tom puffed on the pipe, then withdrew it from his mouth in time to let a single phlegmatic gasp escape.

"I was." He stared across the room. "But that was when I was fighting the idea— Western man's typical reaction. Now that it no longer offends me, I can see the beauty of the process. It's so undeniably fair. Here I am, a single person on a large world bouncing through an infinitely larger time and space. And I'm about to die, just like everything that ever went before me and everything that will ever come after. You think about that long enough, you discover it's God, music and poetry all rolled into one."

Dave couldn't ever remember his father being so talkative, so insistent on conveying his ideas. Was he reacting to the medicine or to running out of time? This was a man he had never known, or at least never noticed. That's when Dave realized his father had stopped talking. He looked up and saw Tom glancing down at his pipe in his hand. He then looked Dave directly in the eyes.

"Listen, enough of this cosmic chatter. Let's talk about you and me." He waved the handle of the pipe. "And, by the way, not a word of this to your mother. She'll accuse me of turning into some sort of heathen on my deathbed."

Dave laughed, making his father grin.

"Know what I keep remembering, David? When you were little how you used to follow me watching whatever I did, then trying to imitate me." Tom started to laugh, which triggered another coughing spell. He blinked back the tears in his eyes as the coughing and wheezing subsided. "The funniest part was that you copied me so well. You would only use the forefinger and thumb of your right hand. Nothing else. You'd open a door like that, hold a pencil like that. I was afraid the other fingers on your right hand would end up being useless."

Dave smiled. "I wanted to be exactly like you. Even overseas, the guys used to make fun of me for screwing a jar shut with my three fingers sticking out."

Both men grew silent again until Tom said, "It's pretty obvious you changed quite a bit in the service. I was worried about you when you were in high school. That crowd you ran with was trouble. You had no use for school; no use for God Himself."

Dave nodded. "I did change. In more ways than one. I guess I see a lot of things

35

differently now—including you. I went through a bad stretch before I left home. I didn't want to be like you anymore. I don't know why," he lied. "Then we all lost so much time fighting the Japs. I suppose I've been trying to catch up ever since I came back." A realization came to him. "And to get you to see me differently. I've been trying to make something of myself, for the sake of my own family."

"You're living a fine life. In fact, you've put your old man to shame. I never was able to succeed the way I thought I should, the way you're doing. Believe me, I'm very pleased." Tom's voice cracked, his eyes glistened. He then reached over and lifted David's chin up, forcing him to look him in the eye.

"But I'm scared for you, David. I'm scared for your whole generation. You're all trying to pretend that all the terrible things you saw never happened. You think you can just ignore all the horror because you were the conquerors, and that there's nothing you can't overcome, if you set your sights on it. And you are all very, very mistaken. There's a very heavy price God makes us pay in this life. Especially for victory. That war's not over yet. It may never be."

Dave sat in shock at the condemnation. How could anyone deny his generation's hard-fought triumph? He needed clarification, but a voice came from the doorway.

"Visiting hours are over. I'm afraid you'll have to leave."

David turned to see a middle-aged nurse standing there, and then back to see his father's eyes had glazed over and his face was drained of color. He stood up, scraping the chair back. He grabbed his coat and hat before approaching his father's side again, taking the pipe from his hand and resting it on the nightstand.

"David," Tom muttered, the hospital gown hanging from his faded frame. "I'm sorry."

Dave leaned in. "For what, Pop?"

"For all the years I let slip by between us. It was my job to start a real conversation." He began to sob. "That night...when you asked to enlist. I had so much to warn you about. You just didn't know what you were getting into. How could you? It should've been so easy to talk to you. I just couldn't. I was too weak."

"How did you know how it would be, Pop? You never went." Dave looked at his father, realizing just how different they were. No one had ever been able to convince his old man that he'd missed out on something. His father had seen things differently. Maybe he had seen everything differently, which was why Dave had never been able to understand him.

He grabbed his father's hand. It was so cold. "Hey, Pop," Dave said, "it's nobody's fault. It's just the way things happened. Okay? And tonight...we really talked, didn't we? That's important to me."

Tom forced a weak smile. "That's good to know 'cause it sure took the starch out of me."

Dave stood up, pulled the blanket up over his father. "I better get going before they chase me out." He gazed down at the shrunken man and didn't know whether to hug or kiss him, so he gave his hand a light squeeze. "See you tomorrow."

His father barely nodded.

Dave turned and started to walk out when Tom cried out, "David!"

Dave stopped and Tom stammered, "Just take care of yourself."

"Sure," Dave replied. He gave a brief wave and dashed out of the room.

*

Dave had lumbered up 107th Street. He hadn't felt this low in a long time, probably not since the War. When he reached the landing to his apartment, he unlocked the door. The lights were out, so he turned on the wall switch, lighting up the living room to the left and the kitchen to the right. The door to the bedroom was shut. He knew Peg, Nora and James would all be asleep inside. It was difficult sharing a room with kids. There was the dread of waking them up and a fear of getting caught in the act if you made a move on their mother. Still, he needed to get in there. The door creaked as he entered as quietly as he could.

"That you, Dave?" Peg whispered.

"Yeah, go back to sleep." Dave opened the closet, got on his knees.

"What are you doing?"

"I just need something from the closet." He groped around in the dark until he found what he was after. When he retrieved it, he closed the closet and went back out into the living room, a baseball glove in his hand. The mitt was wrapped in one of his old white t-shirts, stained yellow from the Neatsfoot Oil he had applied to the glove just the week before when he put it away for the winter. He unwrapped the glove and removed the baseball that had been molding its pocket. As he slipped the glove on his left hand, he felt where the thin interior leather had rotted from his sweaty hand after years of putting it on and taking it off.

He sat on the couch and repeatedly pitched the ball into the glove. The smacking sound gave him comfort as he mentally revisited the conversation he'd had with his father. Of course he knew why he'd tried to become someone totally different. His mother had simply ground down his respect for his father until there had been no choice but to go in an entirely new direction. But then he realized this very night that all the abrasion had never touched a much deeper layer of love between them. Despite everything, it had remained intact, buried just where they had hidden it years before.

There would be no happy ending; Dave had seen too much death to miscalculate its arrival later that night. At least he had learned that his father should never have been an object of his pity. The man had made peace with himself and his God years before. Dave held little hope for as graceful a life and death.

IV
March 1958

S NOW HAD BEGUN TO FALL when Peg looked out the window just after four
a.m. The glass was slightly frosted on the outside, yet sweating on the side
facing the crowded bedroom. The vaporizer hissed and spewed as it filled
the room with moist, thick steam. She went over to James's cot to check on him
one more time. He was breathing heavily. The boy's slightest wheeze made her
anxious. The moving men would arrive in just a few hours, and she could not
afford to have her son's chest cold develop into full-blown croup. She murmured
a short prayer, and as part of the ritual brushed his hair from his forehead. After
checking on Nora in her small single bed, perpendicular to James's cot, Peg returned to her side of the double bed and crawled in.

Dave was more restless than usual. He thrashed about, kicking off the covers.
Probably just the heat in here, she thought. Despite the stress, she couldn't help
feeling excited. *Our own house! That will certainly shush up all the old biddies like
Mrs. Shea.* With separate rooms for the children, the following night in their new
home wouldn't be nearly as stifling. She and Dave would finally have some privacy
and lovemaking would no longer have to be rushed and furtive under blackout
conditions. She pulled the thin top sheet over her and drifted back to sleep.

*

Dave sat up with a start, his pajamas soaked. The empty hum meant the vaporizer had puffed itself out and a sudden shiver shook him. He climbed out of bed
and headed to the bathroom, trying not to wake Peg and the kids. What had he
been dreaming?

He turned on the shower and stripped out of his pajamas. *A good day begins
with an excuse for not shaving*, he thought, climbing into the shower. Moving
would do.

*Sure, it would be a good day. A big day. First, the promotion. Now a house. In
Douglaston at the very end of Queens, practically the wilderness known as Long Is-*

land. He was sticking to his plan. Making it happen, day by day. There was money to be made on Madison Avenue. Big money.

He was entitled to his success. To the cute wife, nice kids. He was only getting back what he had already put in. Yet something was bothering him. Some dissatisfaction he was unable to identify.

Maybe it was the routine. Though it had been so long ago, he still remembered how it had been overseas; to be so focused on reducing your chances of death that you would not even budge in your sleep. The intensity of living in constant jeopardy was over, and that other feeling of mission had dissipated and would not return, no matter how hard he tried to convince himself that what he was doing was important.

He didn't even bother trying to explain the feeling to Peg. She was like everyone else: They all considered him a war hero. Mr. Lucky To Be Alive.

Yes and no. Sure, he was alive. That was more than Johnny D'Amato could say.

Still, there was a catch. He was alive, but he had to go on living, even though he knew the most exciting things that would happen in his life were over and done. Even though he knew he had been responsible for his best friend's death.

It was a nightmare that resurfaced in bits and pieces. Each time, he would relive one snippet of the scene on the beach at Peleliu that was ever so slightly changed. The revisions came out a little more favorable to him each time, but were still unpersuasive. If he hadn't screamed, Johnny would have stayed down. If Johnny had stayed down, he wouldn't have been hit. Simple. Dave was the guy who had cracked. And it had cost someone else.

The worst part of all was that there was no way of setting the record straight. Dave could never square things with Johnny, and he would never forget. At the same time, he would not correct everyone who thought he was a hero. Let them discover his secret for themselves.

The water cascading down his back began to cool. "Get down to business, Devlin," he muttered, turning off the faucet. "You've got places to go. Things to do."

*

Steam from the bathroom rushed into the chilled bedroom when Dave opened the door. A towel wrapped around him, he glanced out the clouded window and saw that the air was crowded with thick wet flakes, the ground covered with snow.

"Just what we need," he murmured.

Peg and Nora were dozing in their respective beds, but James sat up in his cot, bent over and hacking away. Dave went over to him. "Hey, buddy, how you doing?"

James shrugged, his chest filled with phlegm. A beat-up teddy bear lay next to him, face up.

Dave lowered himself and leaned against the cot. "Here's the plan. You and Nora stay here with your mom after the moving men pick up the stuff. I'll leave you one chair you can fight over, okay?" After he paused and saw James's confused expression, he said, "No, really, we'll keep your cot here so you can lie on it and keep warm. Then once I've got everything squared away at the house, I'll come back for all of you and we'll be on our way."

James beamed. "Am I really gonna have my own room?"

"You sure will," Dave said.

James's expression suddenly grew dark, tears gathering in his eyes.

"Hey, what's the matter?" Dave said.

"I want to move, but I don't want to leave Our Lady of the Crucifixion."

Dave put an arm around his son's shoulder. "I know. Nobody likes to switch schools, but you'll like St. Aidan's just fine. I'll bet they've got a lot of great kids there, just like you." He attempted to pat down the hair sticking up in the back of James's head.

"And I'm going to miss Lance."

The earnestness on James's face made Dave's heart jump. "He's been a good friend of yours, huh?"

James nodded. "We stopped playing war because Lance didn't want to be the Jap all the time. But now we take turns and play every day." He hesitated, adding, "Or we did."

Dave stared into space, visualizing two Marines separating him from Johnny D'Amato on Peleliu. James's hacking pulled him back from the memory. He cleared his throat and said, "It's always tough to leave a friend behind, but it's not like you're never going to see him again, right?"

James shrugged.

"You can still come and see him, write him. And he can visit you in Douglaston."

James's eyes widened. "Really?"

"Sure," Dave said cheerfully. "In fact, I saw Lance yesterday and he told me he'd come see you before you leave. Maybe you can plan something then."

James nodded, but still seemed uncertain. It occurred to Dave then that maybe his son was feeling off his game; first with his Grandpa Devlin dying, then being sick and out of school for so long, and now moving from the only place he ever knew.

Dave said, "I guess it hasn't been too easy for any of us lately." He took a deep breath. "Now, let me get these girls going so we all get something to eat before the moving men show up. Try and get some more sleep for now."

James rested his head on his pillow and closed his eyes. Dave then pulled the blankets up under his son's neck.

James was still resting when he heard cabinets opening and closing in the kitchen, the tea kettle whistling, his mother and sister moving around the room. He sat up, craning his neck to peer out the frosty window as best he could, getting a glimpse of the snow. Its silent activity and frozen peacefulness reminded him of the last time he saw his grandpa. He'd knelt by the casket, the body in the upholstered box somewhat similar to his grandpa, but where was the man who'd pinched his cheeks and tousled his hair? He'd reached over to touch the pincer-like hand and was stunned to find it lifeless and cold, its great strength vanished.

"Come on, Jimmy," his mother said, coming into the bedroom. "Time for breakfast." She helped him with his terry bathrobe and slippers, and led him to the kitchen table where Nora was already eating her breakfast and reading the back of the cereal box.

"Mom," Nora said, "where are the scissors? I want to cut off the box top."

"I already packed them."

"But I only need two more box tops before I can send them all in with the coupon for the good prize."

"I have no idea where they're packed."

"It's not fair!" Nora said. "James always gets the prize that comes in the box."

"Knock it off, Nora," her mother said, pouring the last of the milk from the carton into the drain. "Just eat your breakfast."

James had barely begun eating his own cereal when the team of three large black men arrived. The furniture started disappearing out the apartment door. By the time he finished eating, the living room had been stripped of all its furnishings. The bedroom was bare, except for his cot. By the time he was through canvassing the nearly vacant apartment, his father came dashing into the kitchen, brushing snow from his shoulders and stamping his galoshes on the muddy floor.

"Got the last of the breakables in the car," Dave announced. "I'll be back to drive you to the Promised Land in a couple of hours." Then he was off again.

His mother kept a few crayons, coloring books and storybooks handy to entertain Nora and him. Around noontime she served soup in cups that she'd kept out. Nora kept chatting about the move, unable to hush long enough to drink her soup despite Peg's admonitions. In contrast, James was preoccupied, his heavy eyes downcast.

"What's the matter?" his mother asked. When James shook his head, she added, "Come on, out with it."

"Dad told me Lance said he'd stop by before we leave. I don't think he's going to."

"You've got to be patient." She touched his shoulder. "We have time before your father will be back."

James's distress increased by the minute after lunch, until his mother ordered him back to his cot and under the covers. Lying there, fighting sleep, he strained to hear any footsteps on the staircase leading to the apartment. His hopes rose when he finally heard someone. He sat up.

"It's me!" his father yelled as he opened the door without ringing the bell.

James dropped back onto the cot, nearly in tears.

"And guess who I have with me!"

James jumped out of bed. He ran into the living room to see Lance Pritchard standing there. Each boy froze when he saw the other until Lance said, "I came to say goodbye. And tell you I hope you get better soon."

James's father went into the kitchen.

"My Dad says we can still be friends. I can come here and you can come see me."

Lance shook his head.

"Why not?" James said.

"My mom and dad said they would come back again, but they lied."

"I'm not lying!" James said. "You'll always be my friend. We can write to each other and everything."

Lance shrugged and said, "I guess."

Dave walked into the living room carrying the last few household items in a shopping bag. He said, "Lance, could you give your grandma these?" He held out a set of keys.

"Sure," Lance said, taking the keys and putting them in his pocket.

"Well, then," Dave said. "That's about it."

"Come on, then," James's mom said, pulling on her coat. Nora and James did the same. James's father wrapped a blanket around his son and picked him up. Nora took her mother's hand.

James watched Lance follow them down the staircase, then stand at the open front door of the building as his father loaded him into the Plymouth sedan. While his mother walked around to get Nora settled on the other side, James rolled down the window and waved at his friend.

"Roll that window right back up, young man, before you catch your death of cold," his mother snapped.

James reluctantly complied, but could no longer see his friend through the snow-covered windows.

His father honked the car's horn and pulled from the curb. James did not notice that Lance was still waving after the car headed north on 107th Street, signaled for a right turn onto Northern Boulevard and disappeared from sight.

V

March 1958

THE TRIP TO DOUGLASTON through the persistent snowfall seemed endless. The chains on the Plymouth's tires clicked rhythmically as they drove out of Corona and through adjacent communities of Flushing, Auburndale and Bayside. Finally, the car descended into the gasoline alley separating Bayside from Douglaston, then crawled up the slick hill leading to their destination. When they reached the intersection of Northern Boulevard and Douglaston Parkway, Dave announced, "This is it, the new hometown for the Devlins."

From the backseat, James gazed out of the windshield, ignoring the struggling wipers and trying to familiarize himself with everything at once. At the corner of 245ᵗʰ Street and Northern Boulevard, his father made a right turn and stopped in front of a complex of red brick buildings.

"Directly to your left, folks," Dave said, using his best travelogue impression, "St. Aidan's Church and parish school where you, Nora, will start tomorrow and you, Jimmy, as soon as you shake that bronchitis. Now pay close attention, my friends, so you can learn the all-important trick of walking to and from school from your new home."

They continued on 245ᵗʰ Street, entering a residential area. The car wound around an exaggerated curve at Rushmore Avenue, then began to climb a grade lined by identical Tudor-style houses. At the top of the hill, the Devlins crossed Van Zandt Avenue into another flat, mock Tudor block. Halfway to the corner, Dave pulled into the drifts at the right hand curb.

"Here we are," he announced. "Home sweet home."

Soon, with James in his arms, he waded through knee-deep snow, clutching the boy in his arms, then passed him to Peg, who'd already struggled her way to the sidewalk. Dave returned to the car and extracted Nora and a shopping bag, then followed Peg up the path that the moving men had already plowed through.

Peg carried James into the house and up the staircase to the second floor. She hadn't paused to remove the blanket and outer garments from him. "You're going right to bed, young man. This house is freezing from the door being open."

"Where?" James said. "My cot's not here."

Without replying, Peg entered a tiny bedroom. Against the wall was a full-size single bed, assembled and made.

James gave his mother a curious look. "Is that mine?"

"Sure is," she said. She took his boots off and pulled down the spread and blankets and slipped him between the sheets. "Nora has one just like it."

Dave came into the room, wrapping an arm around his wife. "So, how do you like it, champ?"

James grinned, but couldn't speak due to sudden hacking.

"Listen," Dave said, tucking James in tightly," get some sleep so you can get better and get to that new school, you hear?"

James rested his head on his pillow and nodded. Once his parents left the room, he began studying the surroundings. The room was freshly painted. He noticed one of the three cardboard boxes marked "front BR" was opened and he recognized some of his things spilling out from it. Despite loud banging noises working their way through the pipes from the basement to the hissing upstairs radiators, he soon fell asleep.

*

It was five days before James convinced the doctor and his parents he was well enough to attend school. Nora had kept reminding him that kids in the neighborhood didn't believe she really had a little brother. This widespread doubt of his very existence unnerved him. When the day finally arrived, he awakened before sunrise and rushed into Nora's room.

"Wake up! It's time to go to school."

A groggy Nora opened one eye. "Jimmy, are you crazy? It's still dark out."

"Come on, Nora," he whined. "I don't want to be late."

Nora sighed in resignation. "All right, but *only* because it's your first day. And remember, you owe me one really big favor."

"Okay!" James rushed down the stairs ahead of her. He ran into the kitchen where his mother, in her plaid flannel bathrobe, was standing.

"What do you want? Wheatina or Farina?"

"Wheatina," James said, while Nora, came strolling in correcting, "No, Farina."

Peg looked from one to the other and said, "I'll make them both, but you'd better eat it all."

Once James finished his Wheatina, his mother helped him in his newly pressed white shirt and navy blue uniform trousers. When departure time finally came, she helped him on with his coat, hat and galoshes, and issued her instructions for the day.

"Now, remember, you're supposed to be in Class 1-B, and your teacher is Sister Mary Ellen. Pay close attention when Nora walks you to school this morning. She gets out later than you and your father says you should be able to walk home by yourself. All right?"

He nodded, then said for confirmation, "I just stay on 245th Street until I get to our house, the one with the lamppost out front."

"That's right." Peg was still uncomfortable with him being on his own. She kissed him on the cheek and then whispered to Nora, who was standing at the door waiting, "You watch after him, you hear?"

Nora sighed, but then led the way down the snowy driveway with James trailing behind. Sloshing down the sidewalk, he felt like an explorer who just landed in an uncharted region. His head and eyes were in constant motion, grasping for the first time close-up impressions of the naked trees, shoveled walks, and uniform houses he'd studied from afar, now glowing in the sharply angled morning sunlight.

"Wake up, Jimmy, will you?" Nora said. "That door's only for the sixth, seventh and eighth graders. We've got to go all the way around the building to get to your classroom."

James followed Nora down a sloping schoolyard facing Alameda Avenue where they cut across the entrance to the new wing that housed the lowest grades. They entered a large vestibule and stomped the snow from their galoshes onto a long rubber mat inscribed with a big block A. They then pushed through another door and entered a dimly lit hall. James's classroom was the first door on the right.

"Okay," Nora said, "here you are. Whatever you do, don't get lost going home."

"I won't." James pushed open the door and went inside. A craggy-faced nun, whose pinched features resembled an apple left to wither in the sun, looked up from her desk.

"Yes?"

James noticed some students were already sitting up in their seats, their hands folded on top of their desks. Barely above a whisper, he said, "I'm James Devlin."

"Take your wraps off and hang them in the closet in the rear of the room. Then take the last desk in the last row."

Guessing what "wraps" were, he went to the closet, passing by gazing eyes, and struggled to hang his coat and hat on an empty hook. After pulling off his galoshes, he scanned the room and saw the empty desk and headed directly to it. He then sat down and folded his hands like the other pupils did. The shiny desk was quite a switch from the lift-top, inkwell models at Our Lady of the Crucifixion. There wasn't a spot or scratch on it.

"Your books are under the desk," whispered a boy across the aisle.

Puzzled, James bent down and peered into a hollow space beneath the seat.

Sure enough, there was a stack of books, each wrapped in brown paper. "Thank you," he mouthed to the boy. Soon all the seats were filled just as the school bell sounded loudly.

The morning ritual began with prayers. It was apparent to James that his classmates at St. Aidan's were far more holy and knowledgeable than those at Our Lady of the Crucifixion. Hardly restricted to a rudimentary Hail Mary, the standard fare of his old class, these children breezed through the Our Father and even the Apostles' Creed with amazing speed while James observed them in abashed silence.

The rest of the morning only confirmed his initial assessment of the situation. Sister Mary Ellen, a short, round and roving general in swirling black dress offset by white headdress and bib, commanded the class from the front of the room. James couldn't help but notice her sagging breasts, parted by a large wooden cross. Mushrooming in perfect unison, against the flanks of a crucified Christ, they jostled her starched bib up and down with every step she took. Over again, she called upon a small cadre of students to recite the lessons.

James could scarcely believe the feats the nun's inner circle of pupils could perform in arithmetic and spelling. But when the time for reading arrived, he was simply astounded. The reader the class used looked as big as a dictionary. The chosen students effortlessly read aloud sentences, passages and pages James could not begin to comprehend. He tried to follow along, but was unable even to turn the page at the proper time without checking to see what the rest of the class was doing.

James muttered a silent prayer of thanks when Sister Mary Ellen finally sent them to the closet, row by row, to retrieve their wraps at the end of the day. Once they were dressed, they stood next to their desks while she led them through acts of faith, hope and contrition—prayers totally foreign to James. Then the nun left to escort the children who rode buses to their various departure points in the schoolyard. Once she disappeared some pupils began to giggle and chatter.

"Who has been gossiping?" Sister Mary Ellen demanded, having returned unnoticed.

A blond girl pointed in James's direction. "It was him, Sister," she said.

James's eyes widened. He exclaimed, "Was not!"

"There's no sense denying it, young man," the nun said. "Follow me." She pivoted, swinging her skirts around her as she strode down the hall.

James picked up his schoolbag, walking through the gantlet formed by the classmates. He squinted at the girl who'd lied, but she just looked away. Once he reached the door, Sister Mary Ellen pushed it open, telling him to keep following her. They traveled across the icy pavement until they reached a line of bundled children clutching schoolbags and lunchboxes.

"You shall take the Manor bus home, sir," the nun commanded.

James panicked. He didn't know where this Manor was. He only knew how to walk from school to his house. Tears began gushing down his face, but the nun turned and crossed the playground to head back to the building.

"Hey, kid, what's the matter?" called a young man, approaching him. He was wearing a white cloth harness crisscrossing his chest, on which a silver patrol boy's badge hung.

James gazed up at the boy, who was even taller than his father. Pimples dotted his cheeks and chin. "I just moved here," James wheezed. "I only know how to walk home, but she wants me to take the bus."

"Now listen to me. You've got to settle down. That old bitch can't put you on the bus, so don't worry about it."

James flinched at the word "bitch" for a nun. God could strike them both dead. He said, "But...but..."

"Listen, the cops would lock her up if she started shipping kids off on buses when they're supposed to walk home. Just wait and see. In about five minutes, the old prune face will come back to get you. She'll act like she's doing you one big favor by letting you go home. Play along. She's been threatening kids with that wrong-bus routine for years, but she never put one on it yet." The patrol boy then winked at him and trotted back to his post.

Moments later, just as predicted, Sister Mary Ellen stormed back out of the school. "Mr. Devlin, I have decided to pardon you this one time. Should you violate my rules again, however, your punishment will be swift and certain. You may leave now."

"Thank you, Sister," James said, forcing the words from his mouth. He picked up his school bag and hurried across the yard, keeping sight of Alameda Avenue. Later that evening, he outlined the day's disasters over dinner.

"Are you sure you're not exaggerating a bit, son?" His father had changed out of his suit and sat down at the kitchen table.

"James is always making stuff up," Nora sneered. "Everything's always a big deal."

"Uh uh, it's all true," James insisted. "That Sister Mary Ellen hates me and I didn't do anything wrong."

His mother said, "Nuns aren't like that. Why, look at your aunt, Sister Celine Therese. You're crazy about her."

"My sister's a nun, but she's a good egg," his father said.

"And even if you were wrongly accused of talking today," his mother added, "that only makes up for some other time when you didn't get caught. God evens it all out in the end. You'll see."

James shoulders sagged. Maybe he was making what happened into a bigger deal than it was. Later, as he lay in the darkness of his bedroom, he prayed that his parents were right and things would get better. Maybe if he begged God for this one favor, just this one, this Supreme Being with the strange sense of humor and justice would intercede on his behalf. He had often asked God to appear to him at night to let him know that, unlike Santa Claus, He was real. It had never happened, but this time he really needed help. As he looked out the window next to his bed, he tried to mimic his classmates: "Our Father, Who art in Heaven..."

*

The next three days were better. James stayed invisible in his last seat in the last row. While the elite few read, added and subtracted out loud, he drifted into his private dreamland, summoned back successively by the recess, lunch and dismissal bells.

Friday began the same way. Before the children had finished reciting the Apostles' Creed, he was traveling to places he'd seen pictured in the Maryknoll missionary magazine that faithfully arrived at the Devlin residence. His reverie ended during reading period, right in the middle of a story about Zeke the farmer. Sister Mary Ellen stopped a boy who had been unsuccessfully trying to describe Zeke's pig's surroundings.

"That will be quite enough, Mr. Lawrence. Now we will hear from Mr. Devlin."

James wasn't sure how many times she'd called his name, but when he heard her say it in no uncertain terms, he leapt to his feet. He had no idea where the last pupil left off reading. Holding open the book, he stammered and stuttered until Sister Mary Ellen said, "Patrick, show your inattentive classmate the proper place."

A tall boy who sat in front of James turned around, yanked the reader out of his hands, flipped through several pages, then tapped the spot where the recitation had ended.

James began to read out loud as he'd been taught at Our Lady of the Crucifixion, moving his index finger under each word, trying to sound out the many unfamiliar ones, but still stumbling.

"Dear Mr. Devlin, at St. Aidan's School we do not point with our fingers to read like simpletons. Your efforts are woefully inadequate. Please sit down."

James sank into his seat. Sister Mary Ellen stared at him, but addressed the class as though he were no longer in the room. "You must understand, children, the new boy in class is a little slow."

James's eyes filled and his face started to burn. For the first time in his life he felt hate. Its strength frightened him, but as he watched the nun bully other unfortunates that morning, he embraced the feeling. His eyes fixed on the nun, constantly directing his disgust at her crabbed countenance. He was afraid to take his eyes off her for an instant, lest she lash out at him again.

He walked home for lunch, wrestling with his conscience. He would not tell his mother, but quietly plot his revenge. He repeated the awful words: *That old bitch*! But his secret intentions dissolved upon seeing his mother in the kitchen. She placed a sandwich on the table for him, and asked, "What's wrong?"

He immediately poured out his story, sparing no detail. He concluded that he couldn't go back to that classroom, that he hated her and wished she would die over lunch in the convent.

"Calm down," Peg said, "and eat your sandwich. Then we'll talk about what to do."

As she watched James pick at his food, she stewed. A sister wouldn't persecute someone without reason. His story didn't make sense. Surely he was just being oversensitive. She pulled out a chair and sat next to him.

"Listen to me, Jimmy. You have to go back this afternoon. You've only been at St. Aidan's a week. We can do some reading this weekend, if it will make you feel better, but I know you're one of the smartest boys in that class. You've just got to go back and try again."

"Okay," he mumbled. Soon, she was helping him with his coat and hat, and kissed him goodbye.

Dave had a late afternoon presentation at work and would miss dinner again that evening. Peg got the children bathed and in bed, and had a plate of food ready for her husband when he arrived home. It was becoming a new routine.

"Things didn't go well with James again. He says the nun is still picking on him."

Dave pulled out a chair and sat down. "It's probably nothing. We have to give Sister the benefit of the doubt. He's just a kid."

"Well, I think I'll do some reading with him over the weekend, just to make him more sure of himself."

"That's a great idea," Dave said. He washed down a mouthful of food with a swig of water. "I'd really hate for him to feel like he's behind all the others."

On Saturday and again on Sunday, Peg sat with James at the kitchen table and asked him to read aloud from his favorite books. He recited from a children's Bible story about Noah flawlessly.

"That's just the way you have to do it in school," Peg said. "Relax, take your time, and you'll do fine."

"Okay," James said, even though his tone was dubious.

"What's the matter?" Peg said.

"Nothing...but why did God get angry and drown all the people? Even the animals. What did they do wrong?"

Peg removed her wire-rimmed glasses and rubbed her temple. "I don't know, Jimmy. I guess the people hadn't done what He wanted them to do. They made

God angry and He decided to punish them. I have no idea why He drowned the animals too."

James looked like he was going to respond, but then said nothing further.

*

Although James followed the reading conscientiously Monday, Tuesday and Wednesday, the following week passed without a single opportunity to redeem himself. The next day was Holy Thursday, the last day of school before the Easter recess. If he did not get a chance to recite by then, he would have to endure the entire vacation before he got another turn. All morning, James leaned forward in his seat, hoping for a chance to perform, but then the lunch bell informed him that he would have to wait until the afternoon session. His mother had to go to Grannie's, so she'd packed lunches for him and Nora to eat at school.

Sister Mary Ellen's rainy day lunch rules were particularly strict. The pupils were required to eat at their desks in silence. But there was no release to the freedom of the schoolyard as on a fair day. The students were obliged to fold their hands atop their desks when they finished and maintain a monastic silence until the bell to resume classes rang.

Sister's command, somehow related to people starving in Africa, was that no remnant of lunch remain at anyone's desk, leaving James to doggedly chew his warm liverwurst sandwich. When he felt the first contraction in his abdomen, he ignored it, but it was followed by another, and then by a quick ripple of cramps. He raised his hand to gain the nun's attention, but her head was down, focused on a book. He slid out of his seat and approached her.

"Sister," he whispered, "may I please go to the bathroom?"

"No, you may not," she answered. "You must wait until it is lavatory time and go with everyone else."

"But, Sister, I have to go very bad."

"Return to your seat, young man." She turned her eyes back to the book of scripture.

Squirming uncomfortably, James retreated and sat down. Without warning, one sudden sharp twinge released his bowels.

"Ew!" squealed a girl nearest to him, pinching her nose. Others pointed as whispers swept around the room. With tears in his eyes, James looked up at the sound of a sharp rap on his desk.

"Leave this room at once, you disgusting creature," Sister Mary Ellen snarled.

James stumbled off-kilter out of the classroom and down the dark corridors toward the boys' bathroom. Once inside, he locked himself in a stall. Wailing, he pulled his shoes, socks and pants off, then ripped the fetid underwear off and flung them in the toilet. Desperately wiping himself with single sheet after useless single sheet from the toilet paper dispenser, he spat again and again on the tile wall envisioning the nun's face.

His frenzy was beginning to subside when he heard a knock on the stall door.

"Jimmy, let me in," Nora said.

He hesitated, but unlatched the door. Nora surveyed the disarray. Barefoot and naked from the waist down, James self-consciously retreated to a far corner of the stall and cried uncontrollably.

"I'm supposed to take you home," Nora said calmly. "Your coat and schoolbag are outside. Let's get you cleaned up and get going."

After she wiped his smeared crotch, buttocks and legs with the tiny rough slips of paper, she said, "That's about as good as we can do here. Now put your pants and shoes back on. I'm going to wash my hands then I'll wait for you outside."

"But what about my underpants?" James asked.

"Just forget about them, will you?" Nora snapped. "Mom's sure not going to want those things anymore. The janitor will get rid of them. I gotta go before someone catches me in the boys' room."

Once James dressed, he found Nora waiting for him outside. She said, softly this time, "Listen, this wasn't your fault, but don't expect the kids in your class to ever forget it."

Coat buttoned, he followed Nora out of a seldom-used door near the bathroom. They trudged home in silence. It had stopped raining, but the late March wind blew up his pant legs and against his crotch. As he trailed behind his sister, he wondered whether God expected him to obey even when what he was told to do was wrong. He considered the question for some time without arriving at an answer. He only wished he hadn't listened to the nun that afternoon. He wished he had run out of the room, before it was too late.

*

Peg Devlin rang the doorbell of St. Aidan's Convent at nine thirty Good Friday morning.

"I'm Mrs. Devlin. I'd like to see Sister Mary Ellen," she said to the elderly laywoman who answered the door.

"Why don't you have a seat over there in the parlor," the woman suggested.

Peg took a seat in an armchair. She hadn't told Dave of her plans, and could not believe she was there in the convent, ready to challenge a nun's judgment and authority. All her life she had done precisely what the sisters said. She had been raised to believe there was no other option. But this was different. This was her child. This had to be done, regardless of what Dave might say. He was upset by what had happened to his son, but if anything, the Devlins were more deferential to religious authority than the Connollys. She didn't know how Dave would react, but she did not care.

Some five minutes passed before the nun came out to the vestibule. "I'm afraid I do not make appointments with parents during my Passion observance," she stated brusquely.

"I would only like a word with you, Sister."

"I'm afraid you did not understand me—"

"I just want you to tell me what happened with my son, James."

The nun paused. "Since you insist, Mrs. Devlin. It is my opinion that your son is mildly retarded and simply does not belong in my classroom."

Peg felt as though the woman had driven a spike between her eyes. The word conjured up images of mongoloid children confined in attic rooms. She clutched her purse to her cloth coat to keep from doubling over.

"You're wrong," she said as she backed away from the nun, who watched her without expression. "And I swear you're going to see just how wrong you are." She opened the convent's door then slammed it shut behind her.

Peg was nearly home before she regained control. *No sense fuming anymore, not when we know where we stand. Easter vacation gives me ten full days. Plenty of time to set things straight.*

When she got back home, she called James into the kitchen and sat him down at the Formica table wedged in a tiny alcove. She grasped his arm. "I don't really understand how all this happened, but I know what has to be done. When you go back to school after vacation, you're going to be the smartest kid in that class. You're going to show Sister Mary Ellen and every other child who's the best."

Peg had been a top student in grammar school, but her family's finances dictated secretarial school and employment thereafter. She approached James's instruction in methodical fashion. She turned to the first page of the reader. James began reading to her without using his index finger as a guide. He read page after page, story after story. They read morning, afternoon and evening, breaking only for meals. When they completed the thick book once, they started at the beginning again. The initial tedium became a delight as mother and son gleefully shared their secret. Conspirators, they gloated over the trap they would soon spring.

The drill continued for ten full days. The night before classes resumed, Peg sat on the side of James's bed and supervised him as he dressed in pajamas. He then raced through his newly mastered litany of evening prayers. When he crawled into bed, she tucked him under the covers and gazed down.

"You know you're ready, Jimmy." She then flipped off the overhead light. ""And either tomorrow or the next day, or the day after that, you'll get your chance. And when you do, you show them, you show every last one of them."

James looked up, his mother silhouetted by the light from the hall. "I will."

*

Reading was first on Sister Mary Ellen's agenda the following morning. "Well, children," she said, "it is time to shake you out of the doldrums, clear out the cobwebs, and see if you remember anything after such a long vacation. Today's story is a particularly difficult one about a family of otters. Who would like to begin the reading?"

Only one hand shot up.

"Why, Mr. Devlin, I'm sure the children would be thrilled to hear from you again," she said, her voice coated with sarcasm.

James stood and recited without hesitation, maintaining a perfect cadence so that the nun would be unable to call on anyone else. After completing seven full pages, he sat back down at his desk. Teacher and pupil glared at each other until Sister Mary Ellen looked away without saying a word. James just sat wondering if she would take him on again, and vowing to be ready if she did.

*

The last day of first grade was only a half day. As soon as the parish priest distributed a report card to each child, class was dismissed for the summer. Each student would follow his or her bus or walker line out of the classroom, leaving Sister Mary Ellen for good, unless she delivered the ultimate punishment of being left back for another year in her care.

Minutes after dismissal, James ran up the Devlin's driveway to the side entrance. He pulled the screen door open, and walked up the three steps to the kitchen to find his mother placing sandwiches on the table for him and Nora.

"How'd you make out?"

James hung his head down. "Not so hot," he muttered, reaching into his father's old Marine haversack. He handed Peg his report card.

Peg pulled back a metal chair and sat down. She straightened her glasses, a new, vaguely cat's eye-pair, and removed the card from the envelope. She began studying it. Scowling at first, she then broke into a smile. "You little brat. It's all A's!"

James grinned widely.

"I'm very, very proud of you."

"Do you think Dad'll be happy?"

His mother smiled. "I'm sure he will."

That's great, James thought. *He'll be really happy, too!*

VI
April 1961

WHAT IS TAKING HIM SO LONG? James thought as he cranked down the front passenger side window of the Plymouth sedan.

For James, Sundays seemed to be all about waiting. Waiting for Mass to end while he fidgeted in a jacket and tie, even though he'd never seen a picture of Jesus wearing anything other than his play clothes.

Waiting for Sunday dinner at Grannie's to be over. He had to admit it was delicious, and he loved the old woman who always fussed over him, but why couldn't everyone else wolf down the roast beef and dessert like him so they could get on with the too short day off?

Waiting for his Dad to stop being so polite and come down to the car so they could get on the road to Yankee Stadium. If they didn't leave soon, it might be the third inning by the time they arrived in the Bronx.

"Where've you been, Dad?" he asked, when his father finally opened the car door.

"Got to spend some time with the ladies, Jim," Dave explained. "Besides, Yanks are playing two today against the Tigers."

James nodded. They were headed for a doubleheader, twice the baseball for the same $1.25 price. Thank God they didn't have doubleheaders at church, where they would have at least a second collection, maybe a third.

As he settled back in his seat for the short trip up the BQE, Triborough Bridge, and Major Deegan Expressway, his father began talking baseball. Until last season, James had not been interested, but then things changed. James realized that just by answering the question, "How about those Yanks?" a conversation between father and son would get underway.

As Dave drove, he told James about the games he attended with his own father, when Babe Ruth ruled as the Sultan of the Swat and Lou Gehrig was the Pride of the Yankees. The Babe and Lou became at least as real to James as Grandpa Connolly, who had also died before he was born. And he learned to believe some things were true, no matter what all the baseball books said to the contrary—like Yogi Berra tagging Jackie Robinson out when he tried to steal home in the 1955 World Series.

Dave had told him during one such drive the year before that his talks with his father had never really gotten past baseball, and he hoped to do better. James wasn't sure what that meant, but it made him feel grown up, so he listened closely as his father instructed him on what he called "the rules of the game" that included never being a sore loser, and the importance of having "class" by clapping for an opponent's fine defensive play or rooting for the visiting team's pitcher once he took a no-hitter into the seventh inning.

The lessons he had learned from Dave last season had been put to the test during the 1960 World Series. James's first as a fan, it matched the Yankees against the unsung Pittsburgh Pirates. Their swashbuckling uniforms, black-sleeved undershirts exposed by cropped outer garments, looked rather cut-rate compared to the Yankees' staid home pinstripes and gray road suits. Victory for the Bronx Bombers seemed certain, and a more lopsided series could not be imagined. The clubs swapped victories in bizarre fashion. The Yankees pummeled the Pirates on their days to win by scores of 16-3, 10-0, and 12-0. The Pirates, in contrast, emerged victorious from the other preliminary contests by the puny margins of 6-4, 3-2, and 5-2.

It all came down to the finale, played in Forbes Field on a bright autumn afternoon that James would never forget. He had sprinted home from St. Aidan's and knelt on the living room floor within inches of the television for the last tense innings of the seesaw game. The contest was over as soon as the bottom of the ninth began. Leading off, Bill Mazeroski punched at the second pitch, his usual slap that normally produced no more than a quail-like single. This time the ball rose as if preordained, sailing over the ivy-covered wall as Yogi Berra watched helplessly in left field, once again on the wrong side of a memorable play.

Stunned, James had watched with burning eyes as a hatless Maz tried to round third without having his arm wrenched from its socket by the frenzied Pittsburgh fans. Rivers of tears drained down the boy's cheeks throughout the postgame celebration, which he watched in its entirety. If you have class you witness the opponent savor his victory, no matter how much it hurts. Only a bush leaguer, a sore loser, the worst of all fans, would turn off the set and cheat the winner of his triumph.

Now as he stared out the car window heading for their first games of the new season, James still bristled when he thought back to the World Series. Dave seemed to know what he was thinking and tried to console the boy. "It was a tough loss last year, Jimmy. The Yanks are a much better team than the Pirates, in my book, and they should've won. But sometimes it just doesn't work out that way.

The best team doesn't always win."

How can he possibly be so calm? James thought. The injustice of the Series still left him speechless. He had been so certain God intervened in sporting events to make sure that virtue triumphed. He would never count on that again.

"Let me tell you one thing, though," his father continued. "This year there aren't going to be any mistakes, any accidents, bad hops, or fluke home runs by second basemen. We're going to win it all."

After exiting the Deegan on a long ramp, his father parked southeast of the stadium, on the neighborhood streets surrounding the postal depot. The pair walked straight up the weed-lined sidewalk on River Avenue, past a rough board wall. Through its slats, they could spy upon tennis players in spotless white outfits, playing practically in the shadow of the Bronx House of Detention at the corner of 151st Street.

The Devlins picked up the pace at the jail. By the time they hit the tiny bridge over the railroad tracks they were practically running, double-timing down the final blocks, past Baseball Joe, the cutthroat souvenir baron, and rushing across East 157th Street to the nearest general admission ticket kiosk. James stood at his father's side as he purchased two tickets, dreading a cheer or groan that might rise from inside the stadium in response to a spectacular play they would never see. His father gave him a quarter to toss in the collection mitre of the nun sitting at the entrance gate before they pushed through the turnstiles. They purchased a scorecard from the same anonymous vendor as always, then raced up the ramps to the upper level, sprinting along one of the catwalks leading to the upper deck of the right field grandstand. One final climb up the small cement stairs to the last row of Section 17 left them where they could stretch out in comfort.

The Sunday afternoon in the upper deck passed slowly, magically. Signs of an outside world were visible. The scoreboard updated other games around the leagues. The Lexington Express arrived on the el at regular intervals. Shadows crawled from the backstop toward second base, eventually forcing the stadium lights on. But the game moved at its own pace, untouched by any force outside the stadium, measured only by innings, not minutes. James's father quizzed him between pitches with hypotheticals based on the actual number of outs and positions of men on the bases. "You're Tony Kubek. Sharp ground ball to your right. Where do you go? You're Roger Maris. One hop line single to your left. Where's the throw?"

"Hold the runner at second, then on to the Moose. Come up throwing at the cut-off's shoulders," James would bark happily in reply to his father.

"That's the way you do it, kid," his father would say, grinning. "If you use your head and work hard enough at baseball, or anything else, you'll be better than all the rest."

The Tigers' Frank Lary, as usual, had held the Yankees in check through the first six innings, and going into the top of the seventh the score was tied 1-1. All of a sudden, almost half of the Stadium crowd was standing for the visitors' seventh inning stretch.

"Gee, Dad", James said. "There's an awful lot of people from Detroit here today."

"No, Jim," Dave corrected. "They're not from Detroit. They're just Yankee haters."

James was puzzled. "Why don't they just stay home if they don't like the Yankees?"

"It's a sad story. They were either Dodger or Giants fans, until their team left town for the West Coast. They still love baseball, so they come here to root against the Yankees."

James still didn't get it, and he watched one boy his age who had his head down and seemed to be shuffling his feet as he stood next to his father. He felt sorry for the unlucky kid. What fun could it be to root against a team instead of for one?

"It's tough when someone you love leaves you behind," his father said. "They'll probably never get over it."

James glanced sideways at his father. The man sat as always with shoes removed, feet on the back of the empty seat in front of him, watching the action below. James was cracking the shells and peeling the skin from peanuts, quite properly littering the grandstand beneath his feet. He longed desperately to prolong the day, freeze it, anything to make it all last. His father never seemed very happy, but he came pretty close when he was at the ball park. The game was tight. Maybe there'd be extra innings today. James smiled at his father, but Dave did not notice. He was faraway, someplace else....

*

...On October 1, 1944, when most of Peleliu's hills had been secured, what was left of "A" Medical Company had been pulled out. They had only been there fifteen days, but it felt like a lifetime. They'd boarded the U.S.S. Tryon, which was to transport them to the First Marine Division's home base of Pavuvu in the Russell Islands.

With stops, including an unplanned return trip to Peleliu to pick up the latest casualties, the trip took ten days. It was a continuation of the nightmare, aboard a ship loaded with both moaning wounded and silent dead. Despite the invasion's success, even those like Dave who were not horribly wounded were deeply depressed. "If this is winning," he commented to a comrade, "I'd hate to find out what losing is like."

Pavuvu was no paradise. Land crabs and nasty insects were everywhere, but at least none of them would shoot or shell the Marines. For the first two days on the island the collective gloom would not lift. Dave and his comrades were anchored to their tents, some sleeping all day long, others unable to sleep at all, just lying on their cots with a thousand-yard stare, unable to stop thinking about what they'd gone through and the buddies they had lost.

On the third day, a corpsman nicknamed Straw, who was bunked in the next tent, came over in the middle of the tropical afternoon.

"Y'all know," he announced, "it's no good like this. If this is all that's left, we should've stayed on that awful island. No matter what happened, we gotta get on with living. Let's just go play some ball."

Dave looked from his cot at the others. They did not speak or move. With great effort, he swung his feet to the wooden tent floor and pushed himself off the cot. "Count me in, Straw." He pulled his sea bag out from under the cot and began rummaging through it for his fielder's glove. One by one, his tent mates did the same. Word quickly spread and within a half hour sides were chosen and the home team had taken the makeshift field.

Dave stood at shortstop, bare chested, with his dungarees rolled up a few inches and a baseball cap pulled down over his eyes. The hat felt tight since it pressed against the bandage that was still on the back of his head. He held his mitt against his nose and breathed in. He'd thought he'd never smell its well-oiled leather again.

The sun was beating down and steam rose from the crabgrass after the latest Pavuvu cloudburst. But it felt good. Even the humid air penetrating his lungs felt good. In fact, it felt wonderful. So did the sweat, freely flowing from every pore in his body.

He looked over at Roberts, the guy who filled Johnny D'Amato's vacant second base position. *God forgive me, Johnny*, Dave muttered to himself, his eyes welling up. *I'm glad I made it back. I'm glad I'm still alive.*

He wiped his nose with his forearm and yelled, "Blow it by him, Richie!"

*

Just then, a crack of a bat brought Dave back. He looked down to see James riveted. Both life and baseball had gone on, and the roles had inevitably reversed. He had once been the kid accompanying his father. Now he was the father sitting with his son, enjoying a Sunday afternoon game at the Stadium.

*

Nora had listened to the stack of 45s she'd stuffed into her handbag at least three times, even though the Shirelles and the other girl groups she favored sounded scratchier than usual on the turntable in Peg's old room. As "Will You

Still Love Me Tomorrow" played once again, she shook her head, surveying the pinups of Frank Sinatra that hung on the walls. *How could Mom ever have liked such a square?* she wondered. *Now Fabian, there's a guy who's really cute. With looks and talent like that, he'll be a star forever!*

Nora rose from the bed, went into the tight hallway and entered the upstairs living room where her mother and Grannie Connolly were sitting in the mother/daughter house.

"When are they coming back this time?" she asked.

"I don't know," Peg responded. "They usually stay until the end. Why don't you put the game on the radio and find out what inning it is?"

"Because I hate baseball. It's boring." *About as boring as being here. At least Dad could ask me once in a while whether I wanted to go, too.*

"Why don't you go downstairs and take your cousins out for a while? There are usually lots of kids out playing."

"That's boring too. I'm not playing potsy and hopscotch with all the L-7s who live on this block."

"What's an L-7?" Grannie asked. Nora started chuckling.

"I'll tell you later, Mama," Peg said. "Nora, I'm telling you for the last time, stop being fresh and take your cousins out. I don't know why, but they worship you."

"I'll go for half an hour. That's it," Nora countered.

"Fine, half an hour."

Peg waited until she heard Nora stomp down the stairs to the first floor flat where Peg's brother and his family lived. How those three sweet little girls could be so crazy about Nora, with her moods and mean comments, was beyond her.

"An L-7 is a square," Peg whispered to her mother. Grannie either did not hear her or had lost interest. Peg changed the subject. "She worries me, Mom."

"She's at that stage, Peggy. Nothing suits her."

"I know, but I can't have her running wild back in Douglaston when we come here. But I know what she means. There's no clock in baseball, and no telling when Dave and James will come home."

"It's the man's day off, Peggy. He can do whatever he wants. If he wants to go to the ballgame with his son and come home sober, you should be happy. He could be sitting by himself in some bar spending all the money, you know. He wouldn't be home before the game ended anyway, and he wouldn't have a dollar left." Grannie tapped her foot, putting her copy of the *Irish Echo* down on the end table.

"I suppose you're right. I really shouldn't complain." Peg opened the real estate section of the *Star Journal* that lay folded on her lap. *If a man goes to work every day and stays sober, is that all a woman can ask for?* She snorted under her breath. *Maybe that was my mother's dream for both her husband and son, since it never came close to happening. For me, it's not as simple as that.*

59

*

A pennant for the 1961 Yankees seemed a foregone conclusion. The standings became secondary in importance, merely a sidelight to the impossible two-man assault Maris and Mantle were mounting on Ruth's single-season home run record.

The suspense of his heroes' pursuit of Ruth's record was taking a toll on James by August. He and Nora would head off together on the Catholic Youth Camp bus each morning, then go their separate ways. James spent the day painlessly enough, playing softball in Kissena or Alley Pond Park and swimming in one of the camp pools in Whitestone. But on the bus ride home, he could think of nothing but the Yankee game that night, mentally cursing WPIX for refusing to broadcast weekday games on television. Given no choice, he would plan on hearing the conclusion in his dark room after his parents ordered him to bed, stifling any outcry as he listened through the earplug of his transistor radio, hoping for another homer.

Though James steadfastly proclaimed his neutrality to his father, in truth, he was pulling a little harder for Maris. He recognized that the ballplayer was doing the best he could, and his best was very good indeed. You would think people would like him, but for some unclear reason, they did not.

James felt a curious kinship with his hero. No matter what James did, no matter how hard he tried to be nice to the other boys, they never really seemed to like him. Maybe it was his own fault that he had rivals rather than friends. Whether in school, where since his duel with Sister Mary Ellen he was not satisfied with less than top grades, or playing games or sports, he was always competing, even traveling to Pirates Field in Little Neck to sharpen his skills by playing against the older, serious ballplayers who hung out there. He did not like to lose, and he did not lose often. He would not willingly lose, even if it would make him more popular.

August 8, 1961. Maris had 41 home runs, but had not hit one in four days. James had become rundown from his late evenings with the transistor, and a cold had settled in his chest.

As he sat with the family for dinner that Thursday night, he was visibly uncomfortable. His nose was running freely. He could breathe only through his mouth. If he took too deep a breath, however, he experienced the summer wheeze caused by too much dust and humidity. It was followed immediately by a wrenching cough.

His mother had held dinner for his father, who was quizzing his children regarding their camp activities. Nora, who had changed into a sleeveless top and Bermuda shorts instead of wearing the camp uniform she loathed, rolled her eyes at James when her father was not looking.

"You look awful, Jimmy," his mother declared, still in the short-sleeved cotton dress and flats she had worn to Woodside earlier in the day. "You should go right to bed. If you're not better tomorrow I think I'm taking you to the doctor."

"Oh, Ma," he protested weakly.

"Your mom's right," his father joined in, puffing on another cigarette. "Besides, the Yankee game will be over too late for you to stay up listening. And I'm going to be fixing the toilet upstairs and I don't need you cramming into that bathroom with me."

"How about letting me watch Donna Reed, then I'll go to bed?" James offered. His parents exchanged glances. The bargain was struck.

"Help me clear the table, Nora," his mother said.

He left his parents and Nora in the kitchen and climbed the three flights of stairs to the finished attic room where the Devlins moved the television for the summer. He turned on the large Hunter fan in the window, tuned in the show, which he had already seen in the fall, and curled up on the couch. James did not think much of Jeff, Donna Reed's son. But he had a huge crush on her daughter, played by Shelley Fabares. He kept his secret romance well concealed from Nora, who had teased him relentlessly when she noticed him paying too much attention one afternoon to the recently shapely Annette Funicello. To avoid a repeat of that embarrassment, he continued the younger-brother charade of finding all females loathsome creatures.

In the basement, Dave gathered the tools he would need for his latest battle with the constantly running toilet. Attired in his nightly summer outfit of khaki pants, white t-shirt and moccasins, he trudged up the stairs to the second floor, turned off the water by tightening the valve on the floor, removed the cover from the toilet seat, and began dismantling the inner arm and stopper mechanism. Moments later he was sweating profusely in the cramped, muggy bathroom, and in no time cursing fluently at his inanimate foe.

As he watched the television upstairs, James snorted deeply in an attempt to clear his clogged nasal passages. Something dislodged and slipped down into his throat, blocking the airway. He gagged once, twice, but it would not break free. The realization hit him: he was choking to death during *The Donna Reed Show*.

His bare feet slapped the wooden floor as he rushed from the couch toward the staircase. Knees buckling, he pulled himself down the steps grasping the banister, then pitched across the short hallway, crashing into the bathroom, glimpsing his father's startled face before losing consciousness.

Dave spun around when the door hit him between the shoulder blades. He saw his son's brown eyes bulging before the lids flickered, then dropped, locking them inside his pallid blue face. Soundlessly, the boy collapsed on his back on the floor, just missing the side of the bathtub.

"Peg!" Dave hollered, then dropped to his knees. He pushed down on James's

61

forehead and yanked his jaw out. He pinched his son's nostrils with the fingers of his left hand, covered his gaping mouth with his own, and began breathing into him deeply and steadily, oblivious to the horrified screams of Peg and Nora, who stood at the entrance to the bathroom.

Dave was drenched with sweat. He was kneeling in sand again in a scorching Pacific midday. As he paused between breaths, he saw boots and leggings instead of pajamas. His right hand felt the web belt and canteen at the boy's waist. Dave trembled but forced himself to continue the next series of puffs. When he looked at James's face again it was an unrecognizable purple, and he heard his son's bowels evacuating.

"No, Johnny, no!" Dave yelled, pounding the sunken chest with his fist. He blew a desperate, exaggerated breath into the distorted, grinning face, then another, and one more.

The boy retched once and exhaled a foul draft through Dave's parted lips. Dave looked up and James retched again, emptying the contents of his stomach onto himself. He turned James's face to the side, then cradled his son against him on the bathroom floor, weeping uncontrollably. It was James, not Johnny. And he'd be okay. They were still like that when the policemen, summoned by Peg's telephone call, rushed in, quite surprised to find a nine-year-old victim instead of a baby.

The officers helped Dave stand James up. Dazed, he stepped toward Peg and held their son out to her. Sobbing, she took the boy and rushed into his bedroom as Dave supported himself against the hallway wall.

"Nice going, fella," one of the cops said, removing his cap and mopping the sweat from his brow with a wrinkled handkerchief. "If you hadn't been here you would've lost him." He turned and walked toward James's room, where his partner had already gone.

Dave stood rubbing his left forearm, the one that had moments before been caked with sand. He saw his reflection, pale and shaken in the bathroom mirror. He took several deep breaths, wiped his face in his hands, then walked into the boy's bedroom.

The cops had told Peg that James should be taken to the hospital. She had started removing his clothing and cleaning the feces and vomit from his body.

Dave sat next to James, who was looking tearfully up toward the overhead light, shivering as he lay naked before the police and ambulance attendants milling in his room.

"Hey, pal, that's quite a scare you gave us." His wet eyes undermined his attempt at humor. "But everything's going to be all right now, understand? You're going to be all right. You and I are going to go for a ride."

"Where?" James demanded. "Where are these guys taking me?"

"You've got to go to the hospital—"

"I don't want to go to no hospital!" James roared. He began thrashing and tried to leap up from the bed.

Dave held him down until he stopped resisting. "It's okay, Jimmy. They're just going to check to find out what happened, okay? Believe me, they're not going to hurt you."

James nodded, the terror leaving his eyes. The ambulance team picked him up and transferred him to their gurney. They secured him with the belt, then started off down the stairs.

As they went out the front door, they passed Nora. She stood on the front stoop, overlooked in the commotion, crying as she asked where they were taking her brother.

"He's going to be all right," Dave said.

As they carried James down the front lawn to the ambulance, he yelled, "I'm okay, Nora, I'm okay!"

Dave climbed into the back of the ambulance behind the gurney bearing his son. He sat beside him, and grabbed his hand. As the driver slammed the rear door shut, James said, "She really does love me, doesn't she?"

"Sure she does. We all do."

*

Peg and Dave sat at the kitchen table long after they returned from the hospital. "Do you want some tea?" Peg asked. A slight breeze was blowing the sheer curtains off the open window.

"No, don't bother." Dave drew heavily on his cigarette, then crushed it out in an overflowing ashtray.

Peg finally took his hand and led him upstairs to their bedroom. They undressed in silence and piled into opposite sides of the bed. Dave's fear that he would lie awake was well founded. He soon abandoned the effort and rose from the bed, then walked down the hall to James's room. He sat in the small chair tucked in the corner, staring at the vacant bed. *That's what it would have been like if he had died. Empty. For good.* He started to cry once more. *But he didn't die,* Dave told himself, sniffing back the tears. *He's not here, but he's okay. The doctors won't let anything else happen to him.*

He walked around the room, which his son had redecorated himself. Pictures of The Mick, Roger, and Yogi were everywhere. The Phil Rizzuto foul ball Dave had caught years before sat in a clean ashtray. He ran his fingers over the felt of a Yankee pennant on the wall. Then he picked up the catcher's mitt he had bought for James. The boy must have oiled it himself, Dave thought, as he tried to stick his fingers in. They would not fit. James was becoming his own person, he realized. He wasn't interested in playing shortstop like his father; he wanted to be a catcher. That was okay. It was a real man's position.

He remembered what the cop had said to him earlier. The officer had given him credit for keeping his son alive. *Not bad. A pretty good save, like we said overseas.*

Why had it worked this time? He had tried just as hard to save Johnny D'Amato as he did his own son. Why did it turn out differently?

He knew there had to be a connection. Johnny was dead and he was to blame. James was still alive and he got the credit. As he sat alone in his son's room, he tried to reconcile the puzzling outcomes. The similarities were just meant to trick him. The mouth-to-mouth technique he'd used on both Johnny and James was identical. The difference was not what Dave had done during the rescue, but what had happened before. His efforts could never have worked for Johnny like they did for James. Johnny was too badly wounded, and it was Dave's fault. When the critical moment came on Peleliu, he had not been as prepared as he thought. He had choked in the clutch.

In contrast, he had done nothing to cause James's distress, and this time he came through. Still, tonight's test was only some sort of preliminary, not the main event. It could never change what had happened on Peleliu, but perhaps the story was not quite finished. Maybe by saving his son he had earned a chance of at least evening that score.

He had become so captivated by his son, by the very idea of having a son, that he had not been paying attention to his most important task. He resolved to stop acting like a pushover, like his own father had been, and get tough with the kid. There was no more time to waste. If he could train the boy to pass the ultimate test of courage, they would both be in the clear. His son would be brave enough. He would never crack, regardless of the cost. James would become a man, and redeem his father in the process.

The explanation seemed perfectly clear to Dave. It was not his idea. He did not even like it. He was only recognizing the inevitable sequence of events. When he was ready, there would be a dandy little war for James and all his friends. A war in some place no one had ever heard of. War was like that. One of the few things you could depend on.

It would happen all over again.

*

James had held his father's hand for the entire ambulance ride. Although the lights along the way had flashed eerily, he was no longer afraid.

His fear returned, however, when he was placed in the oxygen tent in the darkened hospital room. Although made of clear plastic, the walls of the tent were opaque at night, and all he could discern was the cloud of mist surrounding him. He wanted to scream at first, but the wetness all over his face and arms had a soothing effect. As he calmed down, his thoughts went back to what had happened earlier that evening. He relived the race down the stairs, everything going black, and then somehow awakening.

He remembered the nuns' favorite explanation of such incidents of divine providence: whenever a saint or explorer was spared from a catastrophe such as a plague or shipwreck, it was because he had not yet accomplished the task that God had set for him. His time had not yet come. Instead of simply letting him get sick or drown, God had in mind some more remarkable finish after his mission was accomplished.

As he lay in the darkness, James believed God had something special in store for him. His mind flashed back to the day of his First Holy Communion, when he'd worn the stark white outfit symbolic of his innocence. His soul was already a terrible stained mess, he was certain, not from one huge sin but from a multitude of smaller ones. Lying was a favorite whenever he was in an awkward spot. But disobedience? That was really his specialty. He just had the hardest time doing what he was told, and had become a master of doing what he wanted to do on the sly. Why, if he hadn't broken the rules every night, staying up listening to the ball game when he was supposed to be asleep, maybe he wouldn't have gotten sick in the first place. Still, maybe the harm could be undone and the habit broken. *I'll try to do what You want. I'll really try.* He began furiously praying Hail Marys.

But one thing continued to bother him. He had almost died. Maybe he had died and come back from the dead. Either way, he had seen no trace of an afterlife, no hint of a Being ready to embrace him, to welcome him home. When the shroud dropped over him, he had not seen the face of God. Instead, the last thing he saw before his eyes closed and the first he saw when they reopened was his own father's face. The man who had first given him life had saved it for him that night. The cops had said so; it must be true.

Sitting alone in the tent, wiping his moist face, James realized how scared he was of dying. There was no way he would ever be as brave and capable as his father, who somehow knew exactly what to do and had done it while everyone else panicked. James would never be able to do something like that, and he would be doomed to fail if he tried to follow in this amazing man's footsteps. He would have to figure something else out. That had to be God's plan for him, at least for now.

*

Sunday, October 1, 1961. Yankee Stadium glistened in the bright noon of Indian summer, and the entire area beneath the el buzzed with anticipation. The pennant already clinched, an otherwise meaningless game with the Red Sox was transformed by Roger Maris. He had already tied Babe Ruth's record of sixty home runs in a season. He had one final game to surpass his unseen adversary.

Four more at-bats to hit the unthinkable sixty-first. Yankee fans and haters, fairly evenly divided between those who came to cheer Maris on and those who urged him to fall on his face, milled on the sidewalks outside the stadium.

"I tell you, it'll be historic if Roger can do it," Dave told his son, as they approached the stadium entrance. "We couldn't possibly miss this game." Then he added sharply, "Jimmy, for Pete's sake, stop making that noise."

While in the hospital, James had developed a habit of constantly clearing his throat. Try as he might, he could not control the reflex action. Though his father had told him to stop being afraid of it happening again, in the back of his mind there was a constant terror of something lodging in his throat, an awareness that, at any moment, he could stop breathing again. And what if his father were not there this time? The best he could do was muffle the noise so his father might not hear it and scold him once more.

"Let's get moving," Dave said in a softer tone. "We don't want to miss his first at-bat." James smiled at his father. He was glad to see him excited and hoped he could relax and enjoy the game like he used to before all that scary stuff had happened.

With their usual general admission tickets, the Devlins were banished to the most remote section of the right-field upper deck. The tension throughout the stadium was palpable each time the third spot in the Yankee batting order was reached. The first time up Maris lofted the ball toward left field. The crowd rose to its feet as one and roared. "Pop-up!" Dave cursed as soon as it left the bat. The Sox leftfielder put it away effortlessly, well inside the park.

Fourth inning, Maris got another turn. Tracy Stallard, a rookie right hander, was on the mound for the Red Sox. Two loudly booed waste pitches put him behind in the count two balls and no strikes. Then he threw the pitch that would make him famous. Maris twisted out of his stance, arms fully extended, eyes fixed on the bat meeting the ball. He launched one final shot of the season toward the right-field porch.

"Maybe...maybe..." Dave begged, rising from his seat and pulling James up with him. They held each other's arms, watching the ball intently as it sailed toward them, then dropped out of view beneath the upper deck. The deafening noise of the crowd was their play-by-play announcer: the shot had cleared the fence.

Father and son leapt up and down embracing, their joy undiminished by the well-dressed New Englanders around them who heartlessly remained silent in their seats. They cheered themselves hoarse as the shy Maris was forced out of the dugout again and again by his jubilant teammates. As the clamor finally subsided, Dave turned to the boy and croaked, "Remember, son, you can always say that you were here when he did it."

James looked up at his father gratefully. "I'll always remember that we got to see it together, Dad."

VII
October 1962

J AMES HAD LEFT THE BLIND UP so that the sun's first rays streaming through his bedroom window would awaken him. Father McAlary scheduled the first instruction class for aspiring altar boys from the sixth grade at 7 A.M. Everyone knew that you best not be late. The early starting time was just the first test in the selection process. Father Mack, as he was called behind his back, believed that a boy who couldn't make it to class on time was a poor prospect to serve the early weekday Mass.

James sat surrounded by his classmates, excitedly awaiting the priest's appearance. Each of the desks had one thin red pamphlet centered on it. This was the notorious "book" he had heard so much about from the older boys. It contained the entire Mass in Latin and had to be mastered by heart before a boy was issued his cassock and surplice. James stared at the cover, mesmerized by the amateurish drawing of two kneeling altar boys piously facing each other beneath a cross. He didn't dare inspect its contents.

Father McAlary finally entered the room. He was a huge, ruddy man, wearing his usual black button-up cassock. On this occasion, however, his bushy auburn hair, salted with grey, was covered by a Roman prelate's hat, which was an oddly shaped five-cornered beanie with a black pompom on top. James thought it looked like something Father Flanagan of Boys Town might wear. He would have snickered had another priest worn it, but not when it was Father McAlary.

The priest plucked the hat off his head and placed it on the desk in the room where Sister Mary Anthony tried to tame her class of sixty-six boys Monday through Friday. He then sat one buttock up on the desk and addressed the boys.

"I'm glad to see you're all here on time. That's a good start. I'm sure you've heard I've no tolerance for late altar boys. That's one rumor that's absolutely true. Now, practically all of you have been here with the good sisters at St. Aidan's for five years already—"

The boys nodded their heads in unison.

"—and you've heard each of the lovely Baby Jesus stories they're so fond of telling over and over again, right? And you've memorized the answer to every question in that Baltimore Catechism? And you can tell me how many hours to fast before having Communion, dietary restrictions on ember days in Lent, how many angels fit on the icing of a hot cross bun, and the approximate present population in Limbo?"

Again, the boys nodded their heads.

Father McAlary's voice dropped. "So I suppose by now most of you are thoroughly convinced that Jesus Christ is a cross between Little Lord Fauntleroy and Snow White and the Seven Apostles. And you're certain that religion is about the dullest, tasteless, most senseless concoction ever devised to torture young boys."

James cringed. He finally realized what the nuns meant by the strange word—blasphemy. He glanced around and figured he and the other boys were of one mind: Father Mack must have turned the corner.

"I'm here to tell you to forget all that kid stuff, the fairy tales and kindergarten rules. If you're going to serve as an altar boy, you've first got to become a man. You've got to put aside your childish ways and stand upright at the altar, relating to the Almighty God and His son Jesus Christ as a man. There's no other way. If you're not ready for that, if you can't treat this as the deadly serious proposition it is, go out that door now and don't come back until you are ready."

No one stirred.

"I've been known to lose quite a few recruits right there, but I'm told I have a good crop this year and it seems my sources are correct.

"As far as doctrine, I can tell you everything you'll ever need to know very succinctly. The Catholic Church is based on one fundamental principle: that Jesus Christ, God become man, was born, died for our sins, and rose again. That's it in a nutshell, but if you check, it's all right there. If you profess that short principle, you're admitting there is a God who loves us enough to humble Himself, become one of us and die for our sake. You're also acknowledging that man is puny, sinful and in need of redemption and the only way to overcome death, the conqueror of us all, is through Jesus Christ, the only man to triumph over death. So that's what we're talking about. Jesus Christ, the simple difference between life and death."

James held back a yawn, not wanting to upset the priest while he sermonized.

"Remember what I'm telling you. Think about it, try to understand it. Christ is alive today. He's no sissy or someone to be ashamed of. He's the very best of what we call human. And be aware that a lot of what passes for being a big man in this world, a tough guy in business or on the streets, has nothing to do with manhood and even less to do with God.

"All right, enough preliminaries. Let's get moving. As you've no doubt heard, you've got to know the Book before you make it to the altar. I give you each a couple of oral tests. I stick you in the nurse's room alone with a tape recorder and you begin reciting the altar boy's responses to the prayers, in Latin. If I hear 'oh, shit!' when you get stuck during the test, you become my *inimicus* and you'll get bounced, just like those guys last year. So, if you forget one prayer, just move on to the next one and keep going.

"What's in it for you? Not a whole lot. You get your mother off your back since you won't have to hear that Johnny Jones is an altar boy and you're not. You get free use of a cassock and surplice for all sacramental occasions, except Halloween. You're on your own then, fellas. You may beat a few classes during Holy Week. You get to leave your house when it's freezing and dark all winter when you're lucky enough to serve the 7 A.M. Mass. Oh, I almost forgot. Each of you will come close to drowning in Long Island Sound on the altar boy outing in June. That's when I take extreme care to give each of you the annual baptism by immersion you so richly deserve. Any questions?"

When no one replied, Father McAlary said, "Good. *Ite, missa est.*"

*

James saw his mother and Nora waiting at the prearranged meeting spot outside of St. Aidan's in the new Comet his dad had bought. Nora was riding shotgun so James climbed into the back. His mother pulled onto the street while Nora switched the radio between WMCA and WINS to see which station was playing the better song. He opened the book and stared at the words the priest had read to them: "Celebrant: *Introibo ad altare Dei.* Server: *Ad Deum qui laetificat juventutum meum.*"

"I have to go to the laundromat and stores," his mother said, pulling in front of the Connolly house when they reached Woodside, dropping Nora and James off. "Don't do anything until you say hello to your grandmother, hear me?"

James pretended he hadn't heard his mother while Nora walked up the block toward the candy store. James ran up the stoop and through the front door, which had been left ajar, like always.

The large dwelling, housing his grandmother upstairs and his uncle and family on the first floor, was in rough shape. The staircase leading to Grannie's apartment was always dark, and usually littered with broken toys and other debris. He picked his way through the mess, racing to the second floor and rushing into the living room He kissed Grannie Connolly hello before she could rise from her seat by the window.

"How 'bout the cup of tea?" Grannie asked.

James said, "Sure, Gran, but I have to make it quick."

He followed her across the short hallway to the kitchen, wondering if she'd heard him while she went through the motions of taking a saucepan off the stove, putting it in the sink and filling it with fresh water. She then took a match from a cardboard box, struck it on the scratchy side, lit the pilot and then placed the saucepan back on the stove.

"How's school?" Grannie asked.

"Great," James replied, sitting down and tapping his fingers on the table. "Does the water take longer to boil like that?" He glanced over at the nearby kettle.

Grannie laughed. "You're smart as a whip. The whistle doesn't work anymore," she said, pointing to the kettle. She then pulled two mugs down from the cabinet and added tea bags to them. Once the water came to a boil, she poured the bubbling water into the mugs. She then went to the refrigerator, got a quart of milk and poured some into the mugs. When James asked if he could add his own sugar, she stared at him with her watery blue eyes, then pushed the bowl toward him.

After he added a generous amount and gulped the tea down, James said, "Uncle Rory's waiting for me." He then stood up.

"Don't you want some of these?" Granny pushed a saucer filled with Social Tea biscuits toward him.

"Thanks," he said, grabbing a handful and shoving them in his mouth. He returned his grandmother's kiss and then raced out of the kitchen and back down the stairs, dropping crumbs along the way. Within moments, he was outside the first floor flat banging on the door. Rory Connolly opened it, beaming his crooked tooth grin. "Well, here he is. His Holiness, the altar boy!"

"Cut it out, will ya," James said. "You ready?"

"Sure," Uncle Rory replied. "The kids should be here any minute. Figured you'd be the guy who was late, busy as you seem to be lately."

James ignored his uncle's needling. "You can warm me up before it gets too crowded."

Rory Connolly was the leading football fanatic of Woodside, a pigskin pied piper to the neighborhood kids. Each Saturday morning in autumn the local boys would congregate in front of the Connolly house, confident that whatever chores Rory should have been doing would be abandoned in favor of throwing them pass after pass and organizing them into evenly matched squads for touch football games.

When they reached the street, their concrete field, only Francis Avellini awaited them. Fat Frankie was an overweight redhead several years older than James. He wore black orthopedic shoes instead of sneakers and was the worst football player that side of Woodside Avenue. But he was the funniest and most good-natured kid in the neighborhood.

"Jimmy, baby," Frankie said, sitting on the hood of the Devlin's parked car. "Come here. I got a couple new jokes that'll make you honk up a storm."

James started laughing already, approaching the boy who was draining a bottle of Mission cream soda.

"Forget it, Frankie," Rory barked. "You guys need some work before game time. Line up over by the curb for some buttonhooks at the manhole cover."

"Your uncle's a slave driver, you know," Frankie murmured to James. "And a rotten judge of talent, too." Frankie was almost breathless by the time he reached the metallic landmark. "If he didn't let me be captain of one team each week, I'd tell him to take a hike."

"Stop yapping, Frankie," Rory yelled, "and let's see the buttonhook." He then slapped his hand on the football, the signal to go.

It almost hurt James to watch Frankie as he waddled down the middle of 72nd Street, his flat feet pointed in the opposite directions. He then circled around ten yards downfield at the manhole cover. Rory threw an easy spiral, but Frankie bobbled it, then kicked the ball under a car when he bent to pick up the incomplete pass. He squeezed under the parked car, retrieved the ball, then heaved it back to Rory.

"Good toss," Rory said. "Okay, Jimmy. Break."

James took off at the slap of the ball. Counting off ten strides downfield, he pivoted sharply across from the johnny pump, tightening his stomach in anticipation. As expected, a speeding pass tore into his middle. He grunted, but grabbed it with both hands, turned, and threw a wobbly pass back to Rory.

"Good catch, but your usual nothing throw. Come on, Jim, and crank it up, will ya?"

James nodded, trotting back up the sloping street. His passing left a great deal to be desired even though his uncle had drilled him so he could catch any football he could reach. But, in truth, the whole game left him rather cold. The long stretches without touching the ball, waiting for his play to be called, were bad enough; interminable standing or crouching in a huddle while the older boys dickered and diagrammed ornate, ill-conceived plays was sheer torture. Still, James kept his complaints to himself out of deference to his uncle. Football was the only thing his uncle took seriously enough to put his good humor on hold. If you loved Rory, you must love football. And if playing football was the small price exacted for a Saturday morning with his uncle, James was more than willing to pay it.

The inconclusive pickup game that began once the other boys arrived broke up around twelve-thirty when hunger overwhelmed their interest. One by one they bid farewell, promising to see Rory the following week. Soon James was alone with his uncle. Rory ran him for another half hour, giving him a comprehensive workout he never received in a game dominated by the older boys. James ran continuous buttonhooks, square-ins and outs, stop-and-gos, posts, and straight-fly patterns, the standard street repertoire of moves, each designed to place him breathlessly in front of a smoking pass.

"Okay, Jimmy," Rory finally yelled. "Let me get you some lunch."

Grateful, James chased his uncle into the Connolly house. Rory sat him at the kitchen table. His wife and daughters were nowhere in sight.

"You ready for the big game tomorrow? Giants versus Eagles in Philly? Giants will massacre them!"

"You think so, Unc?"

"Sure. What'll it be, Killer? Bologna or bologna? Cupboard's a little bare again, I guess." He laughed as he opened the refrigerator and pulled out a can of Ballantine beer.

"Guess I'll have bologna," James said. Lunch with his uncle was typically slim pickings.

"That's a good fella," Rory said as he whipped up bologna sandwiches on white bread smeared with Gulden's mustard.

"Where's everyone?" James asked.

Rory cut the sandwiches in half, placed them on plates that looked used and brought them to the table. "Oh, you know, out and about."

James cringed, sorry he'd asked as soon as he saw the sad look on his uncle's face. How did he keep forgetting what his mother called "the tragedy" that had befallen his uncle's family early last spring? The pain was certainly still fresh for everyone else. After three daughters, Rory and Maeve had a boy, little Conor, and Rory was as proud as he could be, handing out cigars all over Woodside. But James's cousin had only been home from the hospital a couple of weeks when his mother found him dead in his carriage, right next to the Connolly's stoop. There was no apparent reason for the baby to die; he was just taking a nap and had been left alone for only a minute.

James's reaction had been to blot Conor's memory from his mind. The explanation he had been given for his cousin's short life simply made no sense. How could it be God's will that Conor be born only to die before he even got to know anyone or do anything with his life? What was Conor's mission: to make all the Connollys sad forever? James hated the words the old women had used to sugarcoat what had happened. Conor's had been just another "crib death," which was supposed to somehow be a happier ending than being "stillborn," when the poor baby was denied its first breath altogether.

James snapped back into the moment when he heard Rory tap into the opposite edges of the beer can with the opener.

His uncle took a large swig, then asked, "So where's that father of yours, working again?"

"Yep," James mumbled, his mouth stuffed with half of the sandwich. After swallowing, he added, "He's still up in Boston. He's been there for weeks, but we'll be picking him up at the airport this afternoon."

"Well, all I can tell you is he better be off Saturdays by the time you're playing for Notre Dame. Can't have it any other way." Rory jumped up and went to the refrigerator. He took out some milk and poured it in one of his daughters' kiddie cups and brought it over to James.

"Thanks," James said, taking a big gulp. He hesitated, before saying, "I don't think I'm ever going to play for Notre Dame."

"How come? Or is it baseball you want to play?"

James shook his head. "Well, I haven't talked to Dad about it yet, but…" He looked away.

"Oh, sweet Jesus, what is it, Jimmy?"

"Well, they're having basketball tryouts at St. Aidan's next week."

Rory nodded. "And you'd like to try something different from baseball."

"But you know how Dad feels about basketball."

"A game for sissy-lalas and freaks," Rory said.

James nodded, his expression glum.

"Listen, Jimmy, don't give it another thought." Rory drained the beer can and rose to fetch another. "I've known your father a long time and I'm sure he won't give you a hard time."

James watched how his uncle opened the can. His father rarely touched beer or liquor for that matter and James was intrigued by the ritual. After Rory took a swig, he said, "Sure, Dave Devlin is the greatest in my book." He grew silent as he gazed across the table, as if he were looking at someone else.

"Do you know your father's a war hero?" he finally said. "He'll never tell you that, but it's true. He was decorated for bravery, and should've gotten the Navy Cross."

James squinted, hearing the story for the first time.

"Yep, he waded across some reef right into Jap machine gun fire and rescued a couple of wounded Marines. Nobody else was willing to do it. Only your Pop. You should be very proud of him."

James stared at his uncle and couldn't help but notice the distant, strange expression on his face.

"Now me," Rory continued, after taking another swig, "I'm a different story. I wanted action so bad I could taste it. A lot to prove, I guess. All I ever heard from your Mom was the different islands Dave was invading. I wanted to be right there with him in the thick of things."

"Why weren't you?" James asked.

"Well, I'm a couple years younger than your dad. It took me forever to lie my way in because I wasn't old enough. Then somehow I ended up the only Marine in the entire Corps that sat the war out on the sidelines, chasing the goony birds off the airstrip on Guam until all the fighting was over."

James wasn't sure how to respond while his uncle paused for a moment.

"It's funny," Rory finally said. "My luck's never been too good. Like they say, can't get myself arrested."

Suddenly, he shook his head and laughed. "Listen, chief. All I'm telling you is never be afraid of your old man like I was afraid of mine. Not with Dave. He loves you like crazy. If you want to play basketball, or even tiddlywinks, that'll be fine with him." He reached across the table and brushed James's hair off his forehead. "You're ten years old now, right? You just have to stand up for yourself and let him know how you feel."

"But it's not like talking to you," James said. "I still feel like his little boy." He remembered prayer time when he was younger. When his father would drop to his knees and James would climb up on his back until his arms reached around his father's neck. Then he would close his eyes while they prayed out loud with Nora beside them. He'd breathe in the after-work smell of his father's starched shirt. "Do you know I still kiss him goodnight?"

"Well, I guess that one does have to go, if you want him to take you seriously," Rory said. "But you can do it, Jim. You're man enough."

James nodded, determined he would talk to his father that night.

*

Peg Devlin's stomach was in knots as she raced through the A&P. She had to finish her mother's marketing and make it back to the laundromat before the wet clothes wrinkled in the washing machine or, worse yet, some impatient customer dumped them in a heap on a folding table. Once she stuffed the clothes in the dryer and filled the slots with change, she'd rush back to her mother's house before the milk turned sour and the frozen food soggy. She would gulp a quick cup of tea while her mother reviewed the price of each grocery item, then would return to the laundromat and retrieve the wash, separating her family's clothes from her mother's.

Even though Rory and Maeve lived downstairs from her mom, it all seemed to fall on her, the big sister, especially since little Conor had died. Maeve would take her three girls and disappear for long periods of time. Rory had never been dependable in the first place. They just could not be counted on to get Mom's groceries and her chores done.

Nora was no help either. She simply refused to accompany Peg on her errands. She preferred moping in front of the television at Grannie's or reading one of her teen magazines. If Nora had come they could have split up. She could have at least done the laundry. *What am I going to do with that girl?* Peg thought angrily as she stood at the A&P checkout. But then her anger faded and turned to worry. She fretted about her sullen daughter who stayed distant and aloof, despite all of Peg's overtures. She was practically a stranger under their roof. And Dave's return that evening would hardly improve matters. When Dave arrived home for his abbreviated weekend, his fuse was extremely short. Just one wrong look, one loud sigh by Nora and the battle would rage.

Regardless of her daughter's misgivings, Peg anxiously awaited her husband's return, dreaming ahead to that night. Once the lights were out, Dave would surely grope for her, commencing the hushed midnight wrestling of parents who still slept within earshot of their children. And she would be waiting, already moist from anticipating his touch. He'd gently pull her nightgown over her head, then lay beside her deeply kissing her lips, throat and breasts until her nipples stood erect. He'd then move lower, squeezing her buttocks with his hands, exploring her.

"Here's your change, ma'am," the pimply checkout girl said, reaching across the counter.

Peg felt the warmth go to her face as she took the receipt, hoping there'd be no errors found by her mother when she tallied up the groceries. She certainly wouldn't tell her what she'd been daydreaming about as an excuse.

*

The Devlins reunited that night at LaGuardia's Eastern Shuttle terminal. Even though he was carrying only a briefcase, Dave dragged himself toward his family as he exited through the revolving door. But he was in high spirits.

His team, hearing rumors again that they would soon be replaced, had knocked themselves out for weeks. Pleasing Gus Holtzin had seemed impossible. Everyone from Oswald & Givney assigned to his account knew what an ignorant slob he was and how difficult he was to work with. He'd ripped up extravagant layouts of his products without any reason, but then the next, with a slightly different combination of graphics and copy, had somehow moved the man. He called it beautiful, even though there was no clear formula that distinguished it from the ads he'd loathed. Dave was sure that the success could never be duplicated, except by another blind stroke of luck, and he couldn't chance it. He finally decided to respond to the headhunters' seductive calls. The issue was resolved on the flight home from Boston and he approached his family with a rare sense of contentment. He kissed his wife, hugged his son and smiled at Nora, thanking everyone for coming. He then added, "I don't think you're going to have to do this much longer," bringing a smile to Peg.

Dinner was calm and Dave even succeeded in getting updates on his children's schoolwork and activities. Later, he watched television and read a book while smoking one cigarette after the next. Jimmy was sprawled on the floor and Peg was beginning to nod out in an easy chair while strains from the radio came from Nora's room. After watching Jackie Gleason and *The Defenders*, James got up and stood in front of Dave.

"Pop?" James said.

Dave looked up and stuck a bookmark in his novel, placing it on his lap. "What's up?" he said, crushing his cigarette in the ashtray on the end table.

James sucked up some air. "Well, there's going to be basketball tryouts at St. Aidan's next week."

Dave raised an eyebrow. "Oh, yeah?" After seeing the crushed look on the boy's face, he relented. "And I take it you want to try out?"

James nodded. "All the other guys are going out for the team. I played a couple of times at the schoolyard with the big kids...and, well, I like it."

While James stood there waiting, Dave withdrew his last cigarette from the pack, lit it with his Zippo lighter and inhaled. Smoke spiraled out of his nostrils before he said, "Listen, it's up to you. Not my game, but if you want to play, be my guest." He set the cigarette on the edge of the ashtray and reopened his book.

"Thanks, Dad." Then for good measure, he added, "Besides, there's no football teams around here anyway." He then shuffled his feet, hesitating. "I guess there's one other thing."

"What's that?" Dave looked up from the book.

"I've been thinking that I'm going to be eleven pretty soon."

"So what?"

The boy's voice lowered. "So I think I'm getting kind of old to kiss you good-night every night."

Dave looked at his son carefully for a moment. "Then what would you like to do?"

"How about shaking hands?" James asked.

James stretched out his hand. Realizing something had changed, Dave took it while his son grinned, pumping his father's arm vigorously. The boy then turned and headed up the stairs. Dave's throat closed up and he blinked, unable to see the words on the page of his book as he poked the ashtray with the remainder of his lit cigarette.

*

The gymnasium at P.S. 107 in Flushing was drafty, yet pungent with the smell of ancient perspiration. Given the gym's structure, its ceiling pressed against the tops of the backboards, only the youngest C.Y.O. basketball teams, the bantams, were condemned to play there. Yet, even the strained shots of these novices frequently banked off the ceiling, adding a few more whistled halts to a game dominated by hacks, walks, double dribbles, palms and held balls.

St. Aidan's "B" bantams in faded red hand-me-down uniforms, were opening their season against Our Lady of the Most Blessed Sacrament in the 8 A.M. game. The starting five for St. Aidan's squatted silently in a huddle, taking last moment instructions from the two coaches. But once the game began, James couldn't hear the coaches or his teammates. He could only see the orange ball, teasing him as it careened up and down the floor. After three weeks of practice, he and his teammates could only chase it, bounce it if they managed to catch it, then fire it at its matching orange receptacle.

When the breathless warriors approached the benches at halftime, the score was knotted at 2-2. St. Aidan's had scored on a line drive shot from the top of the key, released on the run, that had miraculously banked in. His coaches were screaming, "You're playing out of control! You're not hustling enough!"

James was no better than the rest. He stared at the tap play one of the coaches had scribbled on a pad. It did not quite register. Once he heard that the center was to tip the ball to him, the play was over in his mind. With one good long bounce in front of him, he'd have the jump on all the others, outrace them to the basket, and heave the shot home.

At the start of the second half, the referee lined both teams up in proper positions at midcourt. He flung the ball up between the two centers, and it floated back down without spinning. Just as the coach had planned. St. Aidan's center tapped the ball toward James, who grabbed the ball and bolted for the basket his team had been bombarding so harshly.

He stared at the ball as it led him up the court, daring him to dribble it without flaw. Once, twice, three times he slapped it down on the unwaxed floor without bouncing it off his foot or back into his stomach. His pursuit was drawing near and the backboard and baseline were rapidly approaching. With one last glance at the ball he grabbed it and searched above him for his target. All in one motion, he heaved the ball toward the rim, straining backward as he went out of bounds. The ball hesitated on the back spacer between the rim and board, then dropped into the net below.

James smiled, trotting back down the court, expecting cheers and compliments, oblivious to the referee's whistle, blissfully unaware he'd just opened the second half scoring for Our Lady of the Most Blessed Sacrament.

"You're a total moron, Devlin," one of his teammates hissed as the ref lined both teams up again for another tipoff. "You just made a basket for the other team, dummy."

James looked around in disbelief. He double-checked the bleachers to make sure his father hadn't changed his mind and shown up. At least his shame would be private. The final score was 4-2 with Blessed Sacrament's winning margin provided by the perfidious James Devlin.

Stung by his teammates' remarks and coaches' scowls, James walked home alone and went straight to the garage. He took the basketball his father had given him the week before, out of its box. *Boy, have I gotten off to a great start*, he muttered to himself as he began bouncing the ball. He dribbled down the driveway, up the corner, and all the way up to the playground adjacent to Junior High School 67. On a court on the upper level, with no one else in sight, he spent the rest of the day dribbling and shooting. Again and again he would drive to the basket, or pull up short at the perimeter, banking shots against the silvery, perforated sheet-metal backboard. When it was too dark to see the sturdy Parks Department rim anymore, he left the playground and dribbled the ball back home.

*

James left the house at 6:30 in the morning. The late February wind whipped at him as he walked down 245th Street toward St. Aidan's. He pulled the new cassock and surplice, folded over a wooden hanger, close to his chest. To the east, the arching daybreak tickled the undressed trees, and he broke into an awkward run, trying to avoid tripping over the long black robe or wrinkling the short white blouse.

Blocks later, his nostrils and lungs were burning as he rushed past the front entrance of St. Aidan's Church, then turned down the paved walkway that ran along its side. When he reached the heavy sacristy door at the rear, he struggled against the wind to pull it open, only to have it slam into his back and close on his cassock as he dashed inside.

Two tall boys already wearing black robes were leaning against a table in the dimly lit anteroom as he fumbled to free his cassock from the doorframe. The fair-haired one gave him a look of disdain while the dark-haired boy said, "Let me give you a hand with that." He pushed open the door, freeing the cassock, then latched it shut.

"Thanks," James mumbled.

"I'm Mike Cassidy." He extended his hand. "And that's Sean O'Donnell. The friendly one."

Everyone in the whole school knew Michael Cassidy, since he was already a basketball court legend at twelve and a half years old. Though only in seventh grade, he held his own with the best high school and college players in the neighborhood, and was attracting groups of high school coaches to every game he played.

"I know who you are," James said with a grin.

"Oh, Michael, you're just so wonderful!" Sean mimicked in a falsetto voice. "Christ," he muttered. "If Father Mack sends us anymore jackasses like this one, I'm quitting the altar."

James flushed. He was already apprehensive about serving his first Mass. He knew his Latin fairly well, but there was so much more to learn, so many strange gestures to make, if he were to do a decent job. O'Donnell's antagonism unnerved him completely.

"Don't mind Sean the Pill," Michael said. "He likes to eat his heart out for breakfast when he serves early Mass with me." He paused, then asked, "Do you know who won the Knicks game last night? Sean's useless. Doesn't know anything about sports, especially basketball."

"Knicks finally won one," James said. "Richie Guerin caught fire and Jumpin' Johnny Green got a bunch of rebounds."

"Cool." Michael smiled. "Now just hang your coat up in the closet, get your cassock on and I'll show you the ropes. And by the way," he added, "I know your name, too. At least I've heard a lot about some little guy named Devlin who's been tearing up the B league." Michael's eyes twinkled. "That is, once he got his bearings straight."

James blushed again as he hastily donned his cassock and surplice. There was little time before Father McAlary would arrive. Fortunately, Michael was an efficient instructor. He showed James how to light the two candles adjacent to the tabernacle, and gave him hints on how to light the six candles on the top level of the altar as he would before Sunday Mass. "Keep your flame good and long, but don't burn the place down. And when you're putting the candles out with the extinguisher, take it easy and just snuff them out. If you bang that sucker down on the top of a candle, you'll put it out all right. But you'll collapse the wick into the wax and it'll take the poor jerk serving the next Mass 'til the Gospel to get it lit."

Michael led him through a shortcut behind the altar to the priest's side of the sacristy, giving a barely detectable bend of the knee as he passed the rear of the tabernacle. Inside, he showed James the drawers filled with vestments for the priests. He explained how the different colors corresponded to different liturgical seasons, and reviewed the robing idiosyncrasies of each priest in the parish.

"They really run the gamut, but you've got to know what each one wants. Father Rinaldi—he doesn't want you to go near him, which is just fine because he has a wicked pit. Father Driessen, though, he's like a baby you got to get dressed. And if you give him the cincture for the alb with the braid to the left instead of the right, he'll have a conniption."

Michael pointed out the faucet where he could fill the water cruet and a lower drawer that contained a fresh bottle of Christian Brothers sherry at the start of each weekday morning.

"Fill the wine cruet to the brim, whatever you do. And when you're pouring it into the chalice you better not be stingy. If they've had enough, they'll raise the chalice as you're pouring to let you know not to drown them." He whispered," When you serve Sunday Mass with me in the school auditorium, I'll give you a little taste when we refill the wine cruet in the boys' room. It's the most honored tradition of the St. Aidan's Altar Boy Society."

The final lesson for the morning was proper technique for burning incense in the thurible. "This is my favorite," Michael said, swinging the thurible in a complete circle. "You only get to use it in the really big ceremonies. Funerals, High Masses, all the good stuff. The secret is to put enough charcoal in first and, for God's sake, to get it lit right. Don't blow it by starting your fire too soon. Wait 'til right before the ceremony begins. Otherwise, you'll only be halfway through the Easter Vigil with a thurible full of cold ashes, a shitload of incense that won't burn, and a church full of pissed-off priests.

"Oh, yeah, one other thing. Don't leave the top on the thurible longer than you have to. It gets hotter than hell in no time, and when they start lifting the monstrance, you gotta get it swinging and clicking even if your hands are burning off."

Michael was just concluding his discourse when Father McAlary arrived more somber than usual. He looked askance at Sean, who was slouched in a chair, but immediately jumped to his feet.

"Good morning, Father," he said in an uncharacteristically pleasant voice.

Father McAlary grunted. "Let's get moving." He pulled a white alb over his cassock and amice and secured it with a cincture. After saying a silent prayer, he kissed the violet chasuble and pulled it over his head. He remained with his head bowed before the crucifix on the wall. The boys stood behind him, awaiting his signal to flash on the overhead lights and approach the altar. They were an oddly matched trio, yet representative of the community in which they lived. Sean was a resident of the well-to-do Douglas Manor section while Michael lived in Little Neck, in one of the many attached houses. By contrast, James lived in the Park section of town, an area crammed with small single-family homes. Shorter and rounder than his two colleagues, James was the first in his class to master the Latin prayers and be assigned to a Mass as an understudy.

"All right, boys. Let's begin."

Michael flicked on the lights, and the congregation rose as the three boys entered the sanctuary with Father McAlary trailing behind, carrying his golden chalice, covered with a purple cloth embroidered with a yellow cross. All four genuflected at the foot of the altar. The priest mounted the marble steps, arranged his chalice and its accoutrements on the center of the altar before coming back down.

"*Introibo ad altare Dei.*"

"*Ad deum qui laetificat juventutum meum,*" the boys responded with James dragging at least three words behind the more experienced servers.

Father McAlary, Michael and Sean were soon blazing through the Confiteor with James desperately trying to keep pace. With the priest standing and the boys kneeling, swinging their heads toward him in unison at the designated spot, they recited the long prayer so fast that the words all ran together. The novice was only devoutly pounding his breast "*mea culpa, mea culpa, mea maxima culpa*" when the other two had finished and risen.

By the time the boys sat in chairs at the side of the sanctuary for the reading of the Epistles and Gospel, James's face was sticky with perspiration. He glanced up at the Last Supper mural behind the altar. Judas sat on the end of the bench, but his back was turned to Jesus and the other Apostles, and he looked guilty as sin.

"Relax," Michael whispered, thumping James's knee. "You're doing fine. There's a homily today for Ash Wednesday, so catch your breath."

The priest was a master of inflection, skilled in maintaining his parishioners' attention by raising his voice to the rafters, then dropping it to a whisper. He began his sermon in low, sonorous tones, which rumbled back toward the rear of the nearly filled church.

"The people living in our Lord's time were not unfamiliar with death. It confronted them at every street corner in their filthy cities. People had not yet become considerate enough to do their dying in private, like we do, in nice antiseptic hospitals.

"No, death was quite real in all its ugliness, finality and imminence. Perhaps that was most important of all. These simple people had no actuaries, but they understood that their days were numbered. If they reached the ripe old age of forty they had done very well."

James shivered and hoped the others hadn't noticed.

"Naturally enough," Father McAlary continued, "people feared this last, greatest evil, an incomprehensible terror. And, naturally enough, they were receptive to the message of the man who came to conquer death."

The priest's voice rose. "Today, we do not confront death daily. We hide it, and ignore it, putting it out of our minds. We write it off as something you'll only start worrying about when you're too old to function at all. And on those rare occasions when we are forced to face death, because by some quirk it has claimed someone dear to us, we still try to cheat it by embalming, cosmetics, hairdressing, anything we can dream up to make a lifeless corpse seem vibrant.

"Only two days in the liturgical year does the Church pay homage to death. One is Good Friday, where we see its full power, a force strong enough to claim God Himself. Yet, even Good Friday is a horror all of us can brush off, because we know death's triumph is illusory, temporary in the case of Christ. It's nothing to sweat. It's like Jesus took the weekend off. We know he'll be back in action on Easter Sunday in time for the newspapers and the rolls.

"The other occasion when the Church addresses death is today, Ash Wednesday. And it's a whole different story." Father McAlary's voice became barely audible. The parishioners leaned forward in the pews, straining to hear his words.

"Today, we're not talking about God dying because He feels like doing it, certain He can rise again. We're talking about each of us dying, as we most certainly will. And we are not Christ with His confidence and money-back guarantee. Even the most faithful of us has got to have his doubts as to what comes next, if he's given it a moment's honest reflection. Quite frankly, the idea that this life is it, all we get, is enough to make anyone's blood run cold.

"That unspeakable fear is necessary; in fact, it is sublime. For without it, life eternal would be cheapened. Only by arising from the depths of despair can our faith achieve its true glory. Only by confronting the undeniable fact of your own personal death can you give your life any meaning."

The priest's voice rose until he was projecting at full volume. "*Pulvis es, et in pulverem reverteris*. You must make a choice. You can live each day for yourself, pretending you have a limitless supply. Or you can join me in a few moments and receive the black mark on your forehead as a confession of your mortality, an admission of the fact that you will one day render a full accounting to your Lord for your short time on earth. You must decide which path to take. And rest assured, postponing your decision is a decision itself. For the Church is telling us today that time is important, time is of essence. Let us pray."

The priest's footsteps were the only sound as he walked to a side altar and picked up the small urn of ashes. When he returned to the center aisle, he faced the congregation. The three altar boys stood behind him, in the shadow of his power. Aisle by aisle the pews emptied and the parishioners approached.

When he had marked the last of the congregation, Father McAlary faced the boys and rubbed a dark cross onto each of their foreheads with the granular ash. Glaring into their eyes, as though inspecting their souls, he repeated to all three, "Remember thou art dust, and unto dust thou shalt return."

James stared back, thinking he understood while the other boys probably did not. He had experienced the total darkness of death, however briefly. For a long time after the choking incident he had been nervous whenever his father wasn't around. What if it happened again? Who would save him a second time?

But it hadn't happened again. Gradually, as time passed, James had overcome his fear and convinced himself he could live without his father who now seemed as wrapped up in his career as James was in his life.

When he lay in that oxygen tent years before, James had been sure of what everything meant. His father had been able to save him that night because James had a special mission he was supposed to complete. Now he was no longer sure that the incident had any hidden significance at all. James now thought of himself like everyone else and was no longer convinced that he had any secret assignment that should keep him from doing whatever he wanted. If he did have such a divinely ordained task, he had no idea what it might be, so someone had better clue him in soon.

Worse yet, James was not nearly as certain as Father Mack that he would ultimately have to defend his life before God. All he could recall from when he passed out was everything going black. Had God remained out of sight, off-stage because he already knew his father would save him, or was He just not there at all?

PART TWO

VIII
April 1965

NORA DEVLIN LAY IN HER BED, dressed in a pink bathrobe, her head helmeted in curlers, the radio blasting. Self-proclaimed fifth Beatle, Murray "The K" Kaufman, was heavily into the Swingin' Soiree, shooting golden gasser blasts from the past across the airwaves. Nora was dying for a smoke, but reluctant to remove the crushed Marlboro pack from the zippered compartment of her purse and light up for fear of getting caught.

She had a big problem. Not the English theme that was due the next day; that was well in hand. She had come by a composition written by a girl who'd graduated two years earlier, and was copying it with token revisions. Her concern was far more grave. It was already late April and she still had not invited anyone to her senior prom at Immaculata Academy.

It wasn't that pickings were slim for Nora. Quite the contrary. At dances the boys hovered around her, despite her covey of homely Immaculata girlfriends who prayed for a dance with her rejects. Dozens of college-bound seniors from Archbishop Molloy or Holy Cross would flip at the chance to don a white dinner jacket and squire fair-haired, leggy Nora to her prom.

She wanted none of them. Only Billy Elsen would do. But if she ever asked him, her parents would have the ultimate shit fit. Even though he'd told her that he loved school, Billy had reluctantly dropped out of Bayside High three years earlier. The minimal hours and effort required certainly beat any form of work he had ever encountered, but the prospect of being a superannuated sophomore again had forced his move. He bid a sad farewell to Mt. Saint Bayside, and luckily landed an off-the-books job pumping gas at a local service station. It hadn't dawned on his father to tap into Billy's tax-exempt pay for room and board so his pockets remained full, at least from payday Friday until Sunday evening. Peeling through the "Twin Cities" of Douglaston and Little Neck in his 1960 Chevy Impala convertible with huge fins and cavatelli-shaped taillights made him teenage nobility.

The romance between Nora, rebellious Miss Popularity, and her side-burned, duck-assed boyfriend was as inevitable as Billy's running two or three red lights on Northern Boulevard on a Saturday night. Even their first meeting was entirely predictable: it happened at one of St. Aidan's weekly parish dances.

The Friday night affairs were held in the stark grammar school cafeteria where a faint smell of peanut butter lingered. Father Tierney, the most junior priest in the parish, was assigned to "moderate" the dances. A greater euphemism had yet to be coined. The good father would have been more suitably attired in a blue uniform with handcuffs and a billy club than the Roman collar he wore.

Father Tierney made certain that all the teens were properly dressed: jackets and ties for the boys, dresses or skirts, not too short, for the girls. He'd separate any grinding couple with a sharp, "Leave a little room for the Holy Ghost." He took extreme precautions to ensure that no one consumed anything stronger than Pepsi-Cola at the dance. The problem, unfortunately, was never what anyone drank at the dance, but what they had downed beforehand. Neither Father Tierney nor any of his predecessors had found a way to control the pre-dance festivities.

Nora had tired of St. Aidan's dances by the second one she'd attended. Admission was restricted to parishioners and she viewed the male population, with very few exceptions, as twerps or local greasers. Still, she appeared religiously each Friday. The fact was that her father demanded an acceptable destination before letting her step foot outside at night. She would've gone to any dance, ballgame, choral show or chess match, if it meant getting out of that dreaded house for a few hours.

Her feelings about St. Aidan's dances changed once she met Billy Elsen. He'd shown up one Friday night after work, shortly before the dance was over. His blond hair was slicked back, still wet from the shower. He wore a madras jacket with white Levis and black loafers, remarkably collegiate dress for a gas station attendant. To Nora, this new, mature face at the dull dance seemed too good to be true. She pretended not to notice him pointing toward her. Then the band began to play "Tears On My Pillow" and he approached her.

"You want to dance?"

Nora nodded. Billy reached out and wrapped his arms around her, hugging her tight to him, swaying in time to the music. When the song ended, he suggested they go for a ride and by the stroke of twelve, they were far from St. Aidan's.

But now, Nora still had to figure out what to do about the prom, especially after Peg noticed the way Billy and Nora looked at each other when she'd pulled into the gas station to fill up. She reported as much to Dave and the interrogation was underway. "Who is that guy working at the gas station?" he'd asked Nora.

Her evasive answer did not fly with her father and he got more out of her than she'd planned to tell. Billy had lost his anonymity. Dave declared him a young man with no education and no prospects who immediately qualified for the "forbidden dates" list.

Just then, Nora had an idea. *Shit! It's so simple!* She couldn't believe she hadn't figured it out sooner.

She bounced off her bed and flapped across the bare floor in her fuzzy slippers to the Princess phone on her desk and dialed as quietly as she could. Finally, Billy picked up.

"It's me," she whispered. "I gotta make this quick. Listen, I'm going to invite some real square to the prom to keep the peace, but don't worry because I just came up with the greatest idea ever, okay?"

"Whatever you say, babe," Billy said. "I know your old man can't stand me."

Just then, there was a soft knock on her bedroom door. "Gotta go," she whispered, gently placing the phone back in the cradle. "Who is it?" she called out.

The door opened and her mother poked her head in. Nora didn't like the look on her face, but played it cool. "I was just getting ready for bed," she said.

"Your father wants to see you. In the dining room."

The dining room? This can't be good. "I'll be right down."

*

Her father was sitting at one end of the table, smoking a cigarette with an ashtray in front of him. James was sitting at the other end, his homework spread out.

"James," Dave said, "why don't you take that upstairs?"

James looked from his father to Nora, then gathered his papers and left the room.

"Sit down," Dave said, gesturing toward a seat across from him.

Nora did as she was told. Peg sat on the chair beside her.

"We have to talk about your future." Dave loosened his tie. "You'll be graduating before you know it."

"I know that."

"Now, I know you got into St. John's, but the nuns at Immaculata have been telling me for four years that you're not college material."

"That's what they say?" Nora said forcefully.

Dave raised an eyebrow. "Do you disagree?"

Nora paused before replying. "I hate high school. I hate them. I probably could've done better if I tried harder."

"Well, I'm not going to pay a lot of money to St. John's on the hope that this time you'll try harder."

Nora felt her face turning red and wanted to respond, but something held her back.

"Here's the deal," Dave said. "I'll pay for you to go to Katherine Gibbs. They run a classy program. When you finish, you can get a secretarial job with a good company."

"I'm not going," Nora said, sensing her mother flinch.

"You're not going?" Dave tapped the ash from his cigarette.

"That's not what I want to do."

Dave's mouth tightened. He looked at Peg, then back at his daughter. Calmly, slowly, he said, "Well, Nora, what do you want to do?"

"I don't know, but I don't want to be someone's secretary."

"Okay. Then you figure it out for yourself and soon. I'm not wasting any of my money to send you to college while you decide what you want to be when you grow up."

"Fine. Are we done?" Nora rose from the table, glaring at Peg as if to say she knew he'd never let her go.

"Sure," Dave said.

Nora turned and stomped out of the room.

Peg hesitated then said, "You were pretty rough on her, don't you think?"

"She's got to wake up." Dave's voice rose. "You know what that nun said to me the other night? 'Your daughter thinks life is just a bowl of cherries.' Well it's not."

Peg sighed. "Maybe so. But at least when my father told me I'd never go to college, it was because we couldn't afford it. She may never forgive you."

"That's her problem," Dave muttered, snuffing out his cigarette. "Let's go to bed."

*

At 2:45 P.M. on Friday, James rang the first dismissal bell. He simultaneously pushed all five buttons under the large clock located in the principal's office, carefully following the instructions Michael Cassidy gave him before graduating the year before. As he killed the five minutes before repeating the procedure, he wondered if Mike would be at the playground that afternoon. With basketball season at Bishop Reilly High School now over, in all likelihood Mike would be back with the crowd up the park, running full court until dinner time.

At 2:50 P.M. he set off the final bell. He pulled on his cloth harness and badge, left the office, and walked up the staircase to his post where he would supervise lines of students leaving the school building for the buses. Gary Hardy, another patrol boy, was waiting for him at the top of the stairs, fidgeting as usual.

"Hurry up, Devlin, will ya? You're gonna miss her again."

Like almost everyone else in eighth grade, Gary was taller than James. Over the nuns' objections, he was trying to grow his dirty blond hair long like the Beatles. "What are you talking about?"

"Come on, stupid. Donna Bradley, that's what. Donna Bradley. How many times do I gotta tell you?"

"I don't even know her."

"Listen, jackass. She sure knows you. She asks me about you practically every day on the bus home. And I'll tell you everything you need to know about her. First, she is by far the most stacked girl in seventh grade." He motioned his hands in front of his chest. "*Va va va voom!*"

"Oh come off it, will ya, Gary."

"Christ, will you listen to this dope? I'm trying to do him the most spectacular favor in the history of this miserable school and he's being dense." Gary grabbed James by his shoulders. "I'm telling you, this girl has got a great set of knockers. I've seen her in her tank suit a million times at the Douglaston Club and I'm telling you they're the real thing. None of this tissue paper, fill-up-the-bra trick all the skanks use. The genuine article. So go ahead, be thick if you want. Be a snob, see if I care. I'll tell her you can't be bothered."

"All right, all right, you win," James muttered, pulling away from Gary's grasp. "What do you want me to do?"

"Just talk to her, jerko. She won't bite you."

"I've never done anything like that before. What am I going to say to her?"

"Don't worry about it. You'll think of something. Just check her out when she comes by, okay? That'll convince you." Gary walked back up toward his post at the end of the hall closest to the church while James paced back and forth alongside the railing above the stairwell.

Why'd I ever let him talk me into this? he wondered, paying scant attention to the hordes of fifth and sixth graders who marched noisily past him and down the stairs. But when the seventh grade bus riders approached, he searched the crowd and picked Donna Bradley out at a distance, just as he had every afternoon since Gary first mentioned her name. His heart leapt in a totally unaccustomed way as he waited for her to come into view.

Every detail of Gary's description was accurate—but God, how James hated that description. It was unspeakably profane, like saying the Blessed Mother had great tits. In James's mind, Donna Bradley was an angel. Like some beatific vision, her features swam in front of his eyes all day long. Her sky blue eyes peeked out beneath dark pixie hair.

He might have been wrong, but it looked like Donna had spotted him gazing at her. She began chatting conspicuously with the girl next to her on line, and raised her voice as she walked past his post.

"Would you step out of line, please, Miss?" He tried to look stern, but felt his face flush.

Donna stepped to the side and up against the wall, letting the rest of her classmates pass.

James watched the line of students disappear down the staircase, then turned and walked self-consciously toward his prisoner. As he approached, the unpleasant truth became apparent: this younger girl was taller than he was.

James cleared his throat. It was that old nervous sound he hadn't heard in years. "You know you're not supposed to be talking on line," he said quietly, looking at the floor, then up at her.

"I suppose so," Donna answered, her lashes flickering on her lowered eyes.

James could not believe how contrite she looked. "Well, listen, it's really no big deal, Donna."

The girl looked down at him and giggled. James instantly realized he'd blown it.

He cleared his throat again, hating the noise. "Uh, Gary Hardy mentioned you a couple times. It's how I know your name."

Donna blushed. "I was kind of hoping he would...Jimmy."

James grew a little bolder. "How about I walk you down to your bus before you miss it. It's the least I can do after pulling you out of line like that."

Donna gave him a dazzling smile. "I'd like that a lot."

They walked down the stairs side by side, James knees buckling. His stomach felt like it was filled with cotton candy. As they headed toward the exit sign, again and again, he looked over at her. Incredibly, she kept smiling back. He was her slave.

The next few weeks, James's lifestyle altered drastically. His family noticed, somewhat to his parents' dismay and to Nora's horror, his heightened interest in personal hygiene. James took frequent, lengthy showers in their one bathroom. He stood like a statue in front of the mirror, combing and fussing with his hair until he had it just right. He scrubbed his teeth until his gums bled and the bristles on his brush bent backward. He gargled a quart of Listerine every three days.

James's appearance wasn't the only change. He was mysteriously absent from the basketball court where the nuns let the eighth grade boys have at each other after lunch. None of his old buddies understood why it was taking Jimmy so long to eat his lunch and get back to school. He would barely beat the second class bell each day.

Gary Hardy and a few other Manor kids knew where their new friend could be found. He was dawdling on the far side of the school building by the Good Humor truck. He would meet Donna there each day and engage in a little more small talk, a little more laughter. They were growing comfortable with each other. The time would fly by until the first bell rang. With a quick, "See ya later," James would sprint from the playground to his patrol post on the other side of the building. There he would begin a dreamy countdown until dismissal time when he would see her again.

Not coincidentally, Gary became a much more significant figure in James's life. After school each day, instead of heading to the playground where Michael and the other guys would be running full court, he would trek down to Gary's house in the Manor. Gary introduced him to his own circle of friends. They spent late spring afternoons hanging around the residential street corners or roaming up and down the shady roads, hoping for a not-quite-chance meeting with the local girls. If they did run into Donna and her friends, James's day was complete. He was not lucky often. Her parents seemed to keep her closely supervised.

One late May afternoon, Gary, James and several other boys stood down the block from Donna's house. They were leaning against the chain-link fence guarding the rear of the Douglaston Club. A paint crew was putting the finishing coat on the swimming pool, a final preparation for the approaching summer season.

"So," Gary said, "when you gonna ask her out, Jimmy? Everybody's dying to know."

"Knock it off, will you. Ya never let up." James pushed him away.

"I'm just watchin' out for your best interests. You could be the make-out king of St. Aidan's School if you weren't such a coward. I'm telling you, she's ready. You could be slipping Donna Bradley the tongue right now. You're the one that doesn't have the guts. You're Gomer Pyle. 'Gollee, Miss Donna. Could I pretty please hold your hand?" he drawled loudly.

James's blood began to boil. He raised a hand to stop his friend. "All right, Gary. That's enough. I'll ask her out, okay?"

"No shit? You will? Listen now, not one of these quadruple, octuple dates to the World's Fair or some garbage like that. One on one, the real thing, or you get no credit from me. You got to call her up and ask her yourself to make it official."

"Don't worry, the real thing. I'll call her."

"God, you are a lucky man." Gary let loose a loud screech and began dancing across the street corner. The others broke into laughter. James smiled, but then left.

He was tortured all the way home. He rarely called anyone on the phone, and had never called a girl. No, that was not the right term anymore. He had already moved beyond that state with Donna, and had better admit it. She was not just any girl. She was his girlfriend. But what if she didn't recognize his voice on the phone? Worse yet, what if someone else answered? Worst of all, what if Nora caught him on the phone and discovered what he was up to? She would never let him live it down.

As he walked up Douglaston Parkway, his mind gushed forth a million equally valid excuses not to call, but by the time he reached Northern Boulevard, he realized none of them would deter him. He had been challenged and would surely have to report to his friends the next day. No, that was not why he was going to call. He would call because he had not seen Donna that afternoon and missed talking to her. Never mind what Gary and all the other bozos had to say. He would call because Jimmy Devlin wanted to ask his girlfriend out on a date.

That evening after dinner, Nora went upstairs to wash her hair. James knew this was his chance. Nora would be in the shower for the best part of an hour. His parents would still be downstairs. The Princess phone would be left unguarded.

James excused himself innocuously, then tore up the staircase to the second floor. He heard Nora singing in the shower as he crossed the threshold into her room. He tiptoed across the forbidden territory, toward the desk in the corner.

Fear gripped him, as he stood before the phone, its single illuminated eye staring at him in the twilight. *God, what if her father answers?* All James knew about Mr. Bradley was that he was some hotshot businessman. He lived in a house the size of a mansion with a beautiful wife and seven—that's right, seven—gorgeous daughters. James knew that if Donna's father answered the phone, he would choke completely.

He picked up the receiver, put it to his ear, then he placed it back down. Again, he picked it up. Another false start; once more he placed the receiver down. He looked out the window at the last surge of a glorious sunset and imagined Donna sitting next to her phone waiting to answer his call on the first ring. He took a deep breath and exhaled, just as he would before shooting a clutch free throw. He grabbed the receiver, smacked it against his ear and dialed.

A man's voice answered on the second ring with a gruff "hello."

James hesitated, then blurted, "This is Jimmy Devlin. May I please speak to Donna?"

"Wrong number." Then there was a click on the other end of the line.

"Oh, Christ," he moaned, quivering. He couldn't even dial the number straight, he was so scared.

Another deep breath, then he dialed with great care, certain to match the digits correctly this time.

Once, twice, three times it rang. Then he heard a woman's voice answer with a bright "hello." He guessed it had to be Donna's mother.

"Er, hello," James said. "May I speak to Donna? Er, this is Jimmy Devlin."

There was an obvious pause, leaving Jimmy to wonder if she were going to tell him her twelve-year-old daughter didn't accept calls from thirteen-year-old suitors. But then, just as bright as before, she said, "Hold on a minute, Jimmy. I'll tell her you're on the line."

His joy was limitless as he strained to hear Donna approaching the phone.

"Hi, Jimmy."

"Hi, Donna. How ya doing?" He hesitated, then added, "I didn't see you this afternoon. I was, you know, hangin' around with Gary and the guys."

"Oh, I have dancing lessons on Tuesdays."

"That sounds like fun. I'd like to see you dance sometime, maybe." He immediately cringed, thinking he sounded like some sort of pervert.

"That'd be nice," she said.

James tried to hear if the shower was still running, but couldn't tell. He hoped Nora was still rinsing the shampoo from her hair. He said, "The reason I called is because I wanted to know. I mean, I wanted to ask you, if maybe, um, you'd like to go out with me...sometime."

"I'd like to, Jimmy." She then lowered her voice. "But, I don't think my parents would let me go on a real date with anyone."

Jimmy thought about it for a moment, then blurted, "Well, I was thinking since Saturday is Memorial Day. Well, Sunday is, but the parade is on Saturday. Maybe I could come down and meet you and we could go to the parade together. It's not a real date, like going to the movies or something, right?"

"Right," she replied. "I mean, it sounds like we'd both just be heading to the parade alone but ending up going together."

"So, um, would you like to go?" *Ask for the order*, James often heard his father say. Maybe this was what the sales tactic meant; you don't ask, you don't get.

"Sure." Donna laughed.

"Okay, why don't I meet you on Saturday down the street from your house? By the fence to the Douglaston Club. About eleven thirty, okay? That'll give us time to get a good spot."

"You know where I live?"

He laughed sheepishly. "I do. You know, I always end up giving my secrets away to you."

"That's okay. I don't mind. I'll see you on Saturday, about eleven thirty."

"Thanks a lot. I'll look for you at school tomorrow. Goodnight...Donna." *God, I even love the sound of her name.*

"Goodnight, Jimmy. Thanks for calling."

He smiled. "Oh, it was nothing. Goodnight," he said, hanging up the phone and laying his head down on the desk. He was physically drained, but with his eyes closed, he relished his triumph. He had done it! And best of all, he would get to go with Donna to the parade on Saturday. *Please don't let it rain*, he beseeched the ceiling.

"What are you doing in my room, you smelly little worm?"

James jumped up to find Nora standing in the doorway, her head in curlers, dressed in a bathrobe and slippers. "Nothing!" he exclaimed.

"You better not have been on that phone." Nora swung a wet towel at him.

James leapt over her bed and dashed out the door.

"Mom and Dad yell at me enough over the bill without you running it up!" she bellowed.

He floated down the stairs and entered another dimension, a twilight zone, where all his thoughts and emotions were totally directed toward Saturday and Donna.

James's hot streak was still intact late Saturday morning. St. Aidan's grammar school baseball team had won its game, scheduled practically at dawn. James had just enough time to clean the remaining home plate grime out of his hair, nostrils, and fingernails before departing for his rendezvous with Donna.

He pulled on the clothes he'd selected days before—a new madras shirt, white Levis, woolen sweat socks that had turned just the right shade of yellow. And to top it off, the new pair of desert boots he had splurged on with the rest of the allowance money he had saved. He wanted to convince Donna that he wasn't a slob and that he took their non-date seriously.

After combing his hair, he thundered down the stairs, vaulted over the top of the banister, then sprinted out the side door and ran smack into his father, who was coming in from mowing the lawn.

"How about washing the car before you take off?" Dave wiped his forehead with a handkerchief, scarcely looking at his son.

James squirmed at the contact with his father's sweaty t-shirt. "How about I do it tomorrow? I'll even use the Simoniz."

"No good." Dave looked directly at him. "I figured we'd head to Shea tomorrow. Clemente's in town. You might learn something about throwing just watching his cannon." Then Dave scowled, looking up and down at James's attire. "Where you off to?"

"Uh, going to meet some guys in the Manor. We figured we'd go watch the Memorial Day parade. You know, down Northern Boulevard. They're having it today."

"I know. I know all about Memorial Day." He frowned. "What are you running around with that Manor crowd for anyway?"

"I'm not running around with them." James shrugged. "It's just a couple guys I'm friendly with."

"I don't like it. You don't belong over there. You're out of your league and going to end up in some kind of hot water."

"I'm not going to get in any trouble, Pop."

"I don't see why you can't stick around the guys in this neighborhood. I thought you were aiming to play basketball in high school? You're still so short. You'll never make the team if you waste your time with those guys. They're a bunch of rich kids. They don't play ball. They're not friends of yours."

James started to protest, but his father didn't let up.

"You know, you're not the easiest kid in the world for guys to take. You want to be the best at everything—at school, playing ball, anything you try. Most kids you meet will resent you. At least the guys around here are used to you."

James wanted to deny it, to scream at his father that he had lots of friends. But he knew it wasn't true. He did want to win at everything and the guys who never beat him couldn't stand him. Only the real winners, the guys who were sure of themselves, had any use for him.

He looked at his father, stung. He couldn't share the truth with him, tell him his trip to the Manor had nothing to do with other guys at all. He finally collected himself enough to respond, "I promise to take care of the car as soon as I get home, but I'm late and better get going. I'll do a good job, I promise."

When his father didn't protest, James bounced down the driveway and to the street on his new crepe soles. The day was spectacular, a full preview of the summer to come. The scene with his father faded and it seemed only a few minutes more before he'd traveled the two miles and arrived at his destination outside the Douglaston Club.

He paced at the corner, thrusting his hands into his pockets, then pulling them out. He couldn't tell which way looked better, and finally gave up in disgust. Just then, noise from inside drew his attention. It was opening day at the swimming pool and it looked like the Garden of Eden, only more crowded and with a chain link fence. James was sure Gary and the other guys were there, ogling the girls in their swimsuits. He would never get to join them. When his father had received his latest promotion, he had been invited to join but turned it down, explaining to his family that they were not joining any club that didn't allow blacks or Jews.

It didn't matter to his father that there were no blacks in Douglaston or Little Neck and the Jewish people had their own pool in Deepdale where no Christians were welcome; his father's mind was made up, and that would be that. Although he was sure Donna was prettier than all the other girls, he'd never see her in a bathing suit, and it was his father's fault. His father's mind was also made up about the Manor guys. What did he have against them? That their fathers made a lot of money? That's what his own father was trying to do, too. In fact, his mother had told him they would likely move to a bigger house soon, but James was sure it would not be in the Manor but in their same Park neighborhood of modest, detached houses. Dave was making another point, but James didn't get that one either. That was nothing new because, as often as his father's mind was made up, there were other times when he seemed to be saying two different things, or saying one thing and doing another.

They don't play ball. They're not friends of yours. His father's words echoed in his mind. That one was tough to argue. The Manor guys certainly didn't play ball, and any time James brought the subject up, he was pretty much ignored. Instead, they liked to talk about cars and girls. The first topic, James knew nothing about, and the second not as much as he wanted to know. When the Manor guys spoke about Hemis, horsepower, and pink slips, James had nothing to say. When they discussed who had the best tits or nicest ass or, worse yet, who was a skank, James had nothing to contribute either and remained silently thankful that Donna Bradley seemed exempt from their rating system, at least in his presence. In truth, he felt like an outsider. Maybe he was only included in their company because Donna had deemed him worthy, which automatically made him good enough for them, too.

James looked up and saw Donna walking down the sidewalk toward him. His first reaction was surprise. He had never expected their meeting to actually take place, thinking something was bound to mess it up. But there she was, dressed in a shirt with tiny red and white checks, blue jeans, and navy blue Keds. She looked like she'd been to the beach. Her tan highlighted her sparkling teeth. She was radiant and James was quite sure he was going to drop to his knees, like after a painful foul tip at the plate.

"Hi, Jimmy. Sorry I'm late."

He felt himself melting. "That's okay. You all set?"

"I guess so."

"We better get going." He started off ahead of her and she took two quick strides to catch up.

They walked down the tree-lined street for at least two blocks before saying another word. *You gotta talk to her,* an inner voice told him. *You can't ask someone out and then just act like some kind of goon the rest of the day.*

"So what did you do all day?" he blurted.

"All day? It's only eleven thirty", Donna replied.

He stopped walking. "Guess that wasn't much of a conversation starter, huh?"

They laughed out loud together and walked up Centre Drive, exchanging small bits of information about themselves and their families. They even shared some plans for the future. Donna wanted to go to St. Mary's in Manhasset for high school. All her older sisters had gone there.

James mentioned that he was going to Gonzaga Prep in Manhattan in the fall. He confessed that he'd bombed the scholarship test for Regis High School, a far more prestigious Jesuit school around the corner from Gonzaga. Even James was not sure if he had deliberately thrown the test. Nora had threatened never to speak to him again if he became a "Regis fag," which might have influenced his poor performance. But if he had taken a dive, the score had been evened in the end. God and James's father made certain he would not escape the Jesuits, or a daily commute to the City. When James balked at traveling to Manhattan in full military dress as one of Xavier's High School's "subway commandos," Gonzaga was selected by default.

"My dad said he didn't mind paying the tuition because I might be able to make the basketball team there, meet the right kind of friends, and go on to a good college," James confided, as they walked up Douglaston Parkway, and crossed the bridge over the railroad tracks.

Eventually James led Donna up a hill and through the graveyard of the Zion Church, which was not at all ominous in the late May sunshine. He pointed out some of his favorite headstones until he noticed that the wall overlooking Northern Boulevard was filling up with local teenagers. He cut the tour short and selected a prime spot, unobstructed by overhanging tree limbs. With their legs dangling over the side, far above the sidewalk below, it was the perfect vantage point to watch the parade.

As they waited for the collection of marchers to draw near, from flag-waving scout troops to venerable veterans, James spotted members of the Saints, a Little Neck gang. Dressed in snug black chinos and muscle shirts, they were swigging Tango from a quart bottle, and shouting occasional insults at the passersby below. James knew their faces well. They'd been notorious boys' room goose artists at St. Aidan's in their younger days, champions of the forbidden schoolyard game of Mingle, Mangle, Mum, where the unfortunate "it" would be pummeled until he could count to ten and chant the three painful words. These were the same guys who not only refused to cry but laughed out loud while they were beaten by the nuns each Wednesday for some offense during Stations of the Cross.

James only hoped they didn't start anything with him in front of Donna. He had no idea how to respond, but was spared the dilemma when, just as the drums of the first band came into earshot, two girls with teased hair, tight blouses knotted at the midriff, and stretch denim pants came out of Koch's Candy Store, wiggling under the spectators, every step applying tremendous torque to the seams and side zippers of their pants.

The Saints scrambled to their feet, racing off through the graveyard toward the driveway leading to the street below, chasing after the two girls up Northern Boulevard. Their loud whistles rivaled the shrill fife sounds of St. Aidan's Drum & Bugle Corps, which led the parade.

James then looked at Donna who returned his smile. He brushed his hair from his forehead, cleared his throat, then hesitantly reached over and took her hand. She did not pull away and they sat holding hands, bouncing their heels against the wall in time to the music. While he watched the handful of veterans going by, he wondered why his own father wasn't marching with them. He thought of asking his dad when he got home, then dismissed the idea, certain Dave would bark at him that it was none of his business, while commenting negatively about those "barstool soldiers" who did march.

The parade was over all too soon. Once the last kids on bikes bringing up the rear passed, he and Donna retraced their steps to Douglaston Parkway, holding hands the entire way. When they reached the Douglaston Club, James knew he had accompanied Donna as far as he dared.

Reluctantly, he released her hand. "Thanks for coming," he said. "It was a nice day."

"It was," she replied. "Thanks for asking me."

"I'll see you at school on Monday, okay? I'm going to the Mets game tomorrow with my father."

Donna nodded, but just as he was about to walk away, she said, "Oh, there's something I wanted to ask." She was practically whispering, taking a step toward him. "My parents are letting me have a party in two weeks, the day after school gets out. I'd like you to come, if you'd like to."

James thought about it for a brief moment, recalling that his family was supposed to be leaving on a vacation around then, but thought it would be the day after the party. He said, "I'd love to come."

Donna smiled. "Great. I'll send an invitation, but wanted to tell you about it." She then turned, walking up the street. He watched until she disappeared into the large house. Then he took off in a trot for home, for a date with the blue Chrysler Newport, a bucket of soapy water, and a Simoniz can.

*

It was Thursday evening, two nights before Donna's party and James was panicking. He shuffled his way down the dim hallway, eyeing the plaster Madonna sitting on the shelf. "Our Lady, Help of Christians, pray for us." He muttered the prayer aloud. "And please don't let her eat me alive." The "her" in this case was his sister, someone whose help he needed desperately.

He gave a rapid knock on her door, then burst into Nora's room. She was sitting with her feet on the desk, telephone to her ear and hair in curlers. She had the window wide open, but she was still engulfed in a cloud of cigarette smoke, which was James's good fortune.

"Shut that door!" she hissed, while crushing her cigarette in the ashtray sitting on the windowsill. Then, into the receiver, she said, "Listen, I'll have to call you back." She dropped the phone down in the cradle and said with annoyance, "What do you want?"

James hesitated, then blurted, "I need to learn how to dance."

"So? What's that got to do with me?"

James said, "I want you to show me how."

"Not a chance!" she said. "What do you ever do for me? You certainly never stick up for me when Dad starts picking on me. Even though he's your big buddy, right? Now get out."

"I don't think so," he said, feeling desperate. "If you don't teach me, I'm going to tell Mom and Dad that you were smoking in your room."

Nora looked at the half-smoked cigarette he'd made her waste, realizing he had her where he wanted her. Then she looked over at her brother, scowling. "There's one catch before we have a deal."

"What?"

"Tell me her name, Jimmy baby. Who is it? Who's the chickie? Joanie De-Marco with the big boobs? Tricia Fagan with the bleached blond hair?"

James shook his head.

"Then who?"

"Donna. Donna Bradley." James almost choked as he forced the words out. It was as though his throat, lips and tongue rebelled, trying to preserve the secret.

"Never heard of her." Nora snorted. "All right, we better get started. A hopeless case like you is going to take a lot of work. But before we get going, run downstairs and get me a Coke."

*

It took a lot to ruin a Saturday morning for James, who considered it the sweetest stretch of time God had created, but this Saturday morning he'd been assigned the 9 A.M. Mass. His partner was Sean O'Donnell.

When he wasn't thinking about Donna, James was stewing over his misfortune in drawing O'Donnell. What were the odds against such bad luck? There had to be a hundred other altar boys at St. A's. However long the shot, it had hit and he was screwed. This time there'd be no Michael Cassidy to intervene and he would be at Sean's mercy.

James opened the sacristy door, discovering that Sean had beaten him there. *Damn*, he swore, disregarding his sacred surroundings. *This dink must get a ride from home every time he serves Mass.*

"Devlin," Sean said. "Some old guy died the other day and this is going to be his funeral Mass. I'm the master of ceremonies, you're the thurifer. Hurry and get the incense cooking."

James snapped up his cassock. They were under pressure, with no time for snotty remarks.

The Mass proceeded uneventfully. The dead guy must have been really old or very unknown because, aside from his two children, there were only a handful of other old people in attendance. Father Rinaldi had given his usual fill-in-the-blank eulogy and, once they had left the altar, the priest ordered the boys to ready the sacristy for the next day's Masses.

"You guys are lucky," Father Rinaldi called from the foyer. "The family wanted the funeral director to give you a tip, five dollars apiece. You don't usually get it at funerals, only weddings."

Once Father Rinaldi left, Sean assumed command. "Devlin, why don't you get the candles and lights. I'll refill the cruets."

James did as he was told. When he returned, Sean was smacking his lips. If he drank the wine, he hadn't offered James any. Sean pulled the surplice over his head and said, "We made a pretty good team, Devlin. Surprising."

James braced for an insult, but none came. What followed was awkward silence, so James said, "Where do you go to school?"

"Holy Cross."

"You like it?"

"It's school. I do what I have to do and get out every day as fast as I can." He paused, then asked, "Where you going next year?"

"Gonzaga. In the City."

"That's big bucks," Sean said. "You win a scholarship or something?"

"No. My father got a new job and thinks it's worth the extra money."

"Either way, you're going to spend your whole life getting there and back every day."

James nodded. Sean was being a bit friendly. Maybe he'd do the same. He couldn't say anything smart about cars, but he did know something about music. "Hey, Sean, you got a favorite band?"

Sean eyed him, but then said, "The Beach Boys are boss!"

James tried his hardest not to cringe. Trying to find common ground in music was a huge mistake. James had guessed Sean would at worst say the Beatles, since James far preferred the Rolling Stones, holy terrors though they were.

But the Beach Boys? *I'd rather have no girlfriend than one named Rhonda,* James thought. *I can't even tell this guy the groups I really dig are the Miracles and Temptations. He'd never get it in a million years.*

Instead, James lied again in church. "Yeah," he told Sean. "The Beach Boys are great. I love them too."

Sean was heading to the door. "Okay, Devlin. See you around."

"Yeah," James said, adding, "I'm actually going to be in your neighborhood tonight."

Sean turned back toward him. "Why?"

"Donna Bradley's having a party. Were you invited?"

"No," he said. "She's just a kid."

*

It was 6:30 Saturday, Nora's prom night. The Devlins had eaten early. Nora was upstairs making the final adjustments to her hair and gown before the limousine arrived. Peg bounced in and out of her room, offering what scant assistance her daughter would accept. Dave sat on the sofa in the living room, reading the *Star Journal*, smoking a cigarette.

James sat alone at the kitchen table, resplendent in a seersucker jacket, white Levis, and shined cordovan penny loafers. He had a good half hour to kill before leaving for the Manor. If he left before that, he might be the first one at the party. He was anxious to get there, but wise enough not to risk embarrassing himself, so he leafed through a *Life* magazine.

He stopped flipping the pages when he saw pictures of bodies, all clad in black pajamas. The corpses were so little, so young, but unmistakably soldiers. A single American soldier hovered above some prisoners, who also looked like they were dressed for bed, but instead were mixed in with the dead guys. He read the story, but was still confused when he finished. There were U.S. soldiers in this Vietnam place and it looked like there was a war going on. But our soldiers were not supposed to be fighting, according to the reporter. Until recently, they'd been called advisers, whatever that meant. Maybe they were some kind of referee, making sure everyone fought fair. It didn't matter anymore. Now they were calling them soldiers again. Marines.

He closed the magazine and sat in thought. Everybody has a war when they grow up. Dad and Uncle Rory had. So had Grandpa Devlin, except he couldn't go because of his hand. Yes, there was always a war, which the United States would ultimately win. The country was invincible, better at war than the Yankees were at baseball. We never started the war, but we always finished it. We had never been beaten.

James wondered if this were a real war. It certainly looked like the real thing; not at all resembling the fun, pretend war he and Lance used to play. He began to wonder how Lance was doing. Maybe he was a basketball player, too. *Probably is; all black guys shoot hoops, but they play half court "city ball," and don't take the ball back past the foul line after a change of possession. I wonder if he's good? He's probably way taller than me—bet you he plays forward or center.*

His attention went back to the pictures. How long could this war possibly last? If World War II was a World War and it lasted only about four years, then whatever was going on in this Vietnam country couldn't possibly last that long. The thought gave him some comfort. He closed the magazine and stood up. It was 7 o'clock, time to go.

He went into the living room to say goodbye to his father, but before doing so, he asked, "Dad, did you ever hear of Vietnam?"

"Yeah," Dave answered softly. "Things are starting up there. We'll see what happens."

"What do you mean?"

"Nothing." Dave met his son's eyes. "Now, tell me again where you're going."

"To a party."

"Whose party?"

"Donna Bradley's." He started to escape, but his father pressed on.

"And where does Miss Bradley live?"

"In the Manor."

Dave shook his head in disapproval. "I thought we talked about that already."

"It's just a party. I want to go."

"And you're walking there and back?"

"Yeah, is that all right?"

"Okay by me. Your sister's going to be out all night anyway. Don't mention it to your mother. Just go. She won't pay attention to you tonight. Too busy with all this prom nonsense."

James nodded. "See you later."

"Make sure you stay out of trouble, Jim."

James walked down the block, thinking about how his father could address in detail any topic involving baseball, like the infield fly or obscure balk rules, but whenever he asked anything relating to war, James got little if any information at all. He thought back to the men in black pajamas, huddled among the dead bodies, and stifled a shiver that passed through him.

*

James had barely gone out the door when Dave heard two loud beeps of a horn. He got up from the couch and went to the living room window in time to see a long black limo pull up to his curb, the driver opening the back door. The backseat of the limousine was awash with pastel chiffon and white dinner jackets. In a lapse of decorum, two girls scrambled out. When they hit the sidewalk, they just kept going up the front steps to the Devlin house. Three young men trailed behind.

Once inside, Peg took charge. "Dave, I want you to meet John Grady."

The tall young man shook hands with his date's father, telling Dave about his expected major at Boston College and tentative post-graduate plans. Dave listened with marginal interest as he puffed on a cigarette, craning his head around the room and nodding politely. The giggling Immaculata girls and their two gawky escorts were sitting ill at ease on the couch. Dave wondered, *how long is she going to make them wait*?

As Nora descended the stairs, a hush fell over the room. The three boys stood up, awestruck. Her girlfriends rushed to her side, like ladies in waiting fluttering toward their princess.

Dave stared at his daughter, realizing for the first time that she was a full grown, beautiful woman. He didn't know what to think, much less say. He'd never been one to fawn over his little girl. It seemed unnatural, even impure to him, and he withdrew from all physical contact with his daughter once she entered puberty. Then they just grew further apart. He didn't understand her. She had no use for school; no use for him, either, as far as he could tell. All she really seemed to care about were her friends. What her friends were doing or saying had paramount importance, while her family meant nothing. Sending her off to college would be a mistake, even with her threat of going to California. *Why California?* He wondered. Even if she did go, she'd never manage on her own and would be back soon enough.

Peg stood in front of Nora and lined the group up for the obligatory prom snapshots. She buzzed around the room cheerily with Dave watching her, drawing comparisons between the middle aged woman and her teenage daughter. Where did the time go? He and Peg didn't have any fancy prom. They missed out on all that. The War had taken it all away.

"And don't let me find out any of you were drinking," Peg said. "If you get caught misbehaving on prom night, you may not graduate next Sunday."

"Yes, Mom. We know, Mom," Nora said robotically.

Peg kissed everyone in sight goodbye, saving Nora for last. She whispered in her daughter's ear.

Annoyance eclipsed Nora's charm before she said goodnight to her father. They stood on opposites sides of the room. Neither was willing to display any weakness to draw any closer.

"Have fun," Dave said, opening another pack of cigarettes. He lit up and added, "But not too much." Nora scowled at him, then turned away.

As soon as Nora climbed into the limo she blurted, "I can't stay out and go to the beach with you in the morning, John," she said. "My father says I have to be home by 3 o'clock."

John looked crestfallen and his two male companions were stunned by his dramatic shift of fortune.

Nora added, "He's such a drag. He always finds a way to ruin everything." She wasn't lying about that, but used it to her advantage for this particular situation. It was easy to sell.

"Wow, Nora," John said. "He didn't mention anything about that to me. Neither did your mother."

"Mom? Anything Dad says goes for her. She's just his slave who acts like she has no mind of her own." Nora believed those words, too.

"But everyone gets to stay out on prom night—"

One frosty glare from Nora ended his resistance. She then smiled coolly.

*

James waited at the corner, trying to gather his nerve. "Hi, Mrs. Bradley. My name's Jimmy Devlin. How do you do?" He peered through the fence at the Douglaston Club, now empty, looking even more distant in the gathering dusk.

Why did his father keep harping on it? "*You don't belong...You're out of your league.*"

James didn't care what his father said. He wasn't about to disappoint Donna, no matter what.

He walked down the sidewalk to the middle of the block. There it was, the place where she lived. He had never known anyone who lived in such a big house. His mouth was completely dry, but with a final wheeze of determination, he walked up to the front door, pulled on the big metal knocker and released it with a gulp.

A pretty dark haired woman opened the door wide. James stood there, unable to make a sound. She reminded him of Mrs. Kennedy, the assassinated President's wife, wearing a black cotton dress, single strand of pearls and shiny high heels. She bore no resemblance to his own mother.

"Why, you must be Jimmy." She extended her hand in greeting. James grasped it with both of his own. "Donna's been waiting for you. Won't you follow me?"

"Thank you, Mrs. Bradley," James managed to croak. "You look just like you sound on the phone."

She looked at him quizzically. James wondered whether Yogi Berra also blushed when he said something regrettable like that. At least Yogi could hide it under his perpetual five o'clock shadow.

"Nice, I meant," he stammered. "That's all."

She led him out of the cavernous foyer, down a long hallway. They entered what seemed to be a separate wing of the house. Soon they passed through a pair of sliding glass doors onto a patio. Down a few steps was a garden, gaily decorated with different colored Japanese lanterns and fragrant citronella candles.

James strained to make out the faces in the crowd, the girls all in dresses and boys in sport jackets. A few of the kids were from his class, but most he recognized as St. Aidan seventh graders who took the Manor bus with Donna. He didn't even know their names.

"Hey, loverboy! You finally got here!" Gary Hardy's voice was unmistakable. "We all thought you were going to chicken out."

James cringed and shrank away from Gary, who was standing with Steve and Pete, two other eighth graders.

"Hey, daddy. Lighten up, already." Gary smacked him playfully all over his sports jacket and pulled at his tie. "You gotta loosen up, you old make-out artist. We're gonna groove tonight. Look at all the boss chicks, will ya? There's got to be two dozen of them!"

"Keep it down, huh?" James said. Then he saw Donna carrying a tray of Cokes, wearing a white empire dress that accentuated her figure. She was gorgeous and James could not hear another word Gary was saying. His shyness vanished and he walked right up to her.

They stood facing each other, separated by a tray of sodas, drinking each other in, oblivious to all the others. James finally managed to speak.

"It's a great party. Thanks for inviting me."

"I'm glad you could come, Jimmy. Really glad." She pointed to her tray. "Let me pass these out and I'll be right back." Donna smiled reassuringly before she rushed off, and he believed her: she would not be gone for long.

The evening went by in a blur. Twilight became darkness and the lanterns took on a magical glow. James was determined to dance with Donna to every song played on the stereo. Despite being nervous during the first fast dances, his combination mashed potato-cha-cha held up fairly well. But when the first slow song came on, his mind went blank and he struggled to remember his sister's instructions.

"Just put your arm around my back, you dope," Nora had commanded in the Devlins' basement above the music of 'Goin' Outta My Head.' "Like this!" She pulled his arm where it belonged. "And since the party's at her house, just hold her hand up with your other hand, like you're a gentleman, instead of bear-hugging her and getting yourself thrown out."

It all came back to James in the nick of time. He held Donna just as Nora taught him while Peter and Gordon played 'World Without Love.' James thought his first slow dance would be his last. He smelled Donna up close for the first time and felt her warm cheek against his. He closed his eyes, trying to preserve his communion with Donna and the music.

When the song ended, they unraveled themselves and walked to the farthest end of the garden. Donna whispered, "I'm really going to miss you when you leave for vacation tomorrow, Jimmy."

"I'm going to miss you a lot, too. I'd rather not go, but I'd never get out of it. It's going to be the longest week of my life."

Donna gazed at him with sorrowful eyes. "For me too."

"I hate to interrupt you two love birds", Gary announced, somehow finding them in the darkest part of the yard where the lanterns' light did not reach. "But there's a couple of guys here to see you, Jimmy."

James scowled. "For me? You sure?"

Gary nodded. "Jackie Standish and Sean O'Donnell. They said they wanted to talk to you outside for a minute."

"Don't go, Jimmy," Donna said, her tone upset. "That Jackie's always up to something. Tell him to forget it."

James realized he should have never mentioned Donna's party to Sean. Still, he couldn't imagine what he wanted with him. And Jackie Standish? He barely knew him. He'd graduated from St. Aidan's the year before and they'd been on the same baseball team. He was a lousy ballplayer, but a real wild man from a family known to be rolling in the money. But Jackie had never given him a hard time before.

"I'm going to go see what they want," he said. "I'll be right back."

"Oh, I wish my father were home!" Donna exclaimed. "He'd get rid of them."

Ironically, James wished the same thing. The whole scene was straight from a bad movie. Gary, Steve, Pete and James's other friends from the Manor trooped behind him as he left the garden by a wooden gate leading to the street.

"Over here."

James walked in the direction of the voice calling from the darkness. He spotted two cigarettes glowing in the dark. As he got closer, he made out Jackie and Sean standing in front of a large hedge.

"What's up?" James said, attempting to make his voice sound deep and fearless, but as he approached he had to look up at Jackie, who seemed to have grown six inches and put on fifty pounds since the last time he'd seen him.

"We got a little message for you," Jackie said, wearing a black muscle shirt and blue jeans. He stepped up to James, spit on the sidewalk, took a deep drag and blew a mouthful of smoke into James's face. "We Manor guys don't appreciate dirt like you from the other side of Northern ruining our neighborhood, dig? We just can't tolerate shit hanging' around our women anymore."

James felt like an overdressed sissy as he was forced to look up at Jackie. He spotted Sean hanging by the hedge. He had a cigarette in one hand and what looked like a beer can in the other. Sean wasn't talking, but he seemed in charge, as if directing the whole show.

"Face facts, punk." Jackie poked him in the chest with an index finger, waving a cigarette with his other hand. "You know you're a fucking douche bag. And now you're pestering Donna Bradley? You're not good enough for her. That should be obvious even to a fool like you. See these guys here?" He nodded to Gary and the others. "They know you're shit, too. See if one of them sticks up for you."

No one stepped forward to intervene and Jackie grabbed him by the knot of his tie, wrenching him up on to his toes, forcing him to look into his bloodshot, watery eyes. His breath smelled of beer. "I could beat the piss out of you right here and now." He then released James, causing him to fall back a step. "But I'm not going to do that, see. You've got your good clothes on. It'll take your old man months to earn enough cash for another shitty outfit like that."

James was sure he heard his father whispering in his ear: *If a guy won't let you alone, you've got to forget all that fair fighting nonsense. Get your best shot in, right to his nose, and keep punching for all you're worth. If you're going to get beat up, may as well get your licks in first and give him something to remember you by.*

Jackie blew more smoke into his face.

Hit him! Hit that sucker right between the eyes and punch his face in. Let that bastard have it now.

"Go back and say your goodbyes," Jackie said. "Cause if I catch you snarking around here again, I'm going to kick the living shit out of you."

James didn't say a word. He was disgusted with himself, disgusted with those surrounding him. He looked one last time at Sean, smirking in the darkness, then at Jackie. He turned and walked back, opening the gate with Gary and the others following behind.

"What happened?" Donna rushed over to him.

He tried to collect himself. "Nothing much."

"My mother was going to call the Manor cop any minute." Her voice was trembling. "Don't you want to tell me what they wanted?"

"Not really. Just something about my hanging around here."

Donna frowned, but then her mother appeared and announced. "Okay, kids. One last song and the party's over."

"I'll pick the last song!" Gary announced.

James watched Gary place the record on the turntable. As soon as the music started, he knew it would be another slow dance. He couldn't help but wonder whether Gary had been his Judas in the garden. He turned to Donna and asked, "Would you like to dance?"

"Sure," she said, her eyes glistening.

James held her tightly, their bodies swaying as one. James began to think that his father had been right and he really didn't belong there. He was out of his league.

Once the music ended, Donna lifted her head up off his shoulder. He looked right at her and rose to his toes, trying to make himself her height, if only for a moment. He drew her toward him and kissed her once, twice on the lips. She returned a warm, teary kiss of her own.

"Goodnight, Donna," he said. "Thank you so much."

"Goodnight, Jimmy," she replied softly. "I'll be seeing you."

He turned away and hurried through the gate, ignoring all the other guests who were exchanging farewells.

James walked home alone in the moonlight. The soft breeze blowing against his damp clothes felt like a much-needed friend cooling him down. He felt like he wanted to cry but was not sure if he couldn't or simply wouldn't.

Later, sleep would not come and James finally gave up and tiptoed downstairs to the kitchen, flipped on the light, then turned on the radio so low he could barely hear it. It was almost three in the morning. While the Moody Blues sang "Go Now", he sat at the table ruing how he had been intimidated. It was inexcusable, even if he had been outnumbered. He had punked out completely.

His father had been right. Going to the Manor had brought him nothing but trouble. Some fair-weather friends. Humiliation. And what he was pretty sure was a broken heart. How could he ever face Donna again after she found out he had chickened out? He'd been scared, silently enduring every one of Jackie's insults with that prick Sean watching and laughing at him. Maybe Jackie was right: anyone taking that kind of abuse wasn't worthy.

We'll see, though, James swore. *We'll see who ends up the dirt around here.*

He began leafing through *Life* once more and again looked at the corpses and prisoners kneeling before the fierce looking American. It frightened him, much more than before. He realized it was just one Caucasian soldier holding a handgun on so many Vietnamese. Guys with nothing to lose surrounding a guy like him, a person to whom life meant a great deal. The Asians looked and dressed so similarly that they could all be brothers. Their dead were already piled in a heap. But if the survivors got together and rushed the American, he could never fight them all at once. They would triumph. They were bound to figure that out for themselves.

Just then, James heard loud voices coming from the front of his house. He flipped off the light and dashed to the front window to see a limousine sitting outside. He was curious to get some pointers by catching a glimpse of Nora and her date grappling at the doorstep; even though he could barely see them on the stoop, he was able to make out their conversation.

"Goodnight and thanks again," Nora said. She leaned over and gave the guy a peck on the cheek. "You really shouldn't have had that third Zombie at the Hawaii Kai," she added. It looked like she was attempting to steady him.

"Ga night, Nora," the tall boy slurred. "You stuck up, good lookin' thing, you." He then turned and stumbled down the steps toward the limo.

Getting caught spying on prom night would be a capital offense for sure, so James crouched down at the windowsill as he heard the limo heading up the block. When he didn't hear Nora coming inside, he peered over the ledge of the windowsill and saw her walking down the steps to the sidewalk. Just then, a figure emerged from the bushes. A mystery man put his arm around her and they walked together down the block.

James tried to absorb what he'd seen and a few moments later heard the rumble of a souped-up engine starting, Soon, Billy Elsen's Chevy convertible crept past the house and out of sight.

My sister is definitely not chickenshit, James thought.

*

Nora knelt on the front seat of the Chevy as it raced down the Meadowbrook Parkway toward Jones Beach. Her once-teased hair blew in the breeze while she reached over and turned up the radio as loud as it would go. She took a swig from the Schaefer can then said, "Come on, Billy, sing with me!"

Billy smiled and pushed the accelerator closer to the floor.

"Billyee, sing, damn it!" she wailed.

Billy looked straight ahead with a dopey grin pasted on his face.

As she sang loudly, "Time is on My Side," Nora crawled toward him and thrust her breasts against his head.

"For Christ's sake, Nora! Are you trying to get us killed? Cut it out, will you?"

"Then sing, you moron!"

Very timidly, tentatively, he joined in, but as they passed the unmanned toll booths they were yelping the Stones's tune together. He swung the car into Parking Field 9. The big Chevy raced across the empty lot and skidded to a halt at the railroad ties marking the end of the pavement. Nora was out the door before Billy turned the ignition off and she dashed into the dunes, leaving him behind. She held up the bottom of her long silk gown and kept running through the sea grass that blocked her view of the ocean. When it finally came into view, she wriggled out of the dress and dropped it where the dune flattened out. Stripped down to her bra and panties, Nora headed straight for the water. Small, moonlit waves hit her as she edged in and shivered. *The water will be much warmer in California*, she thought.

Despite the alcohol she had consumed, two Pink Gardenias at Hawaii Kai, followed by two Schaefers with Billy, Nora was able to catch a decent wave after several attempts and body surf into the shore. When she came out, she saw Billy sitting at the edge of the dunes. He had spread out a blanket and placed a cooler on its edge.

As she approached, Billy pulled a church key from his pocket, tapped one side of a beer can and hooked the opener on the opposite edge to do the same. Instead of piercing the can in an upright position, he flipped it over as he opened it and shot it, sending its contents gushing into his waiting throat.

Nora was dripping wet, her feet covered with sand. Billy scrambled to his feet to meet her and, without saying a word, embraced her, bringing her to the blanket. She offered no resistance as he clumsily worked on her bra clasp, fumbling to get it undone. When he finally succeeded, she let him wolfishly attach her goose-pimply breasts. She even let his hand roam beneath her soaking underpants. He groped desperately at her crotch with Nora tolerating his awkward advances.

With eyes closed, she waited patiently for some emotion to stir within her, for Billy to pull the right switch and rocket her into ecstasy. But instead, in her mind's eye, she saw herself driving an enormous Country Squire down Little Neck Parkway, with more kids than she could count in the two backseats, all singing "Ee I ee I oh!"

The sound of an unfastening belt buckle snapped her into an upright position. Billy already had his trousers and underpants pulled down off his buttocks. His erect penis was waving at her in the ocean breeze.

"What the hell do you think you're doing?" she hissed.

"But, Nora, isn't this what you wanted? Ditching that other guy and coming out here with me? Ripping off your dress?"

"Put that pickle back in your pocket," she commanded. "I'm not leaving my future in some crummy sand dune with you, Billy Elsen.

IX
June 1967

PEG KNELT ALONE IN A PEW of St. Aidan's Church. The interior of the structure was box-like and far from impressive. The mustard-colored walls were bare and needed a fresh coat of paint. The shabbiness, though, was intriguing. The parish served one of the wealthiest congregations in Queens, yet most ghetto churches were far more ornate. Their impoverished parishioners, whose religious practices traced superstition closer than scripture, lavished much finer vestments and care upon their priests. Christ himself had known a little something about the collection basket—nearly two thousand years later, the widow giving from her need was still the Church's best customer.

Peg clicked through the joyful mysteries of the Rosary, praying like she did everything else: in a hurry. Even when she was giving thanks to God, she was in a rush, unable to slow down.

"And blessed is the fruit of thy womb…" she prayed, thankful for so much. She had two healthy children and a husband who was a good provider. So good, in fact, that she'd calculated that they could finally afford her dream house, not in the Manor where Dave would never move, but in the Park section of Douglaston, located only two blocks away.

From a distance, she'd envied the owners for years and imagined her own family living in the large brick house instead of the elderly couple. When she heard they were putting the house on the market, she made her pitch to Dave.

"Why do we have to move?" he asked. "A big house means more work, the last thing I need. Besides, the kids will be leaving before you know and we won't need all that extra space."

Although she might have let the idea die in the past, this was her only chance. It was too important for her to relent. "It'll be a good investment," she argued. "Besides, when you have your bosses over, you have to show them you live someplace suitable."

Dave hadn't been pleased, but gave in with a shrug. "Do what you want. You will anyway. Just don't make my life more difficult than it already is."

"Don't worry, I won't."

And she hadn't. She'd done everything on her own, dealing with lawyers, banks and movers. She made it all happen by herself. It was totally different from when they bought their first house, back when Dave was in charge of everything. This time, all Dave had to do was show up at the closing and sign some papers. She'd even written the checks herself.

Next had been hiring the contractors to replace the Depression-era kitchen and bathrooms. Living through that had been a nightmare, but she handled it all. Now came the fun part: furnishing the redone home. She recalled the end table she'd seen at Sloane's on Tuesday.

She caught herself, knowing she shouldn't be doing interior decorating while in church. *Thank you, Lord, for the many gifts you have given me.*

But the move hadn't gone totally according to plan. Now she realized that it gave Nora her chance to break with the family. Two weeks before the closing, Nora announced her move to Los Angeles, confiding to Peg that no way would she go to a new house with "him."

Dave had done nothing to try to change Nora's mind. In fact, he'd seemed happy to see her go, and relieved once she was gone. Peg had to admit that the tension level did drop once Nora left. But she wasn't sure that had been a good thing.

Instead of bouncing back to his old self, Dave seemed more withdrawn. He had no enthusiasm for the home improvement projects Peg tried to discuss with him. He just went to work, came home—at whatever time—ate dinner, then went to the den with his book and cigarettes to sit in front of the television before heading to bed. And there? Well, forget about that. She'd never been a sex maniac, but would occasionally put on a little perfume because you just never know. The sex life they had once enjoyed now was pretty much a memory.

When Peg dared voice her dissatisfaction to her mother, she replied, "You complain too much, Peggy. Life's not perfect and the man's doing the best he can." Her mother then pointed a bony finger at her. "Besides, you have a short memory. Before you married him, Father Harkness told you that none of them boys would ever be the same after the War. But all you wanted was that Dave Devlin."

Peg had nodded in agreement. It was true. Dave was not the same person when he returned from the Pacific. Oh, there'd been times when he was the fun-loving, spirited guy she fell in love with as soon as they met, before the War when they were both in high school. But it seemed he had to make such an effort to be that person that he saved it for work and occasions when others were around. Now she hardly ever saw that Dave at all.

"He hasn't taken to drink, has he?" her mother pressed. "So long as that doesn't happen, you have no real worries."

Peg finished her prayers and stuck her beads in the pocket of her purse just as an eighth grade class filed through the side door for graduation practice. Three nuns accompanying them were in control. One clapped her hands and the students genuflected in unison.

Peg stepped sideways across the pew, genuflected on the cold tile floor, and turned to see the sunlight beyond the open rear doors. She then recalled her own grade school graduation years before.

The girls had all worn white dresses and walked two by two ahead of the boys. Peg clutched the medal she'd just been awarded, looking to the left, to the right, searching for her family. She then followed her classmates outside and immediately the graduates were descended upon, their families hugging and kissing them. Peg spun around, looking in every direction, forcing a smile. She must keep smiling, even while the crowd began to disperse. Laughing, the families left for parties they had planned in celebration.

The white dress that had thrilled her so highlighted her shame. She was marked for all to see; Peg Connolly, the girl whose parents didn't bother to come to the ceremony. She ran from the steps, up the block toward Queens Boulevard, unable to hold back the tears any longer. She reached the Connolly apartment, her face smudged and blotchy, bursting into the living room of the railroad flat, her younger brother and sisters in their Sunday best cowering on the couch. Her mother sped out of the kitchen and grabbed her as she headed toward the rear bedroom.

"Where were you?" Peg sobbed, not noticing the ripped shoulder on her mother's best dress nor her disheveled hair.

"He's not well, Peggy. He's not well at all," Catherine said.

Peg broke free from her mother's grasp and flung open the bedroom door to see her father, Rory Connolly, Sr., dangling off the side of the bed, unconscious. His shirt was untucked, his belt unfastened, vomit on him and the bed.

"I tried to get him ready," Catherine had said.

Peg left the memory behind as she walked outside St. Aidan's. Her own children would never face the shame she'd felt. Not while she breathed.

*

"I think the horse needed the riding lessons more than Catherine the Great did."

The classroom full of boys broke up laughing.

"That's very funny, Mr. Devlin. Your classmates enjoy your sophomoric humor as much as you do. I hope you enjoy jug this afternoon nearly as much. It should be a lovely day to walk the courtyard with my other detainees."

The buzzer sounded. "Okay," Mr. DiNoto announced. "Class dismissed. Except for Devlin."

James tried to look unconcerned as the others filed out of the room and he was left to face the short and balding Jesuit scholastic alone.

"Okay, Mr. Devlin. Let's make this quick."

"Yes, sir," James replied without sarcasm.

"I want you to know that I see right through you. You may be able to fool all your classmates and every other teacher at Gonzaga, but not me. You got that?" Without waiting for a reply, he stuck his hands into his cassock's pockets. "Who are you, Devlin? You're like two different kids. One Devlin I like pretty well. Serious ballplayer, doesn't screw around in practice, gives 110 percent in games." Besides teaching World History, DiNoto was the junior varsity basketball coach.

He continued. "The other Devlin, though, you know, the wise ass in class, I really hate that other guy."

James shifted his weight from side to side.

"Who do you want to be, Devlin? The big clown, distracting your buddies who should be paying attention?"

James remained quiet.

"You know what? You don't want to show it, but you actually take the school-work as seriously as the basketball. It's the exams, Jimmy boy. They give you away. You always have to bear down on the exams, don't you? When it comes right down to it, you can't stand to let somebody beat you." The scholastic threw both arms wide in resignation. "I don't care, believe me. I'm out of here next month and back to the seminary for the last time. So you're not going to be breaking my chops anymore. I just think someone ought to give you the facts."

I hear you, Mr. DiNoto.

"You've got a very facile mind. It's your real gift because you're never going to make it as a ballplayer. But let me clue you in. If you squander it, you'll pay dearly."

I understand you, Mr. DiNoto.

"That's the most serious sin of all. Cheating God by throwing your talents away."

But it doesn't matter. Not at all.

James knew the scholastic was right. He would always bear down when finals came along, even to the point of studying instead of sleeping on the bus and subway. Next week the entire school would report to the gymnasium each day. The gym floor would be covered with desks. The Jesuits would assign seats so that the students taking the exam were out of copying range of each other. When it was time to begin, James's heart would start thumping. Flipping over the examination and opening a blank blue book was his secret thrill, one he would never confess to another student. He found it even more exciting than the tip-off of a basketball game. There was no element of chance at all. He'd been given a finite body of material to master. And now the teacher was going to try to best him, sneak in a trick

116

question, an obscure point. It was a challenge James was incapable of resisting.

So DiNoto had guessed right. He knew his reaction to tests. *Big deal*, James thought as he stared back at the scholastic. *You don't know everything. Not by a long shot.*

*

It was uncommonly muggy, even for late July. The perspiration was welling up inside the brim of Dave Devlin's straw fedora. He hated the hat, but it was a concession he made. His hair was disappearing and when he stood beneath the blowers on the BMT subway, he felt the rushes of air on his bare scalp pounding his head. The hat would stay on, for protection, not looks.

His damp t-shirt clutched at his armpits. Dave's discomfort was the only thing keeping his eyes open as he guided the Chrysler toward home from the lot where he'd parked in Astoria, at the end of the BMT line. He refused to pay the astronomical midtown parking fees, but Peg was convinced that taking the bus and subway was exhausting him. Driving part way had been another concession.

He foolishly believed that once he became vice president, he would finally feel like he had it made. Instead, he felt little satisfaction and soon found that his new, more important job was like painting by numbers. Where was the challenge? He could still remember, if barely, what real excitement felt like, when every breath, every thought could be your last. What exactly had been the point of surviving, if life back home was only going to bore you to death?

Maybe there was something wrong with him. By any objective standard, he should be happy. Despite all the setbacks and disappointments his own father had endured, he had always seemed reasonably content, not dissatisfied. What had Tom said on his deathbed: "Your mother was the only woman I ever wanted."

Dave pulled into the gravel driveway, noticing James sitting on the side stoop of the large colonial. How different this house was compared to their first. That one had been for the entire family. This time it was really just for Peg.

Well, there's still the boy. Dave watched his son stand up. *That job's not done yet. You don't like everything you've been seeing. He thinks you're not wise to him, but you know exactly what he's up to. Got to suck it up and keep going, for his sake not yours. You've got to keep an eye on him and give him an example, if he's going to turn out the right way.*

He climbed out of the car as James approached him.

"Hey, Pop. What took you so long?"

"Traffic, I guess. What time is it anyway?"

"Time to eat. I've got to get moving." James said, turning to head inside.

"All right," Dave said. "Let me get my briefcase." He went to the back of the car and opened the trunk. When he leaned in, the heavy hatch swung down and hit him on the back of his head; he dropped down, pressing his hands against his ears.

James raced to his father's side, helping him stand back up. "You okay?" James asked. Dave was breathing hard, his eyes watering. James hadn't seen the terrified look in his father's eyes in years, but recognized it immediately. It happened whenever Dave hit his head, his reaction so extreme that, as a child, James would mimic it whenever he banged his own head.

It took his father a few moments before he replied. "Yeah. I really hate when that happens, though." He reached in, and got his briefcase this time before letting the trunk shut and heading up the stoop.

Peg was at the stove. He went over to her and kissed her.

"You look tired," she said.

"I am." He trudged upstairs to change his clothes. When he returned, the meal was on the table with James already bolting his food. At some forgotten point in time, the Devlins' ritual of saying grace had fallen by the wayside.

Peg placed her paper napkin on her lap. She glanced at Dave and said, "I got a call from Nora today."

James drained his milk and banged the glass down. "See you later!" He jumped up and dashed out the door.

"You're the rudest thing on earth, James Devlin!" Peg yelled after him as the screen door slammed shut. She calmed herself and turned back to Dave, who was staring down at his plate, manipulating his knife and fork.

"I said I got a call from Nora today."

Dave looked up. "How's she doing?"

"Well, she's still doing a lot of typing. But I guess she's gotten to run a few errands for her hot shot agent boss and a few clients. No big names, yet. But the woman has been pretty decent to her and she feels there are some prospects for the future. If not with this outfit, she's at least gotten a start in the business and can move on somewhere else." When Dave didn't comment, but just gazed at her, she continued, "Do you have anything to say?"

Dave blinked. "She's a tough kid. She knows what she wants. I'm pretty sure she'll do okay."

"She's only nineteen," Peg snapped. "I'm not so sure."

"What's that supposed to mean?"

"It means she never really wanted to go to Los Angeles. You practically dared her to by reminding her that's what she said she'd do. Just one word from you, one sign that she was welcome to move with us to the new house, and she would've stayed. God knows there's enough room here for her. It would've been wonderful." After some hesitation, she added, "The two of you would hardly have seen each other."

Dave continued eating, refusing to be drawn into a battle over what might have been. He knew the emotion was being siphoned from his body. Love and happiness were the first to vacate. Compassion and honor followed right behind. The last to leave was anger, the sludge at the bottom of the tank. Even his anger was now in short supply. He must conserve it, make it last as long as possible.

*

James sprinted up the concrete ramp to the upper level of the playground and saw Michael Cassidy and Coney Rogers at the side of the court. He was in luck. They were still evening their teams and were a man short. He'd make the critical first game after all. Missing it meant waiting to play the warmed up victors with a team pieced together from latecomers and first game losers.

James pulled the elastic strap attached to his glasses behind his head and fit them on his nose as he approached the guys.

"Ya look like Spysmasher in those taped-up goggles," Michael said. Coney began laughing.

"I'd wear Coke bottles if they'd make me see well enough to beat your ass," James said.

The same players came night after night. Their strengths and weaknesses, favorite fakes and spots on the floor were well known to all. Crowley was certain to launch a banking jump shot against the backboard if he had an angle from either the left or right. Six Pack would only shoot from the dead corners with no angle at all. Double D faithfully looked to pick off the inbound pass after each basket his team scored. Baby Steps was the master of a running hook shot, the legality of which was open to serious question. Jasper would typically sink shots with two men hanging on him, but always blow a breakaway layup. Bagel would dispute the severity of each hack he committed. Coney would never deny he had fouled and would always volunteer to escort his victims to the emergency room for the repair work they often needed. Stymie would back his defender relentlessly toward the basket, then release the fade away jumper his opponent knew was coming but was unable to block.

James was a scrapper, using aggressive play to compensate for a shortfall in talent. His theory of the game was simple: resist totally on defense, since the opponent was usually lazy and would take the bad shot if it was all that was offered. On offense, drive the lane like mad and, with one exception, refuse to be stopped short of the basket. James kept the defenders honest by popping it in from the top of the key, a half circle he thought he owned. When your man was guessing whether you would put it up or penetrate, he was not ready to stop either.

Then there was Michael. His play was on a different level from all the others. There was something that distinguished him from his opponents. He was a natural and the guy James could never blow by on the way to the basket. James also knew

119

that Michael no longer belonged with the crowd at the park. He seemed to be holding back, reining himself in, at least until the last few buckets. He should've taken his game on the road in search of more talented players who could give him a run for his money. Yet Michael refused to abandon his friends. They were a community, no longer boys but not quite men. They were brothers, jealous and loving at the same time. Whatever the reason, Michael was unwilling to leave them.

That night, Coney and Michael paired off the sides well. The players raced up and down the undersized court, pressing each other over its entire length. The teams alternated spurts of baskets until Michael's team led, 23 to 22, when Stymie bulled through a desperate Baby Steps and banked in a layup for the victory.

"Time for you skins to take the suckers' walk", Michael yelled. The small court sloped distinctly toward one basket, and he was claiming the victors' advantage of playing downhill on offense, worth one or two baskets a game. Coney's squad shuffled off to defend the other basket.

No other players had shown up, so they began the rematch at once, postponing trips to the water fountain. If Michael's team triumphed again, they would be champs for the night. If they lost, each squad had a right to the "rubber," a third game to decide the evening's victors. Any latecomers would be spectators only, barring some injury to one of the sweat-soaked players.

The second game had none of the suspense of the first. Crowley and James were on fire from the outside, pouring in shots from their respective side and top of the key spots. Michael glided through the defense often enough to keep the score respectable, but the game was soon over with Coney's team winning 21-15.

Perspiration dripped from the boys during the five-minute break. The remaining T-shirts were removed, wrung out, then hung on the back of the park bench or through the holes in the chain link fence. The final game would be a battle. Only the ten shirtless players were left in the park as shadows grew longer. Michael's team took the suckers' walk this time, then spun to face the basket at which they'd shoot. The game began.

Elbows and asses. Wet flesh smacking its counterpart. Offense crashing the boards for each rebound. Defense boxing out coldly, leaping for the sphere, slapping it for effect as it was grasped momentarily before the outlet pass.

The two teams fought each other cruelly. Running commentary among the players ceased. They had stopped formal scoring at twenty-one, what seemed like days ago. The contest dragged on as each team struggled to win by the required two baskets. Only one boy looked fresh: Michael Cassidy, who was as cool and energetic as he'd been in the first game.

James knew his team's chances of winning were slipping away the longer the game went on. He crouched at the top of the key, pounding his dribble as Michael guarded him loosely. He felt he had to try to make something happen, but as soon as he began to drive down the lane, Michael lunged and poked the ball away. James could only turn and watch helplessly as his friend went on a break-away, his hand slapping high on the backboard as he laid the ball in.

The game was over. Victors and vanquished alike straggled to the bench and flung themselves down, winded and drenched with sweat.

"Nice game, Mike," James croaked.

"You're still jumping like one of the soul patrol," Stymie added.

"It was a goody," Michael said humbly. "Hey, where the hell was everyone else tonight? There a novena or something we didn't get invited to?"

James laughed while glancing at the approaching storm clouds. They all gathered their t-shirts, wallets, and watches and headed down the ramp. After the pushing and shoving at the water fountain, they strolled out of the playground as the first drops fell. Soon, a cloudburst engulfed them, releasing the steamy smell of overdue rain hitting hot asphalt. When they reached Northern Boulevard, the drenched crowd invaded Mary's Deli. After they all purchased a soda, Mary threw them out and they gathered on the wet stoop adjoining her cellar entrance. Soon, talk went from basketball to girls, with new leaders emerging, before they broke up and went their separate ways.

James accompanied Michael down the Boulevard. He said, "You going to that cookout tomorrow night?" Both boys were counselors at the Catholic Youth Camp.

"Nah," Michael said. "Why? You going?"

"Yeah. My old man said I could long as I get my ass home on time," James said, taking license with his father's actual words.

"Sheet. Ain't that something." Michael furrowed his brow. "Well, I better come along too. Just to keep you out of trouble, Wild Man."

James laughed, then paused before asking, "Mike, how'd you know I was taking that last one to the hoop?"

Michael chuckled. "You're going to be up all night over that one, aren't you, Devlin?"

"Probably."

"When you're going to drive, you start dribbling that ball so hard I'm always waiting for it to explode."

"Are you kidding me?"

"Does a bear shit in the woods? Is the Pope Catholic? I'm not putting you on. But don't worry about it. Maybe you can cool it now that you know. Besides," he said with a laugh, "I'm the only one who's ever noticed and I'll never tell a soul."

*

The following afternoon James shouted out the driver's window of the school bus. "What's the holdup, Mike?"

Michael bounded across the dusty parking lot, then clanged up the metallic steps. "Those assholes in Bus 19 thought they lost a couple kids. They can't even count straight."

"Well, our monsters are all present and accounted for." James tapped the attendance sheet attached to the clipboard. "But if we don't get going soon, we'll be dropping off carcasses. Look at them. They're dying."

The sweltering children, ranging in ages from four to thirteen, had sweat streaking the dirt and residue of grape "bug juice" down their faces. A low chorus of moans replaced the usual din.

"I'm pretty pitted myself," Michael said. "But here comes Vinnie to the rescue."

The large driver lumbered up the steps and bounced into his seat, setting the bus in motion. James and Michael sprawled opposite one another on the front seats, ignoring their charges while the warm breeze rushed through the open windows. Once the last camper was discharged at St. Aidan's, James worked Vinnie for a ride as far as Springfield Boulevard on his way back to the garage. Only after extracting promises to pinch certain female counselors' fannies at the cookout on his behalf did Vinnie agree.

The boys leapt out when Vinnie stopped for a red light at the corner of Springfield and Horace Harding Boulevards. They jogged across the overpass spanning the Long Island Expressway to find Hughie Mulroy waiting for them in front of a deli.

"What kept you guys?" Hughie asked.

"Jesus, Hughie," James said, "some of us have responsibilities. Like getting the little brats home in one piece."

"Oh, they've got you turds' number. I'm impressed."

"You can kill them, but you better not lose them," Michael chimed in.

Hughie was a moody guy who had already worked at the camp for a few summers. James tried to cultivate an older acquaintance or two since he had no proof and no chance for passing for legal. He asked, "Hey, Hughie, you playing in the counselors' softball game next week?"

Hughie gave James a cold stare. "Listen, it's great shootin' the shit with you, but there's some hot young things waiting for me. I would've bought your stuff already, but needed your money, including the buck for me. Let's have it."

"I've got it right here," James said. He handed over three crumpled singles.

"Okay, what'll it be?" Hughie was almost seventeen. Armed with his brother's draft card, he passed for eighteen without question.

"I don't care. A six," James said.

"A six? That's all?"

James flushed. "Make it Colt. Tall ones. And get us some pretzels, too," he yelled after Hughie who was heading into the deli.

"What in Christ's name do you think you're doing?" Michael asked. "Your father's going to kick your ass from here to Timbuktu, if you go home bombed."

"Don't sweat it," James said, leaning against the wall. "Everyone has a few brews at these cookouts."

Michael eyed him warily, but relented. "Okay, Wild Man. It's a good thing I did come along or no tellin' what you'd be up to."

Hughie rejoined them with a large brown bag. The three rushed up Springfield Boulevard to Alley Pond Park. Once they were out of sight from the road, they eased up their pace. Soon, they joined their fellow male counselors at one of a group of long picnic tables. The trio took seats on the table top, their legs dangling over the side. Hughie handed the six-pack and bag of pretzels to James, then set off in search of his female targets.

James pulled one tall can out of its plastic ring and handed it to Michael. He then ripped a second can free, tearing off its pop top lid and taking a deep swig. He'd had his first drink in the streets two years ago and craved it thereafter. The sensation of alcohol was so pleasant that it was as though his body had been playing possum, waiting for his childhood to pass, counting the days until he would discover booze. Now that he had what he wanted, he relaxed.

"Toasty-toast, Mike." He banged his can awkwardly into his friend's.

"Easy, Jimmy. I'm practicing my debonair act," Michael said. "You've corrupted me. I may be looking for a pack of smokes and a half dozen of Hughie's bimbos in a few minutes."

"It'll take more than me to corrupt Michael Cassidy." James drained his first malt liquor while music blared from a nearby portable phonograph and a group of girl counselors posed in front of the picnic table next to the barbecue pit.

James tapped into his second can and lowered himself to the bench while the sunset disguised the grimy picnic area with brilliant orange hues. Michael retreated to talk to some other counselors, short-haired guys who looked like seminarians. James leaned back and inhaled the smell of the fire that would soon be grilling dozens of hot dogs.

"You hiding from me, brown eyes?"

"No," James replied without opening his eyes, "I'm sitting here minding my own business." He then opened his eyes to see Missy Haggerty standing there. She worked on the lunch crew, delivering the Twinkies and Sno-Balls for his campers each day.

"Well, I think I'll join you," she said. "That is, if you don't mind my company, Mr. James." She plunked herself right on his lap. James was startled, but had the good sense to wrap his arms around her. Missy bent his head toward hers, then slipped him her best French kiss.

The Colt 45 had delivered its promised equine kick to his head, but James was savvy enough not to blow a sure thing. Missy had plainly put a few away herself. The Jackson Heights girl was no raving beauty, but in the fading twilight she looked slinky, and Circe herself could not have sounded better to his intoxicated ears.

She began twisting and turning on his lap, their tongues still entangled. James realized if they didn't seek solitude soon, some wise guy would start the catcalls and scare her off.

He murmured in her ear, "How about we go berry picking or something. I got a coupla cans here to go."

"Okay," she said, climbing off his lap.

James pulled a can of Colt off the ring and left it for Michael. He dangled the other two from one hand while wrapping the other around Missy. They stumbled up a rise, moving further into the woods. Daylight was deserting Alley Pond Park.

"Do you know where you're going?" Missy asked.

"Yeah. We won't go far."

They reached a path which ran through the woods before veering off into a clearing where there were more picnic tables. They drank from the open cans as they made their way to one of the tables.

"Here's a good spot," James said, his heart pounding. He was anxious to kiss Missy again but afraid she would have second thoughts if he dallied.

Missy pushed the hair from her face, took a large chug, then put the can down on the table and wrapped her arms around James's waist. "Now, where were we?"

"I think I remember," he slurred. Their lips met and they kissed so hard they ground each other's teeth while their bodies pressed against the table. James brushed his hands against her shirt, slipped his palms beneath it, and began to explore the forbidden regions to the north.

Drunk or not, Missy Haggerty had the natural gifts of a Queens Irish Catholic girl—the defensive instincts of a linebacker and the strength of a wrestler when it came to controlling a pair of wandering hands. Without interrupting their kissing, she pinned James's arms on the picnic table. Unoffended by his shameless attempt to feel her up, she continued the business at hand, dry grinding for all she was worth. But then she blurted, "God, I have to pee."

"Jesus, Missy," James groaned. "We're about a mile from a bathroom."

"No problem," she replied groggily. "I'll just go right over there. Plenty of leaves."

James laughed.

"No peeking either," she yelled over her shoulder.

"Missy," James shouted, "I've found you at last. The girl of my dreams! Please don't wipe with poison ivy and ruin it."

As he swigged some more, he heard Missy swearing. He'd never known any girl who came out of the blocks this fast. He couldn't imagine Donna Bradley drinking so much beer she had to pee in the woods. God only knew what Missy would try next.

Before she came out of the bushes, a pair of flashlights shone on him from the path. He sat still, hoping it wasn't cops.

"Where's Missy?"

He tried to focus his eyes on the two figures before him. He could tell that they were girls.

"My goddamn sandal fell off," Missy said, coming out of the underbrush. "I didn't think I'd ever find it. And who's here?"

"Missy, it's us, Dolores and Rosie. We've been looking all over for you."

Missy sidled up to James. "I been kinda busy." She began playing with his hair. "He's cute, isn't he? And you should see his friend. What's that guy's name, Jimmy? You know, the tall one? Christ, he's gorgeous."

Dolores shone her flashlight in James's face. "Not bad, Missy. Maybe he'd like to try a little smoke with us."

"You guys found grass!" Missy squealed. "Let's do it!"

The short and round Rosie hadn't said a word. She pulled a glowing joint out from behind her back and handed it to Missy, who held it in her mouth and inhaled, snorting a few extra wisps of smoke up her nostrils for good measure.

James stared at her in disbelief. Without exhaling, she thrust the rolled smoke at him, like Eve handing Adam the tempting fruit.

James shook his head. "This has done me just fine," he said, lifting his can of Colt.

Moments later, the joint was puffed into oblivion. The girls giggled at first, but then grew subdued. James took a final swig from Missy's can—nothing but warm backwash. He gagged, then suggested they head back.

The spell had been broken. The sad fact was as obvious as the mosquito bites swelling on his arms and legs. He and Missy walked back to the main picnic area on opposite sides of Dolores and Rosie. They parted at the barbecue pit without so much as a goodbye and she began cozying up to some other fellows.

James looked at the dying embers. There were no hot dogs left on the grill.

"Hey, Don Juan. You're not looking for something to eat, are you?"

He turned to see Michael. "I'm starving," he said.

"I thought you ladies' men could live on love."

James felt a mosquito bite rising dead center in his forehead. "I feel like shit warmed over. I'm hungry, bombed and an asshole in the sight of God and man. Satisfied? Or did I miss something?"

"Yeah, you missed one," Michael said. "Your lips are so swollen you look like Missy punched you. But we'll let that one slide. I tell you what, I snatched a couple of dogs in case you were looking for them when you got back." He led James over to the table where he unwrapped two hot dogs from some paper towels and placed a couple of cans of cream soda in front of him.

"Go to it," Michael said. "They won't be hot, but that's okay. And be sure to drink both sodas. It's called a flush. You'll be up pissing all night, but you won't be stewed when you get home."

James was due home by ten and it was a quarter to nine. He ate the franks and forced down the soda. Over the next half hour, the food, soda and Michael chewing his ear off began to counteract the Colt. As they left the park, James's mouth tasted like cardboard, but his legs were no longer rubbery. He walked alongside Michael and his spirits revived.

There was no bus in sight when they reached Horace Harding so they sat down on the sidewalk, stretching their legs out, their black Cons banging together nervously as the clock in the window of the store behind them clicked closer to curfew.

"You know, Mike, I don't know what it is," James said.

"What what is?"

"Why I'm always chasing girls."

"You must want to catch one," Michael said, scratching a bug bite on his arm.

"Come on, be serious."

"I am serious. You keep chasing fast ones like that girl tonight, pal, you're gonna wind up guest of honor at a shotgun ceremony."

"I know. That's what I can't figure." James belched.

"What?"

"To my mind, women are far superior. I mean, they're better. Of course, there are exceptions, like Missy and Dolores and Rosie, but in general they're much better people than men. Am I making sense?"

"Maybe."

"Listen, women have a knack for doing the right thing. It seems easy for them. They do what they're supposed to and they make it look simple. Now, men. They're a different story. There are a couple I know who seem to do the right thing all the time. You. My old man. But it's rare. Really rare."

Michael had a solemn expression. "You're still shitfaced, Jimmy. And you don't know what you're talking about. Certainly not about me. Probably not about your old man, either."

James shook his head. "The rest of us, God, we just keep getting sidetracked. Good intentions don't mean shit. I keep screwing up again and again. Like girls, I mean, I love girls. Good girls. I worship them. To me, there's nothing better on the face of this earth than pretty, really nice women." He paused, gazing across Horace Harding at the passing traffic on the LIE. "I knew one like that once, but I blew it and fouled everything up. I was too stupid to straighten it out. So what do I do now? I go after the first cheap, trampy thing that comes along. I don't see you pulling that kind of stuff, Mike."

Michael snorted. "Don't ever make the mistake of thinking I'm perfect, pal. You said it yourself, you love women. Me? I'm terrified of them. I can barely say the word woman." He looked James straight in the eye. "I'm scared of girls and a million other things, too. You've just got to learn to accept yourself the way you are. I try to, though I probably don't do it very well. I'm better at accepting myself the way everyone thinks I am, even though I don't believe that's who I really am." He crossed his arms over his knees. "You know, sometimes it seems like none of us are really calling the shots. It's like we're always on the receiving end trying to dodge whatever comes our way."

"Oh, shit." James jumped to his feet. "This is too heavy for a drunken bum like me. How's about a song instead? Let's do the Purify Brothers. It's been a while."

Michael stood up. "Sure. We're out of practice."

As the Q-17A bus pulled up to the stop, the boys were crooning "I'm Your Puppet." When the door opened, James danced knock-kneed up the steps, a bass marionette to Michael's falsetto puppeteer. Once they paid their fares, the tired-looking driver told them to get lost in the back.

Several minutes later as the bus approached his stop, James snapped the wire to ring the exit bell.

"You gonna make it okay?" Michael asked.

"Sure."

"Good luck with your old man. I'm going to stay on to Marathon."

"See you in the morning," James said as the bus came to a stop. He pushed open the rear door and clambered down the steps.

Michael yelled out the window, "And if you get caught, tell him I was hanging out with the merry men of the Nocturnal Adoration Society, not with you."

James heard Michael laughing as the bus drove away. He then mentally prepared himself for the inevitable inspection as he walked the two blocks to his home. When he went in through the side door, he heard the television coming from the front porch, just what he anticipated. As casually as possible, he went into the room and plopped down on a chair next to the TV. His mom looked to be dozing off while his dad had a book in his hands.

"How was the cookout?" Peg muttered through closed eyes. "You smell like fire."

His father put his book down and gave James the once over.

"Oh, fine," James said. "There were lots of people there."

"That's good," she muttered.

"No game tonight?" James asked his father, hoping he sounded okay. He figured staying quiet would only draw attention.

"Yanks are on the coast," Dave replied. "They'll be back this weekend. Want to go?"

James hesitated before replying, "I'm already going to the beach with the guys."

Dave slipped his glasses back on and returned to his book. "Maybe some other time."

Christ, why does he do that? James hated how his father put him on the spot, forcing him to turn down the invitation.

The phone rang from the kitchen. "Who on earth would be calling so late?" Peg asked.

"I'll get it," James said, jumping up, dashing off, and answering on the third ring.

"Jimmy, it's Uncle Rory."

James hadn't seen his uncle in quite a while and he sounded strange. "What's up?" he asked.

"It's Frankie, Jimmy. Fat Frankie," Uncle Rory sputtered. "They killed him, Jimmy, they killed him." Rory barely got the words out due to sobbing.

"What do you mean? *Who* killed him?" James's heart was doing double time.

"Over in Vietnam. Frankie got killed."

"Oh, Jesus." James could hear Frankie's laughter after dropping one of his uncle's passes. "I didn't even know he was in the service."

"He got there a few weeks ago. And now he's back." Rory sucked up some air. "The wake's tomorrow and Saturday they'll bury him."

"Oh, okay," James said, trying to absorb the information. It was like hearing Mickey Mouse was dead, killed by the Vietcong.

"Can you get here then? I could meet you around six."

James nodded. "Yeah, yeah. See you then."

He hung up the phone and made his way back to the porch. After he gave the news to his parents, Peg began to cry.

"That's tough," Dave finally said, staring off. "Frankie was a good kid. Never hurt anyone." He ground his cigarette into the ashtray. "He didn't belong there, but he took his chances like a real man. I'm proud of him."

*

The next evening, Grannie insisted that Rory and James have a bite to eat before heading to the wake. Even though his uncle never drank in front of his mother, James could tell Rory had a few before he got there.

"It's a shame, a crying shame," Grannie said, as she slapped hamburgers between two slices of white bread and served them to James and his uncle. "But it's always the young ones what gets it."

Rory took one bite and then pushed his plate away. "Come on, Mom. Don't talk about it, will ya?" He dropped his head into the palms of his hands.

After James ate a couple bites of his burger, he said, "I guess we should get going."

Rory nodded and they stood, taking the suit jackets off the backs of their chairs and slipping them on. James followed his uncle down the stairs and past the first floor flat. He knew things had never been the same after Baby Conor died. Rory ended up living upstairs with his mother while his wife and daughters remained on the first floor, a typical Irish divorce.

As they walked together toward the funeral home, James felt a sense of dread. He'd been to some before, but this one would be different. This would be someone who was his contemporary and the prospect of seeing him laid out was what scared James.

James didn't usually follow the news in print or on television, whether due to disinterest or fear, but that morning he'd swiped the *New York Times* from a neighbor's lawn to see if there'd been any mention of his friend's death.

The big news that day had been how the riots in Detroit had been quelled by the National Guard and their tanks. *Guardsmen secured the West Side area of the city from Negro snipers after raking roofs and the debris of burned-out buildings with .50-caliber machine guns.*

Frankie and his unlucky comrades had been front-page news as well:

FOE SHELLS BASE
G.I.S ARE DEAD
Vietcong Attack On Airfield Also Leaves 43 Wounded

SAIGON: South Vietnam, Thursday, July 27, 1967. Vietcong guerillas killed 11 Americans and wounded 43 in a mortar and rocket attack today on the Phuocvinh airfield, 56 miles northeast of Saigon, a United States military spokesman reported.

The spokesman said that 137 rounds of 82-mm. mortar and 122-mm. rocket fire were pumped into the airstrip.

American planes attacked the suspected Vietcong positions and United States mortars also opened fire. There was no word of any Vietcong casualties.

The spokesman said there was light damage to military equipment at the airstrip.

As James walked up the funeral parlor steps, he reflected on all he had learned with his brief inquiry that morning. Guerillas were homegrown as well as foreign. The more professional Army had someone count the number of rounds fired at its solders, while the National Guard kept no record of the number of bullets its part-timers triggered. The buildings and gear Frankie and his friends were protecting remained in pretty good shape, while their guardians had been totaled. No one could claim surprise. If tanks were dancing in the streets of Motown, a little firefight on a tarmac in Phuocvinh wouldn't be shocking.

Rory and James were directed to the proper room and signed the visitor's log. His uncle handed him a laminated holy picture crawling with angels. A soldier in full dress uniform stood off to the side, not looking much older than James himself. Frankie's parents greeted Rory, a friend of theirs from childhood, hugging and crying while James hesitantly approached the kneeler set before the box in the center of the room.

He knelt and blessed himself and noticed that the coffin was like none he'd seen before. Frankie had come home in a hermetically sealed casket. James gazed through the glass top at Frankie's face and upper torso. He looked fine. The problem was, you couldn't see the rest of him. Something had gone wrong elsewhere. So wrong that it had killed him. So wrong, you couldn't even show it to those who came to view his remains.

James found he couldn't even say a prayer as familiar as the Our Father on Frankie's behalf. The box was blocking out everything else, as if Frankie had been stuffed, mounted and sent home in a trophy case. James made a quick Sign of the Cross and fled to the rear of the parlor where he sat alone thinking about how much fun he and Lance once had playing war. This war that Frankie had gone to was no game at all.

Rory joined him and they stayed until the priest ran them through the rosary. The wake was a single night and the requiem Mass would be the next day. They left the funeral home and walked down Woodside Avenue.

Uncle Rory broke the silence. "Let's go for a beer. I figure you're old enough."

James had never been in a bar before. He struggled to adjust to the dim light as Rory waved to the bartender and led his nephew to a seat at the end of the bar.

"Give my nephew here a Rheingold draft, Nickie. I'll have the same...and a shot."

The pair drank three rounds before Rory said, "What do you think of the Mets' chances next year?"

James was the product of a mixed marriage, in terms of baseball loyalty. The Connollys had been Giants fans before the team left town. When the Mets arrived in 1962, they switched allegiance from the league-leading Giants to the lowly Mets. Uncle Rory had suffered with his adopted team ever since.

"They're only gonna get better, Unc," James said. "That Tom Seaver could be great if they got him some runs. Some of those other young guys are pretty good, too."

Rory smiled and looked up at the Mets game in progress on the elevated television behind the bar. He then swiveled his stool, facing James and said, "Something's buggin' me, Jim."

James was ready to hit the john, but now the timing wasn't right. He asked, "What's that?"

Rory's eyes filled up and he sputtered each word as if they caused him pain. "Frankie came to me the day he got his draft notice. The token was still Scotch-taped to it. He tells me he's leaving for Canada."

James leaned in, his uncle almost whispering.

"I figure he's joking, right. I say, very funny, Franco. Then I wish him good luck. But he tells me he's serious. That he ain't no Green Beret. He was going to go to Canada. He says to me, 'I'm sure as shit dead meat if they get me to 'Nam.'"

James heard the crack in his uncle's voice, and could tell he needed to get this off his chest.

"I tell him he couldn't do that to his folks. Besides, what did he know about Canada? But then I kept going on, telling him how great the service would be for him, and how it would open all kinds of doors. Christ, I must've sounded like a goddamn recruiter."

Nick placed a fresh setup in front of Rory who flipped the shot into his mouth, then chugged down the beer. He wiped his mouth with the back of his hand and continued.

"I told him how action was the greatest, most exciting and honorable thing a man could experience. I was convincing 'cause I believed it. I really did. Until this happened. But I'd sold him hook, line and sinker.

"When I looked at him in that box tonight I knew I was the one who put him there." He sniffed. "I sent him after something I thought I missed. All that glory I never had when I was a Marine. Something that I didn't have the sense to thank the Lord for sparing me. It was my stupidity that got that kid killed."

Rory waved to the bartender again, then leaned over, pulling James close to him. "Think, Jimmy, think," he said, his voice cracking. "For yourself. Not like me." Tears streamed down his face. "And don't let anyone talk you into it. Don't trust them, like Frankie trusted me. Not for nothing."

There was a sudden commotion at the door. A crowd of other mourners came flowing in. They had already hit several pubs in the procession down Woodside Avenue and were well in their cups by the time they reached the Too-ra Loo-ra Tavern.

Rory pulled out a handkerchief from his pocket and hurriedly wiped his face as his buddies approached the bar. He grinned and began talking up the Mets while James felt grateful to have the men save his uncle from despair, just when James thought it would swallow them both.

James drank glass after glass of draft, watching all the angles in the dark tavern start to turn into curves. Time seemed to bend as well. He wasn't sure if it were minutes or hours after their arrival when everyone began clamoring for Rory to sing.

James was sure his uncle was too drunk to do it, but Rory drained his beer, then gave James a wink. Nick hopped onto the bar to turn off the Mets' game and the floor was all Rory's.

The first notes out of Rory's mouth proved to James that this was an uncle he'd never known. His singing voice was smooth yet defined, like Waterford crystal. Rory's eyes were squeezed shut, as if somewhere, some time, he could see Fat Frankie laughing at him, laughing out loud as he stumbled after the football. He sang the words that turned their grief into sound that would float harmlessly to the musty ceiling of the bar, into hot water that would flow down their cheeks and be gone.

*

James decided to pass on the funeral the next day and go to the ball game at Flushing Memorial, reasoning his friends were counting on him. After all, he'd been recruited by some older Little Neck guys to catch for their CYO team. The night before, Peg had offered to drive him, giving him time to sleep in. His dad bought her a red '66 Mustang when the price had dropped due to the '67's coming out, so James figured she was using his ballgame as an excuse to show her new car off, since he normally had to take the bus.

Dawn brought a beautiful July morning, with cool air and bright sunshine, perfect for a wedding, but pitiful for a funeral. James waited for his mother, sitting on the back steps, next to the catcher's mitt and spikes he'd gotten from the garage. He could block the wildest of pitches, and hit as well as anyone on the team. Still, his throws were disappointing and kept one-hopping into second base. But since the team had no one else to catch, they were stuck with him.

"Sorry I'm late," his mother said, opening the screen door.

Soon, she was backing the Mustang down the gravel driveway while James took it upon himself to change the radio station, even though his thoughts were on the night before: the young soldier standing guard; Frankie in that box; Uncle Rory taking the blame for it all.

The Mustang stopped for a red light. James looked over at his mother, her left elbow sticking out of her opened window. He had to smile seeing her keeping time to the music on the steering wheel while still in her bathrobe and fuzzy slippers.

Scott MacKenzie was singing, advising that if anyone dare come to San Francisco, they'd better wear flowers in their hair.

The light turned green. His mother stepped on the gas and the Mustang raced off. His was obviously a very strange world, and getting stranger by the day. James had very little hope of figuring it out.

X
December 1967

THE HANGOVER ALARM RANG. No bells. No buzzer. No soft or loud music. It was simply nature's way of waking Nora up after a big night out. The shroud of sleep was abruptly lifted. Time to get up, to start hurting from what she drank and smoked the night before.

Nora swung her feet to the floor with a thud. The threadbare curtains waved at her from the open window while she groped on the night table for her cigarettes and lighter, her eyes fixed straight ahead. She barely noticed her throbbing head or sticky mouth, instead trying to recall the dream she'd had, quickly, before it vanished like it never happened.

She remembered being in a doorway, looking at a long rectangular table. From left to right sat her father, mother and brother. Directly across from them, with their backs turned toward her, again sat her parents. She couldn't see the faces of the counterparts, but was sure it was them. To their right, was a sixth, empty chair.

She was puzzled by the duplicate set of parents and surprised that James seemed to think nothing of it. Her father, the one with his back toward her, didn't turn around. The woman at his side, however, slowly swiveled in her seat and smiled at Nora. It was Peg. She beckoned her daughter with a wave to take the seat at her elbow. None of the others acknowledged her presence and she made no move to join them.

The smoke wafting before her eyes stirred Nora from the trance. She straightened the man's t-shirt she wore as a nightgown and moved across the bare floor to the window. She had no idea what the dream might signify. She let it slip from her mind.

It was Saturday, a week before Christmas. She would never forget her first warm December. She would call her mother some time tomorrow afternoon, before the rates went back up. She would endure the thousand questions her mother would ask. But she would ask none of her own. And she would not go home the following week. Regardless of how her mother begged her, no matter what she promised or threatened, she would not return.

*

James stared out the rear window of the Mustang. The bright store windows made Northern Boulevard look deceptively glamorous at night. Peg was driving. Dave was slouched in the front passenger seat. He'd just arrived on a flight from Europe and looked beat. His voice was so hoarse he could hardly whisper.

The car shot past the New York City line and into Nassau County. Gonzaga's varsity basketball team was scheduled to play at 7 P.M. Since he lived so close to the opponent's court, even Gonzaga's coach saw no point in his taking the team bus from Manhattan. Besides, Peg and Dave were probably Gonzaga's most loyal fans and they never missed a game. For some reason, that irked him. It was as though they didn't trust him out at night alone. It couldn't be to see him play, because he never played, except in the final 60 seconds of the contest. Then he was thrown into the fray, with the other junior benchwarmers, after the outcome was already decided.

James thought it was hopeless. That night would be like always, different bench but the same splinters. He'd be picking plenty of them out of his can before the game was through. Then he would ride home with his parents and attempt to explain again why he wasn't getting to play.

They arrived in the parking lot at the same time as the Gonzaga bus.

"We'll meet you in the lobby after the game, James. Good luck," Peg called after him as he scrambled out the back seat. *No luck needed*, he thought.

James tried to blend in as his teammates filed into the gym. One of the managers of St. Mary's team led them to the visiting locker room. Within minutes, they were dressed in their maroon and gold road uniforms, sitting on a bench and listening to the coach's pregame warning that they had better play smart or St. Mary's would bury them.

Soon, hands clapping, the Gonzaga squad ran out on the floor and began warm-ups. James was in the habit of rating his team's drills and thought they looked awful. The game had been left on the bus.

The captains shook hands with each other and the referees before reporting back to their respective benches. The Gonzaga squad huddled. They placed their hands on the top of the coach's and raced through their terse, self-serving prayer:

"Our Lady Queen of Victory, pray for us."

Better make it a rosary, James wanted to shout, but thought better of it, afraid he'd forfeit all his meager playing time for such an outburst. Instead, he took his seat at the end of the bench next to Toad O'Toole.

"Got a feeling tonight, Toadie. You know, if seven guys foul out, you and I are really gonna get to do our thing."

"My plan's a lot more realistic, Jim. If we scrubs can organize, we got it made.

If we agree to foul the shit out of the other guys, we can make the final minute of play last about twenty minutes. It'll be great. Even Coach'll be impressed if I can foul out in less than 60 seconds of playing time."

"I like it, Toad. You may not get back to the bus in one piece, though, if you start gettin' rough. Look around you. The place's packed and nobody's pulling for us."

James surveyed the gym once more. He'd study the two squads and begin mentally coaching for Gonzaga. He'd block everything else but the game. If by some miracle he were told to report, he would be ready.

Then he saw her.

She was sitting directly across the floor from him in the first row. He hadn't seen her since the night of the party. He couldn't believe that Donna Bradley was really there.

Suddenly, his interest in the game evaporated. He just kept staring at her. If anything, he was offended by the inconsiderate players racing up and down the court in front of him, blocking his view of Donna, incensed by the occasional shrill whistling disturbing his concentration on the girl.

Toad kept poking him to stand up at each timeout and join the team. Normally, James paced around the perimeter of the huddle, shouting encouragement and suggesting adjustments to the starting five and the coach. Now he was strictly in Never Never Land. Minutes after the halftime buzzer, he was still sitting on the end of the bench.

"What's the matter, Devlin? You high or something? Devlin? Do you hear me, Jimmy?"

James finally looked at Toad. "Oh, halftime, I guess, huh?" He glanced at the scoreboard. "Yep, down 12. That's too bad."

"Jesus, Jimmy. You're really out to lunch. Come on. Let's get down to the locker room. You know Coach's temper's doubly foul when he's losing. He'll have our asses on toast."

They trotted off the court together, James craning his neck, trying to see if Donna stayed or filed out to the lobby with the rest of the spectators.

He didn't hear a word of the heated halftime tirade. James's mind was back on the floor, praying that Donna would still be there when he returned.

It was so odd. He couldn't remember ever being this thunderstruck, not even when he first met her. He supposed it was just a strange twist of fortune, some astrological quirk destined to incapacitate him that evening. He thought he'd driven Donna Bradley from his memory years ago, after his humiliation at her party. His ties with the Manor crowd had been severed and he'd returned to his life with Michael and the other playground guys. The dissociation was so complete, James hadn't even learned where Donna went to high school. And, yet, there she'd been across the gym from him, at St. Mary's, just as she had planned.

"Now get back up there and give them a second half they won't forget!" The coach's veins rippled in his forehead.

The team burst out the locker room, up the stairs, and back on the court with James in the mix. When he and Toad settled in their seats, he felt as though he'd been punched in the stomach. The gym was alive with chanting and clapping while James looked across to where Donna had been. Then he stood and turned completely around, searching the crowd. She was nowhere in sight. A referee tossed the ball between the two opposing centers and the half began.

James hung his head between his legs. He swore fluently, cursing the coach for scheduling this lousy game and ruining his life all over again. When he finally calmed down enough to look up at the first foul call, he could scarcely believe his eyes. Donna and a girlfriend went rushing down the sidelines during a pause and sat down where they'd been before.

"All right!" James exclaimed.

"All right, what?" Toad asked. ""That's Kelly's fourth foul. Now we're really in a tub of it."

James couldn't stop looking at Donna, from the Peter Pan collar peeking out of her navy blue crew neck sweater to the Bass Weejuns. Meanwhile, the clock ticked down and Gonzaga fell further behind. Coach was never one to throw in the towel readily. Yet down 22 points with 17 seconds to play, even he had to concede the game was out of reach.

"O'Toole, Devlin, the rest of you scrubs, get in there and finish it up."

Toad elbowed James as he whipped off his warm-up jacket. "Let's roll."

James stood up. He didn't want to remove his jacket. During his sophomore year, he'd owned the only pair of bald armpits on the j.v. team. They'd been a source of embarrassment every time he suited up in his sleeveless uniform. Yet, he'd had a good season, at least for a basketball player constantly reluctant to raise his arms over his head. This year he had a few wisps of hair in the pits, but nothing worth mentioning. Certainly nothing worth exposing to Donna for a measly 17 seconds of play. But how could he decline the Coach's invitation to play? While he was going through the possibilities, Toad shook him, yanking on James's jacket.

"Okay, okay," he muttered, pulling off his jacket. He'd play the 17 most hustling seconds in the history of basketball. He would earn the right to shower with the team by getting as sweaty as possible in the minimal time allotted. And if he really ran amok, the coach wouldn't notice his arms never left his side.

When the final buzzer went off, James picked himself off the floor where he'd been grappling with a St. Mary's substitute for a loose ball. *Just in time*, he thought. A second later and he'd have had to fake a cramp during the jump ball to preserve his secret, and a cramp would've been extremely difficult to explain for someone just coming off the bench.

"You were weird as hell tonight, Jimmy," Toad said, running alongside James on the way to the locker room, their brief contribution to the losing effort complete.

James shrugged. All he could think about was Donna.

The Gonzaga players showered with little of the usual horseplay and insults, faced with a long bus ride back with a losing coach. At least James wouldn't have to be with them, pretending the St. Mary's stomping upset him more than it actually did. He put on his suit jacket and tie, something the coach insisted they all wear on game nights, combed his wet hair and gathered his gear into his gym bag. He wished the Toad a Merry Christmas and wild New Year and then walked up the stairs to find his parents. He pushed through a group of students in the lobby.

"Jimmy Devlin!" a female voice rang out. "What are you doing here?"

James felt himself blush, his mouth go dry. He turned around, surprised to find he was much taller than her. "Donna," he managed to stutter.

She gave him the same million-dollar smile he remembered, as if it were just yesterday and not three years ago.

"It's nice to see you," she said. "I forgot you went to Gonzaga. You must be on the team, huh?"

By all rights, she should've ignored him after the jerk he'd been. Yet she seemed pleased to see him. Perhaps as pleased as he was to see her.

"Maybe you could stick around," she said. "We're having the Mistletoe Mixer tonight. I'm on the dance committee, so if you'd like to stay..."

"You sure that's no problem?" He hoped she didn't already have a date.

"It's no problem. Besides, you look like you're already dressed for it."

He smiled, suddenly grateful for Coach's rule. "Just one thing. My folks are outside. I'll let them know."

She nodded. "I'll wait right here."

James dashed into the crowd finding his parents by the door, ready to leave. Breathless, he said, "I met a friend here and they're having a dance tonight. She invited me to stay."

"Absolutely not," Peg replied. "Your father's exhausted and I promised we'd get him something to eat and head right home. *Together*."

James looked from Peg to Dave, hoping his father would come to the rescue. Instead, Dave looked out of it, as if he hadn't heard a word.

"Come on, Ma. Give me a break, will ya?"

Peg shook her head. "I've got more important things to worry about and I'm not going to have you roaming around Manhasset all night."

"I'll get a ride back, no sweat. Besides, it's only three stops on the train." *And Manhasset's not exactly Harlem, Ma.*

"I'm not discussing it anymore, James. That's final."

James glared at his mother before turning on his heel. He took deep breaths as he went to find Donna. It didn't help that she was flashing her huge smile at him as he approached her.

"Got a problem, Donna," he said. "My mother's demanding I go home with her and my dad. She's being really stubborn, too."

Donna's face dimmed with the same hurt expression he recalled. She said, "I was really hoping you could stay."

"Me too. Very frustrating, believe me." He sighed. "Could I give you a call next week?"

"Sure," she said. "Promise?"

"I promise," he said. He wanted to touch her, even to just shake her hand, but instead waved goodbye as he dashed off.

As angry as he was at Peg and as much he wanted to tell her off for ruining his chances with Donna, he couldn't do it when he found her holding his father up. Dave's eyes were just slits, losing a battle to stay opened. Once again, his father had ceded control while Peg became the dictator. It was happening more and more. James seethed during the ride home and forced visit to the pizzeria; the three of them together, just as his mother insisted they be.

*

Peg, sniffling, was lying on her side of the bed, her face partially hidden by a pillow. Dave sat in his underwear on a wooden chair in the bedroom. He looked down at himself. Only 42 years old, he didn't like what he saw. He wasn't fat, but mushy. Muscles once pressing against the surface had sunken. He pulled his nylon knee-length socks off and noticed his pasty skin. He stared at his hairless legs.

"Will it kill you?" he asked bluntly.

"They don't know," Peg replied. "They can't tell until they do the biopsy."

Dave looked up, trying to fix his eyes on his wife, but couldn't. "I don't think you should wait 'til next week. Have it done right away."

"I won't ruin Christmas for the family. A week won't make a difference. Anyway, I'm pretty sure it's been there for a while."

Go ahead, then. Have it your way and be a martyr, Dave wanted to say. He was too tired to argue with her. He stood up shakily and went to the bathroom. He was too exhausted to wash his face or brush his teeth. When he returned to the bedroom, the lights were out.

He pulled down the covers and slid in. Peg rolled over and buried her face in his shoulder. "I'm so scared, Dave," she said, sobbing.

"Me too," he said, unsure of what he was feeling. There was a time when the darkness wrapped them together, hiding where one began and the other left off. When they'd whisper in the dark back then, it was as though there were only

138

one mind at work. Like a person having a conversation with his conscience. But now it was different. The darkness didn't mean communion or melding into some greater whole. They were two separate people, with separate problems, sharing only a common bed. Dave wanted to reach around her and pull her near on the desperate hope that if he squeezed her tight enough he could dissolve the barrier and be safe within her again. But he couldn't move his arms to do so, no matter how much he tried. Then sleep won out, and his eyes closed.

*

James was still in an ugly mood when he arose. He ate, showered, dressed, and left the house by nine-thirty. Around the corner, he knocked on the side door of the O'Reilly house. Stymie O'Reilly opened it. James had made plans to hang out with him, anything to stay out of the Devlin house.

"Come on in, Jamesie. Be right with you."

James walked in and looked around. As usual, the dining room table was littered with football cleats, helmets, cups, and other athletic gear belonging to Stymie and his brothers.

"I gotta drop some books off at Lisa's. She's out of town with her folks, but she's gotta do her term paper when she gets home tonight. She needs these," Stymie said, gathering some books up off the floor.

James griped to Stymie about his mother as they walked down the street. Soon, they reached Lisa's block, which seemed deserted. James figured everyone was attending Mass, something he should've been doing.

"The back door's unlocked," Stymie said. "It always is. These people are nuts. Anyone could come in. And they leave all the car keys on a hook in the kitchen. Come on in."

Stymie was right. The back door was unlocked, letting them right in. Stymie dropped the books on the table.

Rumor had it that Lisa's dad's attic was stocked to overflow with cases of booze thanks to salesmen soliciting his business, whatever that was. James reminded Stymie just by rolling his eyes upward toward the ceiling.

"You're a devil, Devlin. But I'm in. It's Christmas time," Stymie said. "It's probably busting at the seams. And here we are so close."

"So what'll it be, Stym?"

"That's the holiday spirit!"

The boys raced up the stairs to the attic and all the rumors they'd heard proved true. The floor was covered wall-to-wall with cases of liquor. They walked among the cartons like kids in a candy store, weighing their selection.

"By my count, there's more gin than anything else," Stymie said. "What's more, there's an open case of Tanqueray over in the corner. I hear that's good shit."

139

"Lisa's old man'll never miss a bottle," James reasoned.

"All we need's a little mixer and we're in business," Stymie said, pulling one of the bottles out of the box. They went back downstairs, shutting the attic door behind them.

When they got to the kitchen, James sat down at the kitchen table while Stymie rummaged for something to dilute the poison.

"They got ginger ale."

"Should be okay," James said.

"Okay, get a few cubes and I'll get the glasses."

Soon they were taking a large belt for openers. James grimaced. "It's like chewing on the trunk of a Christmas tree." He took another gulp. "But I'm getting used to it."

"It'll do for a Sunday morning." Stymie went to the pantry. "I haven't eaten breakfast yet." He found an open box of Cheerios and discovered enough milk in the refrigerator to wet the cereal. He ate greedily, stopping only for an occasional swig from his drink.

They kept drinking and laughing while James fiddled with the kitchen radio until he found an FM station blasting Stones' music. He danced to it, swigging from his glass every other step as he sang along.

"Least you seem to be in a better mood, Jimbo," Stymie said. "You might even be glad to see Ma Devlin when you get home."

"She's a swift pain in the ass," James shot back, still dancing. "I had a shot at something good last night that she turned to shit. You never get a second bite at the apple, you know."

"That depends on the apple we're talking about," Stymie said.

"You might know her," James said. "Donna Bradley?"

Like God, Stymie knew everybody. "That's some apple. You'd better make sure to get a second bite at that one!", he snorted.

Soon, the fifth was almost finished, its full impact not yet felt. James scrutinized his watch with difficulty. "Maybe there's still time to go to the last Mass."

"Mass?" Stymie countered. "Are you kidding me?"

"I like to take one sin at a time," James replied.

"Well, we could get there in plenty of time. Remember their Country Squire sitting in the driveway?"

James's eyes widened. "Come on, Stymie, we can't take their car!"

"But it's to go to church."

For some reason, it made perfect sense to James, who belched in reply.

"Let's go!" Stymie grabbed car keys off the hook and headed for the door. James followed unsteadily, pulling the door shut behind them.

They climbed into the station wagon, seeing their breath inside the car. It frosted up the windshield immediately. Stymie put the key in the ignition and the car groaned in resistance before turning over. Confidently, Stymie put on the defroster and backed out of the driveway. He swung the wagon onto the street, narrowly missing a parked car on the far side. He threw it into drive and cruised down the block. At 248th Street, the Country Squire looped a right hand turn.

"Shit!" Stymie blurted. "I gotta take a piss. I should've gone at Lisa's." When they reached the middle of the block, Stymie pulled over in front of the entrance to the playground. "Wait here," he said, jumping out and heading into the park.

Further down the street, James saw two men in raincoats walking in their direction. He slid down into the seat. Moments later, Stymie jumped back in and slammed the door. He gazed at the two men, drawing closer, his expression serious. He churned the engine, but it wouldn't catch. He pumped the gas, but the starter only growled, its noise fading every second.

The two men drew closer, keeping their eyes on the boys.

"Let's get out, play it cool," James said.

They got out and walked in front of the car. The men came up to them with the larger one, looking as big as a mountain, asking, "A little car trouble?" He peered in the windows, as though looking for something.

Stymie nodded.

"Maybe you can help us out," the large man said. "You seen any kids hanging around? We're looking for a brother and sister who ran away from home. We got some information they might be around this neighborhood."

Both Stymie and James shook their heads while eyeing the men suspiciously.

"Oh," the large one said, "I'm Detective Rafferty and this is Detective Bardalino." Bardolino craned his neck, looking toward the playground.

"Nah, we ain't seen nobody like that, right, Jimmy? We know everybody around here and there's been no one like that. Right, Jimmy?"

James could tell Stymie was too quick with the cop. Too definite. Too drunk.

"Well, we figured we'd ask." Rafferty exchanged a glance with Bardolino. "Say, maybe we could give you some help with your car."

"Oh, that's okay," Stymie said. "I probably just flooded it. We'll try again in a little while, right, Jimmy?"

"Sure," James chimed in. "Sorry we'll miss Mass, though." He thought that was a nice touch.

"Open the hood and let us take a look," Rafferty insisted.

"Okay, sure," Stymie said. He hesitated, looking at the car. "Jimmy, go on and open the hood for the detectives."

James glared at Stymie. He didn't know how to do it either.

"You boys can't open the hood?" Rafferty asked.

"No, sir."

"You got the registration?"

"No, sir."

"License?"

"No, sir."

"You know you're both in deep trouble?"

"Yes, sir," they answered in unison.

"Come with us."

James's gin-filled stomach was ready to explode. It would be a miracle if he did not barf on the cops when they placed him under arrest. He wanted to make a break for it, but flight was out of the question.

Inside the cops' unmarked car, the boys poured out the whole story. The cops listened with mild interest, then nodded to each other. The tale was so stupid, it had to be true.

"Show us where Lisa lives," Rafferty said.

Stymie directed them around the block and pointed out the house. The un-marked car pulled across the street. They sat and stared at the house and seemed to be thinking.

Maybe they're going to give us a break, James prayed. He gasped and put his hope into words. "Is there any chance of us just getting the car back there and call-ing this off?" he asked timidly.

The cops looked at the house again then at each other. Bardolino said, "Can't do that."

A tear ran down James's cheek. He was beginning to understand just how bad this would be.

"Hey," Stymie said, "do you guys know Detective Ray Costello?"

"Yeah," Bardolino muttered. "We used to work with him. Why?"

"He's my father's law partner now. He's a nice man, isn't he?"

Both officers grew pensive. Rafferty said, "Yeah, Ray's a great guy. Went to law school at nights." He was quiet for a moment before adding, "You say your old man's a lawyer? Ray's partner?"

"Yeah, that's right."

James looked at Stymie, feeling hopeful.

"Well, we're gonna give your father a call when we get to the 111th and have him come down to discuss what you schmucks been up to."

Inside the precinct, Bardalino opened the door to an empty second floor lock-up. "Go on. Both of you. In you go."

James and Stymie entered the cage and were locked in. The detective walked off, leaving them to survey their surroundings. There was an exposed crapper in the middle. It was positioned for emphasis and as Bardalino's footsteps faded, James rushed over and retched into it. Soon, Stymie joined in.

Sweaty, they crawled over to the bench in the corner, huddling next to each other. "What are they going to do to us?" James whispered.

"I don't know. I really don't know, but this is some hell of a mess."

Finally, they heard footsteps drawing near. It was Stymie's father. He walked over and leaned up against the bars. He greeted them pleasantly enough, just as he would any other client in a jam. They came over to him, clenching the bars.

"All right, you guys. I'm going to save all the lectures, all the rest of it until later. I want to know exactly what happened. And you better not hold a single thing back." His manner was professional, not a trace of emotion in his voice.

Stymie gave the details of the escapade once more. His father interrupted him at several points, seeking confirmation or clarification from James. When he was satisfied he had the complete version, he stepped back and said, "You guys are lucky. These cops are pretty reasonable. You were smart to mention Ray Costello's name, Stymie. They're good friends of his, and they're not out to screw you to the wall for pure enjoyment. I'm going to talk to them and see if I can get you out of here. We'll see what happens after that."

After Mr. O'Reilly left for several minutes, he returned with the two detectives. Rafferty did all the talking, directing himself only to Stymie.

"Listen up. We're releasing you into your father's custody. You stay in the house once he gets you there and don't move until he tells you to. Understood?"

"Y...yes, sir."

James began to panic. Stymie was getting sprung, but what did that mean for him? Finally, Rafferty barked at him, "That goes for you, too."

The wind rushed out of him. "Yes, sir," James murmured. "I won't go anyplace."

Bardolino unlocked the bullpen and flung the door back. The boys trailed Stymie's father closely, never looking to either side until they were out of the precinct and next to his car. As soon as they were all in the car, they discovered they'd lost their lawyer and gained an irate parent, reaming them out in no uncertain terms the entire ride, citing example after example of lives ruined by a juvenile record. When they arrived at Stymie's house, he told them to get out of the car. "Go up to your room and stay there until I come back, the two of you. Don't use the phone and don't tell anyone what happened. Don't answer questions from anyone until I tell you. Is that clear?"

The boys nodded and entered the house, doing exactly what he instructed.

*

The Giants game was in the fourth quarter when the doorbell rang. Dave's attention was fixed on the screen. Peg put down her *House and Garden* magazine and got up. She couldn't stop thinking about the tumor growing inside her, regretting how she had ignored it so long, pretending instead that everything was normal and that her home improvement projects were still very important to her. She undid the lock, opening the door to see three men standing on her front steps.

"Mrs. Devlin?" one asked.

She nodded.

"I'm Mr. O'Reilly, Stymie's father."

"Yes? What's wrong?"

"Well, these gentlemen are police officers. It seems the boys are in some trouble."

"Oh, my God! Dave, Dave!" she cried out, tears streaming down her face.

Dave leapt out of the chair, a surge of adrenalin pulsing through his veins. He rushed to Peg's side. "What's wrong?"

"It's the boys," she said. "Are they okay?"

"They're fine," one of the men replied. "Just got themselves into some trouble."

"Why don't you come in?" Dave said to the men. "I'm Dave Devlin." He took their coats and handed them to Peg. He watched as she struggled to hang them up in the hall closet. When she turned, he caught her eye, pointed toward the kitchen, then turned back to the men, saying, "Why don't we sit in the dining room? We can talk there."

Mr. O'Reilly led the procession into the room and showed the cops to chairs. He was clearly in command of the situation. He said, "Well, I'm sorry to meet you under these circumstances, Dave, but let me fill you in on what's happened. Our boys managed to get themselves loaded up at the Ceychelles's house this morning. Then decided to take their car for a joy ride. Said they were going to Mass."

Peg stood in the kitchen doorway, listening, but then ran upstairs sobbing. Dave looked impassively at Mr. O'Reilly. "Don't pay attention to her. They hurt anyone?"

"No, thank God. The officers here caught them by chance. The car stalled in front of the playground. They took them down to the precinct and locked them up."

Dave gazed at the men, unsure what to say.

Mr. O'Reilly took charge and said, "Gentlemen, why don't you excuse Mr. Devlin and myself for a moment." He stood, motioning to Dave. "We'll be right back." He led Dave out to the porch, out of earshot of the officers.

"It's not as grim as it looks," Mr. O'Reilly said. "These guys used to work with my partner when he was on the force and they want to give the kids a break."

"But?"

"But it's Christmas, you know, and they've both got big families, so they say."

"How much?"

"Five," O'Reilly replied.

"Apiece?"

"Apiece. You pay one, I'll pay the other."

Dave hesitated, then said, "Okay. They sold themselves cheap. I would've gone a thousand easy to keep my kid's slate clean."

"Me too." Stymie's father grinned. "Be glad we're not dealing with vice cops. They always know exactly what the going rate is." He paused. "Okay, we'll go back in and get the thing settled. Just leave the spiel to me."

Dave trailed Mr. O'Reilly back into the dining room. The lawyer outlined a plan: the boys would formally apologize to the Ceychelleses. Bardolino would stop by the Devlins on Monday for a "report" on the apology and punishment imposed, while Rafferty did the same at the O'Reilly house.

The detectives rose from their seats. "That should dispose of the matter satisfactorily."

Peg suddenly materialized with their coats. The men slipped them on and shook hands at the door.

"I'll give you a call once I get through to the Ceychelleses. I'll schedule a time when we can go up there later tonight, okay?" Mr. O'Reilly asked Dave.

"That'll be fine. I'll talk to you later."

"Do you want me to send Jimmy home?"

"If it's all the same to you, why don't you keep him until we go to the Ceychelleses'?"

Mr. O'Reilly raised an eyebrow, but then said, "No problem. We'll meet you there later."

After letting O'Reilly out, Dave returned to the Giants game and lit a cigarette, not paying attention to Peg's curious expression.

*

The meeting that night at the Ceychelles's house broke up quickly after the boys apologized and were told by Mr. Ceychelles that he was glad the cops caught them "cause I would've never known you stole from me".

Mr. O'Reilly offered Dave and James a ride as they left, but Dave said, "We'll walk."

"Okay, goodnight then. If you have any problem with Bardalino tomorrow night, let me know."

"Thanks," Dave replied softly. "I'm sure it'll go smoothly." He didn't want the boys to get wise to the payoff.

He walked next to his son down the sidewalk. The night was clear, but a hazy ring circled the full moon, signaling that snow was coming.

James wanted his father to get on with it, to lower the boom, but all he said was, "Did you know the Giants came back and won that game?"

"No," James said.

They fell silent again. Finally, at the corner before their house, Dave stopped, lit up a cigarette and blew the smoke up over his head. He then said, "Let's take care of the simple stuff first. It's three days before Christmas. You will stay in until February. No argument, no exceptions. And by *in* I mean incommunicado. You go to school, but when you get home consider yourself in jail, like you should've been. No phones, no letters, no nothing. Got it?"

"Yes, sir."

"And for the record, I think that's letting you off light. Now, for the important matters. I want to know why this happened."

"I don't know why," James said.

"I don't accept that. You know and you're going to spit it out right now."

James looked at his father. He was as big as the man now, actually bigger. Still, he wasn't nearly his match. A fury burned in his father's eyes. He looked as though he were challenging him, egging him on to defiance.

"I don't know," James said. "I don't know why I do anything anymore. I feel like I'm going crazy. One minute I'm fine, the next I'm outta control. I don't think about what I'm about to do. I just do it."

Dave studied him. It was freezing, yet his son's face looked feverish. "That's what I figured," he said. "I remember being like that."

James scowled, baffled by his father's response.

"You're at a stage when there's only high and low, no in between. Your emotions, your body, everything's in turmoil. It's natural. But it'll pass. Things level off, your reactions ease up. Believe me, there'll come a time when everything in every day feels the same, so that you hardly notice you're alive at all." A flash of memory came to Dave, one of his own father speaking to him with concern. He pushed it out of his mind.

"But don't think you're fooling anyone until then. At least not me. You can't con a con man. I've been watching you for some time now. I know what you've been up to. I know about the booze. I don't say much, but I take it all in."

James started to cry. "Aren't you ashamed?"

"Ashamed? No. Surprised? No. Disappointed? Sure. I wish you wouldn't drink. I thought you were gonna be some kind of athlete. That might've been nice. But you won't be. Frankly, I don't think you can help it. I've always suspected it. You're a Connolly through and through. And you're bound to be a drinker, just like your uncle and his father before him. It'll probably go on forever. Your lucky legacy.

"But you're my son, too. And I expect you to deal with the booze, whatever it takes. As far as I'm concerned, it'll never be an excuse. If you fail, if you're weak like them, it's strictly your own fault. Understand?"

James wiped his nose with his hand and shook his head. He couldn't remember the last time they'd spoken like this and he welcomed it, as much as the words hurt him.

"You're tired of being treated like a boy, right?" Dave asked. ""Well, if you want me to respect you, you're gonna have to earn it. I'm tired of watching you coast. You do fine in school, but you could do better. You want to be a man? Start acting like one. You decide what you want, then go after it. Run for the roses, pal, just like a goddamn racehorse who doesn't even know why he's doing it. Winning isn't everything, but trying your hardest sure is." Dave wiped away a tear. "Try to understand. In my own peculiar way, I do love you." He paused. "Funny, my father could never say that to me."

James shifted his weight. "I'm sure he wanted to say it."

"Yeah," Dave replied, looking away. "I'm sure he did." He sucked up some air. "Here's the deal: you do what I'm telling you and I'll treat you like a man. Don't worry. Put out as much as you can, but I won't settle for less because that's not why your life was spared all those years ago."

His father stared at him. "It's not a game, Jim. You're not allowed to make a single mistake once it's important. You should know that by now. You've got to make sure you're prepared to play for keeps when your time comes." He paused, tossing the butt of his cigarette on the ground, before adding, "There's just one last thing. Seems to me there was a matter of getting even with your mother in a way. I know you were angry with her."

"That dance meant a lot to me. But it didn't matter to her at all. She just wanted to do what she wanted to do."

"Well, you're going to feel like a real bastard when you hear the whole story." He lit up another cigarette. "The Irish are great talkers. About everything except what counts." He dragged on the smoke, flicked off the ash. "We can talk for hours and end up saying nothing. My old man and I were the worst. One day I'm leaving the house for a football game, suited up with a cup, jock, the works. And he looks real serious. So, in front of my mother and sisters he tells me he needs to speak with me before I leave and takes me into the kitchen, tells me to sit down. He sits across from me, but can't look at me. Beet red, he asks if I know what an athletic supporter is. And you know what? I was so embarrassed, I said no. I'm sitting there wearing one and denying I know what it is. So he stands up and says, 'Oh, I just wanted to know.' That's it. End of conversation so off I go."

James wasn't sure what any of this had to do with him or his mother, but he kept quiet.

"At any rate, what I wanted to say was that your mother has something wrong with her."

James' mouth dropped open.

"She's got some sort of growth, Jimmy. A tumor. They're going to operate next week."

"Is it cancer?"

"Won't know till they get at it." Dave snapped the butt into the gutter. "It's pretty cold. Let's go in." He took a step toward the house, then grabbed James by the coat sleeve. "We'll let it pass this time, but don't you ever mistreat her again, understand? Whatever happens, she's mine. More than you'll ever realize. You remember that."

James nodded, filing the warning away, following his father up the block and into the house.

Peg was in the kitchen, the smell of pot roast filling the room. There it was, already on the carving board. Before James could say a word, Peg screamed. "Look at the sight of you! You're still drunk! You and that idiot friend of yours. Two bums, thieves. I'm so ashamed!"

"Ma, I'm sorry," James said. "I didn't know." He started to approach her, but she turned her back to him.

"Don't you come near me! I'm not interested in any apology or sympathy 'cause you couldn't care less." She sputtered, tears streaming down her face. "I won't ever get over this."

Once she finished putting dinner on the table, Dave suggested that they eat. The meal proceeded in silence.

Later that night, James stared out the window of his dark attic room. His mind was reeling, trying to digest everything that had happened in the last twenty-four hours. His father's harsh words kept ringing in his ears. Other images rotated through his mind. First, Donna Bradley, smiling at him in the gym foyer. That was how all this began. Next, he was in the precinct lockup.

What a dreamer he'd been. A drunk. A car thief. He would never call Donna now, even when he finally would be free to do so. At least she'd learn not to listen to lying dirt like him anymore. Turned out Sean O'Donnell and Jackie Standish had been right about him all along.

Then his thoughts went to his father. The man was a mystery. Whenever Dave let him in on his thoughts, James wound up more confused than ever. Nobody else would tell their kid the truth the way he did. Once he got started, his father just let it fly. He compared him to Mr. O'Reilly. Stymie's dad cajoled and maneuvered all the people involved until they saw things his way. He'd hadn't just manipulated them but convinced them he was right. An impressive talent, one he'd never witnessed before. O'Reilly could be persuasive. His charm was real, yet superficial, incapable of moving those on whom it worked in any profound way.

In contrast, Dave Devlin held sway over his son alone. Yet the power he held remained absolute. James had forgotten and mistakenly thought things had changed. His father had reminded him they hadn't: "That's not why your life was spared." When it came right down to it, if his father told him to run through a brick wall, he would still give it a go. Just like the trusting child he'd been. Dave could still make him do what he wanted. Just by saying the word; so great was the debt and James's desire to earn the love of which he was unworthy. He would prove himself yet to the man to whom he owed his life, in more ways than one.

Then he had one final thought, the old question raised once more by his father's reminder. Why *was* his life spared? He still had no idea.

*

Malignant. Benign. Two twenty-five cent vocabulary words understood most anywhere in America. Just like heads or tails, everyone knows what you're talking about.

Peg ignored the nausea that crept in to replace the fleeing anesthesia and repeated the one word that had been spoken by her doctor. "Benign...benign...benign..."

The pain was immeasurable, the fullness gone. So was everything else. She felt incomplete, dismembered. It didn't matter, though. She would have life, a different life, but she rejoiced at her rebirth. She attempted to focus on Dave, but his image remained blurry. She then extended her hand to him, closed her eyes, and imparted a wordless prayer of thanksgiving to the One who'd spared her.

*

"Nora, it's Dad. You're a tough one to get hold of."

"I was out," she said, her tone annoyed. "What's the matter?"

"It was benign," he said.

"What was?" Nora said.

"The tumor. I gather Mom told you what's been going on."

"No! She didn't tell me anything about a tumor. And we talk quite often."

"It's okay. She'll be fine, but they had to do a hysterectomy."

Nora gasped.

"The doctors said that would be a possibility. It will take some time to recover, but I'm sure she'll be back to herself again soon."

"I don't understand why she didn't tell me this," Nora said, suddenly feeling guilty about never asking her mother about her life, when she fended off questions about her own.

"Can I talk to her?"

"Well, she's still in recovery, but I'll call you with her room number when I know what it is."

"Thanks," she said.

"Okay, then, I'll let her know I spoke to you."

Nora said thanks again and then heard the click of the phone. She dropped

149

down on her bed, reached for her cigarettes and lighter from the nightstand, and started to cry. That's when she remembered the crazy dream, the one with the two sets of parents facing each other at the table. She still hadn't figured that one out either. Maybe she'd ask her mother what she thought it meant once she was feeling better.

XI
June 1968

JAMES LOOKED UP AT THE CLOCK on the gym wall. Ten minutes left. No timeouts allowed. He wouldn't need any. There was just enough time to read through his bluebook and clean up any stray omissions or illegible words. After reviewing his answers to the English exam, he closed the book and leaned back just as Father Thomas called, "Time." The proctors collected the papers. James' last exam of the school year was through. It was hard to believe.

Following "the trouble," James tried to reform. He'd had little success with his drinking once Dave let him back out on the street. He had, however, managed to bear down on his studies. During his month's confinement, there was nothing else to do. Success on his exams had become a habit.

"Go, you are dismissed," Father Thomas said. "Those who passed, enjoy God's peace this summer. Those who did not..." He grinned evilly. "...I'll see you next week."

A cheer burst from the lungs of the Gonzaga students as they rose from their desks. They grabbed their blazers from the backs of their chairs and filed out of the steamy gymnasium.

"Hey, Jimmy boy." Toad nudged James as they clattered down the stairs to the basement locker room. "How'd you do?"

"Okey doke, Toadie. All through now. That's all that matters."

"I'll be here next week for tutoring in Trig, but that should be it. I really got my doors blown off on that one."

"You can never tell."

"I can," Toadie replied. "But never mind that. You coming to the party this afternoon?"

"What party?"

"The Ladycliff girls are having a party. I ran into Susie Ruth Simmons this morning. She was trawling around for some Gonzaga guys to come. I figure by the time she's finished spreading the word, the entire junior and senior classes will be there. One huge blast for the road. You interested?"

"I dunno. I'm booked for a little cutting up back home tonight."

"So? Get a jump on it. You been hitting the books too hard anyway."

"When's it start?"

"The ladies expect us in a half hour or so."

"I got my lunch."

"Me too. Let's eat first. I'm starved. We'll pick up some hooch on our way there. I got the address. It's on 69th, off Third."

After they ate and emptied the debris from their lockers into their gym bags, they headed downtown. When they reached 69th, Toad spotted a tiny liquor store a few doors in from Third.

"So, what'll it be, Jim? I feel like Cold Duck. Classy, huh? I'm celebrating since I only flunked one this time. How about you?"

"How about Four Roses? I never tried it before. Everybody in Little Neck's always drinking it." He searched through his pocket and made a quick calculation. "I probably have enough for a pint. Never know when you might want to buy a girl a drink, eh?"

"I like your style, Jimmy."

James grinned. "So, who's going in?"

"You gotta be kidding." Toad smirked. "You look like a kid. Give me the money, will ya?"

"Go to it," James said, handing him the money while Toad handed him his gym bag, and said, "I'll be right out."

James watched Toad cross the street and enter the liquor store then come out a few minutes later, triumphantly. "The nervy son of a gun," James muttered. He walked down the opposite side of the street and then regrouped at the corner, out of the shop owner's view.

"Here you go." Toad thrust the paper bag at his friend.

"You're a real pro, Toadie. Separate bags, even!"

"Hey, look! There's Susie Ruth and a couple of her girlfriends. Come on." He yanked James along. "Oh, yoohoo, girls!"

"Cut it out, will ya, Toad. You sound like an absolute quiff."

Unswayed, Toad tiptoed across the street. James shook his head, but followed.

"All right, Baby Ruth. Introduce us to these fine-looking friends of yours. I'm Toad O'Toole. This is my recently studious but still fun-loving friend, Jimmy Devlin."

"You've got to forgive the Toad, girls," James blurted. "He's totally crazed. Can't seem to handle leaving Gonzaga for the summer."

"Parting is such sweet sorrow," Toad crooned. "Now come on, Susie Ruth, who are your friends?"

"That's better, John O'Toole," the skinny girl crabbed. "You can skip that Baby Ruth stuff altogether."

"Many pardons, fair lady." Toad bowed deeply. "Now, pretty please, who are they?"

"This is Regina Morrison," she said, pointing to a short, freckly, dark-haired girl. "And this is Maureen Cullen."

James gazed at the blond-haired girl who said, "We better be going up, Ruthie. They're waiting for us."

"You guys better wait a few minutes before you come up." Susie motioned toward the building. "Cecilia doesn't want any big crowds in the elevator."

"Okay," Toad said. "But how about carrying our packages up so the doorman doesn't hassle us?"

"All right." Susie took the tall bag from Toad and stuffed it in her shoulder bag.

Maureen looked at James then lowered her sack of books from her shoulder and opened the drawstring.

"Thanks," James said, slipping his bag in.

"We need some more ciggies before we go," Regina chirped. "Let me run to the deli."

Maureen let out an impatient sigh, taking her knapsack off her shoulder and dropping it to the sidewalk. A muffled yet unmistakable sound of glass shattering was heard. Maureen gasped.

"Uh oh," Toad groaned.

"Jesus!" James yelled, as the girl's bag became wet. He grabbed the sack and put it on the curb, pulling the dripping paper bag out and throwing it into the gutter.

"I'm so sorry," Maureen cried.

"Don't worry about it. Look at your bag. It reeks of booze. You can't take your books home in that." He pulled her books out, piling them on the sidewalk.

The girls and Toad were laughing, but James didn't notice. He was too busy checking Maureen out.

"Let me buy you something else to drink," she said.

"No, you don't have to bother," James said, even though he didn't have the money to replace the whiskey himself.

"No, really. I insist," Maureen said. "I have to go back to the deli anyhow for a bag for my books." Her jaw was set, enough to convince James not to argue. "Do you drink beer?"

He nodded. "I love beer."

"Fine. Come on, Regina. I'll go with you."

The others lingered for a few minutes making small talk until Regina and Maureen returned. "Is Miller okay?" Maureen asked James.

"It's my favorite."

"Okay, I bought you the tall cans. I'll give them to you upstairs."

"Fine," he said, wishing she'd smile. "Thanks again."

"See you in a bit," Toad yelled as the three girls walked around the corner to Cecelia's building. He turned to James. "This place is going to be packed with foxes, I'm telling you. Those girls were just a sample. Wait 'til you see."

"That Maureen Cullen looked pretty good to me already. Where's she been hiding?"

"I don't know. Where do all these rich bitches from Ladycliff hide? I sure as hell never see them on the subway. Must get chauffeured to school. Maybe she's an heiress."

James laughed. "Not likely."

They decided it was time to go up and turned the corner, walking into the plush lobby of the building, typical East Side. Half-naked statue. Little old ladies at the mailboxes with their foo-foo dogs. Pudgy doorman, overdressed for June in a maroon uniform of cap and woolen coat and trousers with gold stripes down the sides.

Toad affected his best prep school manners. "My friend and I are expected at the Emerson residence. Which apartment might that be?"

"You and every other punk kid in Manhattan," the doorman sneered. "17-H."

When the door to Apartment 17-H flung open, James stared into the packed living room. It looked like Gonzaga Prep was holding a student body assembly with a few token Ladycliff girls acting as ushers. There was a huge picture window designed to exploit an unobstructed western exposure. The bright afternoon sun struggled to cut through the clouds of smoke draping the living room.

"Ugh, more juniors!" Thunder Thighs Manzarone shouted. Some beefy Ladycliff girl was cuddled on his lap. "Throw Toad and the other weasel out."

"Up yours, anus face," Toad yelled back. "Save your bad breath. You're gonna need it to hoist that load on your lap."

The room dissolved into laughter while Thunder Thighs' fleshy face burned. Just then the stereo blared with Janis Joplin demanding another piece of her heart be taken.

Toad pulled James toward the kitchen where they found Susie and her friends huddled in the corner.

"Baby Ruth, where's my stuff?"

She pointed under the kitchen table. "Help yourself, dippy."

Maureen then reached down and pulled up the six-pack, handing it to James. "They're probably warm, but I didn't dare put them in the fridge with all these friends of yours rampaging around."

"Thanks," James said, taking the cans from her. "They'd have been gone in a heartbeat. You girls want any?" Regina and Maureen looked at each other. "We'll split one," Regina said.

"You can each have your own. You bought them."

"Okay," Regina answered after conferring with Maureen again.

James tore off two cans and handed one to each of the girls.

"If you think I'm sharing any of this precious Cold Duck, Baby Ruth, you're nuts," Toad announced. "I'm getting blitzed all by my lonesome." He popped the cork, shooting it against the ceiling and spilling wine on the floor before racing out of the kitchen.

"What a slob," Susie muttered, following him outside into the hallway.

Regina and Maureen scrambled to wipe up the cheap wine while James attempted small talk, but conversing with them was like pulling teeth. He was unable to elicit more than a monosyllabic answer to any question he managed to dream up. Regina seemed covertly flirty, yet if she had anything to say, she kept it to herself. Maureen was a real doll, James thought as he studied her face, but she was keeping her distance. When a wave of Gonzaga boys piled into the kitchen and crowded around the girls, James realized he was wasting his time, picked up his beer and headed into the living room.

Toad was in the center, inciting a junior-senior riot, just like the ones they staged regularly in the Gonzaga gym. "All right, Thunder Thighs, we juniors are calling you and your pussy classmates out."

"About time you showed some hair," Manzarone yelled back. "What'll it be? Arm wrestling? Chug-a-lugging?"

"Hell, no, you buffoon. We're in a Ladycliff girl's home. Show some respect. I say we have a talent contest. Audience participation. You guys do your performance, we do ours, and the Ladycliff girls decide. All very genteel. Agreed?"

"Agreed, asshole," Thunder Thighs answered.

"Age before beauty," Toad said. "You guys go first."

The seniors huddled at one side of the room while the juniors drank and made time with the girls on the other. James sat on the couch laughing as he watched Toad rush across the room, insulting and antagonizing the seniors. Just then Charity Guisti walked into the room. When she spotted James, she walked over and sat down in the empty space next to him.

"Got a beer for me?" she asked.

James tried not to seem surprised and handed a can over to her. He knew her vaguely from the Gonzaga/Ladycliff school play. She'd been the leading lady and he played a bit role to keep his English teacher, the director, off his back. "Busty" Guisti's old man was probably the biggest leather importer in New York City and Charity wasn't accustomed to slumming with boys from Queens.

While Charity sipped and launched into a monologue of summers here, skiing there, lunch with Daddy, James sucked another can of beer dry. Maureen Cullen came back to mind and James wondered if Toad was wrong and maybe she did ride the subway to school instead of being chauffeured.

Thunder Thighs bellowed until he had some semblance of silence in the living room; the seniors were ready to perform. He had his classmates lined up like a ragtag boys' choir. At his signal, they launched into their class theme song. It was Thunder Thighs' original composition, sung to the tune of "Deck the Halls with Boughs of Holly," entitled "Bendover Prep." It was a touching anthem glorifying the stance taken by a miscreant when Father Phillips, the "Holy Screwdriver," disciplined him with his lacquered wooden paddle.

Toad led the chorus of boos from the junior class. "Same old shit..." they chanted loudly.

James had seen this all too many times before. It was getting ugly. He sunk back into the couch and Charity resumed her chattering.

Just then, he saw Maureen hugging a paper bag full of what appeared to be empty beer cans to her chest, pushing her way through the crowd toward the door. James jumped up and ran over to her, tapping her on the shoulder as she tried to fight her way past two Gonzaga boys blocking her path. "Can I help you with that?"

She stared in surprise. "I guess so." She handed the soupy bag to him. "Be careful, it's leaking."

"Sure is. Grab the door."

The boys cleared out of the way and Maureen led James out of the apartment and down the hallway.

"This way," she said. "The chute's over here." She swung a narrow door open and pulled the hinged chute down. James slipped the bag inside and stuffed it down the shaft.

On impulse, James covered her hand that was on the knob with his own and reached for her other. Maureen didn't resist. He stepped up to her and kissed her gently. After a moment, he pulled his head back.

"I really liked talking to you before," he said. "I didn't think we'd get the chance to talk again. I've been drowning in a sea of bull...." He corrected himself. "... baloney." It felt like her pale blue eyes were piercing him. "Anyhow, I'm glad I met you."

"Susie Ruth told me to stay away from you. She said you're wild and know every girl in Bayside."

"That so? I'll have to thank her for giving me such a fine endorsement." He grinned. "But you didn't listen to her?"

"No. I think for myself."

"So what do you think?"

"I think Susie Ruth is deciding whether she'd chase you herself."

They laughed out loud and then Maureen said, "I think we better get back. My family will wonder what happened to me after school. They know we got out early."

"Wow, it is late," James said. "But it's our turn to perform. Stay for it. The Toad always puts on a great show. And he's in rare form today."

"Jimmy, where you been?" Toad roared when James and Maureen walked back into the apartment. "You're holding up the show. Oh, excuse me, Mr. Devlin and Miss Cullen. What a darling couple you make!"

"Come on, Toad. The talent show."

"Right you are, Jimbo." Toad took a strong belt from some new bottle, having graduated from Cold Duck.

"Ladies and gentlemen," Toad slurred loudly, "I feel I owe you a huge apology. After all their scheming, all the graduating class of Gonzaga Prep could come up with was that worn out, hackneyed song that wasn't funny in the first place, except to someone sharing their severely limited mentality." He took another swig, then continued. "As far as audience participation went, they struck out completely. So I will singlehandedly render a spontaneous, extemporaneous, unrehearsed ad lib performance evoking such strenuous audience participation it will once and for all show up the seniors for the total dips they are."

The seniors hissed as he took a deep breath, a low bow, then began as the din in the room died down.

Toad sang in a mellow voice, asking the crowd what they would do if he had gone off-key. The juniors all cheered loudly, then shouted the chorus back at him.

He was on fire, spinning around the room, his shirt hanging out of his trousers, exhorting each reveler to sing, even the seniors in spite of themselves. Soon after he quizzed whether they would walk out on him, the crowd roared again to confirm they got by with a little help from their friends. Toad conducted them through the whole Beatles song at an ear-shattering decibel level. Drenched with sweat at the conclusion, he accepted the tumult of cheers triumphantly.

"Blow it out your ear, Fatso!" he yelled, walking over to Thunder Thighs who shoved him. Toad reeled backward, smashing into a portrait and knocking it off the wall.

The phone rang and one of the Ladycliff girls answered. Seconds later, she dropped it into the receiver and shouted, "It was the doorman. Cecilia's mother's coming. All you guys, get out of here!"

There was a mad rush toward the door. James fought against the crush, sliding across the room until he reached his fallen friend. He lifted Toad to his feet, threw his arm around him and fled. When he got to the elevator a crowd was repeatedly pounding the elevator call button until the doors finally opened. Fortunately, Cecilia's mother wasn't on it or she would've been trampled by the boys who'd just trashed her apartment. James shoved Toad in and then squashed himself in. After several attempts, the doors finally closed and the car descended, the overload alarm ringing loudly.

The Toad spotted Thunder Thighs at the rear of the elevator. "I'm gonna get you, you pudgy bastard!" He tried to push his way to the back while the Ladycliff girls screamed hysterically. Just then, the elevator reached the ground floor with a bounce. The doors sprang open and the crowd spilled into the lobby, the Gonzaga students sprinting toward the door, hands covering blazer emblems, hoping to thwart identification.

James managed to drag Toad up the block, searching for a coffee shop. They wouldn't be able to manage the subway in Toad's condition. God only knew what stunt he'd pull next.

"My bag!" Toad sputtered. "My gym bag. I left it up there. We gotta go back."

"We're not going back," James said. "I got your bag." He held it up as proof. James had barely managed to grab their bags as they dashed out the door. Leaving them behind would've been fatal. Father Phillips, Gonzaga's prefect of discipline and runner-up to Father Brown as the best detective in the Roman Catholic Church, would surely commence his investigation at the scene of the crime in less than an hour. It was less likely that he and Toad would be fingered on eyewitness accounts alone.

They walked as far as Lexington before they found a coffee shop. James pulled Toad through the door and shoved him into an empty booth.

"Just two coffees," James told the waitress.

"She's not bad, Jimmy. Not bad at all," Toad whispered as he made goo-goo eyes at the middle aged waitress. "Bet ya she's really experienced."

"Shut up or you're gonna experience a shot in the head."

After the waitress brought them their coffees and left, James noticed Toad's glum expression. He said, "What's the matter with you?"

"Had a bad week."

"The trig exam?"

Toad shook his head. "My parents split up this week." He seemed on the verge of tears.

James gulped. "Gee, I'm sorry."

"I guess I've known it's been coming. Still, it kinda hits you when it actually happens."

"Maybe it's just a bad fight," James said.

"Doubt it," Toady said, taking a big slurp of his coffee. "He's been fooling around. I hate the prick's guts." He slammed his cup back on the table. "Do ya know what it's like to lose all your respect for your father?"

James thought for a moment. "No, Toad. I can't even imagine that. There's nobody in the world I respect more than my father."

"Really? Why?"

James shrugged. "I don't know. Maybe it's knowing his history. Where he came from. What he did. How he feels. How he talks to me." It was frustrating to put it into words and James didn't want to have to explain to his drunken friend how his father saved his life when he was little. "Shit, Toad, I don't know why. Because he's my father and I'm so goddamn conceited. If I'm so special, and he's my father, he's got to be special. *Ipso facto*, as Father Cruet would say."

The Toad laughed. "I like that one, Jim." He twirled his spoon, some dexterity returning. "You're lucky you feel that way. I wish I still did."

James finished his coffee. "Think you can make it now?"

"Yeah, I'll be all right. Let's get going." Toad wobbled to his feet while James threw some money on the table.

*

Falling asleep on the Q-12 following an afternoon drunk was a major mistake. As the bus pulled into his stop, James was jostled awake in the unforgiving molded plastic seats. He grabbed for his gym bag, then wobbled from the last row's corner seat toward the rear exit door. The foul taste in his mouth defied description. He felt as though he might puke on the shoes of the riders lining the aisle. However, he made it down the well of the bus and out the door to the curb without a scene. He waited for the stoplight on Northern Boulevard to change then crossed at the green, stopping at Koch's candy store for mints before dragging himself up Douglaston Parkway and finally through the side door of the Devlin house.

His eyes had to adjust to the afternoon light in the kitchen. He noticed the basement door was open and heard the washing machine going. If he were in luck, Peg would be down there, too busy to come up.

"Hey, Ma, I'm home!" he yelled down the staircase.

He heard Peg's slippers scuffing across the concrete floor. She appeared at the foot of the stairs, her shoulders stooped. "How'd you make out on the exam?"

"Okay, I guess." He paused. "I'm really beat. Think I'll go up and sack out before dinner."

"Okay. But exams are all behind you now."

"Right," he said, surprised at her kind tone after months of hostility. He pivoted and climbed the stairs to his attic room, pulled off his shirt, pants, shoes and socks, then collapsed on his bed. About an hour later he was roused by Peg's persistent yelling to get up for dinner.

"Okay, okay, I'm up," he mumbled, his legs moving more like stilts than limbs as he hobbled to the bathroom. A steaming shower did the trick and he felt ready to rejoin the living.

Peg had prepared his Friday "going out" meal of two fishcakes with coleslaw on the side. For some strange reason, she seemed obliging when he was meeting the boys on Friday night. Fortunately, his dad wasn't home yet and James would be able to dodge his mother's less searching questions about the evening's plans without much difficulty.

Peg said, "Uncle Rory will be expecting you first thing Monday morning."

"Are you really going to make me go downtown all summer?" he asked.

"Absolutely. I haven't forgiven you yet. Besides, he says he can pay you three dollars an hour. You can just turn that paycheck over to me for what you cost us..." She paused, realizing what she was about to reveal, then concluded with "... all year long."

James shook his head. He had misread her completely. "The trouble" would never be behind him in his mother's mind.

"And you should find some time to spend with your father. Go to a ball game, like you used to. When he's not working on the weekends, he's just moping around the house."

"Why don't *you* go with him to the ball game? It's not my job to make him happy. If that's even possible." James regretted the words as soon as they left his mouth. "I'm sorry, Ma. I didn't mean that. It's just I'm not a little kid anymore."

Peg sat silently with a look on her face she always got when things didn't go her way.

James got up and kissed her on top of her head. "I gotta go." The screen door slammed behind him as he left.

*

By seven o'clock, James sat on the steps leading to the Howard Johnson's parking lot on Northern Boulevard. Within minutes, the guys began gathering in full force. They had good reason to howl tonight. Michael Cassidy had landed a full athletic scholarship to Dunhill University. A grand scale celebration was in order.

The park regulars were all in attendance, joined by many of Michael's high school friends. Finally, the guest of honor strolled down the Boulevard. Instead of a round of applause, he was greeted by a stirring chorus of abuse, causing him to laugh heartily.

James was bursting with pride for Michael. Stymie seized the opportunity to sum up James' feelings: "Way to go, Mike. Now someday I'll be able to point you out on TV and say, you see how good he is? I taught him everything he knows. He was always a jerk, but could take a tremendous hack with the best of them."

Laughter broke out and they all dragged Mike to Mary's Delicatessen to buy beer, chips and pretzels. Old Mary's charm never flagged. Her young customers had sufficient cash and she wouldn't dream of offending them by demanding to see a draft card.

Like the others, James had a large brown paper bag tucked under his arm, and followed the least conspicuous route to the park. Even though the tall wrought iron spiked gate had been locked for the night, with just two strategic hops, to a railing and then the wall, the guys managed to trespass to the other side without losing their six-packs. Once inside, they scrambled up the ramp to the upper level, passed the basketball courts, and settled on the wall adjoining the grassy junior high school property.

The six-packs were drained can after can. As the sun set beyond the blacktop softball field, the noise level increased. The songs became bawdier. The trips to the latrine area ever more frequent and, as James walked back to the wall after relieving himself, Michael jumped out of a gaggle of the Reilly High guys and flung his arm around his friend's shoulders.

"Hey, guys, this is Jimmy Devlin, the Gonzaga Flash. Maddest dog in this park and the brightest son of a bitch you'll ever meet. We also suspect he and Stymie have a secret organized crime affiliation." James frowned at the mention of the aborted joyride, a matter he'd rather forget. Michael added, "I think he's avoiding me tonight or something."

James leaned into Michael, swaying from the five beers he'd consumed. "I'm not hiding from you, Mr. Popularity. Just waiting 'til your swarm of admirers thins out a bit."

Michael squeezed James' shoulder affectionately. "No problem, Jimmy."

James laughed. "Seriously, Mike. Congratulations. I think it's great. Best move Dunhill ever made. Just remember us with tickets when you get to the Final Four."

"If I'm ever there, you're there, too." His tone somber, Michael added, "I hope going to Dunhill's the best move I ever made. It's awful far away and I'm just not sure..."

James scoffed. "What're you talking about? Anyone who's ever had sneakers on would give his arm to play for Dunhill."

Michael bit his lip. "I'm not worried about the game. It's the books. Did you notice Dunhill didn't commit to the scholarship until my last semester's grades were in?"

"Let's get rolling, you guys!" Stymie interrupted. "Those chippies down the Jug won't be able to last much longer without old Stymie."

Soon the group milled on the corner of Little Neck Parkway at the end of a long line of heavily perfumed teenage girls waiting to get their phony baptismal certificates checked and pay the admission charge to the Jug End.

James laughed and joked while on line with Michael, Stymie and the others, his afternoon hangover completely gone while the latest six-pack made him euphoric. The conversations became difficult for him to follow and he didn't bother trying.

He was eager to reach the dancing crowd, the disorientation of the flashing strobe lights inside.

A shiny new MG sports car raced across Northern Boulevard and screeched to a halt alongside them at the curb, startling James. He spun around.

"Well, hello there, Mr. Cassidy, Stymie," the driver yelled over music blaring from his radio. Oddly, it was Herb Alpert crooning "This Guy's In Love With You", not something like "Sunshine of Your Love."

James couldn't make out the driver's face in the darkness, but he recognized the voice: Sean O'Donnell.

"Hey there, Seanie kid. That's some set of wheels DaDa bought you," Michael said.

"Not bad, huh? A little reward for being accepted to the college of his fourth choice after I came up short on the extracurriculars. Not all of us are athletic celebrities like you," Sean sneered. "But you'll probably have your own sports car soon, plus a little laundry money to boot."

"Those are the breaks. Like the old song says, some cats got it, some cats ain't. And you, Seanie, never had it." Michael grinned as he finished his insult.

James glared at Sean, his all-time favorite person, arriving just in time to spoil the night. The stuck up jerk was back to his old tricks, talking past him as though he weren't there. The car was a beauty but what caught his eye was the dark-haired girl hunched toward Sean in the bucket seat.

"I'm having a graduation party tonight. Why don't you and Stymie and the boys stop by? My girl here is having her friends over and we could use extra guys, even scuzzballs like you."

"I got a big crowd of my buddies here and I'll probably be up the Jug all night keeping an eye on them. But we'll see what happens."

"Suit yourself," Sean said, pulling away.

The girl turned, her eyes meeting James's for just a moment. It was Donna Bradley, wearing a look of disappointment. James was sure she'd expected more from him than hanging out drunk on a street corner. He grimaced when he watched her turn toward Sean as the MG sped off.

James spun on his heel and followed the crowd past the bouncers and into the Jug. Armed with the drink ticket for his two dollar admission charge, he pushed his way to the bar through the patrons who'd been served and were waiting for the band to begin. His face felt ablaze.

James squeezed in next to a short, paunchy fellow wearing a gray t-shirt, blue jeans, and a St. Dunstan's College windbreaker. The guy grabbed James' wrist.

"Jimmy Devlin!" he yelled. "How the hell are you?"

James could scarcely believe his eyes. Many pounds heavier, it was Jackie Standish. "Oh, shit," he said. "What is this, old home week? I just saw your buddy outside, Sean the Prick. I must be on a wicked hot streak."

"Come on, Jimmy. What're you talking about? That night when you were at Donna Bradley's party? That's ancient history. It was only Sean's stupid idea of a joke."

"Maybe it was your stupid idea of a joke, but O'Donnell was all business. He's still trying to put me down. He just ignored me outside like I was invisible. And now he's driving around with Donna Bradley in his hot shit new sports car, calling her 'his girl.' Thought I'd barf on his Brooks Brothers shirt!"

Jackie laughed. "Boy, he really gets to you, doesn't he? Just like he wants to."

"What do you mean?"

"Sean takes delight in breaking your balls. I couldn't figure out why at first."

The bartender arrived and James held out his ticket, but Jackie pulled it away, handing it back to James. He said, "Two Pabsts, I'm buying."

The bartender popped the caps and passed the bottles to the boys.

"There you go, Jimmy. A peace offering, okay?" Jackie looked at him, grinning. "Come on, we got along fine when we were teammates."

James nodded. "I never really thought you were the mastermind of that scene at Donna's. Besides, you said you couldn't figure out why Sean liked busting my balls *at first.*"

Jackie took a strong pull on his beer, swallowed, then said, "I think it had something to do with you and Mike Cassidy."

"Yeah?"

"Sean's always been jealous of Mike. He was just so goddam superior to Sean, so well liked, Sean couldn't handle it. At the same time, he wanted Mike to like him better than anyone else, to be his best buddy.

"Now you and I both know that Mike likes everyone. He would've been happy to be friendly if Sean would've acted halfway decent to everyone else. But he didn't so Mike pretty much ignored him. Seems the more Mike ignored him, the worse Sean got."

Jackie took a break to guzzle from his bottle again, then said, "Then you came on the scene and Sean sees how the two of you play basketball, hang out, all that stuff. How's he supposed to swallow that? You make him feel cheap just by being alive. To make it worse, he finds out you're heavy duty on the books, plus you're Donna Bradley's boyfriend. Sean was always crazy about her. When he found out she invited you to her party and not him, he couldn't let that one slide. That's why he had to fix you."

"That whole story's hard to believe." The words sounded boozy crawling out of James's mouth. "Sean's such a chooch. I almost feel sorry for him, but I'd still like to tap him out."

"So why don't you?" Jackie said. "I'm gonna have a couple of more pops here then head over to his party. My old man bought me a '68 canary GTO. Wild, huh? Why don't you come along for the ride with me? Be worth the price of admission just to see his face when you strut through his front door. Then if he gives you any shit, bang, zoom, you deck him at his own party. Score settled."

"No thanks, Jackie. Not with Donna there. I've made an ass out of myself enough times as far as she's concerned." He pointed toward the rear of the bar. "This gin mill's filled with girls from Flushing and Bayside who are more my speed. That's the one thing Sean's right about. I'm not in the same league as Donna." He pushed away from the bar. "Thanks for the beer, Jackie. Very informative talk. No hard feelings anymore, okay?" He stretched out his hand.

Jackie took it, saying, "Sure, Jimmy. No hard feelings. And if you change your mind, catch me before I leave."

"Tempting, but I won't. Have a good time." James headed for the dance floor just as Jason Garfield was tuning up.

*

James's head was pounding when he came to the following morning, his face covered with drool. He squinted to look at the time. Seven-thirty. He'd have to move if he wanted a ride to the beach. He quickly dressed, then tiptoed downstairs, going into the kitchen. He made an attempt at eating breakfast, afraid to press his luck beyond a few spoonfuls of cereal, before walking out the door.

Mary's Delicatessen was the departure point for Jay Cataldo's outasight '62 Dodge Dart, dubbed the Jones Beach Express. James sat on the stoop, waiting, until he noticed a commotion across Marathon Parkway. He got to his feet and crossed the street to get a look, noticing a crowd of children around a car dumped in the auto collision shop's lot. The kids scattered when they saw him approaching.

The car was yellow, its front twisted up and to the right; no driver's side remained. James peered in the open window. Fragments of glass were scattered throughout the interior. Dried blood was everywhere. James's stomach churned as he forced himself to look into the rear seat at the windbreaker he guessed would be there. St. Dunst...lettering was all he saw. It lay next to a brand new pair of high black Cons. The sneakers were in the box, still unlaced.

He gagged, then started to run, but a pair of hands grabbed him.

"Take it easy, Jimmy."

"Mike!" James stammered. "Did you see this?" His whole body trembled as he waved at Jackie's car.

"Yeah, I stopped by HoJo's on the way home last night and heard all about it. Word is that Jackie was racing around Shore Road to Sean's party. Never came out of the curve by Big Rock. Went right into a tree. Dead by the time anyone got there."

James tried to absorb the information. *Jackie was dead?*

"Did you know he was up the Jug last night?"

James shook his head. "I had a beer with him," he said, certain he was going to throw up.

"Let's go back and wait for Jay," Michael said. "I think Double D's going to drive, too. This way we don't overload Jay's old heap."

"Good idea. Guess everyone's going to be pretty gun-shy about cars for a while."

"At least until next Friday," Michael said sarcastically.

James whispered a prayer for Jackie as they crossed back over the street. Then he thanked God for sparing him again. For whatever reason, He'd kept him out of that car.

*

Michael had been right. By the second weekend following Jackie Standish's crash, it had been all but forgotten. The hordes of uncomfortably attired teens at the funeral parlor seemed a distant memory. James stretched out on Jones Beach, waiting for that evening's next blast. By Monday morning, his red face felt shrunken, as though the sun had fused it onto his bones. He was exhausted, but donned shirt, tie, and sports jacket before daybreak and headed for the bus stop, dreading the commute to Uncle Rory's downtown office, for which he had no one to thank but himself.

He tried to squeeze in some shuteye before the bus's last stop in Flushing where he transferred to the subway, dozing again until the train reached Times Square. He then had to deal with the crowds and heat on the downtown platform and push himself into the packed car, sweat streaming down his sunburned back.

Working with his uncle had been Peg's brilliant idea. She'd dreamed up the punishment for the infamous Ceychelles incident. No more easy life as a camp counselor during the summer. James would make "real money" with a "real job" as Rory's flunky in the accounting department at Batchelder & Company. His mother said she was through financing his dissolute lifestyle. James was expected to pay room and board with the money he earned. Peg believed that if James paid his own way, he'd appreciate what he had. The psychology was lost on him. If his mother said pay, he'd ask how much and give her the entire amount, if she'd just swear off calling him a criminal every couple of days.

But working with his uncle hadn't really been all that bad so far. James was taught how to handle an adding machine and introduced to every man and woman in the office as his uncle's nephew. Rory had even taken him out to a nice restaurant to celebrate his first payday, which proved to be a mixed blessing.

The food was delicious, but James noticed his uncle's mood swing as Rory's first drink led to a second, then a third. He went from talkative to silent to melancholy.

Then to the last stop on his emotional elevator: sentimental. By the time they walked back to the office late Friday, his uncle was attempting to sing some Sinatra tune without knowing many of the words.

That following Monday, James arrived early. The company's quarterly figures had to be completed by noon for pickup by a messenger from the parent company. Rory was to finish them over the weekend and have them typed first thing on Monday. James was then expected to proofread and add the columns of figures a final time before they were reproduced and collated. However, by nine-thirty, Rory still hadn't arrived, and the draft statements were nowhere to be found.

The company comptroller arrived promptly at ten and saw the subordinates' expressions. He approached James's desk.

"Do you have any idea where your Uncle Rory is?"

James tried to catch his breath and willed himself not to cry. "I don't know."

"Find out." Mr. Rifton turned and walked toward the executive offices, calling back, "Come into my office when you have some word."

The silence in the accounting bullpen was conspicuous. James didn't want to pick up the phone, already sure he knew what had happened. His coworkers charitably walked away while he dialed. Moments later Grannie Connolly answered.

"Grannie, it's James. Is Uncle Rory there?"

"Yes, but you won't be wantin' to talk to him."

"I got to talk to him. He was supposed to be here hours ago. Put him on, will ya?"

"I'll try, but he'll be no use to you. None whatsoever."

The phone made a clump. James heard the shuffling of feet then his uncle yelling. A short time later, his uncle muttered into the receiver. "Whatta ya want?"

"What are you doing?" James whispered hoarsely.

"What am I doing?" Rory slurred. "I'm taking a goddamn day off, that's what I'm doing. "bout time, too."

"But, Mr. Rifton is looking for the quarterly figures. Remember? They're supposed to go out this morning."

"I don't give a shit," Rory roared. "I'm owed a lot of vacation time and I'm taking the day off. You can tell Rifton that for me, kid."

James was stunned and didn't know what to say. Grannie was right; he was only wasting his time. "Okay, just come in when you can."

James placed the receiver back in the cradle. He hesitated a second before rising from his chair. He straightened his tie and looked for Mr. Rifton's office. After he was ushered in, he said, "I'm afraid he's not going to make it in, Mr. Rifton."

The man sitting behind the desk didn't look the slightest bit surprised.

"He, ah, he thought he had a vacation day, but said he'd have the figures for you right away."

Rifton removed his glasses and studied the boy. "Okay, why don't you go back and work on the payables?"

Face burning, James nodded and dashed out of the plush carpeted office. At noon, the messenger came but left empty handed. Then the other accounting workers cleared out for lunch. James remained behind. He was reliving the morning's events in his mind when the aroma of cigar smoke drifted in his direction. He looked up to see Charlie Hight from purchasing swing around the partition.

"How you doing, Jimmy?" He smiled between puffs on the Tiparillo. "Hey, that's a real shame about the quarterly figures."

James bit down hard, hoping the creep would go away.

"A real shame," Hight said. "But it's not the first time, you know. Not by any means." He blew the putrid smoke toward James. "It's tough luck for you to end up in the middle of it. Nice kid like you. Too bad your uncle's such a drunken bum. But then, I suppose you Irish are all accustomed to it."

James wanted to scream at him, *Fuck you, asshole*, but instead he grabbed his jacket off the back of his chair and mumbled that he was going to lunch.

"Sure, Jimmy. Maybe you can meet your uncle over at McAnn's for a few. I can spot a future lush like you a mile away."

James hurried out of the building and kept walking. He didn't know what to do. Going back seemed out of the question, but he had to go back, even if it were to quit. But he knew his mother would shoot him if he quit, and probably send him back anyhow. But if he did go back, he might strangle that prick Hight. And he might never be able to speak to his uncle again, assuming Rory ever sobered up and came back to the office.

James stopped for a red light and stood there even after it changed. He paused at the corner, looking for a destination, thinking perhaps Hight was right and a liquid lunch might be the ticket. Just then, a girl with a red sash strung across her chest caught his eye as she tried to hand out fliers to passersby. He found it pitiful the way she had to chase the people avoiding her. Then he realized that the girl was Maureen Cullen, the Ladycliff girl.

"I'll take a dozen," he said, coming up from behind her.

She whirled around. "Oh, it's...you."

"James," he said, reminding her of his name. "Not much luck, huh?"

"I'm having a bad day," she said, waving the stack of fliers in her hand.

"Mine isn't going much better," he said.

"Why?" she said.

"Long story."

"I've got time. I'm due for a break now."

He shrugged. "Let's walk over to Trinity Church. It's pretty quiet there."

While they walked, James filled her in on his morning.

"Why didn't your uncle show up?" Maureen asked.

"Because he drinks. Too much. Not all the time, but when he gets going, well... I never saw him miss work before."

They reached the wrought iron fence on the Trinity property. Maureen said, "In my family, it's my grandfather. We had to send him to the rehab place again last week."

James nodded, grateful she understood. "I just don't know how I'm going to go back to work."

"Remember, no matter how bad your job is, it's better than nothing. And I bet you can put up with any job for the summer." She pulled the canvas sack up higher on her shoulder.

"I guess you're right. I'm from Gonzaga. After that, anything looks good, right?"

They laughed, then Maureen said, "Well, I better get back." She motioned to the sack filled with fliers.

"Me, too," James said. "It was nice talking to you."

They headed their separate ways, and James called out, "Like the song says, see you in September."

James walked back into the office with his head held high, ready for Charlie Hight or anyone else who would try to shame him. He did whatever work he could find until five o'clock then left with the throng, racing for the subway, ready to return to the refuge of the playground at night.

XII
February 1969

P EG FLICKED OFF THE KITCHEN RADIO when the announcer gave the time: Seven thirty. Even with the snow, Dave would arrive any minute. He couldn't stand a moment of the chatter of the evening talk show when he got home.

She wiped the steamy window with a dish towel and peered out at the driveway. The high piles of snow seemed incandescent. In truth, they merely reflected the light of the full moon overhead. The driveway she'd had James shovel earlier formed a black stripe marring the hushed landscape.

She recalled the newspaper article she'd read. It was like an epidemic this winter: Middle-aged executives, men just like her Dave, keeling over like bowling pins, felled by "The Big One" after a snow shoveling session. It wouldn't happen to her husband, she promised herself. *When James goes off to college next year*, she thought, *I'll shovel the driveway myself, if I have to.*

While she kept an eye on dinner, she thought of how Dave's temperament had changed so much over the years. The laughs, even smiles, were spaced much further apart than when the children were young. Maybe it was the blues. Maybe incipient old age. Maybe he didn't find her attractive anymore. Peg preferred to believe that he was just overworked, convinced it was the job.

Always the job. That unseen, intangible competitor that she couldn't destroy without slitting her own throat in the process. The remnants of their social life and conversations all revolved around it. The job drained her husband's physical and emotional energy, like a slut that sent him home to Peg only when it had taken his best. Even then, this cheat was never satisfied, holding his mind preoccupied, somber, solitary.

Peg heard the car turn into the driveway and pull into the open garage. Moments later, Dave came through the side door, stamping the snow off his galoshes.

"Hi ya, Peg. What's doing?"

His chipper fashion caught Peg off guard. She stood on tiptoes to kiss him.

"You're awfully cheery, even for a Friday night."

"I suppose so. I've got big news. Let me get out of my suit and I'll be right down."

He hurried upstairs and Peg set out the dinner. Dave only spoke when he was ready and liked to keep his audience in suspense. He wouldn't be rushed. Moments later, he returned, shirt sleeves rolled up, khaki pants and slippers on. He sat at the table across from a large plate of Kraft's cheese dinner, topped with tuna fish. He'd eaten the dish practically every Friday night for the last twenty years. Even he couldn't explain the meal's attraction.

"So, are you ready?" Dave asked.

Peg braced herself as she sat down. Her stomach squirmed, yet she couldn't deny that he seemed truly excited. She hadn't seen him like this, broad grin and all, for a very long time.

"These trips out of the country the last few years did it. They finally put me in charge of the international division."

Peg smiled uneasily. "Did they offer you the job or say you had to take it?"

"Well," Dave said, scooping up some macaroni and cheese and dropping it onto his plate, "what's the difference? They offered it and I'm taking it. It's a great opportunity. To tell you the truth, we've been kicking tail so badly in the domestic division, it's been getting pretty boring. Our sales would keep climbing if we sat on our hands.

"The international division, though, that's a different story. We've been getting creamed. And now it's my job to roll out some new advertising campaigns and save it. It's a tremendous challenge, selling the company's products to foreigners, instead of people like us."

Peggy tried to hide her dubious expression, but he must've noticed it.

"And more money, too," he added quickly. "It'll be good for us. We'll get to travel together. See the world, now that the kids are grown."

Peg nodded and said, "It sounds nice." She stood up. "I'll put the water on for your coffee."

Dave watched Peg go over to the stove to turn on the tea kettle for his instant coffee. *Money,* he thought. *So what?* He'd been pushing for a crack at this spot for months. The money hadn't been the incentive. It was the save he was after. Ever since he got the promotion, he couldn't shake a vision. As silly, as childish as it was, he enjoyed replaying it again and again in his mind's eye.

He was Allie Reynolds hopping the bullpen gate at the stadium. Blue jacket draped over his warmed-up right shoulder. He strode across the outfield toward the mound as the overhead lights flashed on to chase the dusk. One run lead. First and third. No one out. He whipped the jacket off like a matador and flung it at the batboy. He took the ball from Casey as the huge World Series crowd chanted,

"Chief...Chief..."

Even better, he would get to take on the Japs and the Germans, the old foes. He'd always felt cheated by the way the war had ended. The First Marines had been poised for the final, destined step—the invasion of Japan itself. Then suddenly, it was over. They dropped those bombs. The Japs just called it quits. It was like having the guy who sucker punched you "give" before you had a chance to wipe him out. He and his buddies had been unfairly deprived of their chance to teach the Japs a lesson for starting it all. Now Dave would finally be able to go a few more rounds.

His coffee was placed in front of him, pulling him from his thoughts.

"I always wanted to travel with you," Peg said. "Why don't you go inside now and put the television on while I clean up?"

*

The bowling machine at the Imperial Sportsmen's Grill was on the verge of a breakdown. Its lights flashed, digits flipped, and bells rang. Yet, it was unable to keep pace as Coney Rogers threw strike after strike up its sawdusted alley.

"Come on, Coney," James urged. "Let's go back to the table. The Sportsmen are reliving their annual hunting trip. You know, get drunk and shoot Bambi."

Coney nodded and picked up his mug, following James to the rear of the bar to a booth against the wall. James filled their mugs from the pitcher that was in the middle of their grimy table. He and Coney had been starting their Fridays at the Imperial since September, when Michael, Stymie and the others had left town for college. Usually the pair was alone. Coney was about the same height as James, but powerfully built like the linebacker he'd been at Bayside High until graduating the June before.

"I must admit," Coney said, breaking his customary silence, "I kind of miss those faggots. It's not like it used to be when everyone was together."

James had to agree. He missed them, too. Most were so far away that they never got back for a weekend. In fact, he never heard from them anymore. Like Mike. He didn't even know what he was up to now. He decided to spill it.

"I wonder how Mike's making out," James said to Coney. "I keep following Dunhill's varsity box scores and they could sure use him in the lineup, but they have that stupid freshmen eligibility rule so he's a leper until next year."

Coney nodded. "No word at all. Like he vanished when he went back to school after Christmas. Next year's going to be worse, when you blow town, too."

"Come on, Coney," James said, trying to ward off a sentimental moment. "It won't be bad. You know I'm going to fix you up with some hot little number before I leave, someone who likes the strong but silent type." James smiled at his friend.

His conversations with Coney were unlike those he had with any other guy, including his father. With everyone else, there was the mandatory ritual: sports foreplay. Two guys typically had to discuss the team they both loved—or argue about whose team was better, if they rooted for different ones—before they could address the real subject at hand. Not Coney. He was as macho as God ever made any man. But he was so sure who he was, he had no need to prove it to anyone else, so he said exactly what was on his mind without wasting any words on preliminaries, even if the topic were serious.

Coney chuckled, then drained his mug of beer and poured himself another. "So what have you been up to? Still chasing that city chick you been telling me about?"

"Afraid not." James chugged his beer, then added, "It seems like I've blown it with Maureen Cullen in my typical thick-headed fashion."

"How'd you manage that?"

"Worked hard at it, I tell you. You see, this girl is really cute, right? But she's quiet, so you can't tell what she's thinking. And I guess that got to me. I mean, I had a good time with her. We went out a couple of times to dances. Everything went okay. Took her home. A little kissyface and all that. But something wasn't clicking. I just couldn't get a line on her at all. Do you know what I mean?"

"Not really," Coney said.

"Well, it doesn't matter anymore. This one night, right before Christmas, we were at a Gonzaga dance. And things were going really well. I felt like I was finally getting to know her, getting a little relaxed with her. And it seemed to be like that for her, too. Anyhow, we're sitting on this bench, shooting the breeze about one thing or another, when this goddamn huge fan falls out of the window and hits me right on the head before crashing to the floor. Holy Christ, one minute I'm sitting there making time, the next I'm covered with soot trying to think straight."

Coney poured himself another beer, all the while listening.

"Some of the priests rushed over, see if I needed the last rites or something. But it looks like I'm going to live for a while. Still, we decide it was time to go home. After I walk Maureen to her door she asks if I'd like to go to her Christmas prom the next week.

"Now I think I've been hit by the fan again. I never even heard about this prom. So what do I say? I tell her I didn't think so because I was broke after Christmas shopping and all that."

Coney rolled his eyes.

"Well, it was like I just threatened to murder her whole family judging by the look I got from her, but all she says is that she's sorry before she runs into her apartment. I left, but the next morning, I started thinking a little clearer. I realized I was an idiot and started to figure out different ways to beg, borrow and steal enough dough to bring her. I then call her and apologize and tell her that I changed my mind, but guess what? She's already asked someone else! Man, she didn't waste any time at all replacing me."

Coney couldn't help but laugh, his face bright red. "If you had any brains, Devlin, you'd be dangerous!"

"That's the truth. What's the matter with me?"

Coney poured the balance of the pitcher into their mugs. "Well," he said, you're going to have to eat some crow and start from scratch again." He took a large gulp of beer. "Sounds like a project to me. She worth it?"

"Definitely. I just doubt I'll be able to pull it off."

"Well, there's nothing you can do about it tonight. Why don't we head up to the Jug and check out the local talent?"

James nodded, then finished his beer.

"And why don't you take it easy tonight? I don't want you getting so blasted that I have to go searching for you again."

"I'll keep that in mind," James said, already craving the progressive dulling of his senses he would experience as the night wore on. The loss of awareness was strangely welcome. He had no idea where the ingrained attraction came from. When he drank, it made him feel together, like alcohol was a jock strap for the mind.

He thought about it as he slipped on his jacket and followed Coney out the door. If his buddy felt obliged to give him the heads up about his drinking, he'd better pay attention.

They reached the entrance of the Jug End and stamped the slush from their shoes before going inside and greeting the bouncers. James had to adjust his eyes to the darkness, but led the way to the rear to the bar.

*

May is the month of Our Mother, the blessed and beautiful Queen.

The hymn he'd heard the grammar school children singing that morning still rang in James's ears. He couldn't explain why. It was probably because the day had matched the song so well. It had been a perfect day in May. Spring had so overwhelmed the usually tasteless Manhattan air that he half expected flowers and grass to burst through the cement sidewalks of Park Avenue. It wouldn't have even seemed so farfetched to see the Blessed Mother's own face, smiling gently down upon the young children paying her homage in their asphalt playground.

As he walked toward the subway, his thoughts made a dramatic shift. From Mary the Mother of God to Angie, the red-headed wench from Bayside with the huge station wagon. He couldn't put last Friday's parking episode out of his mind.

He'd been loaded again and the older girl wound up telling him that he drank too much and didn't respect her. After giving him a kiss on the lips, she dumped him, but with some advice: "Find yourself someone, Jimmy. Someone you'll be proud of. Someone you'll change for. That's what you need."

He reached the 86th Street subway entrance and found the two tokens he needed to get home in the bottom of his pocket. The turnstile clattered as he pushed his way through, a stack of textbooks and notepads wrapped under his arm.

Find someone you'll change for...

James hurried down the staircase to the landing separating the local from the express track and waited there.

It's not as easy as she made it sound, though. Reforming seemed beyond him. He couldn't make some personal savior materialize with a wave of his hand. It was not impossible, but you would have to be a total jackass to think you could make it happen by yourself, by just wishing it were so. Did he really want to be different? Or was that idea just a reminder of the little boy he'd once been? Just some relic of the boy who made Mass on nine first Fridays in a row so he'd have a priest at his side when he died. The kid who did extra penance to chalk up indulgences and knock a few hundred days or years off his sentence in Purgatory. Had that person ever been real? Was he still alive within him somewhere? Or was that child just a fantastic creation of his true self, someone who was actually sick of everything surrounding him, and most of all, sick of himself?

Self-pity is best kept a solitary, unobserved activity. James broke his fixed gaze at the sound of footsteps on the stairs. When he looked up, Maureen Cullen was on the third step to the landing. James suppressed a smile, watching as she hesitated. Too late to retreat upstairs to the local track. She was already committed to the express, and continued down the steps to the platform as he followed. He'd be sure to tell the Toad: Maureen actually did take the subway.

They were forced to exchange hellos, then stood looking at each other, the moment awkward.

Jesus, she's pretty. James didn't believe in coincidence. It was just as easy to believe that everything happened for a purpose. Like Maureen's presence. He was being given another chance with her, his to seize or ignore, and knew he'd lose her once and for all if he didn't make some headway before the train arrived. He sucked up some air and spoke.

"So, how's that guy who took you to your prom?"

Maureen stared at him like she couldn't believe he had the nerve to ask the question. She was probably so stunned, she answered truthfully.

"I don't see him very often. He's got a steady girlfriend down at Mary Magdalene High."

"Oh, one of those guys," he said, "All those Xavier and Regis guys have a backstreet girl who puts out." He shivered, realizing what a hypocrite he was, then backtracked. "I'm sorry. I mean, I'm not sorry that you don't see him much. I'm glad about that."

Maureen just stared at him in disbelief.

"Listen, Maureen, I'm sorry about a lot of things. And...well, I was wondering..."

When he paused, she said, "Yes?"

"Well, I was wondering if you'd like to take another crack at it."

The express train came rumbling into the station and jerked to a stop. The doors snapped open, releasing passengers. James then followed Maureen into the car. She grabbed the pole nearest the door. He drew close to her, reaching for the overhead strap, afraid he'd be deemed too forward if his hand slid down the pole toward hers.

The train leapt forward, racing into the tunnel. The lights flickered and dimmed as the car rocked side to side, bouncing down the track. James wanted to speak, but he'd have to yell above the deafening noise. He chose to remain silent, to be satisfied with a glimpse of Maureen whenever the lights flashed back on. When the train reached 59th Street, it braked to a halt.

"I get off here," James said.

"Okay," Maureen replied.

He backed his way toward the open door. *Now or never.* "So, what do you say?"

"About what?"

"A rematch. I mean, giving it another go."

Maureen blushed, trying not to see the passengers' reactions. "I guess that would be okay," she said, barely above a whisper.

"All right!" James exclaimed. "I'll call you tonight, okay?"

"Okay."

He took a step for the platform, but the double door slammed shut, leaving him on the outside, his book-laden arm on the inside. Passengers roared with laughter as he managed to spread the doors with his feet and knee and escape.

*

Stymie made the announcement at Easter time. It had come as a shock to James. There'd been a lot of changes of late, with guys leaving town for college or picking up steady employment to finance their studies at local schools, but there'd been no change so drastic, so threatening to James and his buddies.

Stymie was getting married.

It was nothing against Josie. She was great. It was the basic, undiluted concept of marriage that was troubling. Marriage was something undertaken by old guys. Then he started to realize that this notion was half right. The real problem was that he, along with the gang, was moving toward old guy status.

Arrangements for a memorable sendoff were left to James and Coney. Stymie's dad suggested they have the bachelor party at the Douglaston Club, boasting that he could get them a good deal. James and Coney felt that was too inviting to pass up and went about shaming enough money to finance it out of the invitees.

Those boarding away at school were the easiest targets. James didn't waste a letter on them, knowing that money only flows toward colleges and never away. Instead, he went to the students' parents, explained the situation, and walked away with the necessary loot.

He even managed to collect Michael's share in this sneaky fashion, stopping by St. Aidan's sacristy one afternoon to see Mrs. Cassidy. Sure enough, she was there, hair pinned up high, carefully placing starched linen altar cloths into the shallow mahogany drawers. When she heard why he had come, she promised him Michael would be home from Dunhill by the date they had set for the bash. She reached into her purse and pulled out a crumpled ten-dollar bill, more than James had ever seen Michael carry in his life. She kissed James on the cheek as she handed him the money, and told him to wish Stymie a blessed married life, and to make sure that no one drank too much beer at the party. As he left, James assured her he would see to that himself, and chalked up another lie he had told in St. Aidan's, in addition to all those in the confessional.

The appointed Friday evening in early June finally arrived. The club had gotten its money and had assigned the boys a basement room adjoining the bowling alley. Stymie was being taken to some bar by his father, brothers and future in-laws until everyone arrived. They had been told to arrive singly, instead of in a group, to avoid the possibility of Stymie spotting the gang and realizing something was up.

James walked self-consciously up the steps to the wide Victorian wrap-around porch. He pushed through the door into the foyer, which led to a long oak bar in the rear. An attendant in tuxedo took a disdainful look at his t-shirt, shorts and low black Cons.

"Downstairs to your left."

As soon as the attendant spoke, someone shouted from the bar, "Do you let anyone in this club these days?"

James turned to see Sean O'Donnell.

The attendant said, "Mr. O'Reilly is sponsoring a bachelor party for his son downstairs."

Dressed in a khaki suit, pink shirt, and a blue and gold regimental tie, Sean stepped toward James. "That would explain it. Long time, no see, Devlin."

"Not long enough for me," James said, glaring at his sunburned foe, who was holding a martini in his hand, olives and all. He was wearing tasseled cordovan loafers, no socks.

"That so? Well, you're a little underdressed, even for a stag party. Why don't you get to the basement with the rest of the Little Neck trolls? I've invited Donna and her parents to be my guests for dinner tonight and wouldn't want you to embarrass yourself.

James felt like his head would explode. He muttered, "Very considerate of you," and turned, heading downstairs.

A throng had already gathered in the middle of the party room, next to the two lane bowling alley. They surrounded the large keg centered in a trough filled with ice. James tried to put O'Donnell out of his mind and chugged one paper cup full of beer, then another. He couldn't help but think it looked like worship of the silver idol of Budweiser, instead of the golden one of Baal.

But the pagans were his buddies: Coney, Jasper, Double D, Six-Pack, Kazootie. Everyone from the park crowd but Michael had already arrived. And they were joined by a slew of Stymie's madmen acquaintances from school, Flushing and Bayside, as well.

There was no music but soon they were making their own. The raunchier the song, the louder they sang. *Bang Bang Lou Lou* had just given way to *Barnacle Bill* when Michael Cassidy walked in.

"Hey, Kiss-assidy!" Kazootie screamed, his eyes bulging. "Get that man a beer!"

Michael was pushed toward the keg. Genio slipped him a large full paper cup. In one motion, Michael chugged it down to the roar of approval, turning the cup upside down over his head.

"All right, Father Michael," Kazootie hollered. "It's good to see you got so educated at Dunhill."

Just then Double D burst back in from the men's room. "Quiet, everybody! Stymie's here!"

The boys lapsed into a drunken murmur as they were herded against a side wall and yelled "surprise" in unison when Stymie walked in, looking suspicious. He was rushed from all sides and pummeled on the back.

"Get him a beer! Get him a beer!

Dozens of soggy cups were thrust at Stymie. Beer splashed onto the intended imbiber, drenching the front of Stymie's shirt and pants. James caught Mr. O'Reilly and Josie's father heading upstairs; quite likely for a civilized drink at the country club's bar.

A chorus of "speech, speech" filled the room.

Several boys dragged Stymie through the small lake of beer accumulating on the floor. They forced him up on a rickety folding chair, Stymie holding his hands up for silence.

"All right you smackjobs. Listen up to your emperor. You guys got some jump on me tonight. It's going to take some serious drinking to get as shit-faced as you," He took a pitcher in both hands and drained it without coming up for air. His subjects went wild once more.

"Thank you for the farewell party. This is one totally impressive spread. I mean, bologna, luncheon meat *and* pimento loaf!"

Unaware of the sarcasm, Coney grinned and yelled, "The coldcuts were nothing. The hard part was bargaining for the extra potato salad."

"We're probably gonna need it," Kazootie said, lifting a tray with a mound of the salad high in the air and dumping it onto Coney's head, igniting a conflagration. All hell broke loose.

Within moments, the room looked as though the keg had exploded. Platters of coldcuts were floating down the bowling alley, like barges on narrow rivers of beer. The racks of bowling balls had been knocked over, rolling all over the floor. Coney looked like a week-old snowman.

James grabbed Coney by the arm and led him to the men's room. He stuck Coney's head in the sink, washing the greasy mess off his head as best he could. Coney was laughing so hard, James was afraid he'd drown under the faucet.

When they returned to the room, the din had subsided. Inside the party room, the guests stood at attention. The Douglaston Club manager and Mr. O'Reilly were reaming them out. The sight of Coney Rogers was the last straw.

"And you, Rogers, you're the biggest—"

"Turtle!" Coney shouted.

At the signal, every boy in the room dropped to his belly, arms and legs flapping as prescribed in the bylaws of the Turtles International. It was all over when they got to their feet. Mr. O'Reilly and the manager pointed to the exit, directing them through a winding passageway in the basement, up and out a storm cellar.

Coney was the first up the cement stairs. He pushed open the wooden hatch and stepped out. The swimming pool lay straight ahead beckoning with bright subsurface lights. Coney dropped a shoe by the cellar and the other by the diving board. There was a resounding fiberglass bounce, followed by an unmistakable splash. The others followed Coney's lead and soon the pool was packed with intoxicated bathers.

When the overhead floodlights flashed on, it was obvious the police would soon be on their way. The boys scattered and sprinted across the dewy lawn, scrambling over the chain link fence, the shoes left behind.

Without saying a word, Mr. O'Reilly gathered the footwear and socks and tossed them over the fence. "All right, you jerks. Now get the hell out of here. And for God's sake, stay out of trouble."

Soaking wet, James had what he thought were his sneakers in hand as he walked barefoot at the edge of the throng, down the sidewalk adjacent to the club. He spotted a crowd of adults gathered on the porch watching. Sean O'Donnell, in his sharp suit and glow-in-the-dark pink shirt, was on the veranda pointing and laughing. James knew the people next to him had to be Donna and her parents. He looked away and continued down the street, breaking into a trot.

*

Stymie's stag continued. The boys screamed for "helicopters" at the Salem Inn, a topless go-go joint in Port Washington, but were thrown out when Kazootie tried to pluck a twirling pasty from one of the dancers. Finally, someone suggested they go to the city, but the caravan of cars got separated on the Long Island Expressway.

Around three a.m., James, Kazootie, Michael and Six-Pack walked through the arch at Washington Square. Coney remained behind in Kazootie's Falcon, passed out in the backseat, his bare feet protruding out the window.

A heavy smell of incense hung over the park and faint strains of *Purple Haze* trailed over the bushes from some source they couldn't locate. James felt out of place amongst the freaks. They moved onto Sixth Avenue.

"I got to eat," Six Pack said. "If I pass out on an empty stomach, put me out of my misery in the morning."

"They got any White Castles here?" Kazootie asked.

"Don't know."

None of the establishments they passed resembled a diner or even a bar and grill. Finally, they stopped in front of a dimly lit storefront. It looked to be crowded.

"Celestial Coffee House," Kazootie read from the finger-painted sign. "What do you think?"

"I think the place is crawling with weirdos," Six-Pack commented before spitting on the sidewalk.

"Well, we haven't spotted anything better," Michael argued. "I say we go in. How about you, Jimmy?"

"Fine with me, Mike. Kazoot?"

"Sure, let's go, Six-Pack. We'll make sure none of the fagolas cornhole you in the men's room."

They filed inside and found a corner table, with a fat warty candle on the glass plate in the center. The ashtray was filled with odd-smelling cigarette butts. As the boys settled into their chairs, a Richie Havens album was stopped short and *Handsome Johnny* was left marching across the fields of Korea. Suddenly a dude with a shiny bald head and full beard stood up and began reciting nonsensical verses.

At the same time, a waitress approached the table. She wore a transparent tank t-shirt and long flowing dress. Her enormous tits threatened to bounce all the way down to her navel, as did her braided hair.

"Can I help you?" she asked in a husky voice, peering over her grannie glasses.

"I could really go for a hamburger, rare,"

"We're strictly into macrobiotics here," she said. "We have some fine bean curd—"

"Bean *crud*?" Kazootie asked. "Guys, wake me up when this nightmare is over." He glanced at Six-Pack who had fallen asleep with his head on the table and did the same.

"Don't mind him," Michael said. "He had a long night." He paused, then said, "You have any desserts? We'd probably like that."

"Celestial brownies," she said. "They're the specialty of the house."

"Are they plain brownies?" Michael asked. "None of that hash stuff, right?"

"Of course not. We'd have to charge much more if we made them that celestial!"

"Give us some brownies then and, uh, what have you got to drink?"

"May I recommend our Hermaphrodite tea?"

"We'll take two," Michael said.

The waitress nodded and as soon as she was out of earshot, James turned to Michael. "So, where were you hiding all night? You get in from Dunhill late?"

"No. I got back early. Had to go to Flushing before the party." He paused. "Then I got held up when I got to the club."

"Me too. That douchebag O'Donnell caught me on the way in. God, do I hate that guy. Can you imagine? Drinking a martini at the bar like he's King Shit."

"That's funny. He stopped me, too," Michael said. "He was all excited to introduce me to his girlfriend and her parents, like it was some big deal. They seemed like nice people, though. The Bradleys?" Michael paused when he saw the look on James's face. "You know them?"

"Yeah," James conceded, his face turning crimson, even in the dim light.

Michael noticed his friend's look and laughed. "I never knew you had the hots for a Manor girl, Wild Man."

When James just glared at him, Michael continued hurriedly. "By the way, she's some knockout, and I have no idea what she sees in O'Donnell. Anyhow, it was all very awkward. Sean's making a big show about what great friends we were and how I'm going to start for Dunhill's varsity basketball team next year."

He reached into his pocket and pulled out a pack of cigarettes. He flipped one out, lit it using the candle, and began smoking, as if he'd been doing so all his life. James stared in disbelief.

"I don't know why, but Sean's been playing up to me as long as I can remember."

As the waitress's jugs flapped in James's face, she placed the brownies and tainted tea on the table, barely avoiding Six-Pack's and Coney's heads.

Michael's eyes clouded. "Hey, Jimmy, remember the time Boccinello took us over to Oceania Street to play Little Stevie Antoine and his guys at Madame Curie

Park? Man, that guy had to be six ten. I'll never forget how we blew that lead—"

"Hey, Mike," James interrupted. "You all right?"

Michael mopped his sweaty brow with a paper napkin. "Yeah, why?"

"Well, you got pretty blasted tonight, at least for you. And I never saw you smoke before. When'd ya start that?"

"About the time I flunked out of school."

"What!"

"You heard me, Jim. I actually flunked out at the end of March. It was official yesterday, though. Since the room and board was paid for, you know?"

James was in a panic, not knowing what to say. He glanced at his buddies, grateful they were sound asleep. "Mike," he whispered, "what happened?"

"Well, things went downhill fast after I got hurt. It was right after Christmas break, in a blowout game against Wake Forest – real bad sprained ankle. I was through for the season. All the masterminds in the athletic department told me not to worry, that they could have the exams coming up postponed for as long as it took me to get ready for them. So like a dope, I went along with it. They put them off for a month. That whole time I was falling further behind. Then they suggested I put the exams off for another month. By then, I was totally panicked and jumped at the chance."

Michael crushed his butt in the ashtray, then immediately lit up another. "Then I get this notice to report to Jake Derrick's office. That's the prick who coached the freshman team. Well, he had me sit in this little seat in his office. It's so you're practically on the floor while he struts around you like a rooster. He started telling me that they got the doctor's final report on my ankle, and he hits me with these sweet little quotes. 'Extremely doubtful he can regain former speed. Tenuous hope of complete recovery. Dubious prospect for intercollegiate competition at varsity level.'

"That's what they say," I told him. So he said, 'I just thought you should know about the report and a few other things.'

"By then I was getting pretty hot. So I insisted on hearing about these other things he had in mind. So first, he said, 'Boy, you better get studying because your exams are all on Thursday and Friday of next week.'

"Well, that's just swell," I said to him. And he just laughed at me. And the prick stuck his ugly face in mine and sneered, 'You haven't heard the best yet. Because even if you pass those exams by pulling that miraculous medal of yours out of your ass, your scholarship here is gone, boy. Through. Understand?'

"Yeah, I understand, Jake," I said. "Was that your bright idea? That gonna make you happy? Make you feel like a big man? And he said to me, 'That's right, pretty boy. That's gonna make me real happy because I been telling the head coach what a fucking Mary faggot bastard you were from the first day you stepped foot on campus.'

"And, Jimmy, he stood not six inches from my face, screaming at me. I'll never forget his buffalo breath. There was honest-to-God hatred in his eyes. He was yelling loud enough so someone could hear him down the hall. 'I can spot a sweet one like you a mile away, Cassidy. How come you got no girlfriends, Cassidy? It's 'cause you're out for the other fellas on the team, right, Cassidy? You got big eyes in the shower, ain't that so, Cassidy?'

"I just walked out. I never took the exams. I never went to another class. What was the sense? No scholarship meant no more school. If you're not special at Dunhill, you're gone. I just sat around the dorm. Smoked cigarettes. Drank beer. Watched the tube until I couldn't postpone coming home any longer. Spent an entire year at college, and all I got to show for it is a bummed-up ankle and a pot belly. Don't have a single credit to my name. Some success story, huh, Jimmy?"

James was stunned. "You tell your folks, yet?"

"Yeah. They were really great. I told them give me a chance, I'll get everything straightened out. They said sure, they had no doubt I would."

"So what now?"

"You're going to think it's stupid. You guys always gave me the business about it, but you know I always did kind of want to be a priest. I mean, basketball and church, they're the only two things I ever really paid attention to."

James picked at his brownie, letting Michael speak.

"As a matter-of-fact, I was all set to sign up for Cathedral when the Dunhill scholarship came through. I should've joined up at the seminary. That's pretty clear now. But I just couldn't resist that shot at playing big-time ball. Like you said, I saw Final Four in my sleep."

"Big deal, you made a mistake. Nothing says you can't go in the seminary now, Mike."

Michael blew out a puff of smoke. "You don't understand, do you, Jimmy? I can't go now."

"Why not?"

"Because I'm a fucking dummy, for one thing. I couldn't pass a single college course. Haven't you heard? Priests are supposed to be smart."

"You're plenty smart enough. And it's got to be a hell of a lot easier studying in a seminary than at Dunhill University."

"Maybe so, but I still can't join now."

Six-Pack mumbled something, snorted, then fell back into his stupor. James whispered hoarsely, "Why not?"

"Because what if Derrick is right? What am I gonna be, a stupid *and* queer priest? Maybe they got special assignments down here in the Village for padres like that, huh?"

James clenched his fists. "How could you take anything a redneck prick like

182

that tells you seriously? You're not like that..." He couldn't even use the word to describe the despised condition. He paused, searching his memory for something to prove his point. "I seem to recall that big girl Dolores swapping spit with you at one of the cookouts. You didn't seem to mind that too much, did you" Some queer guy wouldn't have enjoyed that at all. I know you're not like that. Everyone knows it."

Michael blushed. "Jimmy, keep your voice down, will ya? Everyone knows I'm not a homo except me. And until I know it, there'll be no seminary for me." He crushed his last smoke. "Besides, it's too late now."

James was drained from the evening's beer and heated argument and snapped, "For Christ's sake, what are you talking about now? Why's it too late?"

"Because I enlisted. Today."

"*What*?" James yelled so loud that the stoned patrons turned to look and Six-Pack and Coney lifted their heads briefly, before dropping them down to the table again.

"It's why I went to Flushing. I enlisted. U.S. Army. I'm going airborne, like my brothers."

James's eyes burned. He didn't care if he started crying. "That's the stupidest thing I ever heard in my life. That's like buying a one-way ticket to Vietnam. What do you think, there's some sort of tea dance going on over there?"

James turned his head to the side, thinking he might actually puke. He tried to lower his voice. "Some fucking jock with his head up his ass calls you a pansy and you're gonna go Green Beret to prove he's wrong? I mean, we were offered Hermaphrodite tea tonight. What are we supposed to do? Bayonet the waitress for casting aspersions on our masculinity?"

Michael's pained expression flashed across the table. "That's not fair, Jimmy. You know I don't understand when you start talking like that."

Tears ran down James's face. "Jesus, Mike. All right. I'm sorry, but I just don't want to see you get hurt. If someone feels like they've got to go fight, fine. But not for a dumb reason like that."

Michael exhaled another cloud of smoke. "Jimmy, Jimmy? Listen to me. It's going to be all right. I'm telling you. My brother, Johnny, went to 'Nam and he came home okay. I just got to take care of this. Then I'm out from under, don't you see? Whatever I want to do then, I'll be able to do it. But you got to stick by me, pal."

James's legs shook and his hands trembled. That goddamn war hadn't ended on schedule. It had crept closer and now reached out for his buddies. First Fat Frankie. Now Michael. Who next?

He forced a smile. "No sweat," he said barely above a whisper. "I'll stick by you. But then you'd better get your ass back here and become the best goddamn priest the Brooklyn Diocese has ever seen. You hear me?"

*

Springtime is the second chance God gives the world. A divine do-over. An opportunity to commence creation anew to get the job done right this time.

 Maureen Cullen had returned with spring and James had grasped the significance that day at the subway station. He hadn't allowed his reprieve to slip away. Their old aborted romance wasn't exhumed; what transpired between them was something altogether new. The bad memories were dismissed as fears. In a few short weeks, James and Maureen discovered everything about each other they had missed the first time around.

The progression had been gradual. From the dances and parties, to the dates by themselves, to Gonzaga's prom at the Tavern on the Green, and now to Maureen's senior prom, a wondrous evening of dancing at the Plaza Hotel. As he swirled her on the ballroom floor, James knew she'd finally absolved him. Later, they sat in a booth at some French discotheque. The friends surrounding them were all but invisible as they held hands with each other.

Still waters run deep. The nuns' repeated platitude kept coming to James's mind. He'd always dismissed it as trite, but in Maureen's case, the words rang true. He now recognized that the same silence that had irked him months ago was what actually attracted him to her. She wasn't forward and didn't toot her own horn. She knew what she wanted and would have her way. Yet she was willing to bide her time. How could he be fool enough to think he could hold onto her?

Why should Maureen limit herself to a jerk like him, especially when he'd be going to Brunswick College a zillion miles away? She shouldn't. It wasn't fair to expect it. Yet, the thought of her wandering around with some other guy made his stomach turn. He couldn't handle that. Not when she'd come to mean so much to him.

But he was already screwing up their relationship. Maureen's parents were throwing a breakfast party after the prom, but he would have to leave early to catch a plane for vacation with his parents.

Here we go again. Just like with Donna Bradley. James slouched against the red leather padding of the booth.

"What are you thinking about?" Maureen asked, placing her hand on his.

James looked into her eyes. "I guess I wish things could stay like this. You know, indefinitely."

Maureen nodded. "I do, too."

"But things can't stand still. Come September, I'll be in Maine and you'll be in Westchester at Ladycliff with every cadet from West Point, every guy from Fairfield, flocking all around you."

 "The distance doesn't matter to me, Jimmy. I'm not interested in going out with other boys."

184

James gazed at her. "Really?"

"Really," Maureen said, sticking her jaw out, as if daring James to contradict her. "You're the one I want to go out with. Not someone else."

James knew his own mind was made up too. He wrapped his hands around Maureen's. He wouldn't blow it this time.

"You may regret that statement, Miss Mojo Cullen, 'cause I'm never going to walk away from you again."

The words were hardly spoken when a burly foreigner on his way to the men's room staggered into the table, upsetting every drink on it. James and Maureen jumped up, their laps filled with icy liquid, their pledge sealed with a frigid splash, rather than a kiss.

XIII
August 1969

IT WAS SUPPOSED TO BE A CELEBRATION, the young couple's final lunch together before they headed off to college. James found a spot on the crowded
steps of Federal Hall where they could squeeze in. He held a brown bag from
the deli on William Street.

Maureen adjusted her culottes as she sat down. "I can't believe summer's over
so soon."

James pulled out a sandwich and straw, handing them to Maureen. "Some parts
went too fast, some not fast enough."

"What do you mean?" Maureen asked, unwrapping her sandwich.

"The time with you sped by, Mo. The time at work? That was a whole different
story."

"Your uncle?"

"Yeah. He's getting worse. Missing in action every couple of weeks now. The
scary part is, I'm getting used to it. When someone starts yelling, 'Where's Rory?'
I just shrug."

"It doesn't bother you anymore?"

""No, it does. What I really have to do next summer is get a new job."

"That's probably a good idea," Maureen said, biting into her sandwich.

"So much is changing. Last summer I'd bust out of work and head to the park.
This summer, Michael was gone and a lot of the other guys didn't show up like
they used to. Just wasn't the same. I lived for the weekends when I could see you
and now I'm not even going to have that." He then ripped off the wax paper from
his tuna sandwich and took a frustrated bite.

"I'm not happy about that either," Maureen said, wiping Russian dressing from
the corner of her mouth. "We didn't know last year how we'd feel now. But it
won't be so bad if we call and write---"

Commotion at the bottom of the steps interrupted her. "Bring our troops
home now!" a long-haired guy with a bush hat, beat-up fatigues and a bullhorn

chanted. A handful of Vietnam Vets Against the War scrambled up the steps stuffing pamphlets into the hands of the onlookers. One vet with a faded U.S. Army t-shirt walked with a limp toward James and Maureen. He flashed a broad grin, pushing back his stringy hair.

"Better ditch the chick and join us, brother. If we don't get this war stopped, your sweet young ass is gonna get shot next."

James stared back at him without speaking. The Vets then regrouped at the bottom of the steps, crossed Wall Street, and headed for the New York Stock Exchange. James hadn't finished his sandwich, but it was time to head back for his last afternoon of the summer with Uncle Rory, who hopefully hadn't used James's departure as an excuse for another liquid lunch.

Maureen put a hand on James's leg. "What are you thinking about?"

He shrugged. "I don't know what to think anymore. I get what they're saying, but I don't want to be disloyal to my best friend who enlisted, even though he may come back and be right out front with hair down to his ass leading the demonstration. I just don't know anything about what's going on over there."

James had been dealing with the same questions all summer. About Michael. Michael the recruit. Michael the soldier. Where is Michael? How is Michael doing? Have you heard from Michael? Why haven't you heard from Michael? Did you write to Michael? How long ago was that? Michael didn't write back? Do you have any idea where Michael is? Do his parents know? Does anyone know where Michael is? Doesn't that soldier on the news, in the magazine, look like Michael?

James could be anywhere when he'd see him. Michael in long green pants, not shorts. Michael in black combat boots, not Cons. Michael with his curls all shaved so the tiny nicks on his scalp glistened through.

And that same litany of questions he heard at home would continue in his mind as he watched this silent, imaginary Michael. It wouldn't stop until he uttered the prescribed response in his mind: *I would know where Michael is, what he's doing, if I were with him. I'd know where they all are, if I were with them.*

James remembered it always being an expectation. An unspoken assumption. Just like his father's, just like everyone else's, his turn would come, too. It was unavoidable. When the time came, he'd have to be ready to be brave, no matter what, even if he didn't want to. Otherwise, he'd be letting his father and everyone else down.

But had his time already come and he hadn't noticed? He was going off to college, not to war like Michael and the others. What did that say about him? And how was Maureen to know how he felt? Maybe it was something girls had no reason to understand. After all, no one expected them to go trotting off to war.

James hugged Maureen, and said, "I'd better get back and face the music." He then pecked her on the lips and stood up, running down the steps, calling back to her, "I'll give you a real kiss later, when we don't have an audience."

*

Peg and Dave walked away, having said goodbye to James at Brunswick. Peg swore to herself that she wouldn't cry, but she did, just like a baby. She didn't look back at her son. Brunswick College had passed Dave's exacting inspection, for which she was thankful. Prior to seeing it, he kept bringing up Michael Cassidy, and how he'd given up his scholarship at Dunhill to enlist. Now that he'd seen Brunswick and learned of its "Little Ivy" status, he seemed content to have his son go to a prestigious college instead of war, at least for the moment.

They got into the Chrysler and were soon speeding southbound on the Maine Turnpike, Peg glancing at her husband every few seconds. The late afternoon sun seemed to be forcing his eyes closed, but she resolved not to worry about it anymore. After all, a crash would be unlikely. No. There'd be no such drastic resolution of this most recent change of life. Now both their children were gone. She and Dave were on their own. Empty nesters. They would survive the trip and confront the new vacancy at home. Instead of the house, remodeling their lives seemed to be in order.

She closed her eyes. What if James went mad with that hockey-playing room-mate from Boston? But she had to admit that, despite it being "non-sectarian"—a polite way of saying pagan—she too had been impressed with the place and wondered how different her own life might have been had she been dropped off at such a place when she finished high school.

She'd always enjoyed school and wanted to continue, but it wasn't meant to be. Ever since, she felt inferior in the presence of the well-off girls who'd gone to college and spoke on most topics with confidence. She sighed, wondering if at forty-five, it wasn't too late to go back to school. There were so many occupations she might enjoy. So many ways to be of service to others.

But then she remembered her mother who was helpless without her. Besides, she figured, Dave would never approve.

She stole another glance at her husband and then realized why she'd cried, despite the weeks of mental preparation for her son's departure: She'd not completed her job.

She had a God-given task, yet her son had been taken away before she had a chance to finish. He was not an adult yet. There was so much more he had to learn from her, even if he refused to acknowledge that possibility. Society didn't examine the particular case at all to see how hard the job was. It just arbitrarily fixed a time within which the task must be done. If a mother hadn't accomplished all she set out to by the time her son finished high school, he was taken from her, one way or the other. And James had conspired with society against her.

The last few years he'd kept his distance, even refused to argue with her any-more, as though any emotional exchange with your mother was unnatural, un-manly. He had won. He outmaneuvered, outsmarted her. The break had been made. Her claim to him would be a historical one alone. It would fade more every year. She'd ultimately lose him to a girl. She might even lose him to war.

Another quick check on her husband. *I don't know about that one, David. For-give me.* She prayed in silence with her hands unfolded, afraid of incensing him by pulling out her rosary beads as he drove.

*

James walked from Haldane Hall across the quadrangle. In the setting September sun, the large buildings wore orange splashes over their red, yellow, and buff exteriors, looking like giant versions of leaves that would fall in the next few weeks.

He laughed when he realized this was the first time he'd walked to a final ex-amination with a bottle of booze bulging in his rear pants pocket. Yet that was his hopefully future fraternity's theory of education. As the brothers of Delta Tau warned their pledges: "We're the DT's. If you don't have them before you join, you'll have them before you leave."

The fraternity scene had taken James by surprise. He'd not known what to make of it. One thing was sure, it'd been around a hell of a long time.

James's roommate explained the arrangement to him over and over. Eamonn "Bimba" Flaherty knew a lot about things in general, and about Brunswick Col-lege in particular. He was from Charlestown, Mass., an Irish enclave so tough a visitor might expect to see Tommies patrolling it. Bimba had parlayed his hockey talents to a "post-graduate" year at an exclusive prep school, then on to a free ride to Brunswick. He was pushing twenty and knew his way around.

"Just remember this, Devlin: When in Rome, do as the Romans do. When in Brunswick, do as the assholes do."

"Jesus, Bimba. That was profound." James struggled to keep a straight face.

"You liked it?

"Loved it. What's it mean?"

"Elementary, my little jerk-off. It means you aren't at Harvard, sweetheart. And if you're gonna survive this joint in the middle of winter, you better join a frater-nity. Otherwise, you'll go bat-shit for sure."

"You think so?"

"I know so. Now me, I'm gonna join Eta, the hockey house. It's automatic. We got a few token smart guys over there like you to help us pick the right courses and prep for exams. It'll be like having a little insurance policy for my athletic eligibil-ity. I could probably get you a bid there if you want."

"I don't think so, Bimba. I can't tell a hockey puck from a manhole cover. So I can imagine what my role would be over there."

"Wise choice, my man." Bimba gave him his broadest, emptiest grin. "We do hate to lose a good tutor though. But my guess is that you're a little headstrong anyway."

"Well, I sure wouldn't let you guys tool my ass off. And I still don't think I'm interested in any house."

"Listen, Jimmy. Let me put that loner notion out of your head. Do you like to eat?"

"Yeah, I like to eat. Who doesn't?"

"All the yahoos who are stupid enough to come to Brunswick and not drop at a house don't like to eat because there ain't any place to eat up here except at the houses. The student union feeds about forty people. Would ya like to spend your college career on line for shepherd's pie?"

"Okay, oh Wise One. Where should I drop?"

"Try the DT house. You're Irish, so you must like to drink. And I can tell you like to party from those pictures of your girlfriend. She's cute. I'll steal her as soon as she comes up, I'm warning you." He laughed. "But seriously, there's a lot of good shits over at DT. I might have considered it myself if politics weren't a factor."

But politics had been a definite factor for Bimba. He was aware of the need to make the right move at all times. The comparison to Michael Cassidy was inevitable. Without ever seeing him on skates, James knew Bimba wasn't half the athlete Mike was. Yet he knew that Bimba would manage four years on scholarship, the fabled "full boat," and snatch a diploma on his way out the door. And Michael had been eaten alive before he even got rolling. James concluded it was best to take a friendly word of advice from Bimba Flaherty seriously, so he had checked out the DT House.

He liked the members well enough. They were a mixed group and even had several soul brothers, who were in very short supply at Brunswick. James dropped there with less than the usual amount of coercion.

The orientation of his class of pledges hadn't been too bad. Only verbal abuse, various chores around the house, but nothing too strenuous. Most of the work was mental. The pledges first memorized both fair and foul college songs. Then they were given campus tours and lectures by a few upperclassmen, who expected them to digest reams of trivia, real and apocryphal, concerning the college and its illustrious Delta Taus.

They'd been quizzed daily and reminded constantly that "you can't do shit if you don't know shit." This fundamental if ineloquent proposition governed the lives of these pledges. Tonight they'd have an opportunity to prove to the brothers that their hopeless ignorance had miraculously been cured. The pledges had been given four instructions for the final exam: (1) you'd better be on time; (2) you'd better know your stuff cold; (3) you'd better bring plenty of alcoholic beverage of your choice; (4) you'd better wear clean underwear.

James stood on the corner outside the DT house at 7:10. He figured he was in pretty good shape. He was a full twenty minutes early. He knew his obscure facts frontwards and backwards. He had a full pint of rum stuffed into his pocket.

James had heard too many tales of pledges who croaked while chug-a-lugging quart bottles of vodka or gin. Some prospective biology major had explained to him that this caused the equivalent of a flat tire in your medulla oblongata. It was a mixed metaphor, but he got the point and James decided to limit his risk. There was a soda machine in the house. He was sure even the most beastly brother wouldn't deny him a bottle of Coke to dilute his rum a bit.

James even had his clean underwear. That was one instruction that gnawed at the pledges. Why would they possibly need clean underwear?

"Okay, freshman," a gruff voice commanded. "In you go for the final. And I sure hope you wore clean underwear!"

"Yes, sir," James replied, not having noticed anyone approaching. The closed shutters of Delta Tau registered with him. The house was completely dark. This looked like something bigger than a final trivia exam.

He followed the pledge chairman up the walk and through the front door. He was greeted by three large sophomores. The beefy upperclassmen placed a blindfold over his eyes. He was led up several flights of stairs to the top floor, then down a hallway. By the time they sat him down, James had lost his bearings completely.

He was left alone, or so it seemed, for several minutes. Whatever he was sitting on was hard. He let one arm dangle down, as surreptitiously as possible, in case he was being observed. The object felt like a tree stump.

Suddenly a door was kicked open, many heavy footsteps filling the room. Through the blindfold James felt the glare of bright lights.

"You're next, Devlin. And I hope you do better that those other pledges 'cause we just threw them all out. They'll never be DTs."

James didn't recognize the voice of the man who yanked the blindfold off his face. He squinted in the bright light to get a better look, but his face was still not familiar.

"What's the matter? Don't you know me?"

"No, sir," James replied.

"I'm the Most Exalted Archadelphon of the Delta Tau house. The Pink Elephant himself. But you can call me Brother Pink for now. Okay, Devlin?"

"Yes, sir."

"What a cooperative pledge. Is he always such a wimp?"

"Hell no, Pink," one of the onlookers commented. "He's got a wicked New York wise mouth."

"That so, Devlin?" Pink asked.

"I suppose so, Brother Pink."

"Well then, let's just see if you have anything clever to say on your final exam."

Pink began firing questions at him in rapid succession. James spewed back canned responses the pledges' upper-class instructors had provided. Perspiration was rolling off Pink's face, glistening under the spotlight. James felt sweat streaming down his own face as the interrogation continued.

Pink finally paused. "Not bad so far, Devlin. You know the bullshit part much better than the other newts and wombats in your pledge class. But there's one more question, smarty pants. And if you blow this one, kiddo, you're through. Ready?"

James looked around the room at the faces watching him. The sweet scent of alcohol on their breath filled the room. "Okay," he muttered.

Pink pulled a chair up to the tree stump. He leaned forward, his fleshy face practically pressed against James. "Okay, Devlin. Let's suppose for a moment that after a few beers one night, Brother Zeboo takes you into his strictest confidence and confesses that he raped some sweet young thing right in the middle of campus a couple of nights before. And let's suppose further, that the cops question you the next day and they want to find out what you know about the rape. Do you tell them about Brother Zeboo?"

A hush fell over the room. James's mind raced, his eyes darting left and right. "No," he answered resolutely. "If he hadn't been my friend, I never would've known about it. It's like a priest with confession...He trusted me..."

"Asshole! Asshole!" they screamed. "You'd let a rapist walk the streets? Zeboo would do it again!"

When the shouting subsided, Pink stood up and shook his head sadly. "It's a shame, Devlin. You choked on the very last question. But it's the most important one. We DT's aren't too fussy, but we do have some moral standards, you know. After all, that girl could've been my sister." He looked at the others. "Get him out of here. I'm sorry, Devlin."

The blindfold was put back on and James spun around a few times. He was led back down the stairs, relieved that the ordeal was over. *Screw them all*, he thought, satisfied with his answer. He would've given it again and not have betrayed Brother Zeboo's friendship.

"Where you guys taking me?" James asked, feeling as though he'd gone down more stairs than he'd come up.

"Shut up, you'll see."

It suddenly clicked. The final exam, Brother Pink—it was all an elaborate hoax. Had he been willing to inform on Brother Zeboo, they would've exploded for his squealing on a brother. Tonight would be the pledges' initiation. They had to be taking him to the locked room in the basement for the secret rituals.

It was true. Several minutes of ceremonial nonsense later, James was a brother of the Delta Tau Lodge with all the undefined and largely nonexistent privileges attached to that lofty status. He joined the pledges who had preceded him through the maze of hocus pocus. When the last of their number had completed the rites of passage, the brotherhood surrounded them in the basement party room, all magnanimously presented with the booze they'd purchased for themselves.

The upperclassmen saluted them in song as freshmen who were true blue, drunkards through and through. In acknowledgement, each of the former pledges drained the vessel that had been placed before him on the bar.

The crowd thinned out shortly thereafter. Half-drunk upperclassmen wandered off for a futile attempt at studying before passing out. Their less sanguine comrades mingled with the freshmen. The group surrounded the blaring jukebox, gleaming like a large electric monstrance in the dim basement light.

The freshmen were a pathetic bunch. Their minutes of marginal sobriety were numbered. They waited like condemned prisoners for the inescapable punch to the head, kick to the stomach that would be delivered by the quantities of booze they'd consumed.

James sprawled out on one of the wooden benches lining the mottled basement wall. He rotated the bottle of rum in his hands. Before he'd twisted the cap, it had been full of promise. Now the bottle was empty and the illusion became apparent. He was as self-deceived as any drunk. Booze did not make him smarter. But it did make him feel better, much better than he'd felt the moment before. It filled the emptiness, the internal vacuum he'd somehow created.

He was no great ballplayer, like Michael. Maybe a shade above average. He was no real thinker either, just a clever manipulator of information. He could recite, reformulate, recycle, or refute others' ideas and beliefs. They were disposable. James flushed them down his mental drain as soon as they served his purpose, leaving his mind as empty as the bottle of rum.

Where were his own ideas? It was this lack of originality that had left him barren. Like a spoiled child, he wanted it all to be special, all brand new. If that were impossible, he wanted nothing at all.

Yet maybe, just maybe, he now had that first novel idea. One spark that could be kindled and might burst into a whole set of views and beliefs that followed naturally from the first. Maybe he was entitled to half credit for the idea of Maureen Cullen and James Devlin. It was the first truly original idea he ever had. A singular idea that could be developed, that could last a lifetime.

"Hey, Devlin, wake up!" one of the newest brothers shouted. "Let's hitchhike out to McDonald's and look for some townie chicks."

James rose to his feet unsteadily. "Sure," he said without hesitation. "I'll be right with you. I just got to go to the head."

All thoughts of Maureen flew out the open basement window.

*

James slammed his book with a snicker. Maybe he'd write a letter to this Herbert Marcuse guy. Invite him over to the Devlins once he got home. He imagined the invitation: *Dear Mr. Marcuse, I'm sure you and my father would have a very stimulating dialogue. He would find your ideas on civil disobedience very thought provoking. Hah! Maybe even punch provoking. Dave Devlin versus the pinko professor in a fifteen rounder at the dinner table.*

James shifted his feet from his desk, his heavy boots hitting the floor with a thud. His view out the window was obscured. The glass itself was not opaque. The twelve inches of snow piled on the outer sill had covered the entire first row of panes. It was just another nondescript winter day at Brunswick College during "reading week."

Unlike scores of saner institutions, Brunswick postponed first semester exams until after the Christmas vacation. While Maureen and all James's buddies were living the fat life in New York, he'd been forced to report back to the wilderness. In fairness to Brunswick, however, they did give their erstwhile scholars a fighting chance and provided a ten-day recovery period before exams began. With no classes and several feet of snow on the ground, there was little incentive to leave the dorm. James stayed closeted with his books and notes, pulling the semester's work together.

Upstairs, the stereophonic whispering began again. It was a haunting, penetrating sound, played over and over: the Stones' *Gimme Shelter*. The music was his signal. Time for a midmorning break and head over to the student union. Bimba would be in the pool room. James would shoot a couple of games of eight ball with him then check the mail, even though only so much could be said in a letter.

He and Maureen had been trying to cope with their separation. Seeing each other every third or fourth weekend, when he figured out some means of transportation to Ladycliff, had been no solution. The irregular reunions had a pressure all their own. The lovers tried to cram too much of each other into too little time. Coinciding with "big" weekends at Maureen's school, the visits tended toward excessive partying, punctuated by her frequent tears, followed by unkept promises not to let it happen again.

James shook off his thoughts while stomping snow off his boots before entering the student union. He went down the stairs for the pool hall, pausing at the entrance. Bimba was hustling an upperclassman at the center table. He gave James a wink between shots. James waved to him, then headed out the door. Bimba was playing for dough. There'd be no eight ball this morning.

194

His next stop was the mail room. He looked in the tiny glass door and saw a letter. Great! Maureen had written sooner than he'd expected. He spun the combination dial, but when he pulled out the letter it wasn't the typical pastel envelope. This one was tissue thin with numerous stamps and postmarks covering it, the handwriting unfamiliar. Only the one "Saigon" notation gave its author's identity away. He slipped it into his pocket and headed back to Haldane.

After closing the door behind him, James turned on the old stereo, dropping into an easy chair in the corner without taking off his coat. He reached into his pocket and pulled out the letter.

Saigon, South Vietnam
January 1, 1970

Dear Wild Man,

Happy New Year and Decade to you, my scholarly friend. By now you must have figured I'd lost your address or was just too goddam lazy to ever write, which is closer to the truth.

Seriously, I haven't had a good chunk of time to sit down and sort out what I wanted to say. But now I got this two week R&R here in Saigon. It's a great place, just like winning an all-expenses paid vacation to Times Square. At any rate, I finally ran out of excuses not to write so here it is. The first thing comes to me is how little I know about what's going on around me. You ever been on a subway car where everyone's speaking Spanish and you don't understand a word they're saying? That's what it's like here, except worse. You don't look a thing like the people, so there's no prayer of blending into the crowd. And since there's a war going on, you always figure they're saying, 'Let's get this one!' instead of 'Gimme a Cerveza Rheingold and a kiss.' I mean, let's face it. My exposure to Asian culture is zip. There isn't even a Chinese laundry in Little Neck.

The Army. They're no better. All the officers are talking another language too. They're constantly lecturing us on geopolitics and the strategic importance of our position in South Vietnam. I could use you here to translate. Me? I still keep messing up dominoes and Chinese checkers. The guys in my outfit are all pretty decent. But being with them out in the bush reminds me of when I was a kid. You remember, playing guns in the vacant lots. Or like me and my brothers chasing each other around the living room in our pajamas during 'Combat'. Having contests to see who could croak the best.

The sad part is everything is real now. Real uniforms. Real guns. Real people getting killed.

Somehow, it still seems like a game to me. Like a bunch of nut jobs got together and dreamed the whole idea up. Then dragged a lot of people from each side together, told them when it was scheduled to go. 'Here's a gun for you. You go out and shoot a bunch of those guys.' 'And here's a nice mortar for you. You go and blow a few of those other guys up.' 'And lady with the baby? You go out between them and get in the way so we can take a couple of spectacular pictures for Gawk Magazine.' Crazy, huh? If you saw a bunch of bodies lying around after an earthquake, or some other natural disaster, it would be a big deal, real news. When we do it to ourselves, the killing's on purpose. Then it's not so shocking or horrifying. Just routine. I hear they give the body counts on the radio back home, just like the temperature.

It must be a game. I mean we got the uniforms, just like any team. And we got fans, watching the action on the tube back home, rooting for the good old U.S.A. on the 7 o'clock news. And we're even playing against the clock. Not to win, but like Notre Dame—just for the tie. You know, the guys in my outfit come in one at a time and leave the same way. The clock starts when you arrive, and the horn goes off twelve months later if you're still in one piece. It's great for morale. You should see these guys when they start getting 'short'—close to the time they leave. They don't even want to go to the latrine anymore, for fear of getting killed. Let me tell you, that's not too hygienic (I had to look that word up) when you're sitting around the old campfire. And it's sure not the old group mentality back at St. Aidan's: you remember, everyone stays after school until you all know the words to the nun's favorite hymns. I don't understand it. If they told us no one was leaving here until we'd captured Hanoi, they'd have one gung ho bunch of soldiers on their hands.

That's not how it works. So all of us here are just looking at each other, trying to figure out what we're supposed to do. Knowing we're gonna get second-guessed by everyone no matter what we do. Wondering whether you're gonna be the next guy to snap, so the papers will be writing about Mad Dog Cassidy instead of Rusty Calley.

I really shouldn't go on like this. By now you must be screaming out the window, 'I told the dopey bastard not to go.' You were right. I was wrong. Consider yourself entitled to one giant 'I told you so', okay?

I don't mind eating crow, so long as you learn something from it. And so long as you stick by me the way you said you would. Remember, Jimmy?

Now to finally get to why I'm writing. I need your services. Cause I have something to confess. I could probably track a priest down, but it wouldn't be the same. Penance is quite cheap here. 'Father, I just wiped out a village full of women, children and old people.' 'Yes, my son, say three Hail Marys and make a good act of contrition.' I want to talk to someone who still knows what's going on in the real world, who's got a little perspective left.

You remember how I told you about my old buddy Jake Derrick? Well, I haven't been able to put what that prick said to me out of my mind. Don't start yelling again. I just couldn't do it.

So on this R&R, well, all the guys decide that they're gonna go get laid. And they say, 'Hey, Mike, how's about you?' And I shook my head and said no, guys, I'm not terribly interested. Anyhow, we're still boozin' and doing one thing or another in Saigon, and they're all arguing over which whorehouse is the best and where they should go. And they keep after me saying 'What's the matter, Mike? Ain't you ever had any? Better get your rocks off before Charlie blows them off for you.' To make a long story short, I finally said I'd go.

So I went. It was hardly a sacramental experience. I got taken into this tiny room with a bed, nothing else. And there's this little girl there in a negligee. I mean, she was covered with lipstick and makeup and eye gunk, so she would look grown up. But I could tell she was maybe thirteen at best. Anyhow, she undressed me, sucked me and fucked me like a real pro. She was moaning and groaning like she was having the time of her life. And all the time I knew it was an act. She hated my Yankee guts, my Yankee skin, even the Yankee money she did it for.

I did too. I hated myself. I hated her and all her lousy yellow people. I hated the way I pushed myself into it. And I hated the way I pretended to enjoy it.

I've thought it over a lot. It was a very serious sin. Not the part about finally getting my gun off. That wasn't so bad. But the pretense. Cheating on yourself by trying to prove something to someone else. That was the big sin, the unforgivable one. And I didn't prove a thing.

Both of us pretended to be something we weren't. That was the real loss of virtue. She was a little girl pretending to be a whore. I was an altar boy trying to be a whoring soldier.

God always fixes you. And He's devised an extra special punishment for that sin of pretense. You see, the sinners become precisely what they pretended to be. She is a whore now. I am a soldier, a whore myself. Instead of screwing for money, I'm supposed to kill for it.

It's the truth. God forgive me, it's a fact. I'm one of the gang now, heart and soul. I don't think there's any turning back.

Take care of yourself, Jimmy. Do a little work up there, so you don't get yourself drafted if you don't have to. And don't freeze your tail off either.

You be good to that Maureen too. You're lucky. I always had the feeling God was trying extra hard to watch out for you. Don't make His job any more difficult than it already is.

And if you get a chance, say a prayer for me. You know, now and at the hour...

Love,
Michael

An hour later, James was still sitting in the easy chair, staring at the crinkly pages. He'd gotten so involved in college life that he'd lost track of his best friend. *What has he gotten himself into?*

"Little chilly, Jimbo?"

"Huh?" James looked up to see Bimba standing there.

"You got your coat on. I'd expect to see you in your underwear when you get a letter from your sweetie."

"Oh, this isn't from her. It's from a buddy of mine." Needing to change the subject, he added, "How much did you soak the sophomore for? It looked like you had him all hot and bothered."

Bimba laughed. "I got all ten dollars he had. Plus another interesting little item he happened to be carrying." He reached into his pea jacket pocket and pulled out a baggie filled with greenish-looking fiber.

"What the hell's that?"

"You know what it is. The evil weed. Wacky tobaccy."

"He gave you that?"

"It was all he had. Ever have it?"

James shook his head.

"It won't do you any harm. I bet you'd like it. Wanna try some, in the comfort of our little home here?" Bimba pulled out a package of papers.

James folded Michael's letter with care and slipped it into his breast pocket. "Sure, why not?"

*

The outlaw sound of The Jefferson Airplane roaring through the oversize speakers rattled the frayed dorm room on the fourth floor of Pope Hall. The resident *Volunteers of America* were instructed loudly as to the mostly criminal behavior they needed to engage in to get by. James was sitting on an overstuffed couch, next to a fraternity brother.

"Take a hit of this stuff, Devlin. It'll pop your cork for sure," Smegma shouted, passing a freshly rolled joint over to him.

James shook his head. "I must be immune to that garbage, no effect whatsoever. Besides, I got basketball practice in half an hour."

"Tell you what, if you don't get off this time, I'll buy you a six-pack of your choice."

"Okay, Smegs. You're on. And make it Miller, okay?"

"You won't be needing any beer when we finish this, Baby Cakes."

James took a hearty pull. The sweet smoke filled his nose and lungs. He wanted to cough but held his breath, forcing the smoke to remain inside him as long as he dared before exhaling slowly.

Smegma laughed. "You looked like a veteran freak on that one, Devlin." He kicked his legs up on the lobster pot that served as a makeshift coffee table. He held the tiny roach with his fingernails and sucked it into oblivion. This semester he was doing theosophy for credit. No shit, he said, explaining his new endeavor to James.

"Sounds like religion to me," James said.

"It would. You Irish Catholics are all alike. One-dimensional."

"Screw you. You're multi-dimensional. Height. Width. Depth. Filth."

"You're just an inhibited, uptight white boy, Devlin." He then went into a dissertation on the distinctions between theosophy and formal religion.

James listened without interest until he glanced at his watch. "Gotta run, Smegs. It's been real."

"Where do you think you're going?"

"Hoop practice."

"You're not going to be able to practice."

James laughed as he pulled on his knit cap. "Sure I can. Practice wouldn't be the same without me to stir up a little action."

"I'm warning you, Devlin—"

"Just have the beer at the house by dinner. I'm bound to be thirsty," James said as he stepped out the door.

The floorboards groaned as he walked down the hallway toward the staircase. Pope was the only dorm on campus that had never been refurbished. James paused at the window adjoining the landing and saw that it was snowing again. The flakes looked huge, with snowy fingers on each reaching out in every direction, trying to lock themselves with each other.

As he was watching, his legs started tingling, and he knew something was wrong. His legs weren't just heavy, they were being pulled downward, as though the force of gravity had gone berserk and decided to pull him right through the floor. He felt as helpless as a tin soldier drawn within the field of a magnet.

James tried to walk, but his legs wouldn't budge. He finally resorted to lifting them off the floor with both hands. By pushing one leg forward at a time, he inched back down the hall and banged on Smegma's door.

Smegma laughed when he saw James's panicked expression. "If it isn't Chip Hilton, sports star. I thought you went off to basketball practice, Chipper" He then explained that James was experiencing a body rush and offered him a can of Coke that had been chilling in the snow on the windowsill.

James drank the soda greedily. If the last half of the can hadn't been frozen, he would've gulped it all down right away. When the straining sensation on his legs began to subside, he stood up and said, "I'm going to my room. To sleep. I'm worthless as it is."

He crept back up the hallway and lowered himself down the four flights of stairs, clutching the banister with both hands. He shuffled the few yards between Pope and Haldane Halls, making his way up the one flight of stairs to his room. He dropped his jacket on the floor and threw himself on the bed, falling asleep immediately.

"You in there, Devlin?"

Banging sounds on his door woke him. He wasn't sure how long he'd been asleep.

"Your mother's on the phone!"

He sat up, seeing it was five o'clock. He hadn't been asleep for more than an hour. He staggered to the door, confused. His mother always waited for his collect call on Sundays.

"Thanks, Wes," he said, taking the receiver from Westbrook, his eyes cringing from the bright hallway light. "Hello," he muttered.

Muffled noises came from the end of the line.

"Ma? What's the matter?"

He heard the intake of breath. "It's your friend, Jimmy. Michael. Michael...he got killed, Jimmy."

It felt as though all the blood was flushing from his head. James grabbed onto the wall phone, struggling to remain upright. He started pleading. "Oh, Ma. No. Not that, Ma! Not Michael!" Tears streamed down his face. When he could get the words out, he said, "How did it happen?"

"One of those land mines."

The dirty yellow bastards blew Mike apart.

"The wake's tomorrow. The funeral the day after."

He promised to be there before hanging up, and then walked back to his room. He closed the door, leaning up against it. He began to wail—for what he had done, for what he had failed to do, while Michael was busy dying.

*

The next morning James hitched rides from Brunswick. Each driver sped faster than the one before. The Filipino with the giant spongy dice on the rearview mirror. The service man who stopped every few miles to empty a can of oil from the case resting on the rear seat into his smoldering Rambler engine. The self-proclaimed "narc" in the souped-up Camaro, who kept lecturing him not to get dirty with drugs.

Finally, he was walking numbly toward the Imperial and his rendezvous with the others. His suit was tight on him, the pointy shoes next to useless on the rippling layer of ice that covered the sidewalk. He'd planned to have a few drinks with the guys beforehand, but then, as he was passing the funeral home, he changed his mind. Viewing hours weren't until seven. Maybe if he checked it out now, it wouldn't be so bad coming back later with the others.

He walked into the entrance. The attendant wasn't on duty in the foyer. Michael was laid out in the large parlor on the left, according to the directory. With some hesitation, he went into the room. There was no one there. Not even a soldier standing at guard. There was only a large bronze coffin in the center of the room. Its lid was closed. Automatically, James approached it and dropped down on the cushioned kneeler. With both hands he reached out for the box. He ran his fingers over its smooth surface. He'd anticipated the closed coffin. There was something missing, though. That's when it occurred to him. Where was the flag?

He'd pictured the flag draped over the coffin. Bad enough that you had to take it on faith that Michael was really in there. At least the flag would provide scant identification of the deceased. He shivered as he tried to put the question out of his mind.

Say a prayer. Say a prayer for Michael. He remembered Michael's letter. A Hail Mary would have to do. Mike wouldn't mind.

Once he finished, he rose, and turned around. He wasn't alone. Mary Cassidy, dressed all in black, stood in front of the sofa reserved for the family. He couldn't escape her gaze.

She did not look like the same woman he had seen so many times in the sacristy. Her gray hair was not pulled back high in a bun, as usual. She wore it loose, down to her shoulders, like a young girl. It threw James off balance. He had never noticed that Mrs. Cassidy had long hair before. He had never really noticed anything physical about her. Not her well-proportioned figure. Nor her long, shapely legs, now covered with black stockings. It struck him as wicked to be assessing his friend's mother's looks. Particularly at her son's wake.

Yet he did. This fireman's wife could have passed for a high-society lady. She was a beautiful woman, he could tell. For truly beautiful women never lose it. Age, sorrow, even death itself cannot fully destroy their beauty. Mary's face was drawn. Her eyes were so red, they had lost all white. Yet the grace and presence which the woman had passed to her youngest son remained intact, despite Michael's death.

"I knew you would come, Jimmy," she whispered.

James did not know what to do. He was unable to move closer, to touch her. For a long time he had been incapable of the casual kissing and embracing greetings that others exchanged. A kiss or hug had come to signify more for him. It was always a prelude to something further. Affection was not lightly dispensed. It might be taken the wrong way. He stood his ground, hands in his raincoat pockets.

"I don't know what to say, Mrs. C.," he murmured. He cursed himself for failing to master the innumerable expressions of sympathy an accomplished Irish mourner would have had at his disposal. His face began to burn with the shame of the inarticulate.

"There's nothing to say, Jimmy. Nothing at all." She motioned to the sofa. "Come over and sit down." She made the gesture as easily as if she stood in her own living room. As if James had called for Michael and she had told him to wait a minute, her son would be right downstairs.

James nodded and did as he was told. His lower lip began to tremble. He bit it so he would not cry again. So he would not look at Mary Cassidy's crossed legs again.

"All my boys went to the diner with their father," Mrs. Cassidy explained. "Except Michael, of course," she smiled. "I wouldn't go with them. I didn't want to leave Michael alone."

James again nodded politely. The measured tone of her words, the matter-of-fact air were grossly out of sync with her surroundings. She was on the verge of madness.

"But they tell me I will have to leave him alone soon. Later tonight. Then tomorrow for good."

"I suppose they're right, Mrs. C."

"But you know how I feel, don't you, Jimmy? You loved Michael too. Didn't you, Jimmy?"

James swallowed hard. His head was pounding so hard he feared it would burst. "Yes, ma'am. I loved Michael very much. Everyone loved him."

Mrs. Cassidy smiled. "And he loved you, Jimmy. Most of all. He used to talk about you all the time. How smart you were, and how you could play ball too, and were a regular guy. Oh how he loved you, Jimmy!"

James remembered how Michael closed his letter. He had been able to gloss over the fact that it was not the nuns' familiar complimentary closing: "Your friend, Michael." Maybe it had meant more.

"My Michael wasn't so smart," she continued. "He had the hardest time learning how to read. It never mattered to me. I used to tell him his eyes were different from everyone else's. They were, too. Green. And something else. He only saw the good things. Never the bad."

Then her voice began to harden. "Now they're going to put my Michael in a hole in the ground tomorrow."

James couldn't speak. His entire body was quaking as he sat beside Michael's mother.

"I had them close the coffin. I gave them a perfect baby boy. And they killed him on me. And sent him back in pieces."

James sputtered, "I know."

"First they tattooed him. Then they destroyed him. Did you know he'd done that?"

James shook his head.

"It was a fish. An outline of a fish on his arm. A stupid deliberate defacement of his own body, a temple of the Holy Ghost."

A fish. That was Michael, all right. Mr. Christian, even in a tattoo parlor. James wanted to tell her about the Ichthys, to explain that the tattoo wasn't what it seemed. Michael bore the mark of the faithful, a visible sign of his belief that comrade and enemy alike would no doubt overlook. For all her piety, the Rosary Altar lady had missed her son's hidden message. Someday he would explain it to her. Not now, though. It wouldn't matter to her just now.

"Nobody's seeing my baby like that." Her face twisted in unspeakable grief. "Let them remember him the way he was. There'll be none of that military pomp. They were all here before, those soldiers. I asked them to leave. I'll have no part of them standing watch. My Michael was no soldier. He was a good boy.

"And there'll be no flag either. Let him be buried in a plain casket, just like any good Catholic. He was still a baby, taken before his time. I don't need any red, white and blue souvenir of my boy's death."

Voices came from out in the hall. Mrs. Cassidy rose and James did as well. She walked over to the coat rack and pulled something off the shelf. She then walked back to James, thrusting a neatly folded flag into his hands. "You'll be needing it yourself before you know it. They won't be satisfied until they've killed you all."

Numb, James took the triangular cloth and tucked it under his arm. He then rushed out the exit.

*

Despite his dress clothes, James scrambled up the railing and over the pointy wrought iron fence with the flag still under his arm. The checker tables were empty, the handball courts silent as he headed up the slippery ramp to the basketball court. A full moon, low in the sky, cast a watchful eye on the surface where they'd played so often. He sat facing the court, on the park bench where they'd all sweated on summer evenings. He wanted to be warm again. He wanted to sweat, just like he had, just one more time. He unwrapped the flag and draped it over himself.

He couldn't help but think of Michael's last few hours. He'd never really know what had happened – certainly not the Army's bullshit, vaguely heroic version of Mike's death. James was convinced that the dream he had last night was a far more accurate account of what went down.

Michael stared out the open door of the large chopper, listening to the one noise that made him feel at home: the whirring and burping of its blades, a distinctly American sound in a land filled with strange noises.

The copter began its descent into a field of tall, beckoning reeds. Michael's unit was being dropped a mile or so outside some village, and he followed the other members out the door.   He pulled his bush hat down a little further to shade his eyes from the late afternoon sun after he jumped down among the waist-deep rushes, then double-timed behind the others toward a line of trees. The helicopter lifted off, leaving behind a dozen jumpy guys carrying automatic weapons, each of whom, like Michael, had a twisted story of circumstances that brought him to that foreign place that evening.

The unit huddled under the scraggly trees. Their new lieutenant looked very inexperienced. Sweat was beginning to soak through his long-sleeve shirt as he studied a map. The shirts of Michael and the others standing by had been stripped of sleeves, collars, and buttons, and seemed little more than vests.

When the lieutenant gestured at Michael, he moved off down the trail at the point, the others following behind. When they reached a place where the trail widened ahead, Michael motioned behind to stop the procession, then crept forward far enough to see out into the clearing.

He saw what looked like the ruins of a temple. Standing in front of it was a young girl. She had a switch in her hand and was tending an ox. The scene looked very traditional, very Vietnamese. The only thing wrong was that the girl had a t-shirt and pair of short-shorts on. The outfit looked like it came from E.J. Korvettes. Michael watched for a moment. She appeared to be waiting for someone. After several seconds, he spun and returned to the others. He spoke to the lieutenant, and they headed back together toward the girl.

She met them halfway. The lieutenant's choppy attempts at speaking in her native tongue were unnecessary. The girl spoke English quite clearly.

As the lieutenant questioned her, Michael kept staring at her face. She looked about thirteen years old. Like all dreams, no matter how illogical, the silent narrator's explanation of the scene controlled. James knew this girl in his dream could not be the whore Michael had been with in Saigon, but he had to accept that she was.

The girl was laughing and smiling at the lieutenant. She pointed to the other side of the clearing. There were openings for two trails. The one on the left was wide like the trail they had just followed. The other was much narrower. It looked far less traveled. She pointed to the right.

"Quickest way to village, on your right. On your right," she assured them. The lieutenant thanked her. He and Michael returned to the unit.

James had watched Michael arguing with the lieutenant, pointing repeatedly to the left. When the lieutenant grabbed him by the arm, Michael stopped speaking, and lowered his head, "Don't do it, Mike, you know she's lying to him!", James wanted to yell, but he knew he had to remain silent and let the dream unfold, whatever way it was meant to be. The column moved forward again. Across the clearing. Into the small opening for the trail on the right.

The first fifty yards were fairly smooth going. From there on, the narrow footpath began to telescope, and became impassable ahead. Michael looked flustered, afraid to tell the lieutenant he had been tricked. Another soldier stepped up to help him try to push through the vines blocking their path. Together they hacked away at the growth with their knives, tunneling a passageway so those who followed could slide through a bit further.

It was so pronounced: a metallic click, completely out of place in a rain forest. Then Michael's flinch, complete before the explosion.

James had watched Michael lying on his back on the jungle floor, dismantled from the waist down. There was gunfire and screaming all about him. Yet he was silent, as though none of the confusion had anything to do with him anymore. Only his eyes moved, rapidly, like he was watching the end of a movie.

James had even been certain he knew what his friend had seen in his final moments. Michael would have imagined himself out of that hell hole and back where he wanted to be: at the park, midcourt at the showcase upper level. James still watched as the scene shifted, and his friend gave the ball three hard dribbles, their secret signal to hit the boards. Michael was taking it to the hole.

A quick stutter left, and Michael had a first step on the defender as he broke sharply right into the open lane. Someone was switching off, trying desperately to pick him up. It wasn't Coney or any of the guys.

It wasn't a guy at all. It was the girl. That same gook whore, in the real world this time. The gleam in her eye, the smiling teeth warned him. She would not be satisfied with a hack. She'd submarine Mike for sure.

Muscles rippling, Michael left the ground with the ball locked in both hands. As he soared toward the basket, he tomahawked the sphere back between his shoulder blades, then slammed it through the orange rim with a sudden twist as his forearms hit it, rocking the entire backboard, which in turn shook the chain link fence to which it was fastened.

James shivered, tears streaming down his face, realizing he was alone in the park, not actually watching his friend.

Sure, there was a war going on, and James had known that a lot of guys had to get killed. He had selfishly rooted for someone else's friend to die, not his, but Michael had been picked instead. It still didn't feel like this could have really happened. Maybe it was all one big bad dream, and things would go back the way they were, with Michael still far away but okay.

James knew better. The wind was blowing the flimsy fabric of the flag off his legs, pushing it into his face. He then stared across the illuminated court. It was frozen solid. He rose from the bench, the flag wrapped around his hands like a star-spangled muff. As he approached the key, he recognized something in the icy surface.

He went to the foul line and surveyed the area under the basket. The ice was covered with thousands of sneaker prints. He spun around. It was the same up and down the court, as though the guys had been playing full court in the slush when God had gone to the stop-action camera. He'd removed all the players from the frozen frame, leaving only their innumerable crossing and overlapping tracks to mark the paths they'd taken.

James wiped his nose with his flag-covered hands. The gusts of wind seemed to repeat his name through the chain link fence. He remembered where most of his friends' footsteps were actually headed tonight. He thought once more of the friend they'd be unable to see.

Michael had been wrong. He was no whore. It was just that he'd been surrounded by whores so long, they finally convinced him he was one, too. Jake Derrick and the whores at Dunhill who turned him from point guard to point man. The ones in the service, like the ignorant lieutenant who got him killed. The ones at home, the real whores -- like himself -- who were pros at ducking and dodging, so accomplished at slipping away from the truth.

We'll always go on living. Nothing fazes us, not even knowing that somehow deep inside we were glad we let Michael be destroyed. We really wanted his type of innocence blotted off the face of the earth. We just couldn't stand to look at it any longer, and stomach how pitiful we were by comparison.

Michael was the best. It hadn't mattered. He'd lost. Everything.

James knelt down on the ice at the top of the key. Of all the geometrical shapes overlaid on the large rectangle forming the court, that semicircle was easily his favorite spot. It had been almost sacred, the place in the world where he felt most together, nearly invincible, so that he was always surprised when his shot from inside it missed instead of dropping.

James spread the flag across the foul line. It stretched exactly from one end to the other, as if cut to fit, the edge with the stars touching one lane line, the stripes adjoining the other. He reached into his pocket and removed a book of matches he kept handy, just in case he had to light up. He struck one and ignited a corner of the flag. The fire caught without coaxing. The smell was strong, but James couldn't recognize it. It wasn't incense. Maybe it was patriotism, going up in smoke. Or belief in God. Something like that.

After a few short bursts of flame, the flag was obliterated. The transparent footprints it had concealed were gone.

*

"Noo Yawka, phone!"

James ran to the phone. "Thanks, Moosehead." He took the receiver. "Hello?"

"Jimmy, it's me, Nora."

"How you doing, sis?'

"Okay, I can't talk long. I'm at a business dinner, but I've been trying to get a hold of you. I guess those chowderhead friends of yours don't give messages."

"Not really," James said, hearing the click of a lighter over the phone and his sister's intake of breath. He could almost smell the cigarette smoke.

"Anyway, sorry about your friend Michael."

James cleared his throat, paused, and said, "Yeah, me too. The wake was awful, the funeral even worse." He needed to change the subject. "Business dinner?" James was impressed.

"Yes, my boss knows everyone and she loves me. Says I have 'spunk', and hired me even though I can't type fast. We're having dinner with Richard Aronson."

"Who's that?"

"A very well-known screenwriter."

"Oh," James replied. "I never really knew what those guys do."

"You'd better stay in Maine with the other bumpkins, Jimmy. Screenwriters are the most important people in Hollywood. They're the magicians who take a book no one wants to read and turn it into a movie everyone wants to see." She paused, then added, "But I've got to get back in there. We're negotiating our commission renewal and Josie, my boss, is pretty sure Richard has a thing for me. Every little edge, you know?" She laughed. "You should see what he's wearing, a purple Hawaiian shirt and orange Madras shorts. We're in this fancy restaurant in Santa Monica on the beach with a spectacular view of the ocean and you wouldn't believe the looks he's getting."

James laughed. He wasn't used to Nora being so chatty.

"Anyway, I hope you realize that getting killed was Michael's own stupid fault."

"What did you say?"

"I mean, what was he thinking? He volunteered to die. Everybody else was smarter than that. Even Billy Elsen knew enough to sign up for the Navy when he couldn't stall the Draft Board any longer."

His sister's words stunned him.

"You still there, Jimmy?"

After several moments, he replied, "I'm here."

"The point is, I wanted to warn you not to do anything stupid yourself, no matter what Dad thinks or says. He doesn't know what he's talking about. And Michael was a dope who had no idea of what he was doing. But, listen, I gotta run. Stay out of trouble."

James stood there for a moment, holding the phone to his ear, even after hearing the click on the other end.

*

It had been a week since James had seen Maureen. She'd talked a Ladycliff friend into driving her down to Michael's funeral, and then they dropped James off at LaGuardia right after the Mass. There was no way James was going to the cemetery after the heartbreaking service, and he had accepted his mother's offer of paying for his one-way flight to Portland so he'd be back in time for class the next day.

When James got out of the car at the airport. Maureen climbed out too, grabbing him by the sleeve as he'd bent down to kiss her goodbye.

"I'm worried about you," she said.

James gazed at her with red eyes.

"I'm coming up to Brunswick next week when Ladycliff's on spring break,"

James raised an eyebrow. "Oh, really? How are you going to talk your father into that?"

"I'm going to tell him the truth. I have an art history paper due after the break and Brunswick has one of the best art museums in New England."

He smiled. "Is that so? Somehow I haven't found my way there, yet."

"That's no surprise. But it's true."

That had been the whole conversation. Now, he was standing on Pleasant Street as the Greyhound bus pulled in, his Bean boots covered by slush. A few passengers came down the steps, then he saw her. She was wearing a white ski jacket and blue knit hat, her blond hair peeking out. She was carrying a small red Samsonite suitcase that bounced against her navy corduroy slacks.

"Welcome to what's left of the Winter Wonderland," James said, taking her luggage from her and leading the way back to the college.

No one was in sight on the second floor of Haldane Hall when James opened the door to their room, which Bimba agreed to vacate after a suggestive chuckle.

"This is it. The den of inequity," James announced.

"You two are spoiled rotten!" Maureen took off her jacket. "Look at all this space."

"Oh, yeah. Brunswick treats its scholars well. You get to share a living room and a bedroom." He grabbed her around her waist, leading her to the bedroom. He closed the door behind them. They lay down on his bed and he began kissing her, removing one piece of clothing at a time.

They took turns touching each other. Innocent. Embarrassed. Yet curious. Exploring. Trying to convey with fingertips a message their lips would tremble to utter.

"I love you, Maureen," James whispered in her ear. "I loved your first," she responded. "I love you more," he replied to her challenge.

At some point, they dozed off. When James awoke, Maureen looked so peaceful that he just let her sleep. He went into the living room, turned on the desk lamp, and read his government assignment, an excerpt of the Federalist Papers.

A short time later, he looked up to see Maureen standing there in Bimba's white terrycloth robe. "My Grannie would say that's swimming on you," James said.

"Not too fashionable, but cozy."

"Hopefully Bimba washes it now and then. It's his."

Maureen scowled, sniffed it and seemed to find it agreeable. She sat down across from James. "So, how are you doing?"

"Better now that you're here. I never believed it would happen."

"Are you getting over last week?"

"I was. At least until yesterday. My sister called."

"What did she say?"

"You don't know Nora, but let's put it this way. She doesn't sugarcoat anything. She said that Michael was an idiot and it was his own dumb fault he got killed."

Maureen shook her head, her leg rocking up and down.

"I didn't say anything. She went on and on, telling me not to make the same dopey mistake. She thinks she's Howard Cosell, telling it like she decides it is."

Maureen lowered her head. "Do you think she's wrong?"

"I don't know. Sometimes I think I should've gone with him, instead of coming up here and forgetting all about him and all the others. It's just not as simple as she makes it out to be. Maybe it's not about who's smart and who's stupid. Maybe it's about who's brave and who's chicken."

"But, Jimmy," Maureen said, her voice pleading, "you're the one who told him not to go. You're the one who said his reason was all wrong."

"But don't you see, Maureen? It's not just his problem. It's our problem. Everybody's. But we're just picking on a few guys to go take care of it. I mean, this is some neat arrangement. If you're a good boy, mind your business, do well in school, why they just defer you and defer you until you get married or too old, or start making too much money to send you off. But if you get in hot water, you're gone. You flunk out of school, then you're worthless and you're gone. Cannon fodder. Pretty fair, huh?"

"No, Jimmy, that wasn't fair. But now they have a lottery that's fair but sick. And that's the new way it works. You won't change things a bit if you go in on your own. You'll only be making a martyr out of yourself." Her eyes glistened, tiny beads bubbling on her nose. "I think I know you, and that's not who you are. You're not meant to be killing other people. Neither was Michael." She reached for his hand. "But tell me the truth, Jimmy, do you want to go? Because if you do, if it's something you have to find out about, you'll go sooner or later. And there's not a thing I can do to stop you."

James stared at the carpet, listening to Maureen cry. He whispered, "I always thought I would go in a minute if I knew I'd come back okay. But you don't get those guarantees. What I really wanted to be was the invisible soldier. Some guy who walked around not doing anything, not hurting anyone, but watching things, finding out what's really happening.

"But now, even that nonsense doesn't appeal to me. I don't want to leave you." He chuckled wryly. "You're the first person I ever admitted this to, Mo, but I think I'm the biggest coward who ever walked the face of the earth. Fighting's always made me sick to my stomach. But you can't let on to people you feel that way. When a fight breaks out in the locker room, like it always does, you've got to be in the thick of it. If one of your friends is dumb enough to start with the Bell Boulevard Boys, you've got to jump in. If Kazootie has a problem with somebody in the parking lot, you have to get involved, at least to make sure it's a fair fight."

Maureen looked up at him. "And following Michael over to Vietnam's the same thing? Just like rumbling in some parking lot, even though you don't want to?"

James's face burned. "I'm not doing a very good job explaining myself. My point is that you just don't tell people the truth about something like that. People don't understand that you don't want to be John Wayne, okay?"

Maureen nodded, hesitating before she asked, "Are there any other things you don't tell people the truth about?"

James felt that familiar warm sensation. "I suppose so."

"Like what?" Maureen asked gently.

He wasn't about to tell her everything. Especially what he and Bimba and his other dope-fiend friends were up to. "Like I cry. That's right, like you. I try to keep that to myself. I think it's hereditary, anyway, something to do with the genes in your eyes. But I can't even stand to watch an animal die on television, or see a squirrel squished by the side of a road."

"Anything else?"

He hesitated, paused, cleared his throat. "Yeah, I guess I try to talk rough on purpose. Cursing, lousy grammar, stuff like that. I had a teacher who once said I hated the thought of being smart. I know better, but I try to talk like everyone else. I guess it's my way of trying to keep them from noticing anything different."

"Jimmy, I think that if you know what's right, and I believe you do, you just have to go ahead and do it regardless of what anyone else thinks."

James listened carefully.

"That goes for the service, too. You said Michael went in for the wrong reason. That may be, but at least he had his own reason for going. If you went in now, you couldn't even say that. Your reason wouldn't even be that someone else wanted you to go in. It would be that *maybe* someone else wanted you to go in, and I doubt that's true."

James wanted to kiss each of Maureen's tears away, but he didn't interrupt her.

"I know that I want you to stay out. Promise me you won't go unless they make you. As long as you make them draft you, I won't complain. They won't even pull your lottery number until the summer after next. Maybe you'll be the lucky one. Maybe it will go away in the meantime."

*

Maureen spent the night in his bed, across from Bimba's empty one. James knew the rules and hadn't tried to break them. Heavy petting, the perpetually undefined activity blessed by Ann Landers and her equally omniscient sister, was okay; hanky panky was not.

The following morning, while James headed to class, Maureen went to the art museum. They met for lunch in the DT dining room. James could tell his freshman brothers all liked her. Once they finished eating, they got up and James asked Maureen about her morning at the museum.

"That place is such a surprise. It's filled with Gilbert Stuart paintings. There's quite a few by Winslow Homer, too. I think you'd like those."

James nodded absently. "What time do you have to leave?"

"I told my father I'd be on the four o'clock bus. He said it wouldn't take me more than a day to repaint everything in Brunswick's art collection. He was wrong, but he and my mom are expecting me back tonight."

"Got it." James looked down toward the ground, then back at Maureen. "Tell you what. I have a government class at two. Would you like to come? The prof's hot stuff. It only runs an hour. We'll have plenty of time to pick up your stuff from the room and get to the bus depot before four."

"Sounds good to me."

Professor Eden was a crusty old Brunswick graduate himself. With a thick Maine accent, he could even make a discussion of the Founding Fathers' checks and balances interesting. After James had submitted his first paper, Eden called him into his office to tell him what a fine job he'd done. When the class met once a week in small groups to discuss the assigned readings, Eden constantly probed James for his opinions, refusing to let the student slip into the background. The professor's performance that afternoon did not disappoint. When he'd finished, he left the podium and headed toward James and Maureen.

"So, Devlin, how'd you manage to get weekday company up to Brunswick?"

James smiled and introduced his girlfriend, adding, "Came all the way from Ladycliff College."

Professor Eden bowed and extended his hand toward her. "Is that a DT pin you're wearing?"

Maureen nodded. "Jimmy gave it to me last night."

"Engaged to be engaged to a DT? I think you have a tiger by the tail, young lady. You think he's got it, is that so?"

Both Maureen and James were blushing. "I think so, Professor," she said quietly.

Professor Eden's gap-toothed grin broke the tension. "Well, I think so too. He does have it, but doesn't know what to do with it, yet. Maybe you can help him figure that out. I can see him arguing cases in some New York courtroom someday. How about that?"

"I can see that, too." Maureen smiled.

James cleared his throat, explaining that Maureen needed to catch a bus.

"Nice meeting you, young lady. Greater love hath no woman than to ride the 'Hound from Brunswick to New York!" He looked at James. "And be sure to give my regards to all my friends at the DT house tonight, Devlin."

Later, while waiting for the bus, Maureen said, "What do you think, Jimmy? Your professor thinks you could be a lawyer. Would you like that?"

James gazed at her. "I never really thought about it. I figured I'd get some kind of job when I got out of Brunswick. You know, go into business, like my father."

"You could be a lawyer, Jimmy, if you wanted to. I think you'd make a good one."

"Let me think about that," he said, remembering Mr. O'Reilly and that whole bad scene.

When the bus arrived, they kissed goodbye and she got on board. It started to sleet, but he watched until the Greyhound was out of sight. He then walked back up Maine Street, keeping his head down. He decided he'd write to Maureen as soon as he got back to his room.

*

The mood in the DT dining hall was somber. There was trouble. Serious trouble. It had started the previous Thursday, April 30, 1970. Nixon had announced the invasion of Cambodia. The rhetoric was the same: Don't misunderstand. This is just like the reduced draft calls. Just another measure to bring all our boys home sooner. To "secure peace with honor."

Even the densest DT knew better. Cambodia meant escalation. The shit was about to hit the fan.

The last thing the brothers needed was an addition to their list of worries. Spring exams were just around the corner. They were far more dreaded than the first semester ordeals. At least the weather was an ally in January—frigid winds confined the students indoors, the cold limiting the distractions and promoting study.

Springtime was different. The change in weather that had hit Brunswick over the weekend was so drastic it took the students' breath away. But despite the spring fever, despite concerns about the war and exams, the brothers remained calm. The volleyball net they'd strung across their front lawn was as protective as a barbed wire fence. Fluttering in the brilliant noon sunlight, it had blocked all but the most determined students from the library that waited beyond—and had similarly dissuaded all but the staunchest radicals from venturing on campus toward the sparsely attended war protest that the Brunswick Students for a Democratic Society were staging in front of the student union.

The net was like a picket line the DTs refused to cross. The volleyball game had begun after lunch. Shirts and shoes came off. Beer and grass materialized. Players switched and were added to sides. No one kept score. The contest always continued, played to the music of the campus radio station that blared out an open upstairs window.

The bulletin had been repeated several times before anyone grasped its significance: *Students shot at Kent State University.*

James wondered, *where the hell is that?*

Undetermined number dead. Others injured.

"Are you shitting me?" someone said.

National Guardsmen have fired on a crowd protesting the Cambodian invasion...

"Unfucking real!"

All bets were suddenly off. The bravado rock lyrics had come to pass. Students fighting and dying in the streets had become a reality. The gentlemen's agreement that had humanely limited a protester's exposure—a whiff of tear gas, a boot in the ass, at worst maybe a crack in the head with a billy club—had been irreparably broken.

The Brunswick grapevine went into action. Roadrunners were moving through fraternities and dormitories like overalled Paul Reveres. They passed the word. Student rally. Seven thirty. Tonight. At the Union.

The boys crowded into the tube room to see what Cronkite had to say. They watched, astonished. The chaos. The screaming. The diving on the ground or behind parked cars for cover. The senseless deaths in a parking lot of students indistinguishable from themselves.

Someone in the front row stood up and turned off Eric Sevareid in the middle of his even-toned commentary.

They were through listening. The war had gotten out of hand. It no longer had the courtesy to remain oceans away. It had come home. Killing students was far different from killing gooks or even soldiers. This war had to be stopped now.

Shortly after, James pushed into the Union lounge, along with the entire student body. Some were standing on tables or chairs to catch a glimpse of the speakers, leaders that came in all shapes and sizes, freaked out as could be and straight arrows alike. Their message was the same: students across the country would have to bring the government to its knees. They would demand an open meeting of the college community. They would close Brunswick down as part of a nationwide student strike.

The leaders made good on their promise. The students and faculty assembled the following evening in the gymnasium, observing the finest academic tradition. A token debate regarding the appropriate course of action for the college to take was staged. A thickly accented professor reminded the students that "never before had so many paid so much to learn so little." The response was given by a wise-cracking upperclassman. The slight young man had the confidence of a lawyer arguing to a jury he knows has been rigged in his client's favor. Cries of "Right on!" punctuated his plea to send out a message by shutting the college down. The decision to continue or cease classes was a foregone conclusion. The frustrated liberal professors were demanding some sort of statement to Nixon and his gang as loudly as the most desperate student flunking three out of four courses.

James sat among the DTs, silently observing the proceedings. He thought about the students at Kent State. The pictures had been vivid enough. Blood streaming out of the bodies onto the blacktop. Others writhing in pain. They'd been shot because they'd challenged authority. Maybe some hurt were unlucky bystanders, but the student leaders and active participants in the demonstration had defied those in command. They'd been ordered to disperse by the Guardsmen, but told them to screw themselves, so confident had they been of their student immunity. They'd been mistaken.

James thought of Michael, and realized he had been killed for an opposite reason. He died because he did what he was supposed to do and acted just like he thought society expected. Michael had followed orders. Michael had been mistaken, too.

You got one hell of a choice. You disobey, you die. You obey, you die. Symmetrical, but not very satisfying.

He swore he heard Michael laughing as the college president took the podium to supervise the strike vote.

You got to be shitting me, Devlin. Even I know that a strike's when a guy who's paying you to work ain't paying you enough, so you tell him you won't work anymore until he does. In the first place, you guys are paying those faculty guys to make you work. And now you're threatening to refuse to get what you paid for. You ever hear of the boss paying his workers in advance, then not letting them work because he's pissed off at someone else? That may be a bonus or an extra paid vacation for the faculty. But that's no strike. That's crazy bullshit!

James chuckled at the incisive Cassidy logic. He didn't vote for or against the strike when the president called for ayes or nays. The students' rhetoric had been like Beatles' music: it had a very convincing sound, but James was not certain what, if anything, it meant. They could close Brunswick down if they liked. That would hardly be a loss, in his opinion. But he had no interest in clamoring for a strike against classes. He couldn't see any connection between refusing to go to class and stopping the war. It was an idle gesture.

There was only one real way to strike against the war. It was simple, direct. Like Muhammad Ali, you just refused to go when they knocked on your door. You just hoped disobedience cost you less than obedience.

*

By Friday, May 8, 1970, the most strident promoters of the strike had vanished from campus. It was amazing. The more certain a student's assurances that he'd work on campus for the strike until the troops withdrew from Cambodia, the fewer hours he remained in town after passing grades were awarded across the board by the faculty.

James was still hanging around. The college had been closed on the premise that the students would remain in residence. That was the deal. He had stayed.

It had been an unusual week. Once classes stopped, a variety of worthwhile projects had been organized by faculty members opposed to the hostilities. James had attended an open-air seminar given by one prof tracing U.S. involvement in Vietnam. He picked trash off the side of the Old Brunswick Road with a group of students led by another faculty member. He'd cleared trails in the Brunswick town park with a third, outdoorsy professor.

The nights hadn't been bad either. Since many of their number had gone over the hill, the DTs were eating in style on their remaining kitchen funds. With professional hockey and basketball playoffs in progress, and the baseball season just underway, they weren't short of entertainment on the tube.

That Friday night, James was having a beer with other "strikers", watching the news. Cronkite, as usual, was full of good tidings. The highlight that evening was footage of New York City construction workers kicking the shit out of demonstrating students. The protesters had been stupid enough to march past a job site near quitting time. As policemen stood by wearing bemused grins, the hardhats continued their rampage down to City Hall. As a crowd of bystanders cheered, they raised the flag to full staff that had been lowered in memory of the Kent State students by "that limousine liberal Lindsay."

The phone rang from the DT telephone booth. Seconds later, someone shouted, "Devlin, for you!"

He answered with apprehension. It was his mother, but she wasn't crying. She said, "Your father told me to call you. We were watching the news..."

"Me, too," he said.

"He wants you to come home, Jim."

Home? "I can't. We're supposed to be working on programs we have going here. Supporting the strike. You know what I mean, Ma?"

"Not really."

"Well, the idea isn't just to stop going to classes. We're supposed to do something constructive. To educate ourselves, educate people about the war. About what's happening in this country."

"That's all very interesting, Jim. But your father wants you to come home."

James raised his voice. "If he feels so strongly about it, why didn't he call me?"

"Because I said I'd call. Because I didn't want you two thick donkeys screaming at each other over the phone."

"What would he be screaming at me?" James asked.

After some hesitation, his mother said, "He'd tell you he was sick and tired of supporting you up there while you and your no-good buddies screw off to your heart's content. If you're not going to class, get your ass back home. You could be working for Uncle Rory by Monday. There. Does that sound like what he'd say?"

"And what do you say?"

"It's not up to me."

"Why not? Are you his secretary? Or are you my mother, too?"

"Don't start with me, James. I'm warning you."

"Then what do you say about it?"

Peg paused. Her tone softened. "I say I miss you. And I say that things haven't been the same since you left. I think you should come home, too."

James listened, exhaled deeply.

"Are you still there?"

"I'll get my stuff together. I'll be home sometime tomorrow."

"Thank you, Jimmy. I'll tell your father. And I'll make something you like for dinner."

James walked up the Devlins' gravel driveway with his knapsack slung over his shoulder. He noticed his mother's Mustang wasn't in the driveway. He wiped has hand over the whiskers on his face and proceeded up the stoop. He walked in, smelling cigarette smoke. He walked through the house, finding his father on the porch off the living room. Dave was sitting in his spot on the sofa, a briefcase full of work lay open on the floor. The Yankee game was on. James said hello.

His father took off his glasses. He looked at James from head to toe. "You go on strike against shaves and haircuts, too?"

"Not permanently." James sat in the chair across the way. "Who's winning?"

"Yanks, two nothing."

"Who they playing?" James hadn't looked at the television.

Dave looked irritated. "What's the matter, you been too busy protesting to know who the Yanks are playing?"

"I can see we're off to a flying start."

Dave reached for his cigarettes off the coffee table. "You can save the smartass comments, pal. I've already heard more of your smartass generation and their remarks than I care to."

James let the knapsack fall to the floor. "Why don't you just say what's on your mind, Pop? Get it all out. I know you're dying to."

"I have plenty to say. I'm so fed up with the long-haired likes of you running this country down in front of the entire world. You're a disgrace. An embarrassment to your parents. To the whole country. You punks don't do anything. Now you won't even go to class. You're all so brilliant. You don't believe in anything. Except yourselves. How special and wonderful you arc. How precious your little chicken skins are."

"So that's what it's all about, huh? Why don't you tell the truth, Pop? You wouldn't care if we had hair down to our asses and bones through our noses, so long as we were willing to fight your stinking war."

"That's right". Dave coughed loudly, loosening phlegm, before continuing. "There's nothing worth fighting for to you gutless bastards. You're not willing to take your chances. Let your buddies go do the fighting and dying for you."

James bristled. "You talking about Michael?

"Yes, I'm talking about Michael. And all the rest of them. Frankie, too. They were real Americans. Not like you." Tears came to Dave's eyes "How can you march around and say we shouldn't be in Vietnam? That this is a stupid war? If you're right, your friends died for nothing."

In a low, measured voice, James said, "Maybe they did."

"I can't accept that," Dave spat. "I won't accept it. It's a necessary war." Dave's chest heaved up and down as he talked.

"You can accept that, right? If the government says so, then it's good enough for you, right? You don't have to think about it. Right? Just do what you're told. War's just like baseball. Just step up and take a swing when they reach your spot in the batting order."

"Exactly! And you know what? Sometimes it doesn't turn out real well, but at least you did your duty. That's what being a good citizen is all about."

James glared at his father. "Maybe that's what being a jackass is all about. Or a liar. Because I don't believe you never thought about it and never asked a question. You're smarter than that. I don't believe you never noticed it was all the guys like you from the Coronas and the farms in the country who wound up on the front lines during World War II. You didn't catch on to that? No one ever wondered how come all the rich guys, the Harvard and Yale guys, weren't getting their asses shot off? I suppose you all figured that was just a coincidence. Lucky for them, right? They set you up, Pop! You swallowed all that Hun and Yellow Peril shit whole."

"You don't know what you're talking about," Dave shouted. "You're all a bunch of cowards." He stood up.

"And you were all a bunch of naïve jerks. It wasn't all it was cracked up to be, was it? It ruined you all. The ones who got killed. The ones like you who don't know it's over. The pitiful ones like Uncle Rory who are still walking around thinking they're only half a man because they didn't get shot at like the rest of you."

James began to pace. "And Michael? God forgive me, he was a jerk, too." He shook his head. "You're so right. I am a coward." James fists were clenched at his sides. "The worst kind. Your buddy Nixon's got this swell lottery of his going full steam now. It's like life or death Vegas-style. They spin the wheel and bingo, some go to war, some go home for good. I'm such a chicken, I'll go if they call me because I'm even more scared of the other things they do to you if you won't go."

"What do you mean?"

"Prison! And I'm not running away to Canada either."

Dave studied his son while trying to catch his breath. "Why not? I thought you all did that."

"Not me. I got other plans. Plans for right here."

"What're you talking about?"

"Getting married. To Maureen Cullen. Remember her? As soon as I can, if she'll have me. And you can be sure she won't have me if I split to Canada."

"What about school?"

"I signed up for extra courses next year. No more basketball either. I'm getting out of Brunswick as soon as I can.'"

"Then what?"

James hesitated. "I want to go to law school. Some people think I'd make a good lawyer."

Dave smirked. "Maybe you would. You seem to enjoy an argument." He sat back in his chair, tamping a cigarette out of the pack. "How do you plan to finance that?"

"I was going to ask you to help when the time was right. I think my technique needs polishing." He smiled, the tension subsiding.

Dave laughed. "It's a little unorthodox."

James grew serious again. "Listen, Pop, I don't want to fight. There was a time when if you told me to stick my hand in fire, jump off a bridge, anything, I'd have done it. Without hesitation. Not because I thought I could do it, but just because you asked. Because it might make you happy."

Dave clicked his lighter shut and took a deep drag on his cigarette.

'I'm not like that anymore. Maybe you're disappointed, but I'm not ever going to enlist to fight over there. I finally realized there's not a damn thing I can do for Michael by trying to follow him. So forget it, okay? I'll take my chances in the lottery like everyone else. If I get some shitty low number and get drafted, so be it. I'll be there. But I'm making plans as though I'm gonna be around here a long time." He stopped, gazing at his father, waiting for a reply.

"I hear you, Jim," Dave said, snuffing out his unfinished cigarette. It wasn't clear what his nod signified. "I hear you."

XIV
October 1971

"IT'S NOT TURNING OUT LIKE I PLANNED."

"What?" Peg asked groggily. She'd fallen asleep with Fodor's Guide to Germany on her lap.

"Nothing. Just talking to myself," Dave replied.

"Aren't you watching the World Series? I heard they're playing it at night now."

"Nah. I'm sick of watching those Orioles. Probably going to win it again. It's been so long since the Yankees were in it. Now they're not even the best team in New York, much less the world."

Peg straightened up. "Then would you like to talk about our trip to Munich next summer? Maybe we could time it when they host the Olympics. Wasn't Jesse Owens one of your favorites?"

Dave took a deep drag on his cigarette, then rested it in the ashtray. "Yes. And Marty Glickman. He was one of the guys Hitler really screwed. But I don't want to talk about the trip tonight."

Peg rose slowly from the easy chair. "I think I'll head up to bed then. Are you coming along?"

It wasn't a question so much as an invitation. She was attempting to get him to try again. It had only happened once and she hadn't made a big deal out of it. But he had.

"Not tired," Dave replied. "Maybe I'll put on some records for a while. I'll keep them low."

"Okay. Please don't stay up too late. You look like you need some rest."

He didn't reply, but watched Peg walk up the steps in silence, disappointment. As soon as he heard her settle upstairs, he got up and went into the dining room. He knelt on one knee in front of the rolling bar. By feel, he selected a smooth bottle of vodka, then the imprinted bottle of Kahlua. He'd never been a drinker, but discovered "Russo Negros" with businessmen in Europe. The peculiar intoxicated insomnia the mixture produced suited him well. It was Friday night. He was entitled.

He skipped the ice—too much trouble to fight those cube trays—and walked back to the living room with the two bottles and a glass in his hand. He switched on the stereo. *Sinatra,* he smiled when the music came on.

He lit up another cigarette and leaned back on the couch. It had been a really bad day. The second-quarter figures had just been released. The international division had been creamed once more. A second-half turnaround was highly unlikely. With each glassful of the dark liquid, Dave searched deeper for a way to reverse the losses. Just one insight; that was all he needed.

It arrived in an instant, just as he'd hoped. But the insight was not what he expected. Rather than a solution, he'd received an explanation: The Japs and the Germans make better equipment cheaper than his own company could. He could use every advertising and marketing technique, every innovation yet to be discovered, and it wouldn't matter a bit. It wouldn't be long before the competitors began thrashing them in the domestic market as well.

Dave blinked, sure he'd turned the television off before putting the record on. But look at that: one of the old "War in the Pacific" movies. The beach looked familiar. Just like Peleliu.

Dave pictured Johnny D'Amato on that beach. He always envisioned his ageless friend smiling that same cocky smile. Same stubble of beard. Same jagged hole in the neck. It's a good thing you're dead, Johnny," Dave said out loud. "You don't have to see what's happened."

The whole fucking country. Everyone's got amnesia or something. We went and fought, plenty of us dying for this country. For what? So every Jew doctor can drive around in a Mercedes Benz? Are they crazy? The Krauts put their people in ovens. They gassed them! The German bastards would still use their relatives for the upholstery, if they thought they could get away with it.

Dave's restless thoughts wouldn't stop.

And the Japs. Those sneaky, smiling little guys butchered us for the glory of their fucking emperor. They killed you and our buddies and should've had me, too. What did everyone die for? So the whole State of California can drive around in Datsuns? So a million Jap tourists with their stinking little cameras can swarm around Pearl Harbor, taking photos of where they had things their way? Can't anyone remember past yesterday?

And the kids. They turn out to be the worst of all. We sacrificed everything for their sake. Now they just spit in our eyes. They won't take anything on faith. They just laugh at us. "A bunch of naïve jerks." That's what my own kid called us. He thinks his friend died for nothing in Vietnam. Nobody ever said you died for nothing, Johnny. It was important. It had to be done and we had to do it. And that was that.

Dave had been stewing over his son's comments for months. *A lot of time has passed. Maybe things are different now.* Had things been different back then? He thought back to his mother, father, how the world had been when he enlisted. He refused to believe it. The deck hadn't been stacked against his friends and him. No one set them up. He and Johnny had done the right thing. So had Michael. James was the one who was wrong. He was just making excuses. Despite all Dave's influences and efforts, the kid had bailed out. Because it wasn't good enough to go to war if they forced you. You had to want to go and volunteer before they ever asked. That's what a man was supposed to do.

Dave lit another smoke. It might not be entirely James's fault, he conceded. His own father was the same way. Tom Devlin wouldn't have any part of war. Dave knew that, even though the matter had never been discussed. He shouldn't be so shocked that Tom's grandson followed suit.

There was no changing people like them, Dave decided. His father and son. The same guy who'd been his father turned out to be his son. *If they can live their lives scared, God bless them.* He'd just have to deal with it. He'd been mistaken in counting on the boy to correct the past, or at least even the score. James wasn't equipped for it. He'd fail to undo the old mistakes.

"Not to mention the new ones," Dave muttered. Things hadn't stayed the same. They'd gotten worse. He'd gotten the rematch he sought, but the Japs and Germans were winning. Big time. How could this be happening? "We kicked their asses so completely we had to build them up from the ashes. So much for being a good sport. Now they're kicking *our* asses in the marketplace."

Still, he wasn't afraid.

He burrowed down on the sofa. He locked his arms over his knees, trying to make his body stop shaking.

He'd never been afraid since that morning on Peleliu.

At least that's what he'd always told himself. He'd lied. Implausibly, he was still afraid of dying. Even as he aged and his life seemed to diminish in value, his dread of that final unavoidable loss grew.

It wasn't the idea that his life would end that terrified him. It itself, that might be a welcome relief. Death now seemed the only way out from under the guilt that still plagued him. What disgusted him was the knowledge that death would deprive him of his last shred of control. That was the ultimate degradation for Dave, to lose all capacity to act. Like on the beach at Peleliu, but worse. To become so helpless, so dependent, that he would even have to count on some merciful stranger to dispose of his fetid remains.

Johnny had come to help him on Peleliu. Who would come this time? No one. Not if they knew the truth about him. That he was no hero. That he was the guy who got his best friend killed because he choked under pressure.

*

222

"Turn it up, J.T., man, turn it up."

J.T. Gregorio sat grinning, oblivious to the collapsing bottom of his easy chair. James watched J.T., the master of ceremonies, from across the smoke filled room. James was sitting on a daybed, both legs pulled up toward his chin. He had witnessed this scene so many times before, he felt like he could write a script of what would happen next. Still, it felt good to be back with his contemporaries after another tough summer with Uncle Rory, who somehow miraculously managed to dodge one business bullet after another and keep his job.

"You got it, Bing," J.T. said. His long auburn curls shook down over his neck as he reached to his left to turn up the volume on the battered stereo.

"How's that, Bingo?" J.T. yelled above the music.

Bingo began singing along to "Maggie May", rocking his head and strumming on an imaginary electric guitar.

J.T. smiled. He pulled a fresh can of beer from the small refrigerator to the right of his worn leather easy chair, pushed up against the room's sole window. The icebox was strategically positioned. With stereo left, refrigerator right, J.T. only had to leave his easy chair to take a leak.

He squeezed the tall can and tapped its lid three times before flipping the top. It was his hometown custom, intended to minimize the head on the beer. He took a healthy swallow. Then he placed the can on the floor before him, and began rolling a joint from the grass and papers waiting in his lap. He lit it, and passed it along.

One by one, as the joint was proffered, each DT would put his beer can down and take a hit. They had lost some of their trademark diversity when the college opened an "Afro-American Center" the year before. Essentially, it was a subsidized fraternity and all the black DTs were pressured to drop out and hang at "the 'Am" instead. Still, the DTs remained an unusual bunch. In most schools, the freaks and the straights were sharply divided. The freaks would not dream of drinking beer. The straights would not dare touch marijuana. At Brunswick, in the DT house in particular, it made no difference. If something got you off, you did it. It was a simple rule, which brought together overalled freaks like J.T. and short-haired, chain smoking, returning Vietnam vets like Bingo, who was using his monthly disability check from the Veterans Administration to pay his tuition.

Bingo wordlessly thrust the joint toward the DT to his left. James dropped his feet down to the floor when Bingo poked him with his left arm, the one that didn't work too well.

"No thanks, Bingo. I got an exam tomorrow."

Bingo exhaled loudly. Disbelief was written all over his face. "On Saturday?"

"It's not a course exam, Bing. It's the law boards. They're holding them here tomorrow."

"Sheet....! What you wasting your time on them for, Devlin? Uncle's going to draft your butt as soon as you get a diploma."

The album side finished, the stereo clicked off. The roomful of DTs turned their attention to the exchange, awaiting James's response that would break the silence. Bingo was a good four years older than any of them. His combat veteran's status commanded considerable respect.

"Devlin's not going anywhere," J.T. interrupted. "Didn't you hear the number the stiff pulled in the lottery? 265! They'll take women and children first. Right, Jimmy?"

"That's what you keep telling me, J. T." James smiled self-consciously.

These bull sessions invariably turned to the subject of the draft lottery. Who was lucky. Who would go to grad school. Who was not lucky. Who would be draft bait. James really was not in the mood for it tonight.

Bingo turned his attention back to J.T. His voice now had a decided edge to it. He had quickly moved beyond good-natured needling to provocation.

"You sound a little jealous there, Curly. What number did a card sharp like you draw?"

J.T.'s response was inaudible.

"What you say there, Curly?"

"I said 15."

"15!" Bingo's demonic laughter echoed through the silent room. "Did you say 15?"

"I don't see anything funny about it," J.T. retorted. "Only some shell-shocked moron like you would think it's funny, Bingo." J.T. had always been particularly grossed out by Bingo's war stories, especially the one where Bingo is lying in some shallow pool of water, his left arm in tatters, shooting himself up with morphine with his other arm because he was lucky enough to be a medic. J.T. was finally lashing back at him.

"That's pretty tough talk, Curly. Better save it. You'll need it. Me? I don't have to talk tough anymore. So I think it's funny. Someday you will too. If you're still around," Bingo snickered.

"You're a real sick pup, Bingo. You must have been sick when you flunked out of this country club in the first place. And that trip to 'Nam put the finishing touches on you. Tormenting guys like me. You really enjoy that, don't you, Sergeant Rock?"

"I love it, J.T. I love watching cheap punks like you squirm."

James had heard enough. Once the discussion got ugly, it never fully recovered. He rose from the daybed.

"Quitting time for me, guys. I'm going to try to get some sleep. Got to be sharp, and all that good stuff."

J.T. and Bingo were still trying to stare each other down.

"Give them hell, Jimmy," one DT encouraged. The others grunted in accord.

"Thanks a lot, guys." James walked out of J.T.'s room and across the hall to his own.

He grabbed his towel and toothbrush, and strolled down the hallway to the head. By the time he returned, the stereo in J.T.'s room was back on. It was a good sign. J.T. and Bingo must have called a truce, at least temporarily. As he was about to enter his room, Roostook popped his head up the staircase from the second floor landing. "Phone downstairs, Devlin." James hustled down the stairs, expecting it would be Maureen. He was right.

"I wanted to wish you luck for tomorrow," she said.

"Thanks. I'll do my best."

"There's one other thing," she said. "It looks like I'm going to have to go back to school the day after Christmas."

"What do you mean? You always get off for a few weeks."

"Well, I applied for this art program and I got in."

"When were you going to tell me?"

"I never thought I'd get admitted, but I did." She paused. "It's affiliated with the University of Florence."

"Hey, Mo, last I checked, Florence is still in Italy."

"It is, but—"

"Are you kidding me?" he shouted. "Was that our deal? That I take an extra load of courses and bust my ass to get out of here while you have Italian guys pinching your ass in Florence?"

"Jimmy, I'm sorry. I shouldn't have mentioned it the night before your test."

"That's right. You should've mentioned it a long time ago -- or maybe not at all!"

"I'm sorry, Jimmy."

He recognized the sound in her voice; she was starting to cry.

"Sure, but I got to go and try to get some sleep. If that's even possible now."

"Oh, uh, okay. Good luck tomorrow."

"Thanks a lot." He slammed the phone down and stood in the foyer alone, steaming.

Not much later, he lay in bed, listening to the muffled voices and music crawling over his door jamb. He tossed and turned, breaking into a sweat. Finally, he gave up trying to fall asleep and dragged a chair over to the open window. The brisk October night air forecast the approaching winter. He was thankful the chill cooled him down.

Numbers, he thought. *Your whole bloody life comes down to numbers. Draft lotteries. Law boards. You pulled a number and your life changed as a result.*

He'd been pulling lots of numbers lately. First came the draft lottery back in August. After all the years of tension, it seemed so anticlimactic. He'd come home from working with Uncle Rory that evening, as always. His mom told him she'd listened to the numbers announced on the radio and his birthday was selected as 265. Just like that, it was over. The draft calls were diminishing as "Vietnamization" purportedly progressed. He'd made it. He was fat. Golden. Like J.T. said, "Women and children first."

Tomorrow, he'd take a test and again draw a three-digit number. It would be somewhere between 200 and 800. That was about all he knew about the test. Other than that any chance of attending law school hinged on pulling a damn high number out of the hat on the first try. Retakes were futile; the admissions offices reportedly ignored the results. The law boards were like hunting an elephant; you only got one shot, so you'd better put it right between the eyes.

He thought of Maureen and her news, but quashed the thought immediately, needing to stay focused, no matter how upset he was. Then he remembered one of Father Thomas's speeches to the assembled Gonzaga student body.

"Never give a test any credit whatsoever," the Jesuit would say at the beginning of each final exam. "Remember, if you do lousy, you weren't as dumb as it said you were. And if you do well, you're still not as smart as it might lead you to believe. No test can tell who you are and what you can do. Only you can do that. Only you will do it. Take the test and make it your own."

James decided to shut everything else out of his mind and hang on to Father Thomas's advice. He went back to his bed and slipped under the covers. It would be just like taking the law boards in Gonzaga's gym.

*

James walked up the steps to the Senior Center's dining hall. A special early Saturday morning breakfast had been arranged for the legal hopefuls. The seniors' dining hall was foreign territory for a confirmed fraternity rat like James. He'd never eaten there before.

Many of the seniors were already seated, the atmosphere tense. James walked to the food line noticing classmates staring at each other. The sour odor of competition wandered through the air, difficult to pinpoint but as undeniable as a morning fart. He tried to tell himself that no one was looking at him, but saw their quizzical looks, as if asking, "What's that junior doing here?"

Screw them, he thought as he loaded his tray with a plate of scrambled eggs. He spotted a couple of senior DTs huddled at a table in the corner and headed over to them. They were loose, none too excited about law school. They said it was a wait-and-see proposition. Wait until you get your score back and see if you forgot about the whole thing. They shot the breeze and the time passed quickly. Soon, he was hiking across the campus to Threlfall Hall, the ivy covered building where the test would be given.

While sitting at an old wooden desk, waiting for the proctors to distribute the sealed examination packets, he was struck by a thought. He'd always been too psyched before an athletic contest and would combat it with deep breaths and mental instructions to calm himself down. Nothing really worked.

Exams were different, though. They were his thing. A great hitter like Ted Williams could ignore a screaming crowd of sixty thousand and focus exclusively on the pitcher. James's own gift was an ability to shut out all the internal background noise and bear down on the exam before him. As soon as he broke the seal, he knew the law boards warranted all the buildup. He began to concentrate.

When the head proctor called time, James had just completed the last segment. He dropped his pencil – a reflex from years of Catholic schooling, where working on your paper after time was called was worth a definite rap on the knuckles, and a likely failure on the test.

It was over. James stood, stretched, and pulled on his windbreaker. Now he'd drink every last beer he'd stuffed into J.T's refrigerator. He'd drink all the beer in Brunswick, if necessary, until he couldn't remember the test or just no longer cared.

*

By eight thirty that evening, James was in Hardon's room full of flamers. J.T. had told James earlier that they were having a party there. This was after they'd exchanged heated words. James had shouted, "You make like everyone's got the world by the balls except you," after J.T. listed all that James had going in his favor, including Maureen. But after the call James had the night before, he wasn't sure he still had a girlfriend. Now, J.T. was slumped back in an easy chair in the corner, his mouth gaping open. James had rallied once more. He'd teetered on the brink of collapse after dinner, but managed to pull away.

The stereo was recounting the *Book of Job* as rendered by Seatrain. The obscure rock group's claim to fame was a live performance at Brunswick the prior spring. James sipped his beer, eyeing the freshmen women scattered around the room, enjoying the changed scenery now that the school had gone coed. He then sang along with the lyrics. *Instead of getting pissed off again, as usual, this time God dumped wicked shit on poor Job just because Satan dared Him to find out what would happen. I always suspected Old Testament God drank, the way he got crazy angry. Who knew He was a betting man too?*

Eyes closed, James chortled *If J.T. were conscious, he'd be telling everyone how he was on a much worse streak of bad luck than Job.*

"Sounds like you really enjoy that trash."

He opened his eyes to see a lanky girl standing in front of him. "Yeah, Barbara Bagner, right?" He remembered her from when the freshmen were dining around at different houses. She was even taller than he remembered. "And it's not trash. It's very traditional." He leaned against a door jamb, trying to steady himself.

"You call that traditional?" She sniffed and parted her straight black hair with her hands.

"Not the music. The lyrics. You know. Kind of an age-old problem. How come nice guys finish last? They're the ones who always get hammered? Why does God screw people who are just minding their own business?"

"*He* doesn't," she said. "Because *He* doesn't exist. Time magazine let the Silent Majority in on that one."

James grinned. "In five seconds you just put theologians and philosophers through the ages out of business."

"Tough luck for them." Barbara shook her hair off her face. "You don't really believe in that God nonsense, do you?"

"Sure, I do."

"Why?"

"Why not? Don't you believe in anything?"

"Yes. Music. I play the oboe."

"Oboe, huh? I like oboes." He didn't know exactly what an oboe was, but he liked all kinds of instruments, so it really wasn't a lie. "Why believe in music?" When she hesitated, seemingly stumped, he added, "I can tell you why you believe in it. Because it's more important than you are. There's no way of measuring, of course. You just sense it. The reason you believe in music is the same reason I believe in God. That must make us friends."

Barbara laughed out loud. "You're totally whacked, Devlin."

"That shouldn't take you by surprise, Miss Bagner," he said, wondering why she kept parting her hair. "I'm often whacked beneath the pines. I'd go so far to say I'm usually whacked. How about you? I see you climbed aboard the Red Eye Express a few stops back yourself."

"Okay, Devlin." She giggled. "You win. Even I know better than to try to dump on a DT on his home turf."

"Where you from, Bagner?"

"St. Louis."

"St. Louis. Shit! You know Augie Busch?"

"Everyone knows who Augie Busch is."

"You know he makes lousy beer?"

"You're very fresh, Devlin. You'd better stay out of St. Louis."

"Fine by me. I've hated St. Louis since 1964. Say, your father know Yogi Berra?"

Barbara scowled. "No, he doesn't know Yogi Berra."

"Joe Garagiola makes it sound like everyone in St. Louis grew up with Yogi Berra."

"Everyone but my father."

"That's too bad. Yogi Berra and Levi Stubbs are the two greatest team players ever. If I had my choice of anyone in the whole world to pinch-hit in the clutch, I'd pick Yogi Berra every time. Even if they got him out, Yogi'd never strike out. He'd hit a hard liner somewhere. Hector Lopez would be my second choice. That guy could really hit."

"I don't have the slightest idea of what you're talking about." She laughed.

"Okay, let's not talk baseball. The Series is over anyhow. I still hate the Pirates too." He took another swig of his beer. "So tell me about music," he'd said over the organ on the Stephen Stills record rattling the room.

"What do you want to know?"

"What's it like to be able to play an instrument?"

Barbara's eyes lit up. "I find it's a very sensual experience."

The use of the term sent obscene thoughts through James's mind. Lust. The male Esperanto. A language intuitively grasped by men from the beginning of time with hardly a variation in dialect. It occurred to him that despite the façade of learning, he was no better than his forbears. They were all subject to the seemingly unbreakable Law of the Crotch. Fill them with drink or smoke, and they wanted a woman.

He said, "Sensual, huh? What exactly do you mean?"

She shrugged. "It makes me feel good to play it. It's as if I were with someone who understood me completely. Someone who could fulfill all my desires."

James tried to hear her through the haze, to make sense of what she was saying. The few times he'd ever spoken to her, she'd been reserved. Now, as far as he could tell, she sounded like she was auditioning for a skin flick. Definite case of reefer madness, he concluded. Far be it from him to back off. He said, "You never met anyone like that?"

She bent closer and whispered in his ear. "No. I've never even had a boyfriend. Don't let my friends know."

"You're kidding?" When he saw her embarrassed expression, he added, "That's nothing to be ashamed of."

They looked at each other for a moment. She asked, "Would you like to hear some real music?"

"Why not?"

Barbara told one of her girlfriends she'd be back with some decent records. James trailed behind just as *Love the One You're With* ended.

At that moment, as he was following the girl out the front door, he was wondering where Maureen was on this Saturday night. What was she doing? Was she thinking about him? Then he pushed her out of his mind and wrapped an arm around Barbara's waist.

They stumbled across the campus supporting each other, not saying a word. When they reached Douglas Hall, she led him upstairs to her second-floor room.

"Come on in," she said. "Would you like a soda or something? I don't have any beer."

"I'm plenty lit already. Soda's fine." He dropped down onto the edge of her couch. "So, you going to play some oboe tunes for me?"

"Pieces," she corrected.

"Oh, excuse me. Pieces. I won't slip again." He smiled.

She walked into the bedroom and returned shortly with a black case. She sat down at the desk chair and opened the case, pulling out the instrument, cradling it in her lap. She rotated it.

"Are you going to play professionally some day?"

"No. I'd never pervert my talent like that."

"That's a pretty strong way to put it, don't you think?"

"Maybe, but I'd never play for money just the same."

"Well, I've got no intention of paying you so how about playing a bit for me."

She drew the oboe to her mouth and began. The notes were so clear that James sensed them passing through the walls unobstructed. He'd had no idea how long she played. Time had been distorted. It seemed like hours, but could've been minutes when Barbara stopped.

With precise movements she put the oboe back in its case and clasped the lid closed. She then walked over to the couch where James sat. One by one, starting at the top, she undid the buttons on her blouse.

"Tell me you love me, Devlin," she said, dropping the blouse on the floor.

James didn't respond.

She unfastened her bra, slipped it off and tossed it into the corner. "Tell me you love me," she demanded.

*

He woke up with a start. He didn't know where he was. The sunrise that bent under the half-drawn shade poked him in his eye. He wasn't in his room. *Where the hell...?*

Perfume surrounded him. He gagged and swung his legs to the side of the bed, dropping his throbbing head between his knees. He remained doubled over for several minutes. It felt like his brains were bleeding out through his ears, while he attempted to reconstruct where he'd been the night before. He struggled to open his eyes, noticing ladies' shoes in the corner of the room. Slowly, he turned to see long black hair draped over the sheet-covered lump on the other twin bed. It was starting to come back to him, in bits and pieces, like snapshots taken some time apart that are pasted into the same album.

Was she really astride him? Was that him on top of her? Where the hell were his clothes? When he saw them piled in the corner of the bedroom, he shuffled over to them. He gathered them. He saw an empty condom wrapper on the floor next to the wastebasket.

He glanced over at Barbara. She didn't stir and he felt his revulsion grow. There she lay. The temptress. The near occasion of betrayal, or worse? He couldn't remember, but it sure didn't look good. He hoped she wouldn't wake up. He wouldn't be able to speak to her again. *Never even had a boyfriend? What a crock!*

He could almost hear J.T., the resident DT psychiatrist, holding forth. "Transference, Jimmy. It's taking what you hate about yourself and superimposing it on someone else. Then you're free to hate their guts, instead of your own. It's a very clever response. Lets you keep on trucking, you know?"

James wished J.T. had never explained it. Even after he understood and recognized it, he hadn't been able to stop it. It worked much better before anyone labeled it for him. He would still hate Barbara, but not nearly as much as he hated himself. How was he going to get past that?

He closed the dorm room door behind him and forced his shaky legs down the hallway, toward the stairs. The campus was empty. He guessed it was about eight o'clock. Everyone else was still sleeping it off. He wasn't ready to go back to his room. That's when it occurred to him he could make Mass in town.

He'd made Sunday Mass maybe twice in his years at Brunswick, probably Easter both times. The other absences were due to sloth, not guilt. This time was different. He was engaged to be engaged. His transgression was big time. He hadn't violated some commandment or rule dictated by God or man. He hardly considered that sort of precept binding in the first place. This time he'd broken his own vow. This was not the type of thing that could be neutralized by a good act of contrition and skipping Communion.

The wind gusting in his face couldn't overcome the stench of his reeking clothes. He felt so foul he wouldn't dare approach the church. Strange. You were never supposed to get too filthy for absolution. But he'd committed too serious a sin to admit to God. Or Maureen.

He decided to walk over to the student union. Maybe some food could plug the cavity growing inside his chest. He passed his mailbox, noticing a single letter in the slot. He turned the combination and pulled the letter out. He recognized his father's handwriting. He'd never received a letter from his father before. He ripped it open.

Dear Son,

First off, let me tell you not to be alarmed at receiving a letter from the old man. I'm sure you're in shock. Relax. There is no bad news.

I just felt for some time that a few things should be said to set the record straight.

By the time you read this you will probably have finished your law boards. Win or lose, they're behind you.

I just want you to know that I've watched you closely since you told me about this law school idea. And I have admired the way you set your goal and started working toward it.

You always laughed off all those lectures I gave you about 'running for the roses.' You acted like you never heard it. I'm pretty sure you didn't want to hear it. I can tell now that you were listening. Like it or not, that idea is as much a part of you as it is me. You're going to have to live with it, just like I do.

One thing disturbs me. I know you'd deny it, but I can't shake the feeling that, in some way, you've been pushing yourself for my sake. I wonder whether your accomplishments are meant as some sort of message to me. Maybe a peace offering after the battles we've had.

Don't get me wrong. I've very proud of them and you. And I don't think you could have done yourself any harm by trying to achieve something, regardless of the reason.

But do me a favor. I've been taking another look at the expectations I always had for you. Maybe I went a little overboard, like lots of fathers, and wanted you to be more like me than you were. In any event, from now on, be certain that anything you do is because you want to do it. Not because it's going to make someone else happy. Like me or your mother, for instance. I'm resigned to this new arrangement. I won't try to tell you what to do. But I'll always have very definite ideas on how you should tackle the things you decide to do. Find out what's going to be most meaningful to you in life. Then set out after it. All the way.

Believe me, it's not as easy as it sounds. I've been around the block and there are some real surprises. In any event, son, I wish you luck. Remember, I'm always rooting for you.

Love,
Dad

James read the letter over several times before stuffing it into his hip pocket, walking past the small cafeteria and out the rear door. He kept walking until he was alone among the pine trees on the edge of the campus. He stuck his finger down his throat, but the purge wouldn't come. He was still intoxicated. Not really inebriated by booze or drugs any longer. He realized at last he'd poisoned himself with freedom. He hadn't been able to control it. He'd indulged himself with liberty until it became license. He'd already overdosed.

He walked back toward the DT house, knowing he'd have to make the phone call he'd been avoiding.

"I didn't think you would ever call!" Maureen gasped. "I'm so sorry about what happened the other night."

"I'm sorry too." James gulped. *For both nights.*

"I was totally thoughtless springing that on you the night before your exam."

"It's okay. I shouldn't have let it get to me."

"No, I thought about what you said, and you were right. That wasn't our deal—that one person do the hard part and the other just have fun. I'm not going."

"But, Maureen, you really want to go. And, honestly, it sounds like a great opportunity. Don't pay any attention to what I said. I didn't mean it."

"No, I'm not going. We'll get to Florence together some time."

"Are you sure?"

"I'm sure. That's it. Let's agree not to bring it up again." She sighed, then said, "So, what did you do after the exam?"

He'd been dreading the question. "Not much. Drank a couple beers with the guys. Watched some football. I was beat, went to bed early. How about you?"

"At the library. I had a paper due."

He cringed. She hadn't even been out with her friends. In the past, he'd failed to disclose everything to her, but this time he was outright lying to her and it was a whopper. He felt ashamed.

Somehow, he had to clean up his act and never let something like that happen again. He could never make it up to her, but maybe he could scrape money together and take Maureen to Florence someday.

*

James had a relatively mild hangover which would fade during his 8 A.M. class. He thudded down the hallway, down the stairs, hearing a stereo blare behind the closed door to Hardon's second floor room. That was unusual. No one was ever sure when the music died at night, but it was typically well before daybreak. He pushed open the door. The debris of last night's party contaminated the room. Paper cups of skanko beer full of floating cigarette butts and ashtrays stuffed with roaches made a minefield of the floor.

He stuck his head in the bedroom. No one there. Then he noticed the stereo speakers faced out the window. He lifted a leg and slipped through onto the second floor porch outside. J.T. was leaning back on a chair, both feet up on the railing. He was dressed in pants and a t-shirt, no socks, shoes or jacket. His gaze was into the blinding sunrise, turning his face and auburn hair orange.

"What the hell you doing?" James asked. "Working on your tan?"

J.T. didn't respond. He just kept rocking back and forth in the chair.

"Your ears freeze too?" James touched J.T.'s arm.

J.T. turned toward him. He smiled dumbly. "Jimmy! Where you been?"

"Sleeping, dum dum." James examined his friend. The bright sunlight was magnified by the melting snow clinging to the trees, porch and railing. He couldn't manage more than a squint, yet J.T. stared straight into the sun, his eyes wide open. Something wasn't right.

"Hey, J.T. Come on. What've you been doing?"

"What do you care? All you guys left me alone last night. All you scholars wanting to be bright eyed and bushy tailed for classes." His eyes rolled around in his head. "I did some acid."

"Holy shit, J.T.! Are you trying to fry your brains for good?"

"You're just fucking jealous. I finally got something that you don't. Man, I got insight now, Devlin. You'll be in law school while I'm mucking around some rice paddy next year, but right this second I'm seeing things some straight like you will never see."

"I bet you got the answers to the whole world's problems already, right?"

"Don't look at me that way. Don't you go putting me down. You got nothing to say, man. Nothing at all. 'Cause I'm always the one who gets the shit end of the stick. The low grades. That stinking draft number. And you all left me again last night. You left me flat."

"That's right!" James shouted. "And I'm leaving you again. I'm getting some breakfast and going to class. Do me a favor and don't swan dive off the porch until I get back. I don't want to miss it." James shook his head in disgust and climbed back through the window.

James's mind wandered during the history class, unable to concentrate on the morning's lecture. He was still pissed at J.T. for dropping acid. Even more for putting the blame on him. What was he supposed to do? Babysit him every night? James began to worry that J.T. would do something even more stupid, thinking that James had dared him.

He then began to think about what was going on around campus. Drugs, booze, and sex, with the war looming in the background. College life was a bloody free-for-all with everyone working their show on everyone else. Lots of people were getting hurt in the process. There were no rules you had to live by anymore and almost everyone James knew seemed a total space cadet, like J.T., or at least a waste artist like he was. Michael would've suggested they pray to Our Lady of Perpetual Confusion for some guidance.

Now, all James heard in the back of his mind was a song he and his freshman friends used to sing back at Gonzaga, imitating Eric Burdon and the Animals: *We*

234

Gotta Get Outta This Place. He was dying to leave Brunswick, to come home to Maureen and the real world, where a hopefully normal life in law school awaited him.

PART THREE

XV
September 1972

J AMES WALKED OUT OF THE MODERN BUILDING on 116th Street and Amsterdam carrying a shopping bag full of casebooks. He stepped off the curb, edging toward the traffic speeding by on the avenue. At the first break, he ignored the "Don't Walk" sign and ambled to the other side, his technique for crossing the street marking him as a native.

Anyone could recognize New York by looking at its skyline. James could identify it from far more subtle signals. The smells. Street signs, with different color combinations for each borough. Fire hydrants. Even how the sidewalks were constructed. As he entered College Walk, he saw the network of gray octagonal stones crossing the Columbia campus.

This was New York. This was home. He clattered down the stairs to the subway entrance, heading home. He decided to take a detour first and see Grannie, since it would be Thanksgiving before he saw her again, if the studying were as bad as he was warned.

It was a perfect late summer afternoon. Yet from the street all the windows looked closed in the second-floor apartment. He walked in, surveying what was the Connollys' own museum. Everything was exactly as it had always been. Except now it looked smaller to him. The old woman wasn't in the living room, so he walked toward the bedroom, yelling, "Hey, Gran, it's me, Jimmy." From the doorway, he stood and watched his grandmother in the bed.

She looked up. "Well, if it isn't himself." She still lay quietly on her back in her double bed, as if taking inventory of her aching joints and sore muscles. Apparently convinced that she would successfully arise once more, she lifted herself to a sitting position, then stiffly swung her legs from under the covers and off the side of the bed.

As old as she was, Grannie looked peculiarly childlike as her feet dangled above the floor. At a distance, with wrinkles and age spots unnoticed, her thin legs could have passed for those of an eight year old. Her long hair, a jaundiced white, was not yet pinned up in matronly fashion. Her modest flannel nightgown betrayed no contours as it hung over her chest. Her breasts and every other ounce of womanly body fat had deserted her when her stomach went bad, leaving behind a tiny frame overdressed in skin that had proven surplus.

There was no denying her age upon closer inspection. Her face was a stranger to cosmetics. It had withered naturally, accruing a vertical line for each year, and a dozen more for each sorrow. Her hands were even more conclusive. Long, knobby fingers were capped with loose-fitting, muscled pads. They were a reward for a lifetime of servitude: to the rich folks as a greenhorn from Ireland; to Dan Connolly, 'til death did them part; to their children, until her own time drew near.

Grannie finally slipped on her open-toed shoes, then gave an automatic Sign of the Cross to the large picture of the Sacred Heart above her bed. She shuffled to the doorway and embraced her grandson.

"How ya been?" James asked.

"Fine, jes fine. So what brings you by, Jimmy?"

"I figured I'd stop by to see my favorite girlfriend."

"Oh, shush yourself. You're as full of the devil as that famous uncle of yours. How's that Maureen? She's sweet. Looks right off the boat."

"How's Unc doing?" Ignoring Grannie's question, James's tone was somber.

"He can kiss my foot," she said. "You can ask him yourself."

"Isn't he at work?"

"Not a bit of him. He's here as big as life. Has your mother told you nothing? He lost the job. I'd like to brain 'im."

"Oh, Christ," James moaned. "Ma never told me. When did that happen?"

"It's been coming for years. And he's been full of drink ever since. Cursing them all when he's got no one to blame but his own self."

"I'd like to talk to him."

"Go on out into the kitchen. He'll look like the wreck of Hesperus, but I'll see if I can get him up for you."

James put his books on the kitchen table and then sat in the creaky chair, cracking his knuckles, waiting.

"So my nephew the law student decided to grace us with his presence," Uncle Rory said, turning the corner. An unrecognizable barefoot figure in loud Bermuda shorts and a t-shirt entered the kitchen. Rory was disheveled and bleary-eyed, needing a shave.

James stood and wrapped his arms around his uncle's shoulders. Rory felt shrunken, inches shorter, pounds lighter. Like everything else in the apartment, James's memory of his uncle was much larger than the man himself.

"How you doing?" James said.

Rory shrugged.

James scrambled to find something to discuss. He said, "Sorry your Mets fizzled this year, but I'm sure they'll win the pennant next season since Yogi's in charge now. If anyone knows how to win, he does."

Rory gave him a blank look, pulled out a chair and sat down. "I told your mother not to let on about my little 'vacation.' I wanted you to think I was still the big shot you worked for."

James fought to keep his composure. "What happened, Unc?"

"Hell, Jim. Smart fella like you can figure that one out. Maybe I just overstepped myself once too often. Besides, there was a new management team to deal with after some crazy merger we went into. You know, the new broom sweeps clean. They let me go. Just like that."

"To hell with those guys. You don't need them. You'll land a new job in nothing flat."

Rory gave him a grin. He looked like a jack-o-lantern with his tooth missing. "Sure, kid. You and me. Two tigers on the prowl." He looked at the bag of books on the table and nodded. "You're on your way now, kid. Nothing's gonna stop you. Top shelf all the way, right? Just like I always told you."

James cleared his throat. "It's gonna be top shelf for you, too, Unc. Just give it a chance."

Rory smiled. "A chance. That's it, all right. That's all I ever wanted." He got up, pulled a pack of cigarettes from his shorts' pocket, and shook one into his mouth. He shuffled over to the stove and flipped on the front pilot, bending down and lighting his cigarette. He then stood and exhaled.

"It sounds so goddamn silly. But I spent my whole life waiting for my chance to do something spectacular. Just around the corner, maybe tomorrow, maybe the next day, there'd be some accident or a burning building. Rory Connolly's chance to be a hero. To make the sacrifice." He chuckled. "I probably would've settled for finding a tax loophole that would've saved the company a bundle of money."

James wasn't sure what to say.

"I would've been ready, Jimmy. I swear to God, I would. 'Cause it's always in the back of my mind. But my turn never came." He crushed his smoke into the pilfered hotel ashtray, then looked back at James.

"The thing I can't get used to, Jimmy, is that all of a sudden I'm really starting to believe that my turn will never come at all." He shook his head. "It hurts. It hurts to know that not only won't your dream come true, but now you won't even get back to where you started."

*

James sat alone at the highly polished table. The lounge in Maureen's dormitory had been empty for hours. All the girls were out enjoying the early April sunshine.

He leafed through the notes, Bible, and dog-eared missal he'd brought along, pausing occasionally to look out the window.

The afternoon was stretching out, stepping on the evening's toes. At the end of the month, daylight savings time would arrive. This time of year made him think of the playground. The ball games. The guys. James suspected his basketball days were through. He'd be married and living in Manhattan with Maureen by the summer, transformed into yet another playground legend.

He pushed the disturbing thoughts of transience out of his mind. He had to get back to the task at hand. The first year of law school was flying past. Final exams would be upon him soon, but he had promised Maureen he'd put together their wedding ceremony. He'd better do it now or he'd run out of time before she returned from the swimming pool.

He stopped at a reading he didn't recognize. Ecclesiasticus.

[A] man's end reveals his true character. Call no man happy before he dies, for not until death is a man known for what he is.

How did the old guy Sirach figure that one out? Good advice for someone starting out. You don't know the story until you reach the conclusion. With life, there was no cheating allowed. No skipping the middle of the book to sneak a peek at the ending, just to see how it came out.

"How's it going?"

He turned to see Maureen walk in. Her damp hair glistened as she walked past the windows. She bent over and kissed him, then pulled up a chair.

"Not bad. I made some progress. If I get lucky, I'll be close to finishing tonight."

Maureen read from the yellow legal sheets. Several minutes later, she put them down.

"So, what do you think?"

"I like it."

"That's it? Just 'like'?"

"That's it. I can't give you a full-blown critique. I liked it."

"Good. I'm looking forward to using it. Things have been a lot better this year. Despite the work. It's like I finally caught my breath after several years of running out of control. Knowing I'd see you on the weekends calmed me down. I guess I'm getting spoiled, though. Now I'm not even satisfied with that arrangement."

"You won't have to put up with it for long." She smiled, reaching across the table, covering his hand with hers.

James let the idea sink in. "Isn't that something? No more car rides. No more waiting. Speaking of waiting...", he winked. "I'm glad you finally came back, mermaid. I'm starving. Let's eat."

Maureen punched him in the arm. "I knew better than to believe all that lovey dovey stuff I just read. You're as romantic as a doorknob, Devlin."

James lunged across the table and wrapped her in a bear hug while she tried to keep pummeling him. He ducked her blows while smelling the antiseptic soap from her shower at the pool. When she stopped, he pressed her against him.

"You know that's not so. I promised to love you forever. I meant it. I just want to make sure I last that long," he laughed.

*

Later that evening, James sat at his desk in the attic of the Devlin house. He'd completed composing the wedding vows. He was satisfied. With the songs Maureen had selected, their Mass would be the statement they wanted to make. He took off his glasses and looked around the room filled with items he'd collected over the years. Returning home for law school had been a difficult transition. It wasn't like the brief summer stays when he was in college. Now he felt like a guest in his old room.

His parents seemed different, too. Maybe they were. Quiet. Older. Or maybe he was only viewing them for the first time through the eyes of an intruder.

"Jim," his mother called, "I'm coming up. All right?"

"Sure, Ma." Even the simple question and answer seemed unnatural to him. Things hadn't always been so formal. Certainly not when Nora was around.

Peg, wearing a long terrycloth robe and fuzzy slippers, stood in the doorway. "Are you still studying? You'll work yourself to death with those books." Her comments spilled out nervously. "I don't see how you could remember anything at this time of night." She walked over and sat on the edge of the bed.

"I've actually been working on the wedding ceremony."

"Oh. Are you going to show it to me?"

"Sorry, Ma. I'm sworn to secrecy." He thought she looked disappointed. "We just want it to be a surprise. Besides, you'll hear it in no time."

"That's true." She played with the edge of her bathrobe. "In fact, that's what I wanted to remind you about. There isn't much time left, James. You haven't asked anyone to stand up for you yet. Unless you've been keeping that a secret, too."

"No secrets there, Ma. I haven't done a blessed thing about it."

"Well, have you at least thought about it?"

"I've given it some thought. I don't know. Not the way things turned out."

"What do you mean?"

He felt himself being backed into a corner, even though he hadn't moved a muscle. "I probably would've asked Michael, if he were around." He recoiled at his own words. He made it sound like Mike was living on a commune or in Canada. Like he were someplace other than where he really was.

"But what about now?"

"Now, I don't know. That's probably why I haven't asked anyone, Ma. I've run down the list of all the guys. They're my buddies, but nothing too special between me and them." He eyed her. "Something tells me you wouldn't have brought this up if you didn't have a suggestion."

She rubbed her hands together. "I just think you should pick the man who means the most to you."

"You wouldn't be meaning Dad, would you, Miss Connolly?" he teased in a shabby brogue.

"If he's the one who means the most, why not?"

"Well, there's no question he fits the description. I never heard of having your father as the best man before. But that's no reason why not. Do you think he'd do it?"

"Of course he'd do it." Peg beamed. "How could you even ask?"

"I don't know. He might figure I got turned down by everyone else and got desperate."

"Don't be ridiculous, James."

James slipped his glasses back on. "Maybe I should ask Uncle Rory to be an usher. Maureen's girlfriends will love it. Getting stuck with those two old goats."

"Don't count on your uncle at your wedding, Jimmy." Peg stood up, tightening the sash to her robe. "He can come to the church, but I'm not letting him anywhere near the reception."

"You can't be serious, Ma. What's he going to do? Get loaded, like everyone else? That's not the end of the world."

Peg walked over and kissed James on the forehead. "I'm not arguing about it. I just want you to know ahead of time. Your uncle's not going to ruin your wedding day if I have any say." She walked out of the room, calling back, "Goodnight, James."

*

James rocked nervously on his heels. He peered down Eighty-Fourth Street, observing people approaching the church. It was easy to distinguish the wedding guests from the passersby. The suits and ties. You wouldn't be wearing them on a Saturday afternoon by choice. Certainly not on a Saturday as hot as it was. James was sweating already. His pacing wasn't helping. He went back into the sacristy, determined to stand in one place for a while.

Dave Devlin sat on a folding chair in the corner of the mahogany paneled room. "Why don't you sit down, Jim?"

James sat down.

His father grinned. "Kind of nervous, huh?"

"Yeah, I'll say."

"Having second thoughts? It's never too late, you know."

He laughed the suggestion off, wondering why his father asked such a question. "Not about Maureen," James replied. "I never have. The one I have second thoughts about is me."

Dave pulled out a pack of cigarettes, then looked around the sacristy before putting them back into his pocket. "Those second thoughts you're stuck with. I wouldn't worry about them if I were you. You're solid. Like your mother. You always have been. Marriage won't be difficult for you. Your mother, she found it easy, right off the bat."

James sat listening.

"You know, it always seemed to me that man's love is very uncertain compared to a woman's. I think it comes down to something physical."

James scowled at his father. *Where is this going?*

"What I mean is a man's love always starts in his brain. I mean, how does a guy even know so-and-so's his mother or his father? Or his brother or sister? Because someone told him so and he believed it."

"But that's the same for women, too," James countered.

"Yeah, but a man's love never gets past that point. When a woman finally has a child, it's totally different. She doesn't just think or believe the baby's hers. She knows it. For sure. The father, he only gets told again. This time he's told he's got a child to love. Just like he told himself he loved the mother. Convincingly. But it's more remote. It's got to be."

Dave chuckled before continuing. "I often wondered how it is that men came to be the ones busying themselves with great projects and affairs of state and making a buck—all the so-called important things we do—while women were content to stay home with their children."

"It's a new world out there, Pop. Girls aren't ready to settle for that anymore."

"I know. They're the biggest believers in the male myth: that we've monopolized all the fulfilling careers. They'll learn the hard way. It's all just a substitute. All the business deals, the paintings, the books any man ever cooked up. It's a lot of crap that could never match the plainest baby ever born in the world for sheer creativity. The girls your age ought to be careful. A lot of them are going to miss the boat while they're off chasing something that never existed."

James nodded, not in agreement, but merely in hope of ending the discussion.

"I remember years ago," Dave said, his voice cracking, "some days like this. When we knew we'd have to be sitting around somewhere waiting. Funny, it's so long ago, I can't remember why we'd be waiting. But I remember that you'd always beg me to bring the transistor so we could listen to the Yankee game."

The organ in the rear of the church struck up the processional.

"Not anymore, huh, Jim?"

James looked at his father. "I guess not, Pop," he said softly, averting his eyes.

"Come on. We better go."

Father and son left the sacristy side by side. They walked to the center aisle before stopping. James looked toward the back of the church. The bridesmaids seemed half a mile away. Nora wasn't thrilled when Maureen asked her to be in the wedding party, but she now seemed to be okay as she glided into place, along with the others.

James spotted Rory standing between his big sister, the mother of the groom, and his own mother. He was shaven with a fresh haircut, possibly a new suit. James's eyes met his uncle's. His questioning look was unmistakable. Silently, James pleaded. He wanted to explain, tell Rory he didn't think Peg would really insist he not come to the reception.

Just then Maureen was only a few strides away, a dazzling vision in white. His mind went blank. He approached his bride without hesitation.

*

James looked out the airplane's window. It occurred to him that Manhattan was a forest, not of trees but buildings. Small buildings trying to grow tall enough to escape the shadow cast by the giants alongside. Old buildings dying, young buildings pushing them aside to take their place.

Maureen stirred against his shoulder. She wasn't keen on flying, but the trip had been worth the flight. Honeymoon. James wondered where the word came from. It sounded agrarian, perhaps astrological. Like harvest moon. New moon. Rather vague terms, but full of meaning to those who understood them. Now he understood, too.

Preconceptions had given way to knowledge. A lifetime of locker room and frat-house lies had proven to be just that. It had nothing at all to do with pleasing yourself. A man's pleasure took care of itself. Superficial. Fleeting. It paled in comparison to the response of his partner. Simply no contest. A surge from the soul matched against a toot of the testes.

It had little to do with sex at all. Real intimacy was not a physical act but a state of mind. An abdication of privacy. A surrender of self. Granting another permission to share that inner realm which had always been strictly your own.

James had always wanted it. He remembered lying awake in the winter moonlight, praying for God to appear to him, if only for a moment. He wanted desperately to meet this person who already shared his most secret thoughts.

God never showed. Maureen had. James realized that the relationship could be the same. It was up to them. Total knowledge of each other wouldn't come automatically. Yet they could dare to make the necessary disclosures. They could give up themselves for the benefit of each other and receive something greater in exchange. And have a good time in the bargain.

Love is patient. Love is kind. James had heard that often enough. He chuckled at his additions to the litany: Love is fun. Love is practice. And practice makes perfect. He could see that already.

The jet's chimes sounded, signaling the beginning of the final descent and the end of their ten-day trip. The fog that had wrapped them since their wedding day was lifting; the clock would resume running. Time to get on with their married life. Start heading toward forever——that future together that everyone had spoken of so surely, as though it were as tangible as the wedding presents tied tightly in ribbon and bows. He remembered his father's toast, a variation of the familiar Dave Devlin theme: "Now it's time to run for the roses *together.*"

The rear wheels of the plane bounced unevenly on the runway, as the engines churned into reverse. Maureen stretched, looked at him and smiled.

"So your folks will be meeting us, right?"

"Yes, they told me to call only if there were a flight change. Otherwise they'd meet us here."

Once the aisle cleared, the newlyweds left the airplane and headed to baggage claim. James held Maureen's hand while scouring the crowd. Off to the side, he spotted his mother standing alone. He picked up the pace and soon he was kissing Peg on the cheek. She was crying.

"Ma?" James said. "What's the matter?"

"I didn't want to tell you while you were away," she said, sniffling.

"Tell me what? Is it Grannie?"

"No, not Grannie. Your uncle," she sputtered. "He was killed night before last. It was a hit and run, right on Woodside Avenue."

James was having problems processing the information. He looked at Maureen, then back at his mother.

"Oh, Jimmy, what did I do?"

What did we all do? Was the first question in his head. The second was whether his uncle had walked in front of that car on purpose.

*

Rory Connolly's funeral was as grand as any monsignor's, and better attended. Deservedly so. Rory had never offended anyone except his own family. He'd certainly never chided an entire congregation for jingling coins into the collection basket instead of quieter, more precious currency.

The church was standing room only. The family up front. The children's classmates solemnly attentive in their school uniforms. Friends, acquaintances, and curious spectators filled the pews to the rear of the nave. Everybody knew Rory. Everybody learned of his hit and run death, an event important enough to merit a blurb in the Queens edition of the Daily News. Everybody showed for his funeral to give him a proper sendoff.

James sat in the second row, behind Grannie, Maeve, and Rory's girls. Behind his own mother and father. Next to his wife. Next to Nora, who hadn't been happy about coming back from the coast so soon after James's wedding.

The young priest delivered a fine sermon. Everyone either nodded in agreement or sobbed quietly. But, as far as James was concerned, it was all wrong. The priest was talking about someone else. Not Rory Connolly. Not the Uncle Rory James knew. He kept looking around. Was he the only one who noticed? He was on the verge of standing up, shouting, "Enough now, Father Charlie! Let's talk about my uncle for just a few minutes. The real Rory Boy. The guy everybody here remembers."

Grannie kept turning her head, shaking it as she stared at the metallic coffin next to her side. She'd tried so hard to fight the truth. James and Maureen had to break her last embrace with her son in the funeral parlor to pull her off his body while they fastened the casket lid down.

The priest's words didn't matter to her, James knew. Her love for Rory had nothing to do with words. She loved her son regardless of anything he might have been or done. All was forgiven. In her mind, "The Drink" had killed him, like it had so many others.

This "curse"—whatever it was that caused this thirst they all shared—wasn't imagined. First it ruined Rory's life, then it took it. James knew he had to keep his own drinking under control, as he'd been doing since he left Brunswick. It was a matter of life and death. He cried watching the old woman looking at the casket, turning away, then looking again. He couldn't turn off his tears, gazing at the box holding his Uncle Rory, who would never get the apology from him that he deserved.

James had wasted his opportunity to set things straight. Rory would have forgiven him in a moment, outside the church on the receiving line, if only James had bothered to ask. But he'd never said he was sorry. He'd never acknowledged his fault. He'd been too wrapped up in his own life and ignored how much it must've hurt Rory when he joined the rest of the world in ostracizing him, in declaring him a drunkard.

It was the harshest label in the English language. Much worse than "junkie." Everyone gets hooked if they are unlucky enough to start taking smack. But a drunkard is just a drunkard, a weakling who can't handle what everyone else can. James had concurred in the judgment against his uncle: Rory Connolly, a drunkard unfit to attend his nephew's wedding reception. Now James would have to live with it, a cruel act that could never be corrected.

James managed to pull himself together until the solitary tenor in the choir loft began singing *The Impossible Dream*. If every man were entitled to a theme song, Rory Connolly would've gladly shared his with the Man of La Mancha. James fell apart all over again.

Maureen pulled him aside when they'd filed out the door. She squeezed him hard, asking, "Are you going to be able to drive?"

Tears streamed down his face. He nodded. "I'll get the car and pull it up front. Get Nora and my folks, all right?"

Maureen shook her head. "I'm coming with you. You're in no shape to be driving alone."

"Hey, you two aren't leaving me behind." Nora looked like a million dollars, even in the dark suit and stockings. His sister, the Twentieth Century Fox, soon-to-be queen of the big-time Hollywood agents. She glanced around. "Who are all these creeps?"

James looked at her. "They're his friends, Nora. You know?"

"Bunch of old Irish lowlifes, if you ask me. Come on, let's get going."

They found Dave's dark Chrysler. James fumbled with the keys. His hands shook as he tried to place them in the ignition.

"Are you sure you can drive?" Maureen asked, sitting in the middle. Nora was already flicking ashes out her open window.

He nodded, tears still streaming down his face, and wheeled around to the front of the church, nearly plowing into a car ahead of him.

"There they are," Maureen said, pointing to Peg and Dave. They were helping Grannie into the limo.

"Why aren't they going in the limo, too?" Nora asked.

James shook his head. "Not sure. Probably trying to get by with just one. This funeral is costing a fortune as it is."

"The Connollys and Devlins are flying no-frills again. Typical," Nora said dryly.

"Why don't you get the hell off it, Nora," James shouted. "This is what you come from, too. Remember? If it's all so far beneath you, I don't know why you bothered to come back."

Maureen was pressed against her seat, trying to get out of the line of fire.

"You never changed, did you, James?" Nora shot back. "You still have to take everything so seriously. You're depressing. I swear to God you never recovered from when I told you there was no Santa Claus."

Before James could reply, Maureen said, "They're here," motioning toward Peg and Dave.

James jumped out of the car and opened the back door for his parents. Soon, he was edging the sedan into the line of cars for the short drive to Calvary Cemetery. As they turned onto Queens Boulevard, he saw from his rear view mirror the procession stretched for blocks behind them. He said, "There's got to be a hundred cars following us."

Dave swung around from the rear seat to look. "Rory should be happy. He finally got his medal."

"I don't understand it," Nora said. "The guy was such an incredible loser."

"Everyone loves a good-natured slob like Rory," Dave added.

James kept his eyes on the road, but refused to let the remarks pass. "I don't want to hear another word out of you two about Uncle Rory. At least he knew he was a loser. We're all losers. He was the only one honest enough to admit it." His fury built. "You're a real big winner. Right, Pop? Mr. Compassionate. It was all the big war heroes like you that made Rory feel like such a loser. You guys really had him buffaloed. He never figured out he was just as good as you. Probably a whole lot better."

"James, enough!" Peg begged.

"And you. Miss Nora! You're so far above it all that you think you get to pronounce judgment on the rest of us. Michael Cassidy was a dope whose own stupid fault got him killed. Uncle Rory was just an incredible loser. You just think you're entitled to say whatever you like about anyone, just because you decide it's true. What do you say about the rest of us?"

"Why don't you just grow up, James?" Nora snarled. "You can't remake the world the way you want. People aren't going to talk and act the way James Devlin thinks they should. Face it, because you're sure not going to change it." She laughed sarcastically. "I thought it was the male who was supposed to be the realist, but not you, Jimmy. Never you, with all your sanctimonious bullshit. You think you can pray Rory back to life and make all the Devlins live happily ever after together when nobody else even cares."

James pulled the car into the entrance and the Devlins went silent as it wound through the sprawling cemetery. Finally, the hearse pulled over a few yards before the overpass for the Brooklyn Queens Expressway. To the right, up a slight incline, was the Connolly family plot. A simple, modest headstone. No stony archangels or any other fancy stuff. The grave lay open, ready to receive another deceased relative, whose weight would push those who preceded him a bit further toward China.

James stopped behind the limo. He got out and all four doors slammed in unison as it began to rain.

"Jim," Dave called.

James looked at his father, his mouth tightly set.

"I'm sorry. I didn't mean anything by it. You know how I really felt about Rory."

James nodded, but it hadn't escaped him that his father hadn't been with Peg when she'd picked them up at the airport. And that each night he and Mo had come out from Manhattan to Woodside for the wake, Dave hadn't arrived until minutes before the funeral home was scheduled to close. James turned and walked alone toward the others.

The November wind picked up. Father Charlie sped through the traditional service for the dead. There were no more personal references to Rory. He was finished. Just another dismembered member of the mystical body of Christ. The gravediggers were a few yards away, smoking cigarettes and lounging on a few waist-high tombstones, waiting for the priest to finish and the crowd to disperse so they could plant another stiff before lunch.

James stood erect, holding Maureen's hand. His mother was up front supporting Grannie Connolly by the arm. He spotted Dave on the far side of the open grave and Nora in another spot, looking detached, as though she'd just happened by.

The priest walked around the coffin suspended above the hole in the earth, sprinkling holy water from his silver shaker with every step. The rain followed suit, transforming the few blessed drops into a puddle atop the casket.

Ashes to ashes. Dust to dust. He heard Fr. Mack's voice, not Fr. Charlie's.

Nora was right, James realized. The Devlins had disintegrated. They were no longer a family. Just people with a common history drifting in different, conflicting directions, even at a time like this. There was nothing he could do about it. He cried once more.

As the others started to leave, James stayed immobile. His head was down. With the toe of his shoe, he smoothed some of the soil back through the blades of grass below. He looked up to see his father who flicked his cigarette butt to the ground and stamped on it. He then approached James.

"It's okay, kid," he whispered, throwing his arm around James's shoulders and pulling him to his chest. "It'll be all right. Maybe he's the lucky one after all. He's found some peace now."

James looked at his father. "I just don't want any more regrets, Pop. We've all got to get back on track. We can't let everything go to pieces like it just doesn't matter anymore."

"Don't worry, kid, I won't let that happen. No regrets, I promise."

James studied his father. He was sure Dave believed he was telling the truth, but James knew he was lying.

XVI
October 1973

JAMES ENJOYED THE WARMTH of the blankets while straining to detect some noise from the bathroom. It had been quiet for some time. No running water. No flushing toilet. He tossed the blankets off, then stole across the frayed carpet. He flung the metal door open with a flick of the wrist.

"Aha!" he cried at a dozing Maureen. "Caught you again, you potty snoozer."

"Get out of here, you lazy bum!" Maureen squealed, after recovering from her start.

"Get yourself out to work and support me in the style to which I'm accustomed."

She flung a soggy facecloth at her husband's grinning face. "I should've known better than to marry a professional student like you."

"I always dreamt of being a kept man," James said. "It's a shame. In less than two years I'll be turned loose on an unsuspecting public. Expected to earn a living for the rest of my life."

"I cannot wait!" Maureen responded cheerfully as she stepped into the shower.

"What's your hurry?" James asked. "You're making enough money for the both of us. Teaching isn't half bad if you keep your tastes simple. You could support me through a whole 'nother degree program. Something practical this time, like philology instead of law."

"Why don't you have some breakfast and do some studying before your classes?" Maureen asked from behind a steamy shower curtain.

"Aye, aye, captain." James saluted.

By the time Maureen walked into the kitchen, James was bent over a large blue-backed text. He'd poured her juice and coffee. Half an English muffin, grudgingly striped with margarine, rested on a paper towel.

"Saving on dish water again, Devlin? I would've been eternally grateful to your mother if she'd ever managed to housebreak you."

"I'm not lazy, only pressed for time. Getting smart is a round-the-clock project

252

for someone thick like me. I've got to shave corners wherever I can."

"By using paper towels instead of plates?"

"It helps. I was thinking maybe I'd pour the cereal into my bowl the night before from now on. Maybe I could pick up thirty seconds in the morning that way."

Maureen shook her head and laughed. She poured the rest of her coffee down the drain and slipped on her raincoat. James couldn't recall any teachers who looked like her when he was in school. He thought the Spanish fourth graders on the West Side had it made. Our Lady of the Hot Tomato had answered the filthy prayers of the little horndogs. God only knew if their preoccupied preteen minds could retain a single thing the young blond teacher told them.

She bent over James and kissed him goodbye. He threw back his head and tried to lick her nose. "Don't leave me. Don't leave me alone with these books. Not again!" James broke into laughter.

"I'm leaving before you get any of your fresh ideas. Tonight's the parent-teacher conferences, so I'm going to be late. You too, right? Tuesday is the late class in Evidence?"

"Right." James grew serious. "Watch out for the creeps on your way home. All right?"

Maureen narrowed her eyes, flipping her hair back. "I'm the one who grew up in Manhattan. Don't you remember? I know my way around."

"Yeah, City Kid. And I'm the one who knows what they're thinking. Like I said, Mo, watch out for the creeps, okay?"

She placed her hands on his shoulders and kissed him. "Okay, Jimmy."

*

James had showered and changed. He sat hunched over the tiny desk tucked alongside their bed. The small apartment left little choice. Kitchen, bathroom or bedroom. You had to study in one of them. James assumed there was some deep reason why he always chose the last alternative, conditions permitting. He never gave a second thought to what it might be. *No time for that! Have to learn this Dead Man's Statute nonsense.* But then the phone jangled on the dresser. He pushed back from the desk and lumbered across the room.

"Hello," he said gruffly.

For a second, there was no sound on the other end of the line until a low voice asked warily, "James?"

"Ma?"

"Do you have a minute?" She was weeping softly.

Oh hell, not again. He glanced at the open book. "Yeah, I guess so. I've got to head off to class in a little while." His tone was cold. How had it gotten like that?

"It's your father, Jim. He's still moping around, ever since he came back. He won't talk about it. Won't talk about what's bothering him. Oh God, Jimmy," she sobbed, "I think he's going to leave again."

Shortly after Rory's funeral, Dave had simply walked out, leaving Peg a note: *Thanks for everything, but I'd really rather be alone.* He'd rented a room in a multi-family house in the Greek part of Astoria near where he parked his car. Peg had tracked him down after work hours and, following several heated conversations, convinced him to move back home.

Now James listened to her, confused by the emotions rushing through him. At the same time, he was angry with his mother and sorry for his father. It was unfair. He'd be the first to admit that. But somehow, for some reason, he was sliding the blame onto his mother. Maybe because she was the only one who talked about it. Or maybe just because of the upheaval. Peg, the one he remembered as totally in charge, had lost control. The woman who'd taken over management of the Devlin family so completely now wanted him to put things back in order so she could take charge once more. And he was balking.

Disjointed images flashed through his mind as his mother spoke. Finally he said, "You got to get hold of yourself, Ma. Getting yourself all worked up like this won't do a bit of good."

"You don't know," she argued. "You don't know the feeling when your husband treats you like that. Acting like he'd rather be dead than with you."

"No, I don't know, Ma. But I do know that if he's driving you crazy like this, one of you has to get out."

"I'll never leave him" Peg cried. "I made a commitment and nothing will ever change that."

Oh, Christ. Look at the time. Why did I get her started on that again? "I didn't say you had to leave him, Ma. I'm just saying things can't go on like this. It's just no good."

"I know. I know. I can't live like this. But I won't quit either. I'll never quit. You know that."

"I do," he replied. "So what's next?"

There was a pause before she said, "Would you talk with him, Jim?"

"Jesus Christ, Ma! I've got to get to my classes this morning or I'm dead meat."

"I don't mean right now. I mean go see him. Meet him after work. Something like that."

James felt ashamed for snapping at her. "Okay, Ma, I can do that." He glanced at the clock. "All right? But, hey, listen, I've got to run, okay?"

"Okay," Peg said, adding, "When?"

"I don't know. Soon. I'll let you know, okay?"

"All right. Go to school."

He hung up and stuffed his books into a canvas knapsack. He pulled on his windbreaker and went out the door. He twisted the key in the slot, trying to double lock the Devlin family behind in the empty apartment.

He didn't succeed. They were all still with him as he clattered down the metal staircase and trotted toward the subway.

*

The tie chafed James's neck. He'd worn it to school with his one "interview suit" that morning as he tried to line up a job for the following summer. He'd keep it on for his midtown meeting with his father, but would rip it off as soon as he got home. Soon enough he'd put his head through the silk noose for life.

James looked self-consciously around the Lexington Avenue watering hole. Maybe it wasn't the tie that bothered him. He scanned the well dressed, laughing crowd at the bar. This might be his father's hangout, but it wasn't his, despite *Tangled Up in Blue* playing in the background. He felt out of place watching everyone else talking and ignoring Dylan's latest comeback.

He slugged the glass of draft beer down, his eyes fixed straight ahead. He was amazed that a person who enjoyed drinking as much as he did felt so ill at ease in a bar. He didn't want the people around him to mark him as someone who came into bars to drink alone.

"Another draft?" The female bartender pushed a small bowl of peanuts in front of him. She gave him a studied, sexy glance. Definitely suggestive, yet noncommittal.

"Sure," he said, staring down at the peanuts.

"There you are. Sorry I'm late."

James looked up at the sound of his father's hoarse voice. "That's all right." He shifted his stool over so that his father could slide sideways into the open space.

"White Label on the rocks, Sally," Dave called to the bartender. He engaged in some chitchat with her when she brought his scotch, then finally looked at James. "Still drinking beer?" Dave lit a cigarette and unleashed a hacking cough as the smoke filled his lungs. He twirled his Zippo lighter in his fingers a few times before returning it to his jacket pocket.

"I've tried about every drink there is," James said. "Some of them almost killed me. But beer? It's never harmed me."

Dave nodded while James was still speaking. Looking back at Sally, he asked "How's school going?

"Keeping me busy."

Dylan stopped singing in the background and a black man began playing the piano on the far side of the barroom. Father and son fell silent as if on cue. Finally James asked, "So, are you rooting for the Mets in the Series?"

"I like Oakland, except for the stupid white shoes. Weather's great out there. Not like here."

When Dave made no effort to explain his remark, James thought it was time to bring things to a head. "So how are you doing, Pop?"

Dave laughed nervously. "Okay, I suppose. Doing my typical thing, you know?"

"Work's okay?"

"Not bad."

James pushed his empty glass toward Sally. "How are things at home?"

Dave sucked down the rest of his drink, shook the ice cubes that remained, then pushed the glass forward on the bar. Sally refilled it on her next pass by. "Is that why we're here?" His face flushed. "My son the law student to give me some sort of third degree?"

"I wouldn't put it that way," James said. But his father was right; they'd never made it a habit to hang around gin mills together. "I've been hearing from Ma. She's pretty upset."

"She's upset and calls you?"

James nodded. "All the time."

"I'm not surprised," Dave said matter-of-factly. "She's bound to be upset."

James took a drink from his beer. "Well," he said, after swallowing, "what's the problem?"

Dave snorted. "The problem? You want to know the problem?" He turned his head and glared.

The beer was now making James feisty in return. "Yeah, I think I do."

Dave coughed loudly, as if needing to clear his throat. "The problem is," he said, "I'm going to die. You're looking at a guy who's shot his load. I'm finished. Understand?" He took another gulp from his drink.

"You're only forty-eight. That's not so old. You're doing your best to ruin your health with those lousy cigarettes. But you're not nearly through."

"It's already happened." Dave pulled a half-smoked cigarette from his mouth and crushed it in the ashtray.

"What's going on? Are you sick?"

Dave lit another smoke, exhaling in the opposite direction. "Yeah. I'm pretty goddamn sick and tired about how I've got to carry on, keep on doing this and that."

"You're the one always preaching run for the roses. I heard it so often I wanted to puke."

Dave sneered. "Well, maybe you were right. Because I don't want to hear it myself. I spent my entire life after the war trying to make things right and do what I was supposed to do for everyone else's sake. Now I've had it. From here on in, I'm doing what I want. I'm through playing by everyone else's rules." He drew on his cigarette. "The rules. Fuck the rules. That's obvious now. I mean, that crook Nixon had the brass set to lie to us all. Don't think that didn't hurt. Plenty. He was my guy, you remember. And he taught me how real all the things I believed in were. He showed me what a dope I'd been for playing by the rules all along. When I look back, I see my whole life has been a big load of bullshit."

James looked around to see if anyone else was hearing what he was.

"I'm through with it all. I'm sick and tired of playing war hero. Of working my ass off on a job that can't be done. For what? To pay all the bills for a big empty house I never wanted in the first place? Neither your mother nor you is going to shame me into doing it anymore. So you just better get used to that idea." Dave was almost breathless. "Am I making myself clear?"

"Perfectly," James murmured.

"And you'd better get tough yourself. You're nothing but a pushover for your mother and the rest of the world. You could really be something, Jim. You've got all the talent it takes. But you never will because it's not enough to be smarter than the other guy. You were never a fighter, and you'll always come up short until you stop being Mr. Nice Guy and learn to go for the jugular and get bloody when you take what you want. As it stands, you'd rather let some nobody push you out of the way than knock him on his ass, where he belongs."

James remained silent.

Dave picked up his lighter and twirled it in his fingers. "Are we done here?"

"I'm finished." James climbed off the stool.

Dave peeled a fifty from his billfold and left it on the bar. "See you soon, Sally." He then led the way to the door. "I'm meeting someone for dinner. Guess you and Maureen will be by soon, huh?"

"I suppose so."

"Good enough." Dave turned and crossed Lexington, leaving James standing there. A few yards in on 50th Street, he stopped and greeted a woman. He put his arm around her shoulder and they headed toward Park Avenue. James recognized her. It was Rita, his father's assistant.

James headed east and kept telling himself it shouldn't matter. Maureen and he had their own lives to lead. Statistically, it was as commonplace as could be. Marriages break up. There's nothing the people on the outside can do to solve the problem. Maybe nothing the people on the inside can do either. Everyone just watches the relationship unravel, due to one big thing or a million little ones.

He kept walking. *Maybe it shouldn't bother me.* But it did. *To sit on the sidelines helpless, watching everything you took for granted in the world—your parents, your family—go down the tube. For what?*

His father had turned the tables. For years, James had been the master of the senseless screw-up. Regularly, he'd pulled some stunt that was inexplicable in terms of his usual pattern of conduct—stealing a car with Stymie; sleeping with that girl back at Brunswick. Now Dave was the unpredictable one. The old Dave had been hard enough to deal with. But at least you knew where he was coming from. James no longer had any idea what to expect.

He cursed the lingering daylight and the clocks that wouldn't turn back until the end of the month. Nothing would ever change the fact that his father had saved his life. *But I really owe him one this time*, he thought, tasting tears running down his face.

Passersby stared at him, a pathetic sight even hardened New Yorkers couldn't ignore. He wanted to stop. He wanted to swear his father would never make him cry again. He knew it was a vow he was unlikely to keep. Because you're at the mercy of the people you love. They can always hurt you—or the other people you love—whenever they choose.

*

The following night, James and Maureen were having dinner in their apartment's small eating area. The phone rang.

"It's your Mom," Maureen said, her expression serious.

Peg was sobbing. "Turns out he quit his job three weeks ago. He was only pretending to go to work. He never let anyone know."

James felt as though the wind had been knocked out of him. "What the hell happened?"

"They kept losing money overseas. I told him he never should've taken that spot. Now they're trying to sell off the entire division. So they took away his title. Demoted him. He told them if he wasn't a vice president anymore they could stick their lousy job. Then he walked out."

"How'd you find out?" She was still sniffling.

"He must've had it all planned when you met. He moved his things out while I was visiting Grannie's today. When I got back, I called his office and they told me everything."

"Well, he seemed to be knocking down the scotch pretty fast yesterday. Has he been drinking?"

"More so the last few months. But your father wasn't a professional drunk like my father and brother. They could hold jobs for years before they got fired. He threw his away almost as soon as he started."

As he listened to his mother crying uncontrollably, James knew she was wrong. There wasn't nearly as simple an explanation as "The Drink", on which Grannie Connolly blamed everything. He gazed at his wife, who was looking at him with sympathy. All he could think of was his father's words, that awful ironic line about running for the roses together. Dave had deceived him. He wanted to spit.

*

Three weeks went by and there was no word from his father. His mother had been calling James constantly. The emotional stress she was under wasn't going away, but became secondary to the more pressing economic stress. Dave had left her high and dry. With no paycheck coming in, she'd have no way of paying the bills that were piling up.

James got in touch with his father's former colleague Jacob, with whom Dave had worked for years. If Dave would let anyone know where he was, it would be Jacob, whom he regarded as his "maven," a trusted advisor on nearly every subject.

Jacob denied knowing Dave's whereabouts, but James wouldn't let it go. Finally, Jacob promised to get back to him. He did. He called the following night with a phone number in San Francisco, instructing James not to say where he got it. James thanked him, and dialed the number immediately.

"Dad, it's me. James."

"Why are you bothering me? Isn't it pretty clear I want to be left alone?"

James used all his willpower to keep the disgust from his voice. "Don't worry, Pop. I don't intend to bother you again. But you wouldn't leave a dog like you left my mother, so you need to do one thing for me and then I'll leave you alone."

"Your mother's hardly helpless. She's been running the show for a long time now."

"She's broke. That one slipped your mind, I guess. How's she supposed to pay that big mortgage and everything else?"

There was silence on the other end of the line. Finally, Dave said, "What do you want me to do?"

"Here's the deal. First, you tell me your address, which I'm only going to use for one purpose, and it's not to send you a Christmas card. I'm going to send you a deed to the house. You're going to sign it before a notary public every place I put your initials in pencil. Next, you send it back to me with the stamped envelope I'll include so you don't have to bother going to the post office. Then I'll leave you alone for good. I promise."

"Okay," Dave said.

"Fine." James sighed. "By the way, is that woman still with you?" He heard his father drag deeply on a cigarette.

"You know her name."

James laughed harshly. "I don't feel like using her name. Is she there?"

"No. She's gone. Flew back to New York. She has too good a job to lose, even if I'm not the boss anymore."

"Nice talking to you, Pop. Like I said, I won't bother you again." Teeth gritted, he hung up.

*

James knew the realtors were hosing his mother, but there was nothing he could do about it. When they wanted the listing, they told Peg how exquisite her house was. When they wanted her to take the lowball offer, they pointed out all its flaws. The truth was the market was down and Peg couldn't wait for it to bounce back. She had to take what she could get as soon as she could get it.

The closing was a nightmare. His mother was on the verge of tears. The buyers had given her a long list of what furnishings they were willing to "take off her hands." They haggled a separate amount for each item. Peg reacted like a woman selling off her family, negotiating a different price for each of her children. The next day, she moved out of the spacious house and into an attic apartment she'd found in Douglas Manor. James rented a truck and helped her move. When he returned home around eleven that evening, Maureen was on the couch in her pajamas watching television.

"I have a meatball hero for you I can heat up," she said.

"Thanks. It went horribly. There's no place to move in her tiny apartment. It's stuffed to the brim with the things she refused to sell."

"To you, it's just stuff. To her, it's memories."

"I don't get it. If those things are memories, I'd consider them bad ones. I'd get rid of it all." He went over to the couch and sat down, putting his arm around Maureen's shoulder.

"Is that ever going to happen to us?"

"I don't know how it could. You're nothing like him." She pulled James to her and held him against her.

*

A bell rang in the distance. "Okay," the bearded professor said, reaching for the pipe on his lectern. "We'll take it from there tomorrow. Read the next two cases. Don't think you're getting off lightly. *Miranda* will take you most of the evening."

James was finishing his entries in his notebook when someone began massaging his shoulders. Without looking up, he knew it was Joey. "What do you want, Doria?"

"I want to know how my point guard's feeling before the big game tonight. Did you bring your legs, Devlin, or did you leave them back home in the closet?"

"Forget it. You got the wrong boy. I've got too much work to do. You heard the man."

Students left the lecture hall noisily. Joey slid onto the upper row bench beside James. "Devlin! What's this I'm hearing? Disloyal talk from a team player like you?"

"Next time, but I'm not playing tonight. You better round up some ringers."

"Devlin, there may be no next time. Read my lips. Playoffs, Devlin. We lose tonight and we're through. Remember, last year of school. Graduate in May?"

"Playoffs?" James asked. "All right. I'll hang around the library until then."

"I knew I could count on you, Devlin! Once a jock, always a jock."

"Yeah, and once a pest, always a pest. See you later."

∗

The sweat seeping out of each of his pores smelled like memory, reminding him of all those summer nights with the guys, up the park. But the timeout was almost over and James was still trying to catch his breath. He looked at his legs. The mottled red skin told him something new. He was beginning to feel age for the first time in this intramural game.

Only a few seconds remained in overtime. The score had seesawed throughout the game. James tied it at the end of regulation with a shot from the top of the key. He'd laughed as it dropped. None of his law student teammates had wanted to take the last shot. He let it rip, strictly from memory. It was lucky, an unlikely reminder of what he once could do with ease.

The team struggled to keep pace during the overtime. Their opponents were just college students—it looked like half the Columbia football squad was moonlighting. They were in much better shape, and knew it, confident that they would outlast the older grad students.

"Enough arguing," Joey barked at his teammates. "You sound like a bunch of goddamn lawyers. We're down two and only have time for one play. Devlin, take it in. Maybe they'll foul you."

The others all looked at James. He nodded, then grinned.

The would-be lawyers walked onto the court. The undergrads were waiting for them at the far end. When the whistle blew, Joey inbounded the ball to James. He advanced it quickly into the front court, then passed it back to Joey on the left.

Pass and go away. His mind repeated the ingrained command. *Pass and go away.* He turned his back on Joey and headed toward the far side of the key. Then he pivoted sharply and came back for the ball. His breath came in short gasps. His calves throbbed. They were ready to cramp any moment.

Joey bounced the ball to him at the top of the key. James fumbled, but got it back down on the floor before he traveled. He'd have to keep his dribble going. There would be no getting the first step on his opponent from a standing fake.

His teammates cleared out of the lane as planned. James lifted his head as he gave the ball three hard bounces. As he looked toward the basket trying to shake off the telescoping vision that fatigue always brings, he saw Michael Cassidy. Michael was just standing there, his bowed legs bending up and down. He'd read James's telegraphed drive once more. Mike was laughing at him, gesturing with his hands. *Come on, Devlin,* he invited without a sound. *Take it to the hole.*

James took a stutter step right, then shifted his dribble to his left hand. He lowered his shoulder, ducking beneath the specter as he lengthened his stride. He left the ground, both calves cramping, anticipating the contact. *Hold it,* he told himself. *Hold it 'til he hits you.* When the hack was delivered to his right shoulder, he snapped his head back and dished up an underhand shot with his left hand.

When James looked up from the floor, Michael was gone. There was only a beefy undergrad standing over him. The defender looked more amazed that he'd gotten the shot off than that it had dropped through the net.

Only one second was left on the clock. James walked shakily to the line to try the three-point play. He took his time, trying to clear his head, not from the fall, but from the vision. He squeezed his eyes shut for a moment. Three dribbles. A deep breath, then the release.

The ball twanged off the rear of the rim as time ran out. "Oh, shit!" James exclaimed. How many times had Michael told him? He couldn't sink a clutch foul shot to save his life.

*

James sat in one of the two-seaters, pressed against the rail. He reached into his knapsack and pulled out the *Times*. The subway ride home was the only chance he got to read it. The front page had the usual assortment of important and not-so-important information. The stories came and went. But one story was always there, in one form or another, at least as long as he could remember.

Sure enough. The latest from Vietnam. Things looked grim in Saigon. All indications were that our old allies were going to catch it real soon. James glanced below the banner at the date. March 9, 1975. Law school had been some life. Lucky if he could keep track of the day of the week, much less the date.

Suddenly he dropped the paper to his lap. Now he remembered. He understood what had happened. It was five years to the day that Michael had been blown apart. He sat still, staring at nothing.

Now they were all gone. Michael. Rory. Dave. All the men who'd meant something to him. One way or the other, intentionally or not, they'd all abandoned him.

James was alone. His eyes remained dry. He was all cried out.

XVII
March 1977

J AMES STARED OUT THE WINDOW at the East River below. He'd done
so every morning for two years. Soon he'd have a new job. Possibly more
money. Definitely less view. He remembered his first trip to Foley Square
as though it were last week. He'd come out of the subway and blinked up at
that white tower like some country boy. Its golden roof was blinding at midday
and flashed its message above the other downtown skyscrapers: "Make no mistake
about it. This is the Federal courthouse."

James glanced down at his watch. Half an hour early for the interview with
Judge Taggart. He didn't want to enter the courthouse yet. Where should he kill
time? The Municipal Building? The new police headquarters?

He looked straight ahead, noticing a small brick church next to the courthouse,
overshadowed by the buildings surrounding it. He couldn't see the name on the
directory. But the engraved legend above the entrance was plain enough. *Beati qui
ambulant in lege Domini.* He headed over to it.

The foyer was dark, yet somehow familiar. He paused for a moment. It was the
smells that he remembered. Beeswax candles, the real thing. Just the faintest scent
of incense, probably from a funeral mass that morning. He reached into the stoup
and blessed himself. Did the holy water even have an odor all its own?

He pushed through the swinging doors and walked down the aisle, the sights
familiar as well. The church was a throwback to those he remembered as a child.
Nothing fancy. Ebony stained pews, probably the original furnishings.

He slid into the pew and kneeled down. Here and there James spotted figures
moving in the shadows, making the Stations of the Cross. Whoever made the Stations of the Cross anymore? Probably the same people who could still recite the
Five Glorious Mysteries of the Rosary. The ones who knelt down and said the
Angelus at noon.

He smiled. No sense denying it. He was still there, too. In a dark church. In
the middle of the day. Just like all those years ago with his mother, making a visit.

Whenever Peg had cause to bring him to a church for the first time, on vacation or for a cousin's wedding, she reminded him to make a wish. "You always get your first wish in a new church," she assured her son.

Hey, God, it's me again. I gave up praying for things for myself. Maybe you noticed. I figure if You have that much input into what goes on down here, You've already made up your mind how it's going to come out. But if You haven't, maybe this will persuade You. You see, I have this job offer from a judge in Pennsylvania. And I'm going to take it, that is, if I don't get this job today. But I'm kind of worried about Ma still. She's really bouncing back. I mean, back in nursing school now, starting a career when she's nearly fifty. I guess I'm not really surprised. Salt of the earth. She's always had this unbelievable faith in You, while I'm sitting here thinking I'm some sort of screwball who's probably talking to himself.

Anyway, I'm just saying I'd rather not leave here. Not yet. Not until she's gotten a little more time behind her. She's had enough changes. So if I could stay put in New York, I'd appreciate it. That's all.

"What are they unloading on the docks today, Jim?" the judge asked as the washroom door closed behind him. "There's a little smog. I can't tell if today's cargo is heroin or cocaine." The white-haired man laughed. "Never mind. It's all on the Brooklyn side. That's an Eastern District problem until they cart it over the bridge."

Judge Taggart pulled a pack of unfiltered cigarettes from his trouser pocket. He lit one, inhaling deeply. "How's your draft of that *Bacon* opinion coming?"

"I'll have it done this afternoon. I think you'll be satisfied."

"I usually am." The judge smiled. "The question is whether Judge Oswald will be. He'll be looking to dissent on this one unless we have all the holes plugged tight."

"He's going to have to search pretty hard to find fault with the reasoning," James replied.

"That's all we can do." Judge Taggart laughed. "Make old Oswald strain so hard he ruptures himself again."

James smiled. "One more thing, Judge. I'll have to be out of the office this morning. I'm heading over to the U.S. Attorney's office. I finally got a call from Mr. Eliot himself."

"I know. I bumped into Tom the other day. I told him I wrote a lot of letters of recommendation in my time, but yours was the Gospel."

"Thank you."

"Don't thank me. You earned it. Apparently Tom's got a fine crop of candidates this year. Fellows with tremendous qualifications are applying and getting turned away. Maybe it's all the women applying these days."

"I know. The Southern District's the best prosecutor's office in the country, so everyone wants to work with them." He paused. "One of my buddies clerking here with great credentials got shot down last week. But some of the other clerks have already landed spots. I can't figure it out."

Judge Taggart watched James somberly. "Look at everything carefully enough. You'll find an explanation." He crushed his cigarette out in the ashtray on the wide lacquered table. "Good luck, Jim. I know how much getting a spot there means to you. You've been working toward that since the day you walked through the door. You'd be a good prosecutor. I just wish I had more of the clout I once had."

"Thanks again, Judge." James grinned at the old man and dashed off.

*

He crossed the walkway connecting the courthouse to the U.S. Attorney's office, wondering if the judge had been hinting at something. He was concerned about Eliot's failure to call him sooner for his final interview. Other candidates already had their answers. When Eliot's chief assistant finally called, James pressed him: Was he still in the running or had the decisions all been made? Yes, he was assured, he had a very good shot. It would depend on his final interview.

If he were rejected, so be it, James thought as he waited to be shown into Eliot's office. At least he'd take his best shot.

"Jim, come on in!" Tom Eliot greeted him at the entrance to his office. He extended his hand. "I've heard so much about you from Judge Taggart. I'm surprised we didn't meet sooner." He gave James a crunching Wall Streeter's grip.

The intercom buzzed as James walked into the office. Eliot picked up the phone while motioning to a chair for James to take.

Throughout the call, James suddenly noticed just how much Eliot reminded him of Dave Devlin; the age, the features, even the hoarse voice. After about ten minutes or so, Eliot finally hung up.

"Now where was I?" Eliot said. "Oh, yes, I wanted to explain to you myself why we can't make you an offer right now."

James tried to keep his expression neutral.

"I honestly can't remember a year when we had so many 'best law clerks ever' applying for jobs." His tone was wry, as though he didn't believe it for a moment.

"Excuse me," James interrupted. "Are you saying I didn't come over here for an interview?"

Eliot cleared his throat. "That's right. I wanted to speak to you as a courtesy to you and Judge Taggart."

"Do you know your chief assistant told me yesterday this would be my final interview? He said I was still right up there. It all depended on my session with you."

Eliot shrugged, his smile forced. "There must've been some misunderstanding."

James looked away, trying to make sense of everything. Had Taggart been try-

265

ing to tell him this was all politics, that the clerk whose boss had the most pull got the job?

"Don't feel bad. It was a very fast race."

James shot a look at Eliot, plenty pissed at the Dave Devlin lookalike. "I'll admit you guys managed to jerk me around pretty well for a couple of months. But a fast race? I don't know about that. I figure I'm like one of those Olympic guys who got told the wrong starting time for their heat. If you don't get to run, you never really know how fast you are. Isn't that right, Mr. Eliot?"

Eliot's face flushed, his mouth went tight. "I'm sorry you feel that way, Devlin. But it wouldn't have made a difference even if I had interviewed you. Everyone we hired had more experience than you."

"Forgive me, but that's not true, either. We both know you gave out offers to clerks who haven't been around half as long as me. So let's skip that nonsense."

"Listen to me," Eliot said sharply, "I'm not saying no. I'm just saying not right now. You should consider yourself lucky. Only you and one other applicant weren't flat-out rejected." He picked up the résumé from his desk and waved it. "Go down to Wall Street. Work on your pedigree. Then reapply in a couple of years with some solid civil litigation training under your belt."

James stared directly into Eliot's eyes. "Are you making a commitment to hire me in two years?"

"No. No commitments."

"Then no thanks, Mr. Eliot." James stood up. "I'm not interested in going to Wall Street wasting my time on some chance you'll change your mind." He put out his hand, squeezing Eliot's tightly.

"No hard feelings. But you're making a big mistake. I may not have been Law Review or a clerk for a Justice of the U.S. Supreme Court, but I can still remember how the game is played down on the streets. And that's something none of your assistants know. You may have the best prosecutor's office in town. But it's not the only one."

By now Eliot had stood. James let go of his hand and warned with a wink, "I'll be seeing you around."

*

Even two years after taking his first verdict for the Manhattan District Attorney's office, James still reacted physically when the call finally came to his office. He'd pick up the file and walk down to the seventh floor, cross at the checkpoint, then take the stairs back up to the right courtroom in 100 Centre Street. He'd never take the elevator. Probably just a superstition, like Casey Stengel tiptoeing over the foul line whenever he walked to the pitcher's mound.

He followed the routine this time, just like always. It hadn't taken the jury long.

He sat at the counsel table, waiting for the defense lawyer to show up. He noticed the remnant of the motto tacked above the judge's chair. *In God We....* The rest of the slogan had fallen down long ago and no one had bothered to put it back up. Or maybe nobody working in the decaying structure remembered the rest of the interrupted thought.

The irony of it struck him as the court officers led in the prisoner. James had wanted to be a federal prosecutor so badly, but couldn't complain. He was getting to prosecute bank robberies, the bread-and-butter federal crime until the Feds had lost interest in such mundane criminal activity. They'd moved on to bigger and better things: securities fraud; embezzlement, political corruption. The defendants were expected to wear white collars and three-piece suits.

The lowlifes, the guys wearing high-topped purple sneakers or flying their gang colors, the Cecil Davises of this world—their cases were "tossed" to the state prosecutors like James.

The judge yawned loudly. "Madam Forelady, have you reached a verdict on the one count?"

"We have, Your Honor," the churchgoing black woman said. "We find Cecil Davis guilty as charged."

"So say you all?" the judge asked sleepily. "The jurors all nodded.

"Do you want them polled, counsel?"

The legal aid attorney rose and shrugged. "I suppose so, Your Honor."

The judge glanced at his watch. "Your prerogative, counselor," he muttered. He asked each juror if it were his or her verdict. When no one backed off, the judge asked defense counsel if he were satisfied. When he nodded, the judge said, "Okay, ladies and gentlemen, you can go with the thanks of the court. Defendant is remanded. October 30th for sentencing."

James picked up his folder and left. Surveillance photos had put another bad guy away. They had shown Cecil full-frontal, leaping over the counter with his handgun ready while the young female bank teller backpedaled, screaming.

Unlike alibi witnesses, like Cecil's relatives who swore he was home sleeping, the pictures inside a bank never lied.

*

The subway trip home took no time at all. He walked in to see Maureen wearing the jersey dress and black pumps she'd worn to school that morning. Now she was tossing a salad. He slipped off his suit jacket and went to her, kissing her neck.

"How'd it go?" she asked.

"Cecil went down. Don't they all?"

"Good," she said. "Since you chalked up another one, we have the weekend. My mom's wondering if we're coming."

"The whole weekend?" James said, picking a cherry tomato from the salad and popping it into his mouth. He chewed and swallowed. "Can't do that. I have another trial on Monday."

Maureen pushed the salad bowl across the counter, her face turning red. "This is no life, Jimmy. Big plans on a Friday night. You're a real romantic in the bedroom, but the rest of the time I might as well be living by myself."

James undid his tie, tossing it on the chair. "I make my living putting the bad guys in jail. I do it very well because I work hard at it, but if I'm not prepared, they walk at trial."

Tears came Maureen's eyes. "First it was wait until after law school. Then after the clerkship. Now after the D.A.'s office. There's always going to be a reason for putting our life off." She turned to the counter, but then whirled around. "Like having a family. Do you think I'm going to be satisfied teaching other people's children all my life? "

James would've liked to contradict her, but she was right. It was like the future always dominated the present. Whether it was fear of losing or of not doing his best, something drove him, pushed him so hard that putting off Maureen's reasonable requests had become a habit he couldn't or wouldn't break.

He snapped a paper towel from the roll, handing it to her, doing the only conciliatory thing he could. "Here, blow."

XVIII
April 1980

J AMES UNWOUND THE THICK REEL of enlarged surveillance photos one frame at a time. At the first sign of trouble, the head teller hit the silent alarm at Chemical Bank's William Street branch. The film dissected, step by step, the robbery that had ensued.

James gave the robbers names. Grumpy was the stocky one all the witnesses described as vicious, while the skinny one was Dopey, whom they all thought polite.

Then there was Bashful. James considered him to be the reluctant bank robber. The cameras behind the counter picked him up in the background. He lingered at the door, guarding their escape route, looking like he'd rather be anywhere else.

"Come on, Bashful," James muttered. "Just step up a little bit closer. Smile for the camera, you bastard."

Grumpy and Dopey had been caught while Bashful skipped the getaway car and vanished into thin air or maybe down into the subway.

James thought, *Bashful's only problem was he's like us. He works for nothing.* When they brought the other two in, they had all the money. Old Bashful didn't even get carfare home.

James hadn't given up yet. He had another roll of shots from the other camera. Another turn at bat.

He laughed, reminded of what Sarah Kaufman had said to him recently: "There's not a topic I can bring up that you don't relate to sports somehow."

Sarah was acknowledged as the finest lawyer in the Appeals Bureau. Her briefs always caught the attention of every First Department panel that heard her cases. So did her appearance. Her recent friendliness made him uneasy. He was always careful not to make any hint of an overture, but somehow she seemed interested, He found himself looking forward to her unannounced visits to his office, even though he didn't take her up on her lunch invitation.

He shook any thoughts of Sarah out of his mind as he began going through the final roll of surveillance films. There was Bashful again. Slightly different angle, but no real improvement. Average to tall build. Clothing unexceptional, not even the tricolor wool cap like the others wore. Nothing unusual at all. Except maybe the hands. Bashful must be a southpaw.

James moved on a few frames before suddenly rewinding to the best shot of the hands, of the peculiar manner of how Bashful grasped his left wrist. James sat mesmerized by the photo. The shot would've made a professional proud. It captured the unmistakable ambivalence of the robber, the doubts that had surfaced but couldn't sway him from the task he'd undertaken.

But those hands, one placed over the other, belonged to someone James once swore would always be his best friend. Bigger, perhaps, but with palms as pale as before. Because that right thumb, barely visible, should've been black but was as white as his own.

"You were right, Lance," James said aloud. "Always is a long time."

He recalled how they'd played war when they were little, and how Lance had convinced him that zebras were black with white stripes. Then he thought of the millions of things that had to happen since then for Lance to appear in the photo, and for him to sit at his desk inspecting it.

*

James arranged to meet Dopey and Grumpy at Rikers, interviewing them separately in the House of Detention for Men, a relic of a facility used to imprison defendants society presumed innocent but considered too dangerous to walk the streets while awaiting trial, or too poor to come up with the bail that would let them do so.

Dopey turned out to be Damian Rutledge, a career criminal with a rap sheet of low level offenses that was ten pages long, even with the benefit of his sealed juvenile record. Damian told James he'd be more than happy to identify the crowd-control man – he'd snitched out partners before for a sentencing break – but it was no-go this time because of the third member of the team.

Roscoe Brown was now known as Dawan Mohammad, apparently a true believer in the Black Liberation cause. He was never arrested until he was eighteen and got in a playground fight, beating someone badly. The judge offered him jail or the Army, and he was quickly shipped overseas where he became a sergeant, until he was dishonorably discharged along with four other members of his squad. Apparently there had been a small My Lai type massacre in some village in Long An province, but there were no survivors and these guys wouldn't give each other up. The Army threw them out and hushed the whole incident up.

When James asked him to give up their third guy, Roscoe told him to "fuck off and get out". As James gathered the files his investigator had collected on both men, he stole a last glance at Roscoe and said: "By the way, I'll give Lance your best when we pick him up." The shocked look on Roscoe's face could not be undone by a hundred lies.

When James reached the gatehouse on his way off Rikers, he stepped into a phone booth and dropped some change into the slot. His investigator, Detective Houlihan, answered on the first ring.

"Tom," James said, ""I'd like you to bring someone in first thing in the morning. See what you can find out about him in the meantime. No. No current address. Best I have is an old one in Corona. Rikers. Yeah, I know it's a real cowboy move coming out here. Hey, Tom, keep it to yourself. All right?"

*

He went straight home from Rikers, instead of going back to the office. Maybe that would please Maureen. Maybe they could talk a bit, like they used to.

It hadn't worked. He kissed her as soon as he came through the door, but his mind was still focused on what he had seen in Riker's central waiting room. That place was the United Nations of the Poor, filled with anxious wives, girlfriends, and children who had trekked from all over the five boroughs, fearing their next visit with their loved one would take place in some remote town upstate, sent there by someone like him.

"What's bothering you, Jimmy?" Maureen asked when they sat at the dinette table to eat.

"Ah, nothing much. Long day, I guess," he responded.

She looked disappointed, but said nothing, turning her eyes away from him.

James began wondering when he had developed the habit of keeping things from Maureen. Certainly it had started when he was at Brunswick. He had always tried to limit the nondisclosure to his darkest secrets, the things that had happened there that he did not want her to ever know. The booze. The drugs. Other girls. Now it seemed like the rock pile of secrets was constantly growing, as he would casually toss another on rather than let his wife know what was really happening.

"Mo, that's not quite accurate. There is something on my mind."

"Then tell me." Maureen sat up straight, and slid her chair in closer.

James exhaled deeply. "Okay. It's a very strange story. I'm handling this bank robbery down on William Street, and we already have two of the perps in custody."

"Well," she said. "That sounds like good news."

"Yeah, it's fine. But the third guy got away. He had tape on his face, so no one is going to be able to identify him, and the surveillance photo isn't too hot."

"Sometimes people get away with it. That's what you always tell me. You'll get him next time, because he'll probably do it again."

"You're right. But it's more involved than that."

271

"How come?"

"Because I'm pretty sure I know who he is," James said quietly.

"How is that possible?" Maureen asked, turning from the stove and undoing the apron that covered the dress she had worn to work.

"Because he was my best friend when I was a little kid in Corona."

"This is really serious, Jimmy. Does anyone else know about this?"

"No. I haven't let on. I keep telling myself I'm not sure it's him, but I am. Then I keep telling myself that no one could ever tell who he was if they hadn't been his best friend growing up, and they couldn't."

"What are you going to do, Jim? If you don't tell, it could jeopardize your career. Not just this job; your entire future. Do you realize that?"

"I know that. What I don't know is what I'm going to do," he answered glumly. "I'm going to have to figure it out somehow."

He had made his confession to Maureen, but it wasn't a good one. It was a terrible one. He had come clean about the whole business with Lance. But he had not mentioned Sarah Kaufman at all. This thing, whatever it was, that was going on at work.

No one but he would have noticed that the third black robber's thumb was in fact visible in the surveillance photo, but it happened to be white. His fellow robbers would not identify Lance. Roscoe was no snitch; he had proven that in Vietnam. Damian was petrified of Roscoe, so he wouldn't tell. Houlihan? He could care less. He was loyal to James and, if he found out, would figure that if James decided to cut someone loose he had a good reason, and it was none of his concern.

Maybe there was a good reason to cut him loose. James had no idea what kind of hand life had dealt Lance. All he knew for sure was that he had promised to remain Lance's friend, but had dumped him as soon as the Devlins moved from Corona. Uncharacteristically, James could not make up his mind.

∗

Tom Houlihan rose as James walked in. The large detective snorted and motioned toward the sullen young man sitting in the corner. "There's your guy. I read him his rights already. You need me anymore?"

James shook his head.

"Good, going for coffee. When should I be back?"

"Don't bother," James said.

Houlihan raised an eyebrow and walked out the door.

James slid behind his desk and sat down. Lance Pritchard turned and glared at him. "You mind telling me what I'm doing here? Your fat friend just picked me up when I was going to work. He wouldn't tell me shit."

Lance wore a short leather jacket, dress slacks, and shined shoes. He was fashionable, but not flashy. James enjoyed the advantage since Lance didn't recognize him.

"We're investigating a bank robbery," he finally said. "It took place down on William Street last week. Chemical Bank."

"So what's that got to do with me?" Lance's expression never changed.

"Nothing much, by the look of things." James fingered the dossier Houlihan had compiled on Lance overnight. "I see you're a high school graduate. Decorated Vietnam vet. Employed at Cosgrove Brothers. That's the investment banking house. What do you do there?"

"I'm a page."

"How long?"

"Since I got out of the service."

James nodded. "Where's the office?"

"Down Wall Street."

"Not too far from William, huh?"

Lance jumped out of his seat. "Fuck this, man. I don't have to listen to your bullshit. Am I free to go?"

"Anytime. I only wanted you to come in so I could show you something." James pushed a glossy enlarged photo across the desk. "Thought I recognized that guy by the door. The one with the gun. But I wasn't all that sure. I thought of your grandma, though. And figured she'd be able to spot that fellow anywhere."

Lance's hands trembled as he held the picture. He sat back down. "I don't have a grandma anymore." Then, he examined the face across from him. He finally asked, "Jimmy?"

They sat staring at each other, as though there were nothing else to say. Conflicting feelings clashed in James's mind. Now was the time in any interrogation when he always moved in for the kill. He waited until he had almost convinced a suspect that conviction was inevitable. He would have the guy commit himself just a bit more, so there would never be a real chance of turning back. Something now held him up. Then he thought about it for a moment. It was simple. He was just glad to see Lance. It wasn't Maureen's fault, but his life had become so solitary, at least as far as other guys, that he was surprised to be speaking with a man he could describe without hesitation as a friend, not just an acquaintance or co-worker.

"Been a long time, hasn't it, Lance?" He cleared his throat. "So, how'd you get involved with those two beauts?"

"What do you care? Why don't you just tell me what your next move is."

"Never mind that. I do care."

"Bullshit! Look at you, Mr. Hot Shot D.A. Probably went to some fancy school. All that good shit. Right?"

"That's right, Lance. Just like you said when I left Corona. You were so right.

I never looked back once. White neighborhood. White schools. I only knew black guys on the basketball court. And when the game was over, we didn't have anything to do with each other. Isn't that something? You were a seven year-old prophet. Now, let's look at you. So you never had the big breaks. But you never had it so bad either. What happened? You had your high school diploma. What next? You get a low number and get drafted?"

"Number three, man. I was number three. So don't tell me about luck."

"A lot of guys got screwed. You came out in one piece. A big war hero. You could've had the world by the balls when you came back home. Employers are turning handsprings for bright black guys like you. How come you've kept the same shitty job for years? Sharpening white boys' pencils. Getting them coffee. You like that kind of work?"

"Fuck you, Jimmy. You've got no idea what I'm like. You don't know what I've been through."

"You're right," James said. "I've been told that before. Sometimes you're at a real disadvantage in a discussion when you haven't been black all your life. Or when you haven't been shot at in battle." He shook his head. "Still, it seems to me that if we had to have exactly the same lives to understand each other, they shouldn't have bothered inventing talking. It would be totally useless."

"Maybe you've got a point," Lance conceded.

"Maybe." James smiled. "Sometimes I get lucky."

Lance chuckled. "You're funny, Jimmy. All these years, and you haven't changed so much."

"You either," James said. "I feel like I've had this conversation with you before."

Lance grinned. "I shouldn't come down on you too hard. You white folks ain't exactly what you once were."

"That's for damn sure."

Lance's eyes danced as he spoke. "You're getting just like us now. No one staying home with the kids anymore. Except you call it single parent families and that's supposed to make it all right."

They shared a hearty laugh.

"Well," Lance said, it's been nice rapping with you, Jimmy. But, like I asked, what's your next move?"

James said, "I'm open to suggestions. How do you think I should play it?"

"You go to the grand jury yet?"

"Thursday."

"How's it work? I mean, if I flip for you. Rat on Damian and Roscoe, you put me in as a witness. I get immunity, right? I'm in the clear?"

"Yeah, if I put you in the grand jury without a waiver of immunity. Then if I asked you if you did the job, and you said you did, my office can't come after you.

Why? You willing to testify? What if your buddies with the *dashikis* find out?

"Who's got to know? I mean, Damian and Roscoe will probably cop, right?"

James thought it over. "It's a clever idea, Lance. But it won't work. Two problems. One is that I don't need to give you any deal. I already got them on a silver platter. If I put you in the grand jury and give you an immunity bath like that, there's going to be some real questions raised. My ass ends up in a sling." He stood and began to pace.

"The second problem's related. If I give you immunity, the state can't prosecute you. That's true. But nothing would stop the feds from going after you. That's one of the little fine points of our beloved federal system. All they have to show is an independent source for the case against you. They would have the surveillance photos for starters. And if your buddies got wind of you testifying, they'd be dropping love letters to the U.S. Attorney before you know it."

Lanced looked glum. "So you've got to put it to me?"

"I didn't say that." *Christ, how is this happening? I'm in a room with an armed bank robber, scheming up different ways to put him in the clear.*

"What do you mean?"

"Your two accomplices aren't willing to testify against you. Roscoe's stonewalled before and Damian's scared shit of Roscoe. I spoke with them yesterday. No victim would be able to identify you. So the case against you is that an assistant district attorney who hasn't seen you in twenty years thinks he sees a resemblance to some average-looking guy in a surveillance photo. Sounds pretty thin, huh?"

"When you put it that way, yeah."

"Let's face it," James said, "the only reason you're here is because you made the mistake of being my friend a long time ago. Otherwise, you're home free. What am I supposed to do? Screw you over for old time's sake? Let's just forget it." He pushed his chair in. "So split. Go and sin no more."

Lance stood. "That's it? Nothing else?"

"Go on, before I smarten up and get Houlihan back here."

Lance started for the door, but then turned and sat back down. "Thanks for the favor, Jimmy. Now it's my turn to even the score. You never know. It might be another twenty years before we run into each other again."

James's interest was piqued. "What have you got?"

"It may be nothing. That's for you to find out, but I've been keeping it to myself for a while now. Something to deal if I ever got jammed up."

James went over, pulled out the chair and sat down. "I'm all ears."

"A few years ago when I just got back and was looking for work, I happened to see this Wall Street dude on Sutphin Boulevard meeting with Paulie Granelli on the sly. Everyone knows that fat punk Paulie's connected. His uncle was big shit in the mob. Ran all the local action."

James leaned in.

"Now these two guys don't belong running together. But what's that to me? I just make a mental note. You never know what's going to be useful. Anyhow, I finally get this shit-ass job at Cosgrove. A steppingstone, according to the personnel lady. Stepinfetchit is more like it. And don't you know who turns out to be working there?"

"The white dude?" James said.

"You're a good listener, Jimmy. That's who's a rising young star there. And I sharpened his pencils extra hard and fast, 'cause like I say, you never know. And we became tight man. I mean as tight as a lord and his lackey can be. He told me I should use my G.I. Bill and go to college at night. And I yessed him. Kept an eye on him. Inside me, I knew this dude was still talking to Paulie. The guy is up to no good."

"What kind of work does he do?"

"Mergers. The guy does all the top-secret bullshit."

"Sure beats getting tips on horses, but what makes you so sure he's talking to Paulie? You ever see them together again? Actually overhear a phone conversation?"

"Nothing like that. The man's too slick to make a poor move like that. I just sense he's involved."

"But why? The guy's a fat cat already. Pulling down the big bucks, right? What's he need Paulie for?"

"That's it, Jimmy. That's the angle. I figure he's scoring dope from Paulie. Coke, more likely than not. All this kindness shit to me. That's where he's coming from. I'll bet on it. He wants me to connect him, too. He's just a little too shy to ask."

"So you've got some heavy suspicion, but nothing solid."

"Nothing solid."

James thought a moment. "Want to help me get him, Lance? Just background stuff. No direct involvement."

Lance reached across the desk. "You're on, Jimmy."

"Great. It'll be like our old war games. We'll make this guy the Nazi and forget about bank robberies for a while."

"Deal."

"Just one more thing," James said. "I want to get Houlihan digging right away. What's the guy's name?"

"O'Donnell," Lance replied. "Sean O'Donnell."

For a moment James felt paralyzed. When he could speak, he said, "That's truly amazing, Lance. What did you guys used to say in Vietnam? Payback's a bitch?"

XIX
June 1980

LANCE HAD MISSED HIS CALLING as far as James was concerned. The records he kept were as meticulous as any accountant's. The file he'd gathered on Sean O'Donnell during the five-plus years he worked with Cosgrove Brothers was impressive. James considered it as thorough a job as Houlihan had ever done. Lance had hardly played the background role in the investigation he'd been promised.

The details were disclosed their first evening meeting in James's office. Lance had compiled a list of every merger and acquisition O'Donnell had worked on since 1973.

"It wasn't easy," he'd said. "Everything's coded while the tender is being prepared. Memoranda. Letters. The works. All the pages like me know enough to steer clear. You show a little too much interest in what the takeover kids are up to and everyone knows what your game is. You'd be on the sidewalk that afternoon. But after the deal is done, the wraps come off. Everyone's got to know who the heroes are. So in no time flat, you find out who the honchos were on each deal. Me? Like I said, I was hedging my bets. I never knew when I might need something to swap with the police, given the Mosque crowd I was hanging with. So I kept a little scorecard on what my friend Mr. O'Donnell was doing."

"But," James asked, "what if Sean isn't tipping on his own deals?"

Lance nodded grimly. "You and I think alike. I mean, if we're lucky, he's doing it the easy way. Dealing Paulie information on the deals he definitely knows are going down. But if he's cagey enough, he's been covering his tail. Then we've got to do it the hard way."

"What do you mean?"

"Look," Lance said. "It's numbers, pure and simple. If they've been trading on his deals, there's just a limited number to check. It's a pain in the ass. Sure. But if we examine them closely enough, we're going to see the moves he makes. If they're trading on the office dirt, you know, the good solid info Sean picks up from the other merger-and-acquisition guys, then we've got trouble. He could have a string on every deal Cosgrove's done since he's been there."

James was visibly disturbed. "How many's that? Hundreds?"

Lance nodded.

"We don't even know what they were," James muttered in disgust.

Lance expressed mock dismay. "Do you think I'd overlook something so elementary, Watson?" He reached into his briefcase and pulled out a loose-leaf binder. "Here they are. Every public merger and acquisition Cosgrove has done since I spotted O'Donnell there. It's amazing what a page can learn when he's a little nosy and good listener."

James took the binder. "I see what you mean about the hard way. Aren't there any shortcuts?"

"Not that I considered too promising. I mean, you could come straight down on Sean like Dirty Harry or something. Hold a gun to his head and make him talk. Or you could go after his bank records. Phone records. See if you could tie him to Paulie that way."

"So...you don't think it'd fly?"

Lance shook his head. "He's no fool. You may hate this guy from the last movie, but he'd never make a call from a phone that wasn't safe. He's sharp."

James stared at Lance.

"And I don't think you'll see any cash going into his accounts either," Lance added. "He and Paulie got themselves a little barter club. His gives Paulie info. Paulie gives him dope. No money changes hands. No banks. Nice clean transaction."

"But you said he's coming on to you for coke. That means he's still hungry."

"Maybe, but he never came out and asked me to connect him. I'm sure I'm reading him right, but he still doesn't quite trust me. He knows I can score it for him, but he's still checking me out. He's that careful."

James threw up his hands. "We could be chasing this bastard 'til kingdom come."

"How bad you want him?" Lance asked.

"About as badly as you do. Where should we start?"

"Let's start with his own jobs. He may be lazier than we think."

The process began almost immediately, after the short return date of the subpoenas James served on the Stock Exchange. He received less flak than expected from in-house counsel. *Subpoenas duces tecum* had become an everyday occurrence. Probably a quarter of the Exchange's records at any given time were sitting in cardboard boxes in the U.S. Attorney's office somewhere in the cycle of being produced, ignored, examined, labeled, discarded, returned or, most frequently, lost. No one noticed that James's subpoenas bore the caption of the New York

State Supreme Court instead of the U.S. District Court. He typed them himself to avoid any questions from his superiors, and each evening he and Lance waded through the records. However, Sean's deals led them nowhere.

If the records of the Exchange suggested anything, it was that Sean O'Donnell was a tight-lipped investment banker, but James wasn't ready to award him a medal just yet.

"You don't give it away when you're selling it," James surmised, and Lance agreed. Yet there was nothing in the patterns of trading in any of Sean's targets to suggest he was divulging information at all. Rather than wasting any more time on the obvious, they gambled and pushed on, but their nightly efforts continued without success. Lance and James had to finally grapple with the doubts that had arisen.

*

Late one Thursday evening as they left his office, James asked, "Okay, Lance, you ready to pack it in for good? Admit that old Sean grew up straight after all? "

"You believe that, Jimmy?"

"Of course not. He's a prick. I told you that from the start."

Lance smiled. "We've been busting tail. But some parts haven't been so bad, eh?"

James grinned. "No, it's almost been fun. It's like we're kids again."

"True. Hey, you thirsty?" Lance said.

They skipped the usual watering holes and headed north to Chinatown where neither would be recognized, entering the Lucky Dragon Lounge on Mulberry Street.

Lance ordered a double rum and coke. James followed suit, ordering a gin and tonic, immediately regretting his decision. He hadn't had hard liquor in years.

They drank the first round while discussing the Knicks' dismal season, and the Mets' and Yankees' prospects for the summer that lay ahead. By the time Lance ordered them a second round, the gin had hit James hard.

Lance drained his drink. He said, "Remember how we used to play war when we were boys? Well, it found me quick enough after I screwed up my last year in high school. I'd been high scorer on the hoops team as a junior, but then I started with the weed. Blew the whole sweet college deal. Next thing you know, I'm tromping through rice paddies."

James sipped his drink, nodding.

"It seemed like that was something that was always waiting down the road for us someday." He paused, then asked, "So, Jimmy, how'd you manage to skip all the excitement?"

James looked inward, his voice faraway. "I remember I was still in grammar school when I first paid attention to what was happening in Vietnam. I figured it couldn't possibly still be going on when I was old enough to fight. But it just kept going and going. At the start, the country was all gung ho on how we've got to stop the Communists there. I had one old friend get killed when everyone still thought like that. But then, everyone decides we made a mistake and have to end that War and get out of Vietnam."

The bartender poured another round.

"Lance, you remember that *everyone* who ran for president in '68 was a peace candidate who said we had to get out? Well, that decided it for me. The Green Beret days were over and no young guy in his right mind was going to enlist anymore because no one wanted to be the last man killed for a lost cause. Except for one of my friends, who didn't see it like that. He came home the hard way."

James took another sip.

"Long story short, I pulled a high number. Life went on for me right here, my father never forgave me and I never got over my friend getting killed."

"You didn't miss anything good," Lance said, pulling a cigarette out of an opened pack of Camels. "That medal I got was for next to nothing. Went back for a friend who was hit; he would have done it for me. Heroes were in real short supply over there."

"Well, I'm grateful you came back in one piece."

Once they finished their third round, Lance said, "That's it for me, Jimmy. Cosgrove Brothers will be expecting me early as usual.

"Good idea," James said. But he felt the longing inside him—he hadn't had his fill yet.

They headed out the door. "Hey, Jimmy," Lance said. "That was nice. We must've missed each other all those years."

James looked down at the sidewalk, then back at Lance. "We must have. It was a long time, but we caught up in a hurry." He stared off into space for a moment before blurting, "Holy cow!"

"What?"

"We've been going at this thing with Sean bassackwards!"

"What do you mean?"

"The only thing we know so far is that if Sean isn't honest, he's one cautious son of a bitch. So we've been coming from the wrong direction. He was never going to tip on one of his own deals. Or someone else's small deal where it'd be too easy to spot. He's going to do the exact opposite. He's going to bury the insider trading but good. Sean's going to hold out for the really big deals. The jumbo issues, big headline stuff, where he's protected by the large volume every day. And somewhere, hiding in all those trades, there's someone who bought when the fix was in. The only thing in our favor is that this certain someone had to pick up enough shares to make the whole swindle worth Paulie Granelli's while."

"You're right," Lance said, his eyes wide. "The more active the issue, the less you notice that someone. Let's start with the biggies tomorrow. I'm tired of ripples anyway. Maybe we can find ourselves a few waves, Surfer Boy."

"Don't look at me, Pritchard. I was strictly a Motown man in my day. Must be the Corona in my soul."

*

James walked into the apartment feeling pretty hammered, but elated by the new theory of how Sean and Paulie operated. He hung up his raincoat before walking into the living room. It was dark. He went down the hallway and stood in the doorway to the darkened bedroom listening. Maureen had gone to bed without him. He couldn't blame her; it was about one in the morning, and she wasn't happy about this business with Lance. He strained his eyes, trying to spot her, but couldn't make her out. He was too keyed up to sleep so he pulled the bedroom door closed.

He went into the living room, pacing. He was certain he and Lance had pieced the whole scheme together on the subway ride uptown. They'd assumed Sean had been compromised by drugs. It was the only plausible explanation for his relationship with a hood like Granelli. And Granelli had to be more interested in Sean's information than his money. The conspirators' problem was how to keep their partnership from being unearthed by the many investigators constantly checking stock exchange transactions. How to keep from becoming just another exposed "insider trading scheme?" Their solution was a conservative, professional one, which utilized Sean's knowledge of unpublished takeover plans and Paulie's mob connections to full advantage.

They didn't shoot for the one enormous score. They satisfied themselves with a modest killing every time out. A sure thing. Their trading was confined to the largest issues on board. Sean would give the signal when the gradual "collection" process should begin. Slowly, imperceptibly, with funding provided by numerous other illicit ventures, the "partnership" would accumulate shares of a large corporation that would soon become a target of Cosgrove's bidding client. When the public announcement of an impending takeover was finally made, a handsome premium would immediately attach to the market price of the shares they'd surreptitiously gathered. The sure profits could later be taken with little risk in the general selloff that took place after investors decided the stock price had peaked. It was a classic "twofer" for Granelli. He was able to capture another neat return while reinvesting and laundering the profits of the illegal family business.

James was certain the Exchange records would back him up. Given what he knew, he'd be able to perceive significant, otherwise inexplicable activity in the shares of the major targets attacked by Cosgrove's clients. Then he'd have to dig into the trade slips. Find out which brokers had executed the trades. Subpoena each of their records in turn to determine which customers had actually placed the orders

There would be a long paper trail, but if he and Lance were right, it would lead directly to Paulie Granelli. Some clue, some pattern in the tidal wave of documents would reveal a disciplined network of buyers who traded at Paulie's command on Sean O'Donnell's inside information.

James's mind wouldn't rest. It had been a mistake to come home. He should've gone back to the office, started examining the records surrounding the biggest Cosgrove deals right away.

He needed to calm down. He turned on the TV for distraction and flopped in the easy chair. *The Honeymooners* was on. It reminded him of when the Devlin family would watch Jackie Gleason on Saturday nights. He'd be in his pajamas, smelling popcorn his father was making in the kitchen while his mother brought him a glass of soda.

He watched the credits roll, the show over. The memory disappeared, like it hadn't ever really happened.

He knew it was stupid. Unfair. There was no connection to the unraveling of the Devlin family; to the distance creeping into his own marriage. Yet James couldn't shake the notion. The past was taunting him lately. Teasing him with people and events he'd thought were long buried. Like the one time he'd chickened out at Donna Bradley's party all those years ago. Or was it really two times, as his father would surely count them, since he had accepted his high lottery number and not followed Fat Frankie, Michael, and Lance overseas?

If he could just reach out and grasp this piece of the past, maybe he could undo those mistakes. And maybe he could use it to rectify everything else that had happened.

"I'm going to nail you, Sean," he whispered.

∗

It was five-thirty. The end of the day in the district attorney's office. A time when everyone was back from court. The assistants could relax, if only briefly. Trade a few war stories. Applaud or condemn the latest sentence that had been handed down.

James sat alone in his office. He closed up a trial folder and tucked it into his briefcase. He tried to recall where he'd left off the night before with the unauthorized investigation of possible securities laws violations. Lance and he believed their theory had proved out. They detected suspicious increased trading in the shares of Cosgrove targets prior to major developments. At least they'd convinced each other that they saw it. Maybe they'd been kidding themselves.

The brokers' records gave them no reassurance at all. For months, they'd examined the slips of each trade they'd pegged as potentially tainted. The pattern they'd counted on had failed to develop. No one street name had done an unusually heavy traffic in the target stocks. There was no suggestion that the inside traders were steered to a particular brokerage house, as they'd hoped.

The customer records of the executing brokers provided even less comfort. Their last hope for making a case against O'Donnell and Granelli lay in linking them to a few of the limitless names appearing on the customer sheets. They'd combed the slips tirelessly, searching for the telltale connection. In truth, they could hardly remember ever seeing the same name twice. The trading in the target companies appeared to be random. Maybe purposely random.

A cough caused him to jump. He turned to see Sarah standing there.

"What's up?" he asked.

"Thought I'd come down and see how my friend's been doing. Haven't seen you around much lately."

"I've been hiding."

"Working the night shift?"

"Why?" he asked. "People beginning to talk?"

Sarah sat down across from him. "Let's say there've been a few comments. The hours, the company you've been keeping."

"That it?"

Sarah shrugged. "Like your mind must be on something else. Maybe things aren't right at home."

He nodded as if there was an element of truth to what she'd said. "What do you think?" he asked.

"I try not to think about you, Devlin." She smiled. "Okay, I don't think anything of it. I just want to know how much longer you're going to pursue it because I cannot help but wonder how much longer you'll last."

James squeezed his face. "Christ, I must look worse than I thought."

"I'm serious, Devlin. No one can continue at this pace. You and your mystery man friend are playing a hunch, true?"

"We like to think it's more than a hunch."

"Right," Sarah replied. "Obsession is a better term." She scanned the banker's boxes lining his office wall. "And what if you turn out to be right? Have you figured out what you do next?"

James cleared his throat. "Never gave much thought to that. Figured I'd nail down the facts first, then decide what crimes to charge."

"Well, you'd better start thinking about it. You and your buddy must be tracking insider trading if you're dropping *subpoenas duces tecum* on Wall Street firms.

Even the feds have trouble with those cases. They use the mail fraud statute and Rule 10b-5, but those don't fit too well. What are you going to charge them with, assuming you can ever put a decent case in the grand jury? Robbery one? You've got a serious problem, Devlin."

James knew she'd made sense, convincing as always. Yet it wouldn't matter.

"I hate to be a party pooper," she continued. "But I don't want to watch you killing yourself for nothing. Knocking yourself out to build a case you'll have to give away to our competition down the street. Whoever this guy is, he isn't worth it. This office can't afford to lose you in the process." She stood, looking pointedly at James.

"Thanks for the warning, Sarah."

"You didn't hear a word I said!"

He saw how angry she was. "Just the ones I wanted to."

She sighed and walked toward the door. "Will you at least put a time limit on it, Jim?" She turned, and looked at him. "And I'm still waiting for you to accept my lunch invitation."

He couldn't look her in the eye.

"I'll stick up for you, but if they find out you've been freelancing, there's not much anyone can do for you. After all, they're paying you to get the guys in the Cons, as you put it. Not the guys in the pinstripes."

"Thanks, Sarah. I know I'm breaking the rules. I'll appreciate whatever you do."

*

Lance would be late that night. If nothing else, there'd been one positive result of the whole ordeal. Lance's aptitude for securities work had become so obvious that he could no longer deny it and finally enrolled in college at night. Sean had been delighted when Lance informed him he was following his advice. He wouldn't have been nearly so pleased with Lance's other nocturnal activity.

Even though Sarah tried to warn him, he was too far down the road to back off now. He flipped through the customer sheets subpoenaed from Grable, Todd & Co. It was hardly one of the big brokers on the Street. Yet it had executed a few of what Lance and he had identified as "advantageous" trades. Its records had to be checked, just like the rest.

He made his way down the list. Fighting sleep, fighting boredom, he heard Sarah's words again: *Obsession. For nothing. Maybe things aren't right at home.*

Maybe things aren't right at home.

He shook his head, hoping to force each customer's name to register in his mind. He yawned, eager for Lance to show up. Having someone to talk to would wake him up. He forced himself to keep reading, finally finding that he was staring at one line on the long customer sheet. His fingers were practically crumpling the paper.

It was the second best name of all. Sean O'Donnell's own name would have been best. Proof positive, as the nuns used to say, that he was trading on inside information.

James leaned back into his chair, smiling broadly. No more bullshit paperwork! No tortuous process of selecting and assembling disparate trades into a coordinated, coherent design. Sean would now do all the work for them. He'd gotten careless. He'd given them the whole case on that single line.

James said it out loud, savoring the sound it made, the satisfaction it would bring: "Cassidy, Michael J.: 1000 shares Congelton Industries, Inc. common at $21 7/8; trade date: August 1, 1977; settlement date: August 8, 1977."

*

Houlihan escorted the tall young man into James's office. He pointed toward the straight-backed chair, the command implicit: *Sit down, buster.* He then shot James a sly wink. "You want me to stick around?"

"That won't be necessary, Detective. Mr. O'Donnell will be free to go whenever he chooses."

Houlihan nodded and went out the door.

James turned to Sean who looked just like James had pictured him. He had the finely hewn, tanned features of a model and the wardrobe to match: plush blue cashmere coat, opened far enough to display a gray herringbone suit. The black tassel loafers, regimental tie, and blue oxford shirt completed the image: youthful, casual success. Sean let loose a tremendous, moist sneeze.

"God bless you," James said automatically.

Sean did not respond. He just leered at James.

James tapped his pen against the desk. "You know, it's really impolite not to thank someone when he blesses you. Even if you think it's a ridiculous custom. But then, you've always been a very impolite guy, Sean. You always ignored me. But now it's just you and me in this room. And you're going to tell me the whole story about what you've been doing. Then when you're finished, you're going to tell it to me all over again in front of the whole bloody world. And when I'm through, there won't be a single secret you have that won't have been exposed. Do you understand, Sean?"

Sean practically spit. "You're loony, Devlin. I don't have any idea what you're talking about." Then, as an afterthought, he added, "I want to call my lawyer."

James shoved the phone toward him. "Be my guest. But why don't you take a look at this first." He slid a copy of the incriminating trade slip with Michael's name highlighted in yellow in Sean's direction.

Sean glanced at it, maintaining composure. "What's this cheap bullshit?"

"Just something that struck me as real peculiar when I was investigating a little trading that went on in some stock of a company by the name of Congelton Industries. You know that outfit? I gather the French company that took them over is one of the Cosgrove Brothers' clients. That's where you work, right?"

Sean didn't reply.

"Anyhow, like I was saying, it struck me as peculiar. How Michael Cassidy's been dead all these years. And yet there he is, big as life, making a smart play like that on the market. It really doesn't sound that much like the Michael we knew, does it? I mean, scoring on the market. He was never bright like you or me. And his luck never ran like that, did it?"

Sean cleared his throat. "Cassidy's a very common name."

"Sure it is. But you know my buddy Houlihan? I asked him if he'd look up this Michael Cassidy for me. So, he did a little gumshoeing back at Grable, Todd, and came up with the most peculiar fact of all." James paused, then continued. "He found out that the Michael Cassidy who placed that clever order to buy Congelton was a dead ringer for you."

Sean shifted in his chair.

James lowered his voice. "Now I know you've been selling inside information to Paulie Granelli for years, Sean. But I really never thought you'd actually trade on it yourself. That really surprised me."

"Fuck you, Devlin," Sean replied.

"It's taken me years to merit such a candid assessment directly from you. I mean, you used to let it go with one of your stooges telling me what a dirt bag I was. By the way, I owe you a lot for that. It was great motivation."

Sean snickered, motioning around the room. "It was true, Devlin. Look at this dump you call an office. Look at the rags you're wearing. You were the big star brown nose at St. Aidan's, Devlin. Where'd it get you? A shitass job like this? I could buy and sell you fifty times over."

James forced a laugh. Like Yogi said, it was "<u>déjà vu</u> all over again."

"Don't tell me you don't care either, Devlin. You got a wife? What's it like for her to live with a nobody like you who can't give her shit? When we started playing for keeps, you wound up the biggest underachiever of all."

What had his father told him years ago? The best team doesn't always win. We'll see about that, James thought.

"Score the basket, kid. You read me one hundred percent, Sean. Sure, I hate your guts for walking in here like you stepped out of Brooks Brothers' window. I won't deny it. In fact, that's going to make this all a little more enjoyable for me. You know, I caught an earful from Jackie Standish the night he died. He laid the whole picture out for me." James shook his head. "That's what kills me. That trading slip. It all comes back to Michael, doesn't it? The fact that you had it all, but

Mike picked me for his friend. Isn't that something? You never quite got over that one, did you? All these years go by and Mike delivers you on a silver platter to his old buddy."

"I could've done something for him," Sean said. "Michael was a dumb fuck. Had to be to wind up getting himself killed in Vietnam. There were a million ways to beat that."

"Maybe," James replied, rubbing the back of his neck. "But this didn't happen by accident. We didn't just cross each other again by coincidence."

Sean exhaled. "How'd you find out? That's my only question."

James gambled. He lied convincingly to protect Lance. There was no telling what reprisals Sean or Granelli could arrange. "The narcotics guys got the lead. One of their snitches, a user, said Paulie Granelli was dealing to you. That started the ball rolling. Once we found out the mob had their hooks into an investment banker we figured there might be big things brewing."

Sean looked down, lowering his voice. "It was a mistake, starting with coke. The circles I travel in, though, it's no big deal. Big party drug. But I needed it all the time. Paulie sized my problem up in a hurry. Before I knew it, I was his. Once you gave up that first tip, you'd be through in the industry. He let me know it."

"You guys had a perfect arrangement," James said. "I knew what you were do- ing. Yet I studied those slips until I was cross-eyed and still couldn't prove any- thing. What made you place that order in Mike's name?"

Sean shrugged. "I don't know really. Bored maybe. Paulie was squeezing me, complaining the information I gave him was no good. He kept reminding me how a little suspicion might be raised at Cosgrove as to my integrity if my productivity didn't improve. He thinks he's a real management expert." Sean banged his fist on the desk. "Shit. I made this sleaze a fortune and he's telling me the information's no good. This turd thinks he's a genius because his uncle the Godfather told him so. Imagine the fat slob started to tell me how the trades should be made!"

James took in all the information, noting how Sean's face lit up.

"I'm telling you, Devlin. You didn't see anything. A drop in the bucket. If Pau- lie had let me call the shots, use my touch, we'd have made several million dollars more and you still wouldn't have been able to spot a thing. I would've started pick- ing up the shares sooner, using what I'd describe as an extremely educated guess. He wouldn't go for it. Each purchase had to be a lock or Paulie wasn't interested. He wasted at least half the information I gave him."

"I made the trade in Mike's name because it should've been harmless enough. Probably would've used the money to buy more coke. At that point, I just didn't give a shit anymore."

It was time for James to pop the question. "So, are you going to work with me? Testify against Paulie? Drag his uncle down, too?"

Sean shrugged. "May as well. If they find out our arrangement is in the open, they'll waste me anyway. That's the way they operate." He glanced at his watch. "Can I leave now?"

"Sure."

"You'll call, I suppose?"

James nodded.

Sean stood. Reluctantly, he extended his hand toward James. "I still don't like you, Devlin, but it looks like I'm stuck with you for a while."

James shook his hand firmly before Sean pulled away and headed toward the door.

"Hey, Sean, one last thing," James called out. Sean turned, looking at him. "I always thought the Beach Boys really stunk."

XX
March 1981

IT WAS ST. PATRICK'S DAY. Spring was tantalizing close. James passed the Supreme Court, then turned before reaching the crowd of street people congregating in front of 100 Centre, each waving a court appearance reminder in his hand. He went through the revolving door on Leonard Street and soon was on the elevator up to his office.

He spotted her right away. A little girl, maybe five years old, dark hair, bright blue eyes and plenty of freckles. She sat sideways in a chair in front of his desk. She stared at him as he approached.

A woman was standing in the corner. He took her in all at once. The flat heeled shoes, navy tights, camel hair coat, and face fashionably suntanned for March. It was the prematurely gray hair that threw James for a moment. It had been a long time. He looked back at the little girl.

"Hi. What's your name?"

"Delia O'Donnell," she replied.

James fixed on the mother's eyes, awaiting confirmation. She nodded. He squatted down to the little girl's level. "I bet I know your Mommy's name."

Delia studied him without replying.

"Would it be Donna?"

Delia looked over at her mother and grinned.

"Is there any place Delia could go for a few minutes so we can talk, Jim?" Donna asked.

"Sure," he said. "Delia, how'd you like to do some typing? My secretary would be happy to teach you." He just guessed at what might interest the girl.

Delia looked at her mother, who gave a nod of approval.

James took Delia by the hand, leading her to the office next door. He said, "Your Mommy will be right in there. Okay?" He introduced her to the secretary who immediately took over.

When James returned, Donna was sitting in the chair, clicking her fingernails.

He walked around his desk and sat down.

"It's getting to be like old home week in this office."

She looked at him and laughed. "Another Devlin ice breaker."

He smiled. "Nice to see you, Donna." He meant it. "What's on your mind?"

"Sean told me what's going on. At least some of it."

"Which parts?"

"What he was doing with this Granelli character. And how you caught him. And that now he's working for you."

"Do you know about the drugs?"

She looked down, playing with her pinky. "Yes," she said, barely above a whisper. "He told me about that, too. I suspected it for some time. I didn't know what to do."

"Did he tell you anything else?"

"Why? I'm not sure."

"Sean seems to forget some of the biggies now and then."

"Like what?" She met his gaze.

"Like you. He never mentioned that to me."

"Oh," she said, looking away again.

"Hey, it's none of my business, but it makes me uneasy when I don't know everything. I hate surprises from my star witness when he's on the stand."

Donna fidgeted in her chair. "Are you surprised?"

"That you're here? Not really. At this point, I'm waiting for Jesus Christ to come bopping through that door one of these days."

"I meant, are you surprised about me marrying Sean?"

"No. I should've seen it coming. But that doesn't mean I have to like it."

Donna looked to be trembling.

"I take that back. If he hadn't married you, I probably never would've seen you again."

She blushed, crossed her legs and turned her gaze toward the grimy window.

"How long have you two been married?"

"S..six years," she stammered. "I broke it off a few times because of his drinking, but my parents thought he was a good catch." She cleared her throat. "I love him, Jimmy. I really do. Delia does, too. He's not as bad as you think." Tears slipped down her cheeks. "Sean's always had this need to distinguish himself, but wasn't athletic or as smart as he wanted to be. So he latched on to money. With some people, that's all you need." She wiped away the tears. "But not you. Or that boy from Little Neck."

"Michael Cassidy."

She nodded. "Sean couldn't impress you two. You never noticed."

"I noticed. Plenty. Sean knows I did. He knew how I felt, and played on that.

He still does a good job working that old inferiority routine on me."

"It's just an act, Jimmy. Besides, it never seemed to bother you."

"I understand Sean a lot better now. I think that over the last couple of weeks we've found we had quite a bit in common." *Maybe I just managed to stay slightly more sober.* "I'm guessing he's believes you'll leave him when he loses his job. When the money stops rolling in."

"And there's nothing I can do to convince him that's not true," Donna sputtered. She then looked at James. "And what about you?"

"Married. Her name's Maureen. She's great. She teaches at a little Catholic school in Chelsea, Guardian Angel. Remember when we all used to have one of those? Mine died from overwork."

He paused, then added, "I suppose Sean and I have been equally misguided. I always thought you could earn someone's love. If you deserved it, you got it in return. I've been as far off base as Sean. He tried to buy love, I tried to earn it."

"It's got to be free of charge." Donna smiled weakly. "Not because someone owes it to you, but just because they want you to have it."

She was right. He was reminded of Roger Maris. No matter what the guy did, he couldn't win over the fans. He said aloud, "Love's peculiar. The more you give it away, the more there is to spread around. Amazing."

After a moment's silence, Donna said, "I didn't know how you'd act today, Jimmy. I even envisioned seducing you somehow. Anything to make the whole situation disappear."

"I really don't think that's your style, Donna."

She smiled. "True. Besides, the way things were left, you obviously weren't that interested in me. You never called me when you said you would after that night at St. Mary's."

He met her gaze. "Not because I didn't want to. Let's just say I was seriously detained. Again, right? But I always cared about you. First cut's a deep one, right?" He shot her a wink. "But let me give you a tip in case you decide to go that seduction route with someone else. Don't bring your daughter with you."

She laughed, then sobered. "I'm still scared, Jim. Sean got mixed up with some bad people. I'm afraid something awful is going to happen if he testifies."

"He's going to testify, Donna," James said firmly. "There's no way around that." He wasn't prepared to surrender his prisoner. Even for her.

Donna stood. "I was afraid you'd say that." She looked around, then said. "I'll get Delia now."

"I'm sorry, Donna."

"I know." She slipped her bag over her shoulder and walked out of his office. He heard her voice turn gentle as she spoke to Delia, and their footsteps fade down the hall.

What was Sean's daughter to him? An image of what used to be and might have been? He had no idea how to relate to the child. Hopefully her father did do better.

He pushed away thoughts of all the O'Donnells. It was time to concentrate on what needed to be done. To fish or cut bait. Figure out what crimes to charge the Granellis with or hand the case over to someone who could.

Sarah had been perceptive enough to raise the issue. It was as serious as she'd indicated. A federal prosecutor had several malleable statutes under which he could indict the participants in such a sophisticated securities fraud. An assistant district attorney seemed to have no similar weapons at his disposal. So far, James was shooting blanks. So the search for a viable legal theory of culpability had continued for weeks. He'd found a few possibilities, but they all turned out to be dead ends.

James flipped through the supplements, the annual stapled paper inserts stuffed into the pockets of the bound volumes of the Penal Law. He came to a stop when a new statute captioned "Scheme to defraud" caught his eye. First degree was an E felony with penalties sufficient to justify the risk Sean would be taking in testifying against the Granellis.

He skimmed the language. It actually might fit. *Scheme...systematic ongoing course of conduct...intent to defraud ten or more persons or to obtain property...false or fraudulent pretenses.* It sounded just like the federal mail fraud statute he had wrestled with so often with Judge Taggart. He glanced at the annotations to see what cases had construed the law. None at all, a clean slate. The statute had only become effective January 1, 1977. It couldn't have been better timed if someone in Albany had known the detection of Sean's scheme was imminent and had made sure a conveniently tailored charge was available. It would give him the hammer he needed.

The phone rang and James picked it up, continuing to read, stunned by the lucky shot that had dropped again.

"Yes, sir. Yes, sir," he said. "I'll be right down."

*

District Attorney Martin Stafford was sitting behind his large desk when James entered his airy office. With an exaggerated wave of his hand he motioned to the seat next to his desk.

"Hiya, Jim," Stafford said, a slight lilt clinging to his low-toned voice. It was rumored he was born in Ireland. "How're you doing?"

"Okay," James replied. The midday sunlight flashed off Stafford's bald head.

"Still happy with us?"

"Yes, sir."

Stafford nodded. "Good. I wasn't sure you'd be. Moving down the block like you did. Let's be frank. The job's a bit of a step down from clerking in the Southern District." He smiled. "Listen, I don't intend to take up a lot of your time. You've been carrying a heavy caseload for me and I know better than to step in front of a dray horse. But I'm curious. I've gotten complaints about your bureau monopolizing the grand jury time the next few weeks. I did some checking to see who the hogs are. And it looks like it's all yours. Now that's surprising to me. I know you spend as little time in the grand jury as possible. I mean, five minutes per bank robbery, in and out. You don't want to turn over any more to the defendant in discovery than is absolutely necessary, right?"

"Yes, sir. I try to keep it thin in there. Just enough to establish each element of the offense."

"So what have you got cooking, Jim?"

James stared at Stafford. As Grannie Connolly would say, he doesn't miss a trick. There was no sense trying to con him.

James said, "I think I'm on to something really big, sir." He gushed forth with the entire story, except for one minor detail: Lance Pritchard's participation.

Stafford nodded. "You did quite a job uncovering it. I guess we'll never understand how you pieced it together."

Shit, he even knows that. "No, I guess we never will", James sputtered. "Let's just say it fell into my lap."

Stafford waved his hand. "Fine. We'll let it go at that." He studied James. "Can you make the case stick? You're about to open one big can of worms. I want you to be fully aware of what you're taking on."

"To be honest, if you asked me this morning, I wasn't so sure. There's been a new development, though. Now I've got a legal theory. You'll have a conviction."

"Terrific." He took a deep breath. "That pretty much exhausts it. It occurs to me, though, your prior relationship with O'Donnell is bound to come into question. I'd ask you to step aside and let another assistant try the case if I thought O'Donnell would cooperate. I doubt he will. So, it's your game to win or lose." He gazed at James. "But the defense lawyers are going to attack both of you when he testifies. They're going to claim you took it light on him for old times' sake. So promise me he'll be treated like any other witness would be. If you can't do that, then we'll have to pass on this one altogether."

Take it light on Sean O'Donnell? Not a chance. He faced his boss as he rose from the chair, "Just like any other witness? I'll make certain."

Stafford nodded. "We'll have to let the U.S. Attorney and State Attorney General know what we're undertaking. Protocol and all that. But I'll back you all the way."

James's heart pounded. It was all coming together.

*

James watched Maureen from across the table. It had been ages since they had dinner together at home. There'd been a time it was a ritual, but now, just a few years later, he felt like a guest at the table. He wanted to enjoy it while he could. It would be the last such dinner for another long while. Sean's first appearance in the grand jury was scheduled for the next day.

"I said, I had a visitor today after school," Maureen repeated.

He looked up at her. "Who?" he said, wiping his mouth with his paper napkin and tossing it on the table.

"Donna O'Donnell."

James kept his gaze on Maureen, unsure how to respond.

"She said she was an old friend of yours. We went to the playground so we could chat while Delia played on the monkey-bars."

"She had no business going to see you."

Maureen scowled. "That's against the rules of whatever game you're playing?"

He cleared his throat. "Don't bother telling me about the rules. You don't play the game; you don't make the rules."

She clenched her fists. "Your quick comeback that's supposed to end all discussions isn't going to work this time. That woman told me everything. She was the first old girlfriend of yours I met who wasn't a tramp. I didn't think you knew any nice girls." Her voice rose. "She was begging you for help."

"She understands I can't just let Sean walk."

"Would she have understood if she knew how you let your friend Lance off the hook on a bank robbery?"

"That was different—"

"Hold everything! The great prosecutor can distinguish that case?"

The rage gathered inside him. "I'm warning you, Maureen, you'd better ease off."

"I guess I don't know you at all anymore. You're some stranger who thinks he's God. Someone who can let a bank robber off because he's his old friend. Then turn around and throw the book at some other guy because he's always hated him." She laughed sardonically. "That's it! How could I have overlooked it? I married God, not a man. You and your crucifixion complex. Maybe James Devlin thinks he's Christ reincarnate, searching for something worth being nailed to a cross because he needs to suffer. Or maybe it's some wrathful God of retribution, doling out sentences to anyone who dares offend him. When is it ever going to end?"

"I don't know!" He jumped up from the table. "I don't know anything anymore. Except that I'm going to finish this case. I'm going to see this goddamn thing through."

"Of course! James Devlin doesn't start things he can't finish!" she yelled. "No matter what, he'll teach everyone a lesson for messing with him. Well, guess what, Jim. Nobody's watching. No one else will even care. You'll be the biggest loser of all!"

James threw the table over, knocking Maureen backward. He was poised over her, before the last cup and saucer crashed to the floor. Then he smashed his fist into the wall, inches away from Maureen's head.

"Now me," she cried. "Get it out of your system. As long as it's someone you love, it shouldn't matter that it's not your father."

James turned and thundered out of the apartment.

*

Moments later, he was gasping as he crossed under the viaduct. He didn't know which way to turn so he went straight, sliding into the shadows next to the ancient sanitation garage, creeping along the deserted building like a fugitive.

He sat on the bulkhead to the East River, dropping his head down between his knees and staying that way for a long time, trying to piece together how he'd wound up in such a state. He'd stopped going to confession years ago, unwilling to spill his guts to another man, but never learned how to forgive himself. As a result, his guilt over sins of commission and omission never went away, it just lingered. His wastrel life at Brunswick had been full of lying and cheating, at a time when his friends were fighting and dying. Now the lying and cheating were starting all over again at the office.

And tonight's episode? He felt nothing but shame. What had the nuns called it? The first step toward penance. An examination of conscience. In his case, maybe a cross-examination of conscience. Sarah would undoubtedly laugh. Maybe it was outdated. Maybe long overdue. His turn to sit in the witness chair and tell the truth, nothing but the truth. He recalled how he used to catalogue his sins before entering the dreaded dark box at St. Aidan's. It was as dark on the river as the most tightly hewn confessional. There was no one there to deceive except himself. He swallowed hard. Where would he begin?

Hypocrisy. He was a former burglar, car thief, drug user and drunk. Although he'd been shown mercy along the way, he found the nerve to prosecute others.

Disloyalty. He'd become a master of betrayal. He'd dumped Rory Connolly. Ignored his mother as much as he could. Maureen was next in line. When he put the rationalizations aside, it was clear he flirted with Sarah, for the sheer thrill.

Revenge. The targets were almost too numerous to list, most recently Sean O'Donnell. He needed to avenge any slight, real or imagined.

Denial. He'd intentionally removed himself in time, space and emotion from his sister. Now he had set to work on his father. Just as he'd done with Nora, he was willing to sacrifice all the good memories so long as he could destroy the bad.

Pretense. Like Michael said, the most serious sin of all. From the time Dave left, James had pretended to be something other than what he was. To prove he was not soft, he played the role of an unfeeling prosecutor, inflicting more punishment on defendants than they truly deserved. His own punishment would ultimately fit his crime. He would stop pretending not to feel. He would become incapable of feeling anything at all.

He rose from the damp, rotting timbers. The list had been there, easy enough to review, plain enough to see. He'd refused to look until Maureen forced him.

He started back. To the apartment. To his wife. He had done it to himself. It would be his decision where he went from there.

*

Maureen was sitting on the floor in her bathrobe, alongside the table that tottered on three legs. She had a newspaper spread open and tube of Elmer's Glue-All in her hand while trying to glue one of the dishes back together. She glanced in his direction then looked back at her project. After a few moments, she slammed the dish, scattering the pieces over the paper.

"Let me help," James said,

Reconciliation. That was what the sacrament was called now. Confession had always been misnamed; if they had called it "Forgiveness", a lot more people would have gone. The point wasn't about telling your sins, or even the penance you were supposed to do, but rather the absolution that you received. Confession had to be directed to your victims or it wasn't worth the bother. Never mind God. The people you had done dirty were the ones who had to be told. They were the ones who had to forgive you. He lowered himself across from Maureen.

"You're pretty good at figuring things out, Mo," he said. "A lot better than I am. Like the business with my father. I've let it change me. I've let it come between us. You don't know how much I loved him when I was a kid. Or how much it hurt when he asked why I was bothering him." He took a deep breath. "But there's more you've got to know. Maybe you don't know me. Maybe I'm not the guy you think I am." His lip quivered. "I've lied to you often. I was cutting up with girls at Brunswick when you were playing by the rules. Back then, I'd smoke any sort of dope that came my way when I told you I wouldn't."

Maureen was sobbing. "Why didn't you tell me before? While it was happening? I could've helped you."

"Why? Because I was afraid. I can't remember the last time I felt worthy. I was afraid you'd see that you were wrong about me, that I wasn't good enough for you. I hoped once we got married I'd change and put it all behind me." He closed his eyes, then opened them, staring into hers. "Well, I've changed. But it hasn't been for the better. I've been drinking big time when I'm with Lance. My romance with alcohol wasn't over; just a trial separation. I'm afraid where it's heading. Once I start I don't want to stop. I wonder if I'm determined to force you out that door."

He sucked up some air, knowing the last disclosure would be the most difficult.

"I don't know why I'm like that. I'll give you an example and you'll have to decide what to do. I've been hanging around with someone at the office. He paused for a moment. "Her name is Sarah Kaufman. Nothing has happened, but I'm worried."

Maureen remained quiet, looking down at the broken pieces of the dish.

"I guess that's it. I've let my past paralyze me. I was convinced I would never deserve your love, no matter how hard I tried to make up for the past." He rubbed his eyes. "Donna Bradley, Sarah Kaufman – they're not real. You're the only thing that's ever been real in my life, Mo. You're the only one who could ever cut through all the make-believe and get me to tell the real secrets. You're the difference between yesterday and tomorrow."

He looked down to see Maureen's hand on his. "None of it matters to me, Jim. I love you. I can overlook it all, too, if you're willing to start over again. That's my only condition."

"You know I am, Mo." He spoke slowly. "I'm sorry. I'm sorry I misled you so long. I'm sorry the truth took forever to come out." Tears ran down his cheeks. "You love me for no good reason at all. Now I realize it. I don't have to earn your love. I only have to learn to accept it."

Maureen made her way to him and they embraced, tumbling onto the floor. She lay across him, pressing him against the hardwood floor, his wet eyes scanning the ceiling. He squeezed her as tightly as he could.

*

For the second consecutive day James sat in Martin Stafford's office. Circumstances had changed drastically. This was no chummy chat with his boss. He was on the firing line. The shiny oak conference table was as long as Stafford's office was wide. James sat on one side, the three biggest law enforcement officials in New York County sat on the other.

U.S. Attorney Thomas Eliot exhibited no pretense of cordiality, no dead-fish handshake, much less his typical knuckle-cracker. State Attorney General Fischbein kept scowling without looking at James. And Martin Stafford sat back in his leather-lined chair with a noncommittal expression. It was Tom Eliot who took the lead.

"Let's not beat around the bush, Devlin. Martin was good enough to inform us of the case you're planning to bring. Mel and I have both voiced our strongest protests."

James shrugged. "Sorry to hear that. I didn't think you'd have any problem with it."

"Well, think again. We have real problems with it. Your office has no business being involved in a securities fraud matter. That's the bailiwick of the U.S. Attorney."

James looked at the men. "All I know is that there have been several violations of the Penal Law of the State of New York, which I'm empowered to prosecute. So that's what I intend to do."

Fischbein faced James and barked, "Don't give us that garbage! The only reason you're bringing this case is for your own career advancement."

"Of course," Eliot chimed in. "You overstate your sense of duty quite a bit, Devlin. From what I understand, this little solo investigation of yours was completely unauthorized. You broke every rule, disobeyed every office directive that exists. Martin could can you this very minute. And we intend to request that he do so if you don't turn over this matter immediately."

James watched the grim faces from across the table. He could swear he smelled Jackie Standish's smoke in his face. He'd been intimidated once, and regretted it ever since. It wasn't going to happen again.

He took a deep breath and said, "You raise some valid points. I understand that you question my motives. I have myself. Truth is, they probably weren't the best at the start." He faced Eliot. "I'd be lying if I said you didn't enter into it. In retrospect, I was dying to show you what a mistake you made by not hiring me. What better way than to beat you at your own game. By stealing the hottest white-collar crime case in this city right out from under your nose. I admit, that was appealing to me." He then turned his attention to Fischbein. "And you may be right, too. I've always been ambitious. Maybe that was part of the master plan, as well. Get a lot of good press with a conviction. I could be on my way, off and running politically. But that's behind me now. I have no intention of elbowing my way in front of you in the race to the Governor's mansion."

Eliot said, "So you'll follow orders, Devlin? Hand the case over?"

James shook his head. "No. It's my case and I'm going to run it my way."

Eliot's face darkened. "Then you're going to be fired, Devlin. That's a promise."

"Excuse me, Mr. Eliot, but I don't think so." James raised his voice. "Because I've got all the cards. The witnesses trust me. I'm the only one who knows who the defendants are going to be. What are you going to do? Bounce me out of the office and throw me into my own grand jury to find out the information you need? Those folks are fond of me, you know. They'll think it's peculiar that all of a sudden that nice young Mr. Devlin has his own fanny in the fire. Your beloved media is bound to get wind of it. And when your friends with pens and cameras do, there'll be a lot of explaining to do. I think the man in the street is really going

298

to be surprised that this sort of shit goes down in so-called high places."

Eliot and Fischbein were visibly shaken. Stafford, with a hint of smile, turned and said, "So what do you propose, Jim?"

He looked at Eliot and Fischbein. "Mr. Stafford made me guarantee that my witness would get the same treatment as anyone else. He thought I'd be too easy on this guy because of our past...relationship. Actually, I would've been just the opposite. But fair is fair. This guy's going to be blowing the whistle on the mob. He needs protection. Anyone else would get it." He nodded toward Eliot. "You make the federal witness protection program available for him and his family. He'll agree to testify for you as soon as we finish the state case. The way I see it, you've got nothing to lose. Even if you're right and I'm lousy enough to screw my case up, it's just a dry run for you. You get a second clean shot at the bad guys for all the federal securities law violations you like once you indict them down the street."

Eliot glared while Fischbein asked, "What about my office?"

"It's not too promising," James said. "The best you can drum up is a misdemeanor charge. You'll have to settle for table scraps. Sorry about that."

After a moment's silence, Stafford asked, "Are we in agreement?"

XXI
October 1981

J AMES DROPPED THE THICK trial folder on his desk. The painstaking
preparation in the grand jury, the constant interviews in his office, were
now paying off. Sean O'Donnell's skill was remarkable. On direct, James
asked a question, then stepped back out of the jury's way. Sean did the rest,
providing them with a natural, spontaneous detailed exposition of the scheme he
and Granelli had concocted.

On cross, Sean was unshakable. The veterans of the criminal bar retained by
Paulie and his uncle hammered away at his credibility to no avail. Sean refused
to be drawn into an argument, to volunteer additional information. He acknowledged his culpability and the favorable treatment he sought by cooperating. He'd
be through with this case in another day or two. Donna and Delia had already
been spirited out of town by the U.S. Marshals. Sean wouldn't join them until his
next command performance for the federal government was over. Then he'd fade
out of sight. A new name. A new man. A free man.

Houlihan and the handwriting expert would handle the mop up. They were
the only other witnesses on the prosecution's case in chief. They'd supply all the
corroboration the jury might need. Sean hadn't been privy to the mechanics of
the Granelli's procedures for collecting their insider profits. Yet he sensed where
Houlihan and his men should look.

The investigators hadn't uncovered the host of fictitious names they'd expected. The Granellis were more clever than that. Their controlled stock purchases
were all by real people. Only dead. Fairly recent departees whose inventories of
assets and social security numbers were conveniently available in estate tax peti-
tions that had been filed in the various Surrogate's Courts in New York City. Like
Queens County. Right on Sutphin Boulevard. Up the block from the luncheon-
ette where Lance spotted Paulie and Sean and the scheme first emerged.

It was a beautiful way to confuse anyone tracking them. Title examiners and
others were constantly reviewing these public records, so no suspicions were

aroused when the Granellis had them inspected, as well. They could select the name of a decedent who'd owned some of the target's shares when he was alive. Then, while his estate was being wound up, they purchased additional shares in the dead man's name.

The Granellis had found a way to exploit the IRS's own division of responsibilities. Since the federal estate tax audit had already been completed before the Surrogate's Court filing, those agents would never learn that additional, tainted shares had been purchased. The fiduciary income tax unit, seriously understaffed, was practically run on an honor system. It made only a token effort at enforcement, rarely auditing a trust or estate. As long as some income from the stock issue were reflected on each return, as it invariably was for the shares shown on the estate tax inventories the Granellis had selected, there was no reason to suspect that income was understated.

No scheme is foolproof. Yet this one came close. Without the lucky break in the case, the few odd belated purchases or sales that came to light wouldn't have attracted sufficient attention. They could easily be taken as an estate's transactions in assets already on hand. No one would have checked to see who deposited the brokers' dividend and proceeds checks. No one ever would've been able to trace the money into the Granellis' pockets. Once anyone could have become suspicious, Paulie and his uncle would have been long gone.

All the transactions were run through a revolving series of post office boxes. Proceeds checks payable to the deceased stock purchaser when the shares were dumped were sent to post office boxes "in care of" fictitious law firms. The checks were then deposited in estate checking accounts that the decedent's true fiduciary and heirs never knew existed. With a death certificate from the Bureau of Vital Statistics and a certificate of letters testamentary or letters of administration from the same Surrogate's Court where the estate had been targeted, both anonymously obtained at a nominal charge, the Granellis could open such accounts in any bank in the city with their own signatures recorded as that of the fiduciary. They could then disburse the funds, paying the estate's "debts," making "distributions," ultimately channeling the money to the real beneficiaries: themselves and their illegal operations.

Houlihan had collected all the necessary documentation and would demonstrate the operation of the scheme to the jury in a detailed manner. The signatures memorialized in the banks' records were the defendants', according to the People's expert who'd testify based upon his analysis of the handwriting exemplars the Granellis were compelled to give. The links established between the Granellis and the various payees of the "estate" checks made the prosecution's case impossible to refute. Grabbing his briefcase, James headed out the door.

Everyone carries their past with them, James thought, as he picked a path through the living room of his mother's attic apartment, crammed with furniture he recognized from their old house. *But you can't let yourself become its prisoner, like I did. You're better off traveling light. Keep it to a few select memories. Don't dust them off and reexamine them unnecessarily, or you might lose them altogether.* He had discovered that rule only that afternoon, when he had visited the wreckage of the playground. He had come up empty when he tried to visualize one of the old full-court games with Michael and the other guys. He had finally given up and left for his mother's.

"I always liked your spaghetti, Mom", James said. She'd called him earlier in the week, inviting him for dinner, but he knew it had to be for another reason.

"That's nice to hear. You were never too free with the compliments."

James wiped his mouth with a paper napkin. "That doesn't mean I didn't notice." He folded his paper napkin in half. "I know I should tell you I love you, that I admire what you've accomplished. I know going to nursing school, getting a job wasn't easy for you. You probably figured people were talking about you, but you kept going."

Peg began to cry. "You're like that too, James. You always were."

He shrugged. "I like to choose my battles a little more carefully, if I can." He pushed his chair back from the table. "So, was there another reason you asked that I come over?"

"Your father's in the hospital. He had a prostate operation."

"Probably means pecker failure. Didn't Grannie always say that's the last thing to die?"

"More likely from overuse," Peg commented dryly. They laughed before Peg grew serious again, "You don't know the half of it." She sighed. "But he's all by himself out there."

"Isn't that what he wanted? He's got some nerve calling you when he gets sick."

"He's my husband. I'm all he has."

"He doesn't deserve you." He studied her, realizing his mistaken idea was surfacing again. "But you'll never give up on him, will you?"

She shook her head, blew her nose with her paper napkin.

"He's lucky. Most anyone else would never catch a break like him."

"Probably because they don't need it," Peg replied. "Maybe God always give you enough to get by."

James nodded. What was the sense in arguing? He asked, "So what do you want me to do?"

Her voice dropped to a whisper. "He was asking for you. Several times. Do you think you could go see him this weekend?"

James rolled his eyes, and his face flushed. "I could be summing up in this case next Monday morning." He finally sighed with resignation. "Okay, I'll go."

"No, forget it. It was unfair of me to ask."

"Of course it was unfair, Ma. It's all unfair, but since everything else is coming to a head, I may as well face him, too." He stood. "I'd better be getting back." He mellowed. "Anything else you need before I go? Like change water into wine?"

*

After Nora made it very clear to James that she had no intention of visiting their father "after what he did to Mom," James hung up the pay phone and headed back to his father's room. He walked in noticing again that his father's prostate wasn't his only health problem. The cigarettes were eating him from the inside out. He pulled out a chair next to the bed.

They discussed the room, the cards, and the flowers. When those topics were exhausted, they sought refuge in sports. The lineups were slightly different. They now had to add the Giants and A's to the list of baseball teams whose past errors and future prospects they were obliged to discuss. Yet the talk was strangely hollow, as though it were recited from memory, not delivered from conviction.

"I should've brought you a book," James said.

"I wouldn't be able to read it anyway," Dave said, his voice weak. "The medication knocks my eyes out."

"I could read to you," James said. He spotted a Bible on the nightstand, which made sense for a Catholic hospital. He went over and grabbed it, bringing it back with him to his chair, leafing through the pages.

"Here's a good one," he said. "Abraham and Isaac. Remember how Abraham struck this deal with God, how he was going to offer up his son, just to get God off his back?" He looked up at his father. "All the priests and teachers always talked about Abraham, but I always wondered about Isaac. He noticed they went all the way up the mountain without a lamb to sacrifice. He was a bright kid and I wondered if he figured it out. What if Isaac realized that the old man has flipped out and is going to kill him, and he decides to beat feet?"

Dave's washed out face looked older at that moment. "Is that what you thought, Jimmy? I'm like Abraham?"

James shrugged. "Something's been bugging you as long as I've known you. My gut tells me it was something that happened during the War." He closed the Bible. "Let's face it. You saved my life, remember? Maybe that gave you a right to reclaim it. Was that what you were thinking?"

He looked away. "Something bad did happen. I thought I'd be tough enough for anything, but I was kidding myself. It was worse than anything I had ever imagined, and I was way over my head. I cracked and it cost someone else. Then I spent the rest of my life reliving that one moment, trying to see how I could've made it come out differently." He began coughing. Once he stopped, he continued. "I thought if I got you prepared when your turn came, I would be able to correct my mistake. My second chance would be you. But when your turn came, you didn't go."

James shook his head. "It's no good like that, Pop. Don't you see? Abraham got himself all confused. What kind of crazy caveman's God would tell a man to kill his son for nothing? I always thought Abraham should have told Him to go jump when He told him to do that. It's always a disaster when you follow a bad order. If Abraham were so sure God needed a human sacrifice, he should have torched himself, just like one of those Buddhist monks, rather than kill his own kid."

James cleared his throat. "I always knew you felt war was something I'd have to experience to become a man. But when the time came, I didn't see it that way." He picked the Bible up. "I wasn't willing to kill anyone for some vague idea. I wasn't willing to die for the past, not even your past. That's not what your war buddies died for. They died for the future. So Vietnam? That was long over when my turn rolled around. All we'd been doing there for years was killing time, in more ways than one. Just running the clock down until we saw who was left standing." He tossed the Bible on the nightstand.

"Truth is, I'll never know if I would've had the nerve," James continued. "I'm not tough. When the other guy's down on the pavement bleeding, I'd rather walk away instead of finishing him off. That's probably a disappointment to you. But I made my choice and I think I can live with it." He thought of Uncle Rory, who never could handle the idea he might not be as tough as the next guy, and never realized that the heroic act might be more adrenalin than courage.

Tears streamed down his father's face. He gasped as he spoke. "I never wanted you to get killed, Jimmy. That would've been a terrible waste. I just wanted you to take your chances and come home okay. That would've made it all right."

"I did take my chances, Pop. Except they changed the game. My crap shoot was in the qualifying bracket, the draft lottery. I never even made it to the finals."

"You must hate me," Dave sputtered through sobs.

"No, I don't." He pulled his chair closer, face to face with his father. "But there are a few things that really bother me."

Dave wiped his eyes, the IV tube taped to his wrist stretched to its limit. "What's that?"

"How you just gave up. I mean, really, Pop. If there was one thing you pounded into my head was never to quit. Why, shit. We've been talking in sports riddles all my life. And you weren't alone, either. Even the Church gives you a goddam pep talk about not quitting. St. Paul, bragging away. Not that he won the race.

Just that he ran it. That he finished. But despite everything you taught me, when the time came *you* stopped running. That's what irks me." He gazed at his father, realizing the balance of power had shifted.

"It irks me because I know you still care, as much as you pretend you don't. I remember that moment when I woke up in your arms on the bathroom floor with you crying and hugging me. You loved me then, and I knew it. But now there's some perverse twist in your head keeping you from thinking straight, from feeling normal. And if you keep pretending you don't care, soon enough you won't."

Dave shook his head, shuddering.

"I know I shoved you away first. I had to stop being your little boy, but I wanted you to be there when I came back as a man. Why wouldn't you wait?"

"I don't know, Jimmy. I couldn't help it."

James dropped back in his chair, his anger spent. "No, I don't believe you could. It's not your fault", he said looking at his father. *Fathers and sons are natural enemies. We must be paired off to inflict maximum pain on each other. Maximum disappointment.*

"I should've seen it all along," Dave whispered. "You were no Marine. That wasn't your fault." He forced a grin. "It was my old man with the last laugh. For the times I put him down for being soft, he came back to haunt me. You're him all over. The two of you are stronger than I'll ever know how to be. I know that now."

"Yeah, but if you're a quitter, what's that make me?" James replied. "You tried to start over with a son of your own. I've been so afraid that things would get botched up that I haven't been willing to take that chance at all."

He glanced at his watch. He'd have to leave if he were going to catch the last flight to New York. He got up. "I have to go. I just want you to know I don't believe it matters. Any of it. The lessons weren't wrong, even if the teacher doesn't believe them anymore. I love my family. Despite anything else that happens, that won't ever change. Whatever we've done has nothing to do with it." Leaving was difficult, seeing his father slumped in the bed crying.

"Maybe love's like baseball, Pop. Remember what Yogi said?"

"What's that?" Dave's swollen eyes were fearful.

"It's not over 'til it's over. Maybe it's never over, no matter what."

James approached the bed and grabbed his father around the shoulders, kissed him on the cheek, then dropped his face onto Dave's hospital gown. He then raised his head and smiled. Choosing his words carefully, he gazed into his father's eyes and said, "Goodnight, Dad. I'll see you soon."

XXII
November 1981

H E LOVED SUMMING UP most of all, James thought as he hunted for the right keys on the typewriter. To him, it was the single artistic aspect of a trial. Only in summation could the case be presented in a coherent, integrated fashion. After all the evidence had been presented, the closing argument was the lawyer's final chance to demonstrate his skill. His adversary's argument had to be anticipated and neutralized. The jury had to be provided with a version of the events so inherently plausible that the advocate's side must prevail.

It was always spontaneous. No matter how detailed James's preparation for summation, he changed it once he got on his feet. A new inference or a new phrase would invariably enter his mind. He would always run with it, following his instincts, dragging the jury along to see where the unexpected idea might lead. He was seldom disappointed. It seemed like the winning argument, the devastating counter to the proffered defense, was already inside his mind, waiting to be born if he would only trust enough to release it. That morning's summation had followed the pattern. Sean had supplied him with a complete arsenal against the Granellis. While preparing, James realized this summation wouldn't have to be built so much as pared down.

He still felt it, moving about the courtroom, maintaining eye contact with the jury. Every motion, inflection, was entirely by design, keeping the jury on the edge of their seats. It was the ultimate balm for the ego.

And poison for the soul. Some people just couldn't handle the exhilaration. He was one of them. He'd get so caught up in the argument that he'd forget it was supposed to be reality, with authentic characters and a true story, not just a convincing one.

He rolled the paper out of the typewriter, checked it for errors, and signed it.

"I caught a little of your closing this morning."

He looked up to see Sarah standing in the entranceway to his office.

"I was quite impressed."

"We had a real good case. I expect the Granelli boys are sweating bullets right now...or maybe boarding a plane."

"There was more to your performance than a real good case."

He smiled. "Maybe it was like the time I knew I was playing my last basketball game. I came out flaming. I don't think I missed all night from the top of the key."

"What are you saying?" Sarah asked.

"Sorry, top of the key is the semicircle behind the foul line."

She nodded. "A semicircle symbolizes everlasting life."

"I never heard that before. I knew there was something special about it, but never knew what it was." He folded the letter, stuffing it into an envelope. He saw her watching him. "My letter of resignation," he said, waving the envelope.

Her dark eyes got teary. "Are you kidding? I hope that offers an explanation."

"Not really," James mumbled. "It's too long a story. It's pointless to rehash it all. Let's say I did some bad things and I don't want to do any more. It's time for me to go."

She didn't say anything right away, but then asked, "Will I still see you, Jim?"

James shook his head. "No, Sarah--"

Just then the phone rang. A court officer. Already a verdict.

He hung up and stood. Sarah was still there. James picked up the trial folder and said, "It occurs to me that a terrific appellate lawyer like you should have a little trial experience. How about taking your first verdict?"

"Do you mean it?" she asked wide-eyed.

"Of course. Do you think I want to be in the same room with the Granellis when they're convicted? We'll confuse them. They won't know who to put a contract out on." He laughed, then added, "Seriously, Sarah, these guys are gentlemen. Kind of. They wouldn't do that sort of thing to you. I'll go along just to be sure they whack the right guy."

"What do I do?"

"I can teach you everything I know in the time it'll take to go across the street to the courtroom."

*

James came through the rear exit of the Criminal Court building and paused on the steps overlooking Baxter Street, the November wind fluttering through his suit jacket. His briefcase was bursting with books, a coffee mug, Maureen's pictures and other items he'd accumulated over the years.

He spotted a small, solitary figure in the playground across the street. It was a boy. He crouched down, then heaved the basketball up at the hoop with great effort. The sequence he followed was relentless. Three dribbles. Shoot. Retrieve. Repeat.

James hardly remembered how it was done as he approached the court. How did you invite yourself to play? Still, he drew nearer. He stopped at the faded sideline and put down his briefcase. He folded his jacket and placed it on top. He rolled up his sleeves as he walked toward the basket.

The dribbling stopped. The Asian boy looked at him warily.

"Mind if I shoot a few baskets with you?" James asked.

He threw James a deliberate bounce pass without answering.

James caught the ball, bouncing it to his left hand, to his right. Then he jumped as high as his wingtip shoes would allow, releasing the shot at the top of his leap. It passed through the netless rim. The boy snatched the ball on its first bounce.

"Shoot 'til you miss?" James asked.

The child nodded reluctantly, then passed the ball back.

James's dribble grew more intense, his shots more frequent. Again and again he launched himself and the ball through the air, a sweating, overgrown kid with his shirttail hanging out of his suit pants. Soon he was winded, grateful the boy decided to hold the ball.

"You used to play, huh mister?" the boy asked.

James smiled. "Yeah, but you should've seen my friend Michael play. He was something else."

The boy nodded then said he had to go.

James tucked in his shirt and rolled his shirtsleeves back down, buttoning his cuffs. He looked around the park, dotted with thick beige trees. There were piles of dead leaves, crinkled victims of early summer storms, pressed against the chain-link fence. Other leaves, still yellow and orange, lay pasted to the blacktop where they'd just fallen. Despite the calendar, the remaining leaves clung to the tree. They'd continue changing colors until they were brown and lifeless, finally dropping without a struggle to the ground.

"LIFE SUCKS" had been scribbled on the backboard back at his old playground. James disagreed. It just hurts like mad sometimes. And while there may be such a thing as a conscientious survivor, there's no such thing as survivors' guilt. The guilty aren't survivors. They're only prolonging their dying.

James slipped on his jacket, picked up the briefcase and walked toward Chatham Square and the bus, not the subway. For a change.

He and Maureen would go out tonight. Maybe he'd give Lance a call sometime. They could go shoot the rock. It was high time to find out how much game his old friend really did have.

He would visit Grannie Connolly in the morning. He wouldn't complain, no matter how she drowned his tea with milk or buried it with sugar. He had a lot to learn from the old woman. She was a survivor. He would be one too. There was no more time to waste.

Epilogue
December 1988

THE WIND WHISTLED behind the granite blocks like many voices refusing to be forgotten. The man in front ignored the call, except as a signal to turn up the collar of his overcoat and pull his tweed cap down tighter. He ambled alongside the wall, glancing down repeatedly at the paper in his gloved hand, then back to the wall for names he was hoping to find on the panels the directory had specified.

The crowds at the Vietnam Memorial had thinned over the years. The squads of veterans who'd gathered at its opening had dispersed. James Devlin could move at his own pace on the frigid winter afternoon. There'd be no one to challenge his presence. None of his contemporaries would ask where he'd served.

He thought of how the battle had continued to the bitter end. Even when the nation conceded a memorial for those killed in its longest war, it remained divided over the form it should take. The abstract design surrounding James had been opposed. A giant, ambiguous V. What did it mean beyond the place where they'd all died? Nixon's old "Victory" sign that he stole from Churchill? Or the converse peace sign James's generation had flashed? Virility? Vengeance? Vanquished? Vindication? It would take much more than the addition of an interracial Yankee Doodle Dandy statue to answer the questions the wall raised; like the biggest riddle of them all: the chronological listing of the dead.

How many people had it taken to put the thousands of names in the right order? Or could some software package now assemble the list in seconds?

He found the first of several names he sought. He paused, then walked on. He passed tablet after tablet filled with names, each ticks of a second hand on some infernal timepiece. He stopped occasionally and bit his lip at the sight of a familiar name before moving on.

The symbolism struck him. It was like Michael said: like basketball, they had been playing a game against the clock. The soldiers, each hoping to survive their personal 365-day war and earn a plane ticket home. The nation as a whole, spending money and lives until time ran out on the roof of the embassy in Saigon.

James stopped before the designated panel. It was near the end of the wall. A block of latecomers. Close to the end, but not close enough. He scanned the wall for the name. There. Right on the first line. That was Michael. Top shelf. Just like always. He stood staring at the name chiseled into the black stone.

"I the robber!"

He was tackled from behind the knees. He hadn't heard the approaching giggles.

"You're coming with me, Mister," a gruff little voice said.

"Michael, Mommy said to leave Daddy alone!"

James crouched down to the level of the two children. "It's okay, Deirdre. I need a hug. Bad." The kids scrambled into his arms. He closed his eyes and wedged between them, pressing his face against their cold woolen dress coats.

Deirdre pulled away. "What is this place, anyway, Daddy?"

James smiled. "Something that's supposed to help you remember some people who died."

"Mrs. Meenan's cat died last week!" Michael exclaimed.

Deirdre poked her brother in the belly. "He's talking about people." She looked at her father. "Who died?"

"Soldiers. Lots of them. In a place called Vietnam. It's a long way from here. It was beautiful, but very different from our country. They had a terrible war there and it lasted a long time." James scooped up his son and daughter, one in each arm, so they could reach the highest names on the wall. "Here, I'll show you the name of one of my friends." He pointed.

Deirdre leaned in, touching the letters with her mitten. "Michael. Hey, Michael! Just like yours."

Michael beamed.

Deirdre continued. "Michael...J...Cass...idy. Is that him, Daddy?"

"That's him all right. Michael J. Cassidy. He was my friend and would be proud that you read his name all by yourself." He put the children back down on the ground.

Michael sniffed, his nose runny. "Were you a soldier, Daddy? I want to be one too!"

James took a handkerchief from his picket and had Michael blow into it. "No, I was never a soldier." He spotted Maureen approaching.

"How come?" Michael asked.

"Things just didn't work out that way." He tucked the handkerchief back into his pocket.

"Are you ready?" Maureen said as she approached. "They're liable to catch pneumonia." She nodded toward the children.

James nodded. "I'll catch up in a second."

Maureen gave him a comforting hug then led the children away. James turned once more toward the wall. He hadn't known what to expect. The wall was the whole nation's way of beating its breast. He figured he'd be pounding his own, too. Just like the old days, kneeling at Fr. Mack's feet. But he hadn't felt that way. No tears. No guilt. It was all gone. The war he'd fought inside himself was over. It was finally obvious how it began: The innocent childhood image. In church. With his mother.

He now understood why he'd clung to that memory. It was the source of the question that had disturbed him so long. Was his life some giant Crackerjack box in which God hid a special prize he was supposed to find? Like a secret message for his Captain Midnight decoder?

James had wasted years searching for it. He'd believed it was there, just waiting to be discovered. Like so many others, he'd misled himself by forcibly reading some meaning, some connection into random, unrelated events. In his case, trying to figure out why his life hadn't been taken when he was a child. Now he stood alone, knowing better.

He wasn't condemned to a treasure hunt, a lifelong struggle to sort the conflicting clues. James was convinced that people were made in God's image and likeness. Not in looks. Nothing so obvious that a distant aunt or uncle could spot. No. Each person was a miniature creator, expected to mold a life, his own life, out of whatever surrounded him.

The wall, the past, would always stay the same. Michael's name. Uncle Rory. His own father's face. He'd see it all in his mind's eye until the day he died. But none of the people, places or incidents he remembered meant a thing unless they changed the present and the future.

He wouldn't retract his own choices. There are no real second chances because you can't change what happened the first time. You just have to get over it, because living means making one mistake after another, keeping up your nerve enough to make one mistake more, and just hoping that you don't make the same mistake twice.

Looking back, he doubted that any of it could have been avoided. People never really change. The blackjack player always takes a hit in the same situation. His only hope is for the next time. Maybe someone will shuffle the deck, so he draws a better hand.

"Goodbye, Mike," James whispered.

He spun and rushed to find his family, to try to make it come out right this time.

THE END

READING GROUP GUIDE

for Edward T. Byrne's

LOVE'S NOT OVER 'TIL IT'S OVER

1. In the prologue's conclusion, James questions whether he should have returned to the park, believing some things are better left alone. Do you agree?

2. Dave Devlin's relationship with his father had been tenuous. How do you think this affected his relationship with his son James?

3. Sports is a running theme throughout Love's Not Over 'Til It's Over. Do you think this worked as a metaphor for the novel? Why or why not?

4. World War II and the Vietnam War both play an important part in Byrne's novel. Do you think Dave was right to be upset with his son for not volunteering to go to Vietnam?

5. Lance Pritchard shows up unexpectedly later in the story. Why do you suppose James let him off the hook?

6. Why do you suppose Nora gave her father such a difficult time?

7. The Catholic Church has a major role in this work of fiction. How do you think the author represented it?

8. This is a generational novel, filled with lots of characters and storylines. Which ones stayed with you? Do you know any families like the Devlins?

9. Do you subscribe to the novel's major premise that once love truly takes root it can never be eradicated?

10. What do you think happened to James beyond these pages?

CPSIA information can be obtained
at www.ICGtesting.com
Printed in the USA
FFOW03n0328230218
45174992-45681FF

9 780692 873502